GRAVITY WELLS

GRAVITY WELLS

SPECULATIVE

FICTION STORIES

James Alan Gardner

An Imprint of HarperCollinsPublishers

Page 345 serves as a continuation of this copyright page.

HarperCollins books may be purchased for educational, business, or sales promotional use. For information please write: Special Markets Department, HarperCollins Publishers Inc., 10 East 53rd Street, New York, NY 10022.

FIRST EDITION

Eos is a federally registered trademark of HarperCollins Publishers Inc.

Designed by Cassandra J. Pappas

Library of Congress Cataloging-in-Publication Data has been applied for.

ISBN 0-06-008770-6

05 06 07 08 09 WBC/RRD 10 9 8 7 6 5 4 3 2 1

To Algis Budrys and Kim Mohan,

who both discovered me

Contents

Preface

In his preface to *Three Plays for Puritans,* George Bernard Shaw extols the virtues of prefaces and berates Shakespeare for never writing one. "I would give half a dozen of Shakespear's[1] plays for one of the prefaces he ought to have written."

Far be it from me to take sides in the famous (one-sided) fight between Shaw and Shakespeare; but I confess, I like prefaces and enjoy reading what writers have to say about their writing. One of the great formative influences in my youth was the *Dangerous Visions* anthology edited by Harlan Ellison. Every story in the book started with an introduction by Ellison and ended with an afterword by the author—some of them chatty, some of them evasive, some of them talking about what goes through a writer's head as he or she tries to make a story work. It was the first time I really got a sense that people sat down and wrote this stuff: real people with real lives, not godlike beings who exuded words effortlessly. In *Dangerous Visions,* Ellison talked about getting together with these people, shooting the breeze, or maybe just walking with them down the streets of Greenwich Village . . . and the authors themselves talked about rewrites, struggling with characters, *inventing* details, and putting them down on the page.

[1] Shaw had his own unique way of spelling things. Shaw had his own unique way of doing practically everything.

This was a revelation to me when I was twelve or thirteen. It made writing real; it made the *writers* real. I won't say it made me think *I* could be a writer—I'd been writing stories since kindergarten, so writing was already in my blood—but it made me think of writing in a different way. Instead of tossing off imitations of stuff you saw on television, writing could be something you *thought* about: something you put your heart into rather than scribbling words as fast as possible so you could show off to all your friends.

Therefore, when I started to write the introduction to *this* book, I wanted to offer the same kind of inspiration to anyone reading this preface. I wanted to tell potential writers there's no magic involved: just work and discipline, gradually developing your insight and technical skills. There is, no doubt, some indefinable quality called talent, but neither you nor anyone else will ever be able to tell if you have it. All you can do is write and write and write—and of course, read and read and read—in the same way that Olympic marathoners simply run and run and run. (Yes, I know marathoners do more to train than just running . . . and there are useful training exercises for writers, too. But the heart of running is running, and the heart of writing is writing. Everything else is auxiliary.)

Unfortunately, when I tried to write that kind of inspirational material for this book, the results truly sucked. They reeked. They blew dead bears (as teenage boys were fond of saying around the time I read *Dangerous Visions*). The whole write-up was god-awful claptrap, so utterly pompous and idiotic my computer started to make gagging sounds. It only went to prove another thing Shaw said in his introduction to *Three Plays for Puritans:* the reason many writers don't publish prefaces is that they can't write them.

So what can I say? If you want a *good* preface, go read Shaw or *Dangerous Visions* . . . or another of my favorites, Samuel R.

Delany's preface to *Distant Stars*. All I'm going to do is talk about the stories in this book: how they came to be, why I wrote them, and perhaps what I think of them now.

One more note about talking about one's work. There's a story (probably false, but I still like it) that the first time Beethoven played his *Moonlight* sonata, someone came up to him afterward and said, "The music was very beautiful, sir, but what did it mean?"

Beethoven answered, "An excellent question. Here's what it meant." Whereupon he sat down at the piano and played the whole piece again.

I agree with Beethoven on this one—some things ought to speak for themselves. That's why I decided not to clutter up the stories themselves with forewords or afterwords. Instead, I'm putting all the chat right here in the preface, and it's up to you to decide if or when you want to read my commentaries.

A Note on the Text: It turns out short-story collections aren't magically assembled by pixies. This particular collection was put together by yours truly, starting with the story manuscripts as I originally wrote them, *not* as they finally appeared when published. In my experience, editors sometimes make tiny cosmetic tweaks before stories go to print . . . which only makes sense, considering these people are called *editors*. Anyway, I didn't want to go through the slogging dog-work of comparing my original text to the final printed version in order to make faithful copies of what was actually published. Instead I went through the slogging dog-work of perusing all the original texts and making my own cosmetic tweaks. In other words, I've lightly edited every story in this book to tighten up the language, make a few points more clearly, and so on.

That's the nice thing about being a writer—you can keep working on stories until you get them right.

And now for the commentaries . . .

"Muffin Explains Teleology to the World at Large": This is my most reprinted story, based on an idea I'd had for years before I finally found the right way to put it together. Believe it or not, the first time I tried to write a story on this premise, it was a sordid tale about a shipwrecked sailor and a dockside whore. I won't even try to explain how the one story changed into the other—I like Muffin too much to sully her reputation.

Incidentally, this was the first story in which I decided to have fun with the title. Science fiction stories typically have terse no-nonsense titles . . . and for a long time, I thought titles like that were absolutely necessary if you wanted to be taken seriously as a writer. Finally, of course, I realized what a ridiculous notion that was—not only did many great stories have out-and-out *florid* titles, but one doesn't always want to be "serious" anyway. Therefore, I chucked out my preconceptions on what titles "must" be and have felt better ever since.

"The Children of Crèche": Once upon a time, there was a thing called gonzo journalism. It's not entirely dead—I still stumble across delightfully over-the-top pieces of supposed reportage that are really just an excuse for mouthing off in extravagantly purple prose—but I fear the glory days of gonzo are gone, gone, gonzo. Readers of "Crèche" have told me they're sure I'm imitating some-one, but they can't tell who. Sigh.

(The answer is I'm not imitating anyone specifically; I'm simply having flashbacks to Hunter S. Thompson, Tom Wolfe, Harlan Ellison in Tick-Tock mode, and a whole bunch of other writers who fed my gonzo cravings in the late sixties/early seventies. Hee-whack indeed.)

By the way, this is my earliest story featuring a scalpel. Don't ask me why, but scalpels keep popping up all over my writing . . . scalpels and mutilating corpses. It's a good thing I despise Freudian psychology, or I'd be really, really worried.

"Kent State Descending the Gravity Well: An Analysis of the Observer": This is the one story I've written as me, Jim Gardner, rather than from some fictional point of view. It's not quite a true story—I never actually sat down and wrote out the "scribbles" as they appear—but the ideas did cross my mind as I saw how the press tried to deal with the twentieth anniversary of the killings at Kent State University. Our beloved media (as they so often do) wrote *around* the facts without ever truly connecting to the reality of what happened.

The shootings seem like ancient history now; but for the sake of our souls, we have to remember that history is about real people with real lives and real deaths. There's something disturbing about the air of unreality with which we often view the past—as if anything that happened more than a few days ago took place in some alien dimension that doesn't have much to do with who we are now. I'm certainly guilty of feeling that way, too . . . which is one reason I wrote a story about fading memories and trivializing other people's tragedies.

"Withered Gold, the Night, the Day": I'm normally a pretty cheerful guy . . . but when I saw the movie *Se7en* in 1995, this story just came blurting out over the next three days. A story in which the world is withered, thinned out, shriveled. Where Everyman is a despairingly unbalanced vampire who seeks moral guidance from the Devil in a bus shelter.

I should know better than to see certain types of movies. If I'd seen a movie about the Care Bears, heaven knows what I might have written.

"The Last Day of the War, with Parrots": A story from a woman's point of view. People ask why I use female narrators so much. My answer is (a) I don't use them any more often than I use male narrators, and (b) why *shouldn't* I use female narrators, provided I'm not a jerk about it? To be sure, men often do lousy jobs of portraying women—but I have to believe that's just sloppiness and inattention, not an inevitable fact of gender. I don't accept that the only type of character I can legitimately write about is someone very much like myself . . . because frankly, I'm bored with middle-aged middle-class white men, and there are far too many of those guys in science fiction already.

Therefore, I resolved long ago that whenever I wrote about the future, I would show it containing just as many women as men, not to mention people of diverse cultural backgrounds, old, young, straight, gay, rich, poor, and every other variation I could make fit within the story's logic. That's the sort of future world I wouldn't mind living to see.

One more thing about this story. It takes place in the League of Peoples universe, and readers who know about the League might be wondering how two groups of aliens could descend upon a planet and start waging war against each other. Isn't that against the fundamental law of the League? Yes, it is; and someday, at the proper time, I may tell the story of what *really* happened on Caproche.

"A Changeable Market in Slaves": Sometimes it takes a number of rewrites before I find a good tone of voice for a story. And sometimes the rewrites get out of hand . . .

"Reaper": In 1989, I attended the Clarion West Science Fiction workshop. Each student was required to write a story a week. This was my first story of the workshop, written longhand in the depths of Seattle.

I'd had the idea of Reapers for some time before, but had never made a serious attempt to write a story about them. At first I thought the central character was going to be a brash teenager like the Hooch character; but after a page or two, I realized it wasn't working. That's when I switched to the current despicable narrator . . . and the story practically wrote itself.

"Lesser Figures of the Greater Trumps": This is what one calls a prose poem . . . or at least what *I* call a prose poem, for lack of a better name. At the time I wrote it, I could be pretty confident most readers would be familiar with the Rider-Waite tarot deck. I don't know if that's true anymore. The world seems to have acquired a disdain for such things; and not for healthy reasons like sincere rationalism, but simply because disdain comes so easily. Pity.

"Shadow Album": In the 1980s, I did a lot of theater: writing, acting, directing, and improvising (which is writing, acting, and directing combined). Somehow in the middle of that, I got involved in a mask workshop—possibly because said workshop was taught by my wife, Linda Carson.

Masks are powerful things, which is why they feature prominently in shamanistic religious traditions. Donning a mask is often the first step to donning an alternate personality. Masks are therefore used in some types of theater training to help students learn to set aside their mundane selves and become something Other.

If this sounds hokey when you read it on the page, let me assure you it's very effective in practice. Masks can have a powerful psychological effect . . . if you let them. In some sense, you can "become" the mask: someone you'd never let yourself be otherwise. There are obvious risks in this process, which is why mask workshops should always be led by people who know what they're doing; but taking risks is one of the great exhilarations of acting, and when it works, you can be transformed.

In this particular workshop, we constructed our own masks. The mask I built, and the personality I discovered within that mask, are exactly like the character ToPu (pronounced "toa-poo") as described in "Shadow Album." The mask of poor sad ToPu still sits in my study as I type these words—the closest thing to a magical object I've ever made.

"Hardware Scenario G-49": Another Clarion West story. ("Shadow Album" was, too.) All I can say is that my grandfather ran a hardware store and I worked there for several summers. The rest followed naturally.

"The Reckoning of Gifts": Back when I was doing theater, I wrote a one-act play called "Gifts" that was performed by my old high school. Years later, when Lorna Toolis and Michael Skeet asked me to submit a story for *Tesseracts 4,* I resurrected the idea from the play and this is what I got.

I should point out the story is substantially different from the play. For example, the play had none of the Vasudheva/Bhismu subplot. There are subjects that high schools prefer to avoid . . .

One last thing about "The Reckoning of Gifts"—the story is science fiction. *Science* fiction. Just because the tale is dressed in fantasy clothing, just because the characters talk about gods and demons and dreams, don't automatically believe them. Science-fiction readers should know better.

"The Young Person's Guide to the Organism": The title comes from Benjamin Britten's *The Young Person's Guide to the Orchestra* or *Variations and Fugue on a Theme by Purcell.* This is a musical work written in 1945, designed to introduce children to the various instruments in a symphony orchestra.

Structurally, the piece starts with the entire orchestra playing a simple tune composed by Henry Purcell in the 1600s. Then each different instrument plays a variation on the tune, demonstrating the sound of the instrument, the range, something about playing technique, and so on. When Britten has finished taking apart the entire orchestra, he puts it back together again in a fugue that has all the instruments taking the melody line in the order they were first presented. Finally, while the fugue continues in the background, the brass section soars in with the original Purcell tune playing over top of the rest of the orchestra (which is still belting out the fugue).

If that sounds complicated when described in words, it's quite straightforward when you hear the music. You can probably find a recording of the piece at your local library—check it out and listen for yourself. Most recordings have narrators who explain what's going on throughout the music, so you won't have any trouble following the structure.

I followed the same structure in writing "The Young Person's Guide to the Organism." In my case, the initial "theme" was one of science fiction's classics: First Contact. The story consists of a number of individual "voices" describing their moment of contact with an enigmatic alien organism that drifts slowly through the solar system. Each of these individuals imposes his or her own interpretation on what the organism is—the organism serves as a blank slate on which personal concerns are projected. At the end of the story, in the fugue section, the individuals are brought together again for a climax, and then the original theme of First Contact comes back for the grand finale.

It's worth noting that "Organism" tells the story of First Contact between humans and the League of Peoples. That makes it the foundation for all of the novels I've published so far.

"Three Hearings on the Existence of Snakes in the Human Bloodstream": It's seldom that I can actually trace the genesis of a story, but "Three Hearings . . ." is an exception. The night of January 1, 1996, I couldn't sleep; and when I got out of bed to find something to do with myself, I happened to pick up a how-to-write-poetry book I'd been meaning to read. (There's this nagging voice in the back of my head that keeps saying, "Jeez, I really should know something about poetry. And microbiology. And Chinese folklore." That voice is why I keep writing science fiction instead of something respectable, like murder mysteries.)

Anyway, I opened the poetry book at random and found a short poem called "The Oxen" by Thomas Hardy. The poem is based on a folk tradition that oxen supposedly kneel on Christmas Eve, just as they knelt before the baby Jesus on the first Christmas. Hardy wistfully thinks about the legend and says he would like someone to say to him, "Let's go into the fields to see the oxen kneeling." Even better, he'd like to see that they *are* kneeling. To me, the poem was about becoming tired of modern sophistication: nostalgically wishing for simplicity and simple proofs of faith.

This led me to think of a point in history where a simple article of faith was suddenly exposed as a lie. My notes say, "Someone has invented a telescope or a microscope which shows the belief is not true; that person is pulled in front of the High Priest to judge his heresy. The High Priest is a sophisticated man and feels the symbolic truth is more important than the literal; but he knows that for some people, this tiny thing *will* undermine their faith."

It's a stock situation in science fiction: the moment when science confronts religion. But then I decided things would be more interesting if, for some people, the microscope/telescope *did* confirm their simple faith. Some metaphoric claim of something in a person's blood . . . and with the poor quality of early microscopes, some people saw what their religion claimed would be there. Over the generations, those who did see something would intermarry with one another, tending to reinforce the trait within that population . . .

A pattern immediately presented itself: first Leeuwenhoek with the microscope; then Darwin explaining how selection processes emphasized the trait; and finally, a modern scientist who could lay out the whole situation with real chemistry. The parallels with Rh-positive and Rh-negative blood were just begging to be exploited . . . and the story wrote itself from there.

"Sense of Wonder": A while back, the editors of a proposed new sf magazine called *Sense of Wonder* sent mail-outs to various science-fiction writers, inviting us to submit stories. The editors wanted "big" stories that worked on a cosmic scale, stories designed to evoke the famous "sense of wonder" that many people believe is the heart of science fiction. The letter specifically mentioned Dyson spheres and other large-scale props of classic science fiction as examples of what the editors were looking for.

I certainly have nothing against Dyson spheres, ringworlds, and the like—I've read plenty of good stories that use such knickknacks. However, I was feeling in a contrary mood the day I received the mail-out. My first response was "Big stage props aren't what you need for sense of wonder. I'll show you sense of wonder!"

Which is why I wrote this little scene of two boys on a summer afternoon.

And why I wrote all the other stories in this book, too.

JIM GARDNER
Kitchener, Ontario
July 29, 2004

Muffin Explains Teleology to the World at Large

I told my kid sister Muffin this joke.

There was this orchestra, and they were playing music, and all the violins were bowing and moving their fingers, except for this one guy who just played the same note over and over again. Someone asked the guy why he wasn't playing like the others and he said, "They're all looking for the note. I've found it."

Muffin, who's only six, told me the joke wasn't funny if you understood teleology.

I never know where she gets words like that. I had to go look it up.

TELEOLOGY [teli-*ol*oji] *n* doctrine or belief that all things or actions are designed to achieve some end.

"Okay," I said when I found her again, "now I understand teleology. Why isn't the joke funny?"

"You'll find out next week," she said.

———

I talked to Uncle Dave that night. He's in university and real smart, even though he's going to be a minister instead of something interesting. "What's so great about teleology?" I said. He looked at me kind of weird, so I explained, "Muffin's been talking about it."

"So have my professors," he said. "It's, uhh, you know, God has a purpose for everything, even if we can't understand it. We're all heading toward some goal."

"We took that in Sunday school," I said.

"Well, Jamie, we go into it in a bit more detail."

"Yeah, I guess."

He was quiet for a bit, then asked, "What's Muffin say about it?"

"Something big is happening next week."

"Teleologically speaking?"

"That's what she says."

Muffin was in the next room with her crayons. Uncle Dave called her in to talk and she showed him what she was working on. She'd colored Big Bird black. She has all these crayons and the only ones she ever uses are black and gray.

"What's happening next week?" Uncle Dave asked.

"It's a secret," she said.

"Not even a hint?"

"No."

"Little tiny hint? Please?"

She thought about it a minute, then whispered in his ear. After that, she giggled and ran upstairs.

"What did she say?" I asked.

"She told me we'd get where we're going." He shrugged and made a face. We were both pretty used to Muffin saying things we didn't understand.

The next day I answered the front doorbell and found three guys wearing gray robes. They'd shaved their heads too.

"We are looking for her gloriousness," one of them said with a little bow. He had an accent.

"Uh, Mom's gone down the block to get some bread," I answered.

"It's okay," Muffin said, coming from the TV room. "They're here for me."

All three of the men fell facedown on the porch, making a kind of high whining sound in their throats.

"You know these guys?" I asked.

"They're here to talk about teleology."

"Well, take them into the backyard. Mom doesn't like people in the house when she's not here."

"Okay." She told the guys to get up and they followed her around the side of the house, talking in some foreign language.

When Mom got home, I told her what happened and she flat-out ran to the kitchen window to see what was going on. Muffin was sitting on the swing set and the guys were cross-legged on the ground in front of her, nodding their heads at every word she spoke. Mom took a deep breath, the way she does just before she yells at one of us, then stomped out the back door. I was sure she was going to shout at Muffin, but she bent over and talked quiet enough that I couldn't hear what she said. Muffin talked and Mom talked and one of the bald guys said something, and finally Mom came in all pale-looking.

"They want lemonade," she said. "Take them out some lemonade. And plastic glasses. I'm going to lie down." Then Mom went upstairs.

I took out a pitcher of lemonade. When I got there, one of the bald guys got up to meet me and asked Muffin, "Is this the boy?"

She said yes.

"Most wondrous, most wondrous!"

He put both hands on my shoulders as if he was going to hug me, but Muffin said, "You'll spill the lemonade." He let me go but kept staring at me with big weepy eyes.

"What's going on?" I asked.

"The culmination of a thousand thousand years of aimless wandering," the guy said.

"Not aimless," Muffin cut in.

"Your pardon," he answered, quickly lowering his head. "But at times it seemed so."

"You'll be in the temple when it happens," Muffin said to him.

"A million praises!" he shouted, throwing himself flat-faced on the ground. "A billion trillion praises!" And he started to cry into our lawn. The other two bald guys bowed in the direction of our garage, over and over again.

"You want to pour me a glass of that?" Muffin said to me.

The next day it was a different guy, with a big beard and carrying a sword almost as tall as me. When I opened the door, he grabbed the front of my T-shirt and yelled, "Where is the Liar, the Deceiver, the Blasphemer, the She-Whore Who Mocks the Most High?"

"She went with Uncle Dave down to the Dairy Queen."

"Thank you," he said, and walked off down the street. Later, I heard on the radio the cops had arrested him in the parking lot of the mall.

————

The next day Muffin told me I had to take her down to the boat-yards. I told her I didn't have to do it if I didn't want.

"Shows how much you know," she said. "You don't know any-thing about teleology or fate or anything."

"I know how to cross streets and take buses and all, which is more than I can say for some people."

"I have ten dollars," she said, pulling a bill out of the pocket of her jeans.

That surprised me. I mean, I maybe have ten dollars in my pocket twice a year, just after Christmas and just after my birth-day. "Where'd you get the money?" I asked.

"The monks gave it to me."

"Those bald guys?"

"They like me."

"Jeez, Muffin, don't let Mom know you took money from strangers. She'd have a fit."

"They aren't strangers. They're the Holy Order of the Immi-nent Eschaton—the Muffin Chapter."

"Oh, go ahead, lie to me."

"You want the ten dollars or not?"

Which wasn't what I ended up with, because she expected me to pay the bus fare out of it.

When we got to the boatyards, I thought we'd head down to the water, but Muffin took out a piece of paper and stood there frown-ing at it. I looked over her shoulder and saw it was torn from a map of the city. There was a small red X drawn in at a place about a block from where we were. "Where'd you get that? The monks?"

"Mm-hmm. Is this where we are?" She pointed at a street cor-ner. I looked and moved her finger till it was aiming the right place. "You should learn to read some time, Muffin."

She shook her head. "Might wreck my insight. Maybe after."

I pointed down the street. "If you want to go where X marks the spot, it's that way."

We walked along, with sailboats and yachts and things on one side and warehouses on the other. The buildings looked pretty run-down, with brown rusty spots dripping from their metal roofs and lots of broken windows covered with plywood or cardboard. It was a pretty narrow street and there was no sidewalk, but the only traffic we saw was a Shell oil truck coming out of the marina a ways ahead and it turned off before it got to us.

When we reached the X spot, it was just another warehouse. Muffin closed her eyes a second, then said, "Around the back and up the stairs."

"I bet there are rats around the back," I said.

"I bet there aren't."

"You go first."

"Okay." She started down an alley between one warehouse and the next. There was lots of broken glass lying around and grass growing up through the pavement.

"I bet there are snakes," I said, following her.

"Shut up, Jamie."

The back was only a strip of weeds two yards wide, stuck between the warehouse and a chain-link fence. Halfway along was a flight of metal steps, like a fire escape leading to the roof. They creaked when you walked on them, but didn't wobble too badly.

On the roof we found a weird-looking airplane. Or boat. Or train. Or wagon. Whatever it was, it had wings and a tail like an airplane, but its body was built like a boat: a bit like our motor-boat up at the cottage, but bigger and with these super-fat padded chairs like maybe astronauts sit in. The whole thing was attached to a cart, but the cart's wheels were on the near end of a train track that ran the length of the roof and off the front into the street.

"What *is* this thing?" I asked.

"The monks made it for me," Muffin said, which didn't answer my question. She climbed up a ladder into the plane and rummaged about in a cupboard on the rear wall. I followed her and watched her sorting through the stuff inside. "Peanut butter. Bread. Kool-Aid. Water. Cheese. Diet Coke. What's this?" she said, handing me back a roll of something in gold plastic wrapping.

I opened one end and sniffed. "Liverwurst," I said.

She made a face. "Is that like liver?"

"No, it's peanut butter made from bologna."

"Weird. Do you see any hot dogs?"

I looked in the cupboard. "Nope."

"I should phone the monks. We need hot dogs."

"What for?"

She ignored me. "Is there anything else you'd want if you were going to be away from home for a few days?"

"Cheerios and bacon."

She thought about that. "Yeah, you're right."

"And Big Macs."

She gave me a look like I was a moron. "Of course, dummy, but the monks will bring them just before we leave."

"We're going on a trip?"

"We're on a trip now. We're going to *arrive*."

Early the next morning, Dr. Hariki showed up on our doorstep. He works with my dad at the university. My dad teaches physics; he uses lasers and *everything*. Dr. Hariki is in charge of the big telescope on top of the physics building, and he takes pictures of stars.

"What's up?" Dad asked.

"You tell me," Dr. Hariki said, spreading a bunch of photographs on the coffee table.

Dad picked up a picture and looked at it. Turned it over to check out the date and time written on the back. Sorted through the stack of photos till he found whatever he was looking for and compared it to the first. Held the two together side by side. Held one above the other. Put them side by side again. Closed his right eye, then quick closed his left and opened his right. Did that a couple of times. Picked up another pair of photos and did the same.

Muffin came into the room with a glass of orange juice in her hand. "Looks more like a dipper now, doesn't it?" she said without looking at the pictures.

Dad and Dr. Hariki stared at her with their mouths wide open. Muffin said, "The dipper was too spread out before. Don't you think it looks better now?"

"Muffin," Dad said, "we're talking about stars . . . full-size suns. They don't just move to make nicer patterns."

"No, but if they're going to *stop* moving, you might as well make sure they look like a dipper in the end. Anything else is just sloppy. I mean, really."

She walked off into the TV room and a moment later, we heard the *Sesame Street* theme song.

After a long silence, Dr. Hariki picked up one of the photos and asked, all quiet, "Something to do with entropy?"

"I think it's teleology," I said.

That night Uncle Dave was over for Sunday supper. Mom figures that Uncle Dave doesn't eat so good in residence, so she feeds him a roast of something every Sunday. I think this is a great idea, except that every so often she serves squash because she says it's a delicacy. Lucky for us, it was corn season so we had corn on the cob instead.

After supper we all played Monopoly and I won. Uncle Dave said it made a nice family picture, us all sitting around the table playing a game. "Someday, kids," he said, "you're going to appreciate that you have times like this to remember. A perfect frozen moment."

"There are all kinds of perfect frozen moments," Muffin said, and she had that tone in her voice like she was eleventy-seven years old instead of six. "Right now, people all over the world are doing all kinds of things. Like in China, it's day now, right, Dad?"

"Right, Muffin."

"So there are kids playing tag and stuff, and that's a perfect moment. And maybe there's some bully beating up a little kid, and punching him out right *now*." She banged her Monopoly piece (the little metal hat) when she said "now." "And that's a perfect moment because that's what really happens. And bus drivers are driving their buses, and farmers are milking their cows, and mommies are kissing daddies, and maybe a ship is sinking someplace. If you could take pictures of everyone right now, you'd see millions of perfect little frozen moments, wouldn't you?"

Uncle Dave patted Muffin's hand. "Out of the mouths of babes . . . I'm the one who's studying the Wonders of Life, and you're the one who reminds me. Everything is perfect all the time, isn't it, Muffin?"

"Of course not, dummy," she answered, looking at Uncle Dave the way she did when he tried to persuade her he'd pulled a dime from her ear. She turned around in her chair and reached over to the buffet to get the photograph they'd taken of her kindergarten class just before summer holidays started. "See?" she said, pointing. "This is Bobby and he picks his nose all the time, and he's picking his nose in the picture, so that's good. But this is Wendy, with her eyes closed 'cuz she was blinking. That's not perfect. Wendy cries every time she doesn't get a gold star in spelling, and she knows three dirty words, and she always gives Matthew the celery from her lunch, but you can't tell that in the picture, can you? She's just someone who blinked at the wrong time. If you want someone who should be blinking, it should be dozy old Peter Morgan, who always laughs too loud."

Uncle Dave scratched his head and looked awkward for a bit, then said, "Well, Muffin, when you put it like that . . . I suppose there *are* always some things that aren't aesthetically pleasing . . . I mean, there are always going to be some things that don't fit properly, as you say."

"Not always," she said.

"Not always? Someday things are just going to be right?" Uncle Dave asked.

Muffin handed me the dice and said, "Your turn, Jamie. Bet you're going to land in jail."

Next morning Muffin joggled my arm to wake me up. It was so early the sun was just starting to rise over the lake. "Time to go down to the boatyards."

"Again?"

"Yep. This time for real." So I got up and dressed as quietly as I could. By the time I got down to the kitchen, Muffin had made peanut butter and jam sandwiches, and was messing around with the waxed paper, trying to wrap them. She had twice as much paper as she needed and was making a total botch of things.

"You're really clueless sometimes," I said, whispering so Mom and Dad wouldn't hear. I shoved her out of the way and started wrapping the sandwiches myself.

"When I rule the world, there won't be any waxed paper," she said sulkily.

We were halfway down to the bus stop when Uncle Dave came running up behind us. He'd been staying the night in the guest room and he must have heard us leaving. "Where do you think you're going?" he asked, and he was a bit mad at us.

"Down to the boatyards," Muffin said.

"No, you aren't. Get back to the house."

"Uncle Dave," Muffin said, "it's time."

"Time for what?"

"The Eschaton."

"Where do you pick up these words, Muffin? You're talking about the end of the world."

"I know." The first bus of the day was just turning onto our street two corners down. "Come to the boatyards with us, Uncle Dave. It'll be okay."

Uncle Dave thought about it. I guess he decided it was easier to give in than to fight with her. That's what I always think too. You can't win an argument with Muffin, and if you try anything else, she bites and scratches and uses her knees. "All right," Uncle Dave said, "but we're going to phone your parents and tell them where you are, the first chance we get."

"So talk to me about the Eschaton," Uncle Dave said on the bus. We were the only ones on it except for a red-haired lady wearing a Donut Queen uniform.

"Well," Muffin said, thinking things over, "you know how Daddy talks about astronomy things moving? Like the moon goes around the earth and the earth goes around the sun and the sun moves with the stars in the galaxy and the galaxy is moving too?"

"Yes . . ."

"Well, where is everything going?"

Uncle Dave shrugged. "The way your father tells it, everything just moves, that's all. It's not going anywhere in particular."

"That's stupid. Daddy doesn't understand teleology." She waved her hand at the world out the window. "Everything's going to where it's supposed to end up."

Uncle Dave asked, "What happens when things reach the place they're going?"

Muffin made an exasperated face. "They *end up* there."

"They stop?" .

"What else would they do?"

"All the planets and the stars and all?"

"Mm-hmm."

"People too?"

"Sure."

He thought for a second. "In perfect frozen moments, right?"

"Right."

Uncle Dave leaned his head against the window like he was tired and sad. Maybe he was. The sun was coming up over the housetops now. "Bus drivers driving their buses," he said softly, "and farmers milking their cows . . . the whole world like a coffee-table book."

"I think you'd like to be in a church, Uncle Dave," Muffin said. "Or maybe walking alone along the lakeshore."

"Maybe." He smiled, all sad. "Who are you, Muffin?"

"I'm me, dummy," she answered, throwing her arms around his neck and giving him a kiss.

He left us in front of the warehouse by the lake. "I'm going to walk down to the Rowing Club and back." He laughed a little. "If I *do* get back, Muffin, I'll have your parents ground you forever!"

"Bye, Uncle Dave," she said, hugging him.

I hugged him too. "Bye, Uncle Dave."

"Don't let her do anything stupid," he said to me. We watched for a while as he walked away, but he never turned back.

Up on the warehouse roof, there was a monk waiting with a McDonald's bag under his arm. He handed it to Muffin, then kneeled. "Bless me, Holy One."

"You're blessed," she said after looking in the bag. "Now get going to the temple. There's only ten minutes left."

The monk hurried off, singing what I think was a hymn. We got into the plane-boat and I helped Muffin strap herself into one of the big padded seats. "The thing is," she said, "when the earth stops turning, we're going to keep on going."

"Hey, I know about momentum," I answered. I mean, Dad *is* a physicist.

"And it's going to be real fast, so we have to be sure we don't run into any buildings."

"We're going to shoot out over the lake?"

"We're high enough to clear the tops of the sailboats, then we just fly over the lake till we're slow enough to splash down. The monks got scientists to figure everything out."

I strapped myself in and thought about things for a while. "If we go shooting off real fast, isn't it going to hurt? I mean, the astronauts get all pressed down when they lift off . . ."

"Jeez!" Muffin groaned. "Don't you know the difference between momentum and acceleration? Nothing's happening to us, it's everything else that's going weird. We don't feel a thing."

"Not even wind?"

"The air has the same momentum we do, dummy."

I thought about it some more. "Aren't the buildings going to get wrecked when the earth stops?"

"They're going to stop too. Everything will freeze except us."

"The air and water freeze too?"

"In spots. But not where we're going."

"We're special?"

"We're special."

Suddenly there was a roar like roller-coaster wheels underneath us and for a moment I was pressed up against the straps holding me down on the seat. Then the pressure stopped and there was nothing but the sound of wind a long way off. Over the side of the boat I could see water rushing by beneath us. We were climbing.

"Muffin," I asked, "should one of us maybe be piloting this thing?"

"It's got a gyroscope or something. The monks worked absolutely everything out, okay?"

"Okay."

A long way off to the right, I could see a lake freighter with a curl of smoke coming out of its stack. The smoke didn't move. It looked neat. "Nice warm day," I said.

After a while, we started playing car games to pass the time.

The sun shone but didn't move. "If the sun stays there forever," I asked, "won't it get really hot after a while?"

"Nah," Muffin answered. "It's some kind of special deal. I mean, it's stupid if you set up a nice picture of kids playing in the park but then it gets hot as Mercury."

"Who's going to know?" I asked.

"It's not the same," she insisted.

"How can we see?"

"What do you mean?"

"Well, is the light moving or what?"

"It's another special deal."

That made sense. From the way Dad talked about physics, light was always getting special deals.

The water below us gradually stopped racing away so fast and we could sometimes see frozen whitecaps on the peaks of frozen waves. "Suppose we land on frozen water," I said.

"We won't."

"Oh. Your turn."

"I spy with my little eye something that begins with B." Right away I knew she meant the Big Macs, but I had to pretend it was a toughie. You have to humor little kids.

We splashed down within sight of a city on the far side of the lake. It was a really good splash, like the one on the Zoomba Flume ride when you get to the bottom of the big long water chute. Both of us got drenched. I was kind of sad there was no way to do it again.

Then I thought to myself, maybe if we were getting a special deal on air and water and light and all, maybe we'd get a special deal on the Zoomba Flume too.

We unstrapped ourselves and searched around a bit. Finally we found a lid that slid back to open up a control panel with a little steering wheel and all. We pushed buttons till an inboard motor started in the water behind us, then we took turns driving toward shore. Every now and then we'd see a gull frozen in the sky, wings spread out and looking great.

We put in at a public beach just outside the city. It had been early in the day and the only people in sight were a pair of joggers on a grassy ridge that ran along the edge of the sand. The man wore nothing but track shorts and sunglasses; the woman wore red stretch pants, a T-shirt, and a headband. They each had Walkmans and were stopped midstride. Both were covered with deep dark tans, and as Muffin pointed out, a thin coat of sweat.

I wanted to touch the joggers to see what they felt like, but when my finger got close, it bumped against an invisible layer of frozen air. The air didn't feel like anything, it was just solid stuff.

Down at one end of the beach, a teenage girl was frozen in the act of unlocking the door into a snack stand. We squeezed past her and found out we could open the freezer inside. Muffin had a couple of Popsicles, I had an ice cream sandwich, and then we went swimming.

Lying in the sun afterward, I asked Muffin what was going to happen next.

"You want to go swimming again?" she said.

"No, I mean after."

"Let's eat," she said, dragging me back toward the boat.

"You can't wiggle out of it that easy," I told her. "Are we the only ones left?"

"I think so."

"Are we going to freeze too?"

"Nope. We got a special deal."

"But it seems pretty stupid if you ask me. Everything's kind of finished, you know? Show's over. Why are we still hanging around?"

"For a new show, dummy."

"Oh." That made sense. "Same sort of thing?"

"We'll see."

"Oh. Where do we fit in?"

Muffin smiled at me. "You're here to keep me company."

"And what are you here for?"

"Everything else. Get me a sandwich."

I reached into the basket and pulled out the sandwich on top. It was inside a plastic sandwich bag. "Didn't we wrap these in waxed paper?" I asked.

Muffin laughed.

The Children of Crèche

So it's good-bye to New Earth and <BINK> hello to Crèche."

Inter-World Vac/Lines is such a mind-slogging Mom-and-Pop outfit they think their good-bye/hello trick is cute. Halfway through the welcoming spiel from the burstingly mammalian Coffee-Tea-or-Kama-Sutra Flight Hostess—and speaking of sexual pandering, Inter-World, must we be so heavy-handed with the airborne pheromones in the cabin? I for one am more comfortable buckling up the seat belt when I don't have a point-lessly throbbing erection—halfway through the opening mono-logue with all its openly oozing female fecundity, they hit the cabin stasis field, and <BINK> it's six weeks later, we're dirtside on some colony where every particle of air has been through one lung too many, and Miss Wouldn't-You-Like-to-Know-If-I've-Been-Surgically-Enhanced is finishing off a sentence that started a cou-ple of dozen light-years ago. I mean, really, Inter-World, can't you see how smarmy the whole thing is?

No, you probably can't, you pitiful geckos.

It was with this lapse of taste in my mouth that your in-trepid Art-Critic-cum-Role-Model-cum-Provider-of-Vicarious-Savoir-Faire donned the traditional leather jacket of his profession and sallied forth into the Vac/Port for a first recce of the fabled planet of Crèche. I was not entirely surprised to find that a Vac/Port is a Vac/Port is a Vac/Port, all of modern semiotics notwithstanding. You have your usual gaggle of tourists from the colony one star system over, the ones with no particular idea why they're here, except they just *had* to get off-planet or go mad, and this place was cheaper than Morganna's Semen-Sea Whack-Me World; and you have your traditional traders from your favorite alien culture that doesn't see in the visible spectrum, blundering around with incomprehensible accents, asking humans to read the signs to them; and alas, you have your mass of parochial flibberties who shouldn't be allowed to read our dear old *Mind Spurs Weekly* but do anyway, who have pilgrimaged to the V/P to maketh the Big Embarrassing Frenzy of Gratitude that J*O*N*N*Y! T*H*E! S*C*A*L*P*E*L!, Knower of Taste and Taster of Knowing, has deigned to descend upon their terraformed little Nowhere to partake of their pathetic drippy lives and report same to the Cosmos at Large (i.e., You, Devoted Reader, currently feeling superior to such hicks, for reasons that are more obvious to you than to Yrs Trly).

Still and all, the Crèche mob of droolies were a touch outside the normal run: old as dry beavers, the lot of them. Of course This Reporter was aware of Crèche's famed shortfall in the production of mewlies and pukies; but you don't plug into the *reality* of a child-poor world until you wander into a Vac/Port expecting the usual horde of training bras, only to find their ecological niche has been filled by the saggy-sack set. At least these postmenopausal minks weren't packing those sharp little tissue-sampling spatulas that the gigglers bring to scrape off souvenirs. (Honest-to-Boggie, kids, if you really want to impregnate yourselves with my DNA, break down and shell out the bucks to one of the fine mail-order houses that advertise in this very magazine. You get professionally prepared guaranteed-viable sperm, a certificate of authenticity, and a hyper-sincere form letter produced by a state-of-the-art computer that fakes my signature better than

I do; and I get to have an epidermis that doesn't look like a land-use map. Bargains all 'round.)

For all their graysies, the Raging Aging were still cut from the typical Scalpel-worshipping mode—each and every one of them was waiting to be discovered. Crèche's idle idolizers came unto me bearing their children that I might bless them . . . said children being sketches and sculpture, mosaics and masks, tapestries, filigrees, etchings on flasks, holograms, cameos, prints wet and dry, ceramics and beadwork and oils, oh my!

Cherished Reader, perhaps you have recently heard Crèche lionized in song and cinema as the Mecca of all artistic perfection. Mine own ears too had been visited by paeans to the planet's sublime accomplishments, which is why I felt it incumbent upon me to visit said colony-size cathedral to Aesthetic Excellence and there do homage. Nevertheless, in those moments when I was besieged by the untalented Crèchian unwashed waving their pathetic attempts at self-expression like whores who want you to smell their panties, it came to me we must never forget that every cathedral is surrounded by pigeons screaming for crumbs and crapping on the architraves. Thus endeth the gospel according to Jonny.

I was saved from the gaggle of gleanies by my contact on Crèche, one Philip Leppid, Ph.D., Ph.D., Ph.D. (in Music History, Art History, and Pharmacology—the Three Graces). As those who claim to be au courant with the Contemporary Art Scene should know, the good Doctor-Doctor-Doctor is the man who first brought Crèchian objets d'art to the attention of Those-Whose-Opinions-Are-Thought-to-Matter, in a gala showing last year at Buddenbrooks & Bleaks. Since that time, he has made himself buckets of booty huckstering the work wherever empty lives and full wallets are found. He is not Crèchian himself—he hails from the hinterlands of a world named after some bottom-of-the-barrel Greek god who wouldn't have rated a pico-asteroid in the old Sol System—but Leppid is Crèche's foremost Advocate-

Slash-Publicist-Slash-Pimp, and therefore was the natural choice to serve as my Sherpa during my Ascent to the Peak of Human Ahhh-tistic Achievement.

When he sighted me foundering on the shoals of a blue rinse ocean, Doc Leppy (as I never heard him called the whole time I was there) waded in with heroic disregard for his own ship of taste, scattered the minnows with the indiscriminate barging of his 300+ pounds, and dragged me to the safety of his waiting Lava Cruiser Deluxe. To be accurate, the cruuz was a cherry red Ourobouros Devourer 4.3BSD from the Wildebeest Motor Works, with manual steering, a logarithmic tachometer, and two dangling wires where the anti-collision computer used to be. The uphol-stery was taut white, covered with the bleached hide of an endan-gered species that I probably shouldn't name because it would earn Leppid a visit from ecological guerrillas with a nasty How-Would-*You*-Like-to-Be-Tanned-and-Sat-On attitude. Ah, what the hell, it was an alligator. (Sorry, Phil—the Public's Need-to-Know wore down my resistance. Anyway, what have you done for me lately?)

With Leppid at the wheel, we peeled out of the Vac/Port at a speed that didn't quite break the sound barrier but opened a hair-line crack or two, and one exit ramp later we were spattering through the local lava fields fast enough to throw up a peacock tail of molten rock directly behind us . . . except it wasn't directly be-hind us too often, because Phil was weaving like a tripped-out spi-der: hard to port, hard to starboard, through our own wake of stony slush, one grade A skidding donut that bid fair to roll us Ass-over-Teacup o'er the burning plain, one six-G deceleration that buried our nose so deep in volcanic phlegm I found myself wishing I'd brought a periscope . . . and finally I had to say, "Phil. Enlighten me. Are we taking evasive maneuvers from snipers, or are you just jerking off?"

"Come on, Scalpel." He grinned as he gave the wheel a twist

that heeled us over far enough to scorch the door handles. "I read that piece you did on the Overdrive Overlords of Omicron II. They drove around like maniacs and you wrote the most glowing review of your life."

"It seems to have escaped your attention, Phil, but the Overdrive Overlords were engaged in performance art," I told him. "They did not drive like maniacs, they drove like artists. The distinction may be subtle, but I like to think it's important."

Leppid snorted as if he knew what I really meant.

"If you recall any fragment of the article," I insisted, "from the moment they made their commitment to Art, it became the most important things in their lives. They made *sacrifices,* Phil. They were willing to Bleed for the Cause. Need I remind you the couple who drove *Ballet of the Sand* had abstained from Vigorous-Convexity-in-Voracious-Concavity for six wanking months because they thought the yearning would make the performance more poignant? And even though I am not of the school that believes celibacy is a nonconsummation devoutly to be wished, I must confess there were tears in the Scalpine Big Browners as I watched them dance. Yes, the dancers were driving cars across salt flats, and yes, they were smashing fenders and sideswiping each other at velocities most speedometers only dream of; but they were expressing deep things, Phil! Two souls locked inside metal hulks, trying to make contact, trying to come together, turning near collisions into ballet, and eventually using the cars themselves to make soaring gentle love. Magic! Art! Spirit, Phil, greatness of spirit! The material is immaterial, the artifact is arbitrary. The heart, the soul, and the life of Art is what counts." I paused. "Is any of this sparking neurons, Phil, or am I just impersonating a tree falling in a forest?"

"Come on, Jonny, I know what you really want is to get totally wild."

I sighed. The difference between a Sensitive-Critic-Known-

Respected-and-Feared-in-All-Corners-of-the-Galaxy and an Opportunistic-Boor-Who-Might-Have-Three-Degrees-but-Doesn't-Know-Titian-from-Turds is that one of us has eyes that see and ears that hear, while the other has an assortment of prejudices he waits to have confirmed. "Phil," I told him, "*you* are getting wild, the car is getting wild, and the lava is getting positively livid. I, on the other hand, am sitting here passively, save for the occasional reflexive jerk to prevent my skull from making forceful contact with the dashboard."

Leppid laughed loud and long at that, all the while playing Jiggle-Me-Juicy with the steering wheel. The world is divided into two groups: the people who listen to what you say and ponder it deeply in their hearts; and the people who think every word that issues forth from your mouth is utterly facetious, and can even write down your clever turns of phrase and quote them in articles, without ever allowing it to penetrate their brains that you are trying to make a *statement*.

So Leppid pursued his attempts at wooing me by wowing me, until Crèche's sun moseyed off to see if there was anything doing on the other side of the planet and the stars showed up to see what had changed since they left. At first glance, lava-leaping in a cruuz looks even better after dark because of the weaving strips of black and flame, the fountaining of sparks, the gouting arcs of hot planet blood . . . but all that brucey imagery loses its charm damned fast if the smoky shadow you drive into is a jag of recalcitrant bedrock too pigheaded to melt. At last, even the good Triple-Doc had to admit further monkeyshines in the murky magma were just a shade closer to suicidal than good taste allowed, so with tears in his eyes he called it a night.

We pulled up onto the highway at a spot apparently made for the purpose: something like a boat launching ramp, only gnubbly with flecks of dried lava dripped off by other hot-hot-hot-rodders who'd passed this way before. There was a bevy of Bloat-Belly trucks sharing the road with us, all coming from the Vac/Port and no doubt filled with the gewgaws of a hundred worlds, belched up from the cargo holds of the same Vac/Ship that brought Your Obedient Servant. The trucks we passed were all bot-driven, which was just fine with me—if Phil had seen one of those Bloaters under human control, he would have drag-raced the rig in order to demonstrate his testosterone level to his captive member of the Press. (Ah, children, the world is full of people who want to impress the old Scalper with feats of derring-do. My advice is, derring-don't.)

Nascence City, the colonial capital, nestles halfway up the side of a volcano everyone swears is extinct (this surrounded by a lavid plain that seethes with fumaroles, geysers, and the like . . . suuurrrrre). You can see its lights winking, blinking, and nodding among the crags when you are down on the flats, but when the road actually begins climbing the mountain, your line of sight is blocked by assorted igneous effusions that welled up some thirty million years ago—this geological travelogue courtesy of *Nascence Alive!!!*, one of those End-Every-Sentence-with-an-Exclamation-Point publications whose natural habitat is the top drawer of hotel night tables.

The hotel in question was the Nascence Renaissance—redundant in name, and redundant to describe for those who have stayed at its kin throughout our wart on the galactic arm. Squatting by the main highway, just inside the environment dome's airlock, surrounded with carefully tended greenery that would look more natural if it were plastic . . . anyone who has traveled on expense account knows this same hotel follows you from city to city, running on ahead so it has time to put down its foundations and change its makeup in the hope you won't recognize it from the night before. Everywhere, the same covered entranceway, whether you drive up in a lava cruuz, sand-crawler, or gondola: so dark and shadowed by the overhanging portiere they need lights during the daytime (globe-lights in simulated antique fixtures), and as you are helped from your vehicle by a grizzled male in pseudo-military livery, you see assembling a battalion of bellhops who wash their ruddy cheeks each morning in a fifty-fifty aqueous solution of eagerness and cynicism. Professional small talk ensues momentarily; then, into a plush lobby befitted with oaken desk, crystal chandelier, and round-the-clock concierge (always a middle-aged woman who is the epitome of courtesy and dispatch, but who you can tell was a Grade A heart- and ball-breaker in her day).

You can count on two artpieces in the foyer: one some sort of sunset, the other an historical motif, neither aggressively representational or abstract. The Nascence Renaissance held true to form on the first, with a hooked shag-wool tapestry of one (1) regulation red giant about to take its roseate leave behind a near-naked horizon clad only in a tastefully placed cactus. But what to my wondering eyes should appear on the wall above the neo-Victorian pseudo-hearth? Not the black-and-white Battle of This, nor the blue-study Treaty of That, nor even the sepia Discovery of the Other Thing: it was a layered assemblage of vertical Mylar and buckram strips, the Mylar a wispy mercurial foreground that tinseled several planes of fabric behind it (like a curtain of mist in a dream? a glittering spiderweb? bars of a gossamer cage?), and the stiff cloth backgrounds painted with dyes to give a textured three-dimensional picture of a nursery—playpen, cradle, toy box, stuffed animals scattered about the floor, dolls toppled over on a window seat, a closet with its door ajar and filled to overflowing with tiny, carefully hung clothes.

At first, there was no one visible; but as I examined the work, I thought there was a small movement behind one of the nursery curtains. When I looked directly at it, nothing; but out of the corner of my eye, I caught a tiny quiver of motion behind the closet door, ducking out of sight too soon for me to see. Then in the toy box; then from behind a pile of dolls; then under the blanket tossed carelessly beside the cradle—the piece was alive with children peeking from behind every strip of fabric, but hiding too fast to leave more than the ghost of their passing.

"Computer-controlled," Leppid said at my elbow. "Hidden cameras keep track of your eye movements. You can watch all day and the little buggers will never be where you're looking."

"Could get bloody irritating after a while," I said.

"If it was done badly." He shrugged. "But it's not." And even though I was not kindly disposed toward the Doctor[3] at the time, I had to admit he was right. The work had a subtlety and a sly naturalness that made it both haunting and haunted.

"Who's the artist?" I asked.

"Vavash," he answered. "Earth mother type—long straight silver hair, shapeless tie-dyed dresses, would rather wear glasses than have corrective surgery . . . a textbook classic. One of the First Colonists, of course. They're what make Crèche what it is. Since the Rediscovery, a lot of lesser lights have settled here to bask in reflected glory, but no one of any stature. Most of the new immigrants are . . . well, the group at the Vac/Port were typical. Black Velveteers."

"We'll stick to the First Colonists," I said hurriedly.

"I thought you'd feel that way." Leppid grinned. "I've set up a visit to their retreat tomorrow morning. It's in the Upper City— poshly Spartan. Entirely state-supported too; the other colonists treat the Firsties like royalty. Not much interaction between old and new, except at official ceremonies. It wouldn't hurt you to be a bit deferential around them."

I gave him a look that was intended to wither his fat-beribboned carcass right in its pointy-toed shoes. He laughed and slapped me on the back as if I'd told a joke.

My internal clock was scarcely in the sleeping mood when I retired to my room, so it seemed like a good time to refresh my memories about the sordid history of Crèche by looking up the colony in *Auntie Agatha's Encyclopedia of All Those Things You Should Have Learned in School, You Jam-Headed Git, But No, You Were Too Lazy to Apply Yourself and Now Look Where You Are . . .* a reference work I have recommended many times in this column, whenever I use it as a cheap expository device.

The First Colonists landed on Crèche some sixty years ago, the vanguard of what was intended to be a grand colonizing caravan that would bring hundreds of thousands of other nouveau Crèchi and Crèchae to this toasty-warm lava-ball. For Reasons That Have Never Been Adequately Explained (i.e., a computer error the sneaky machines managed to cover up before human auditors arrived), all of the subsequent colony ships were diverted to the beautiful planet of Mootikki, famed for its semisentient water spiders that eat anything with a pulse. Forty years passed before some minor functionary stumbled across records of the original Crèche expedition and dispatched a scout to peek in on their progress.

Crèche had not done badly, all things considered. There had only been ninety people on the lead ship, but there had been a full complement of builder-bots, plus all the materials needed to erect a life support dome and get the food vats pulsating. In fact, with only ninety people to support, there was an embarrassment of supplies, and more than enough bot-power to keep the staples stapled.

All skittles and beer then . . . except for The Problem. As reported by the Crèchians to the scout four decades later, no children had come. Hell, yes, they had tried to make babies, with total lusty devotion; and according to medical analyses, they were as fertile as Teenagers-Who-Think-It-Can't-Happen-to-Them; but

something in the water/air/topsoil/Van Allen belts was prevent-
ing Mr. Sperm and Ms. Ovum from producing nicens little baby
Zygote, and year after year went by without those little feet
a-patterin'.

Now our old friend Sigmund the Shrink would be cocky as a
cigar to hear what happened next: the Crèche colony turned to
the solace of Art as compensation for lack of littl'uns. (Isn't that
always the way? Every time you think Freudian psychology has
finally achieved its own death wish and the world can move on to
something loftier than the Poopoo-Weewee-Slurp School of Human Behavior, along comes some pack of clods giving their all to
make the All-World Sublimation Team and you're right back in
Libido-land. The human psyche is pretty damned anal-retentive
about Freudianism.) Still, I thought to myself, the Crèchians
hadn't chosen either their situation or their hang-ups; the important question was what they had made with what they were
given.

Morning arrived with an artillery barrage of photons on my eyelids and a cheerful computer voice saying, "This is your wake-up
call, Mr. The Scalpel."

"I didn't ask for a wake-up call!" I bleared from under a pillow.

"This is a free service of the Nascence Renaissance Hotel. If
there is any other service I may perform for you, I would be happy
to comply."

A less experienced traveler would have retorted with a suggestion both vulgar and topologically challenging; but I knew better.
I once used a pithy colloquialism in response to an annoying hotel
computer, and an hour or so later, room service was at the door
with a huge agglomeration of feedscrews and suction pumps that
was apparently capable of doing precisely what I'd specified. Not
only did I have to pay for materials and transport costs, but there

was a hefty fee for custom molybdenum tooling that had had to be done in a low-G L5 colony.

I have to admit, though, the contraption did work as advertised.

Breakfast came with a complimentary copy of the *Crèche Colony Chronicle* (alliteration is the soul of journalism). The front page was splashed with many of the same articles slopping around on the stands the day I left New Earth . . . no big surprise, since all the news must have come in with me on the Vac/Ship. However, there was one interesting tidbit: Miss All-the-King's-Horses-and-All-the-King's-Men Flight Attendant had apparently caused a major uproar by sneaking away from the Vac/Port and visiting one of Nascence's night spots. Oh, the outrage! A fertile female at large amidst the Barrens! The Colonial Cops had clapped her in irons posthaste and transported her in utter ignominy back to the V/P, there to remain in quarantine until her ova-rich ass could be kicked off-planet.

"Computer!" I called. "Do you do legal information?"

"I am fully prepared to make small talk on legal matters, none of which should be construed to imply, suggest, or covenant that information imparted in such wise constitutes qualified advice from the Nascence Renaissance Hotel, which will in no way be held liable for any damages, costs, expenses, claims, actions, or proceedings that may result directly or indirectly from this little chat."

"Just confirm for me that women of childbearing age aren't allowed on Crèche."

"Human females below the age of fifty may not immigrate to Crèche unless they are certified incapable of reproduction."

"And why's that?"

"For their own protection. Some factor in Crèche's environment makes childbearing impossible. The First Colonists do not want others to suffer the infertility they themselves endured; and as the authorized colonial government, the First Colonists have benevolently forbidden off-planet women from subjecting themselves to such risks."

"What about men?"

"Men of all ages are welcomed."

"But, computer, I thought no one understood the sterility. How do the First Colonists know men are safe but women aren't?"

"Have you enjoyed your breakfast, Mr. The Scalpel?"

"You didn't answer my question, computer."

"Did you notice how evenly we spread the marmalade on your toast? The Nascence Renaissance Hotel kitchen-bots take great personal pride in attending to the smallest details."

"Am I to assume I'm venturing into areas of the data banks that are missing, classified, or both?"

"The sauce on the eggs is a special invention of the chef's. He's won prizes for it."

Ahh, a quick prayer of thanks to Elizabeth of Hungary, patron saint of the hasty cover-up. It is a far, far tastier sauce for a journalist's breakfast than some soupy pseudo-Hollandaise that probably came from the rear end of some bacterium.

By the time Leppid came to pick me up in his manic-mobile, I had rented a vehicle of my own: a docile town car that understood it was a mode of transport, not a kinetic emetic. When Leppid got into the passenger seat, I believe he thought the car was a dragster incognito; all the way up to the First Colonist retreat, he was bracing himself for the moment when I would press some hidden button and go FTL. His face was red with nervous perspiration by the time we reached the front gates.

Now if we are to believe *Mind Spur Weekly*'s demographic studies, you, Gentle Reader, are likely to be an upper-middle-class inhabitant of the more frequented worlds, a youngish college-educated pseudo-intellectual who fancies him- or herself weird and unconventional, though you wouldn't know real weirdness if it bit you on the bum and licked . . . in short, you're a byte-pusher and probably a civil servant. As such, you have no doubt imagined the life you intend to lead when you achieve supremacy within your employment oligarchy—the dining room suites made of gold, the platinum bathroom fixtures, the black velour drapes speckled with diamonds in patterns that mimic the local star map—and you believe Everyone Who Wields Power must share your dreams of wallowing in the mud-pits of flagrant excess.

The First Colonists owned Crèche as thoroughly as you own your monogrammed handkersniffs; but they had more Style and Taste and Class in their nostril hairs than the entire populations of several planets I could name. There was no showy Imported-Vegetation-Intended-to-Look-Lush-While-Not-Straying-a-Millimeter-Out-of-the-Kidney-Shaped-Flower-Bed-Where-It-Belongs or Mansion-Built-to-Ape-Some-Blissful-Historical-Period-When-Culture-Was-in-Full-Flower-and-Peasants-Knew-Their-Place. Their retreat consisted of dozens of two-room prefab huts spread over a tract of unadorned twisted sheeny-black volcanic cinder, and a mammoth central building that looked like a Vac/Ship hangar and served as refectory, general store, and studio.

The plainness of the buildings was offset by a profusion of statuary: at the top of every rise, at the bottom of every hollow, on the side of every cinder slope stable enough to support weight. Just inside the gate (which opened automatically as we approached), we passed a life-size hologram of an ancient metal swing set—at first sight, brand new, painted in bright reds and yellows, but aging rapidly as we drove forward until it was rusting and pitted; then back again, freshly reborn. A little farther on, a copper-green man and woman stood side by side a short distance apart, with their hands held out and down as if they supported an invisible child between them. Not too far beyond that, a tree of dew-slick steel pipes supported a host of mirrored cylinders that dangled on silver cords and swayed in the morning breeze; within each cylinder, some light source gave off a golden glow that shone up on the pipes' wet sheen.

"Something's happening over there," Leppid said, pointing. Some twenty people were walking in slow single file across the slaggy landscape, following a pair of bots who carried something I couldn't make out. The humans were all old, in their eighties or nineties; even the bots were elderly, obsolete models not seen in the fashionable part of the galaxy for many years. One of the bots was playing a recorded flute solo through speakers that crackled with age.

Doc-Doc-Doc Phil and Your Ever-Curious Correspondent got out of the car to investigate. Walking across the gnarled terrain was an open invitation for the Gods of Twisted Ankles to give us a sample of their handiwork; but like most gods, they didn't exist, so we managed to reach the procession with tibiae untouched. The man at the end of the line said nothing, but nodded in recognition to Leppid and motioned for us to follow.

From this new vantage point, we could see what the bots were carrying: more perfectly polished than the finest mirror, the silvery ovoid of a stasis field with the size, shape, and probable functionality of a coffin. Perhaps the same stasis chest had housed one of the First Colonists on the voyage that had brought them to Crèche—in those early days of Vac/Flight, travelers were wrapped in individual containers instead of the full-cabin One-Field-Immobilizes-All systems used now.

The parade stopped at the edge of a cloudy pool that thickened the air with the smell of sulfur. The bots tipped the coffin and stood it on end as a plump woman at the head of the line reached into her apron and produced a copper wand with a ceramic handle. She touched the tip of the wand to the surface of the stasis field, and <BINK> the field popped like a soap bubble on a sharp toenail. Revealed to the gloom of an overcast day was the naked, emaciated corpse of a woman in her nineties, liver-spotted hands folded over her flat-flap breasts. She had coins where most of us have eyes, and a small butterfly tattoo where many of us have small butterfly tattoos.

Suddenly the woman with the wand proclaimed in a belly-deep voice, "There are some among us who have compared Life to Stasis. In our trip from birth to death, we are locked inside a body that can be frozen with sickness or age or fear. If this is so, death is the moment of liberation, of release, of reaching our long-awaited destination. We wish our sister well in her new world."

The woman bent over the body and kissed the dead cheeks with that airy Two-Centimeters-from-Contact Kiss that was so much in vogue sixty years ago. The corpse accepted it in the spirit with which it was intended. Then the line began to move, and we all got a chance to scope out the bare-ass carcass and take what liberties we chose. As we filed along, watching others shake the deceased's hand, stroke her flanks, and so on, Leppid murmured to me, "The dead woman called herself Selene. She specialized in collage . . . very personal stuff. This whole thing is a surprise to me—I saw her a couple of days ago and she seemed very healthy."

"She wasted away pretty damned quick then, didn't she?"

"Oh, she was always very thin. If you'd ever seen her work, you'd know. She often incorporated photos of herself into pieces."

"Ahh." Self-portraits have a long and noble history—Art will let you pick a self-indulgent subject as long as the self-indulgence stops before you get your brushes gooey. When I drew close and had my turn to pay my unfamiliar respects, I intended to give a quick smooch and walk on; but something caught my eye and held me there much longer than protocol required. Dim and camouflaged by the mottled old skin, stripes of stretch marks chevroned down both sides of her belly.

Esteemed Reader, there are only a few conditions that stretch abdominal skin enough to leave permanent marks. One of them is obesity, from which the scrawny Selene apparently had not suffered. The only other common cause is pregnancy. It was an enigma I pondered deeply as Selene's remains were remaindered into the steaming maw of the planet's digestive system.

In the main building, a retrospective of Selene's work had been hastily mounted on one side of the Dear Departed's studio: a collage of collage. There was a canvas covered with gears and gems and alphabet blocks . . . a volcano-shaped mound of plaster wrapped in wrinkled tissue paper, dabbed with blobs of solder and melted crayons . . . the great bowl of a radar dish sequined with thousands of tiny dolls' eyes opening and closing in accordance with a cellular automaton schema described in an accompanying booklet . . . but no, no, no, it is not the Old Scalper's intention to describe too many of the Art objects on Crèche. Quick jump to the earliest piece in the collection: by luck or deus ex machination, a life-size double photograph of Selene herself at twenty, front and back view, in the buff. Titled *Birth, Re-Birth, and Its Consequences*, it was the usual sort of work colonial artists seemed compelled to produce when starting off fresh on a new world: an assessment of who she had been and what she was now.

The two full-length photographs were black and white, very clinical, tacked to a corkboard backing. Every scar on the artist's body was carefully circled with red paint; black surgical thread connected each scar on the photos to an accompanying card that explained the circumstances surrounding the scar. (Judging from her knees, Selene had been one of those children who should never be permitted to play on gravel.) Since I know what you all are wondering, the answer is no—her taut little tum-tum showed nary a sign of stretch, hurt, or lesion.

"See something you like?" a woman asked from behind my back. Her voice sounded amused. Without turning around, I knew she must have been watching me scrutinize the photo of naked young Selene; no doubt she thought I was staring with lascivious intent.

"I see an interesting lead to an article I'm writing," I replied, making a point not to turn away from the nude photo. "The moment I arrive, I become part of a funeral. Later I come across a picture of the same woman sixty years younger. I should be able to use that somehow: irony, contrast, the usual glib literary nonsense."

"Oh."

I finally turned around. The woman behind me was, of course, Vavash—more or less as Leppid described her, and more rather than less. She loomed a head taller than I and a beefy bicep wider, the product of one of those Fringe Worlds that dabbled in übermensch breeding programs. For all her eighty years, her eyes were as clear as the cry of a hawk and her spine as straight as a teenage erection. She wore a shapeless tie-dyed dress (pink on green), not to mention huge round spectacles, leather sandals, and a gold mandala on a chain about her neck. A naïve observer might call her an anachronism, a clichéd throwback to the Stoned Age; but there was too much intelligence in her for anything so trite.

She'd been the woman who led the funeral, and to all appearances she was the First of the First. Frankly, the other First Colonists were a sorry-looking lot: over half had already died of old age, and most of the rest were only a shuffle-step away from Worm Chow. I doubted that more than a handful were actively working anymore. A functioning studio is filled with more smells than a Fomalhaut Flatutorium—oils and turpentine and damp clay, hot metal and etching chemicals, tart developing fluid, fresh sawdust, the crinkle of human sweat—but the studio building I stood in carried only the ghosts of effluvia past.

"Was this Selene's first work?" I asked.

"Earliest surviving, I would guess," Vavash answered. "She was fresh out of art school when she signed up for the Crèche colony. I'm sure she had many student pieces, but I doubt if they're still around. Not on Crèche, anyway. That's not the sort of frippery colonists were allowed to bring with them in the old days."

"So Selene planned to be an artist all along?"

"Oh, we all did. Crèche was intended to be an artistic commune. What was called a Second Wave colony. The earliest colonies, the First Wave, were founded solely on economic grounds—which planets had the most valuable minerals, which were the cheapest to terraform, that sort of thing. The Second Wave was an idealistic backlash: hundreds of special interest groups wanting to set up utopias to show everyone else how it was done. Pure ideology, with no materialistic bullshit. I got invited to half a dozen Art-oriented colonies before I finally decided on Crèche."

"What distinguished Crèche for you?"

Vavash laughed. "I had a boyfriend and he liked the name. That's the truth as seen from the objectivity of old age. At the time, I would have sworn I made my decision out of unsullied idealism, and my Tomas would have said the same thing. What distinguished Crèche after the fact, of course, was that those of us who landed here had forty years to work without outside interruption, and with such a surplus of supplies we never had to do nonartistic labor."

"You had all you needed?"

"We had the essentials, but we didn't have everything. Very little technology beyond the basic terraforming machinery. You can see that in our Art, of course . . . we work in media that are centuries old. And almost all the medical supplies and medic-bots were on one of the other ships. We were lucky the authorities put us through rigorous decontamination procedures before leaving

New Earth. If any of us had brought in a single little plague germ, the whole colony would have been defenseless."

"You were also lucky you never had children. Pregnancy can get very dicey, medically speaking."

I knew I was taking a bloody great risk bringing up such a touchy subject. The First Colonists *were* the government on Crèche, and Vavash was their leader. If she decided to cut off my head and parade it around the Vac/Port on a pike . . . well, in place of reading my pellucid prose you'd probably be skipping over some unctuous obit on the late Scalpel, Jonathan The, by that self-important Gretchen What's-Her-Name whose incoherent ramblings blight these pages when I'm away on assignment. (By the way, that picture they run above Gretchie's byline isn't really her—it's just a stand-in. Our Valiant Editor is afraid if he shows the Gretch as she really is, the *Weekly* will get slapped with an injunction for Harboring the Product of a Genetic Experiment Counter to the Public Interest. Hi, Gretchikins. Kiss kiss.)

But as you have probably guessed, Vavash did not choose to take extreme rancor. She simply stared at me with piercing eyes and said, "You are rude, Mr. Scalpel. I can't tell if you're being rude because you don't know any better or because you intentionally want to provoke me. Which is it, Mr. Scalpel? Are you a pugnacious little brat or some scheming Machiavelli?"

"I'm an Art Critic, ma'am," I replied. "Brat and Machiavelli all in one."

"Does that justify taunting a woman to her face?"

"Politeness is the enemy of both Art and Criticism. It tries to color true perception, dilute strong emotion, and replace genuine compassion. To pursue bad manners is childish, to pursue good ones is emasculation."

"Are you quoting someone?"

"Myself," I said, wondering why it wasn't self-evident. "How can you people call yourself artists if you don't read my column? And why would you let a Critic through your front gate if you didn't respect his judgment? I feel like I've washed up on one of those islands where the lizards have never seen a predator."

She looked me up and down once more with a critical eye. Suddenly, I had the impressions she was assessing me for my proficiency in the Slap-and-Tickle Disciplines. I knew the colonies Vavash called the Second Wave were rife with the belief that Genital Interlock could solve any problem, from How-Can-I-Show-This-Cocky-Little-Punk-He-Doesn't-Know-Everything to Oh-God-I'm-Bored-and-Everyone-Around-Me-Is-Senile. I was rehearsing my standard speech #24 ("I'm sure it would be delightful, duckie, but I only review people on one Art at a time") when Vavash shook herself and said, "You are many things I dislike, Mr. Scalpel; but I believe you have integrity. Feel free to wander where you choose."

The woman departed in a pink and green swirl. Leppid, with his toady-suck way of hovering in the background, came out from behind an installation piece (a mound of rag dolls, each with a picture of Selene spiked to the chest by means of a voodooine hatpin) and mopped his brow, saying, "Ye gods, Scalpel, I thought I told you to be deferential."

"You did. I ignored you."

We spent many hours touring the studio building—Leppid looming behind my shoulder, pointing out the obvious and the obnoxious, punctuating his every remark with a pudgy finger poking at my chest. For your delectation, allow me to present a typical Leppidine diatribe, held in front of a trompe l'oeil picture of a shadow-bedecked wooden chair with a teddy bear carelessly sprawled on the seat.

"See this, Scalpel?" he said. "An oil painting. Colored pigment on canvas. Showing something you can immediately recognize. That *sells*, Scalpel, that sells on any planet, Fringe World, or colony you want to name. Why? Because Art consumers recognize it as Art. Yesterday you were saying Art isn't artifacts, and you hit the nail right on the head. Art consumers—*my* Art consumers—aren't buying artifacts, they're buying into the Human Artistic Tradition. And this Crèche stuff, it's classic. Painting, sculpture, tapestry, illustration . . . that's what Art was, for thousands of years. People know that. They want to be part of the greatness. So you tell me why that damned Inter-World is so chintzy with cargo space they're only allowing me eight cubic meters on this next flight out. At that rate, I'll need decades to get a good volume of Crèche's work on the market!"

Well, Precious Perusers, whatever there may be off-planet, there is a whacking great volume of work in the Crèche studios, and it is quite beyond the capacity of this reviewer to critique a comprehensive catalog. Some of it is quotidian—all the time and freedom in the Bang-Crunch cycle won't wring masterpieces from the determinedly mediocre—but much of it is high quality stuff . . . if you like being chopped in the chin with childlessness. Wham, we don't have children; whap, we *can't* have children; powee, we'll never again *see* children.

How much Crèchian work has actually found its way out to the World at Large? A tiny fraction of the amount that is still on their planet. And on any given world, there might be at most twenty pieces, distributed over several collections. No one out there has experienced one iota of the cumulative impact of a sortie through Sterility Studio-land.

For example, empty cradles were an egregiously popular theme, especially when embellished with some unplayed-with toy trying to look pathetic. Wooden cradles; macramé cradles; molded glass cradles with marbles embedded in them; wicker cradles fondly tucked up with bunny rabbit blankets; cradle sketches in pencil, charcoal, India ink, sepia, silverpoint; cradle paintings in acrylics, watercolors, oils, gouache, tempera, and several home-made concoctions that looked like crushed lava particles suspended in white glue; and this is not to mention all the collages, assemblages, and installations that managed to sneak in cradlelike objects amidst the battered packing crates and out-of-context magazine clippings that traditionally provide the backbone for such works.

There were indeed pieces without obvious reference to barrenness—mirrored cylinders were very big, for example, and it didn't take someone of my keen intellect to see they represented the stasis chests that carried the colonists to Crèche—but there was no escaping the overpowering presence of the underage absence. It was a scab these people couldn't help picking, psychological vomit they had to keep revisiting.

With brief stops for lunch and supper at the refectory (bot-staffed and culinarily uninspired), I plowed on undaunted until we saw twilight through the skylight. In that whole time, I had encountered none of the other colonists; Leppid said they were probably holding some kind of post-funeral vigil for Selene in the hut where she'd lived. Considering my usual working conditions, trying to do my job while sandwiched between artists and agents groveling, picking fights, or both, I was quite chipper to be left on my own.

Naturally, I put off what I hoped would be the best till last: Vavash's studio. Several times during the day I had caught a whiff of it, a tingly tangle of herbs and chemicals with the fragrance of the back room of an alchemist's shop. When I stepped through the door, I immediately saw where the smells came from: vats of fabric dyes, extracted by hand from roots and leaves and flowers and seeds that Vavash must have brought with her and grown hydroponically. Above the vats were festoons of freshly dyed yarn in long skeins as thick as my arm, cones of thread stuck on pegs, and wool bats hanging from hooks like fuzzy Ping-Pong paddles. On the opposite wall were shelves all the way up to the roof, thick with bolts of felt and broadcloth and muslin. In one back corner, a spinning wheel stood beside a cherrywood loom with more pedals than a pipe organ; in the other, a sturdy table two fathoms long supported a gleaming new sewing machine with so many dials and levers and robotic attachments it would probably qualify for full citizenship under the Mechanical Species Act. And in the middle of the room, Vavash had left a small collection of her work. It brought tears to my eyes.

Honored Reader, Genius is rare. True talent is sparse enough, but Genius . . . the kind of monumental vision where every picture tells a satori. . . .

Some psychologists contend that inside every soul, there is Genius waiting to spring forth in strength and passion and beauty . . . and some sentimentalists would have it that many a Genius is born to blush unseen and waste its sweetness on the desert air. All I know is that billions upon billions of human beings have been squeezed from wombs throughout history, but there are less than a thousand who we can scrupulously say had Genius.

Vavash had Genius.

And she had squandered it.

Doll clothes. A tapestry strung with toys. Empty cradles.

So damned close to being a profound statement of loss or yearning or bitter tragedy . . . but ultimately the whole shebang was devoid of heart. Some step of emotion just wasn't there to take. I saw entirely new ways of combining textiles and dyes, ideas as eye-opening as pointillism or cubism or scintillism were in their day . . . but once your eyes had been opened by the woman's wonders of technique, she had nothing substantial to show you. These were the visions of a towering artist who had stared into the very depths of the Abyss . . . and in response, all she'd done was make pretty wallpaper.

Empty cradles. Empty fornicating cradles. Vavash had the eyes of Genius, the hands of Genius, the brain of Genius. But not the purity. Not here. Not in these works.

"There has to be more," I said hoarsely.

"What?" asked Leppid.

"The woman's been working for sixty years. She's done more than this. Where is it?"

"I think there are storerooms in the basement . . ."

"Show me."

Leppid peered at me nervously, as if I were a bomb about to go off—not a bad assessment of my mental state. Keeping fidgety watch over his shoulder, he led me through bare cement corridors to a thick metal door. "Down there. I've never been myself." He tried turning the knob. "No, no good."

"Get out of the way," I told him.

"You can't go down there," he said. "It's locked."

"Nonsense," I said, looking at the latching system. It had been obsolete for centuries. "A lock is a security device. This old thing is just to stop the door from banging in the wind." I reached into my pocket and pulled out my totem, the most magnificent solidinum scalpel that influence-peddling could buy. By grandiose claim of the manufacturer, it would cut through anything short of White Dwarf material.

"What do you think you're doing?" Leppid moaned.

"Vavash told me I could wander where I chose."

"I'm not going along with this," the Doctoral Triumvirate muttered and stomped off. I suspected he was going to get Vavash, but I didn't care. I'd got it into my head I was being played for a fool. For some reason, Vavash had only put out her failures for me to see. Perhaps she was trying to test my judgment after all. Perhaps she'd been in a nasty mood one day and tossed together some bathetic Oh-Our-Terrible-Totless-Tragedy garbage to sell to off-planet yokels through D-D-Doctor Wouldn't-Know-Art-If-It-Carried-

I.D. Perhaps someone else with hideous taste had chosen Vavash's display, and there were good and powerful works just on the other side of this door.

I started cutting. My blade upheld the Scalpel family honor with speed and grace. In something under a minute, I was descending a long flight of steps into a darkened basement the size of a steel mill. Halfway down, I passed through an electric eye and a bank of lights turned on in front of me.

Blinking my eyes against the brightness, I saw a jungle of artworks, some packed in crates, some covered with tarpaulins, most just sitting out gathering dust. They stretched off into darkness at the far end of the cellars, where I could just make out a shimmery glimmer.

I walked through the silent collection, harsh overhead lamps turning on automatically whenever I approached the edge of the next darkened area. Flash, lights up on a flock of life-size papier-mâché pygmies, some standing up, some lying on their backs, one squat little androgyne fallen over onto a terra-cotta jar whose rim was now deeply embedded in its throat. Flash, and there were long vertical racks that held canvases slid in on their sides; I pulled a few out, saw stuccoed prickles of color in abstract patterns. Flash, and echoing glows ignited in dusty stained glass, vases striped wine red and frosty white, engraved with tall, slim men wearing the sharp-edged styles of long ago, casually embracing one another.

Flash, flash, flash, then Vavash.

Unmistakable. Unforgettable. Genius.

Utter simplicity: a tapestry hung from a tall wooden arch. A sun-crowned rainbow bursting upward in joyous fountain between the legs of a prone woman. Truth. Beauty. Purity. A clamping knot of hunger untied in my chest, like the release of doves at High Festival. Yes. Yes. In the hands of someone else, it would just be hackneyed vomit, trite images done to death by the sentimentality squad. But this . . . exquisite workmanship, flawless clarity, profundity in naïveté, artless artless Art.

"Mr. Scalpel!" Vavash stood halfway down the stairs, one hand clutching the railing tightly, the other shading her eyes as she tried to catch sight of me amid the clutter.

"You've been hiding your light under a bushel, madam," I called to her.

Her gaze hardened and she snapped, "Get out of my things." There were perhaps fifty meters between us; her voice sounded thin and shrill.

"I can't imagine why you've been keeping your best work down here," I continued. "Of course it's blatant birth imagery, but why should that bother you? Humans have been expressing their feelings about pregnancy and childbirth since Adam had Eve. There's nothing to be ashamed of." I picked up a bulb-shaped basket made of bright ribbon woven on a wicker framework, and held it high enough for Vavash to watch me examining it. Through the vulva-shaped opening at the top, I could see an effusion of stylized flowers made from colored felt: cheerful, bubbly happiness embodied in fabric with love and spirit. "This makes the rest of the work here look like bot-work."

"Leave that alone!" Vavash cried.

"Why should I?"

She glared at me with a hatred clear enough to see even at that distance. "You have the sensitivity of a thug!"

"That's it exactly," I snapped back. "Every critic is a thug, and we work for that merciless godfather called the Spirit of Art. A long time ago, old Art loaned you a wheelbarrow full of talent, didn't he, lady? But recent-like it seems you ain't been keepin' up the payments. So Art sent the Scalpel-man to chat wit' youse an' have a look-see how to get you back on the program."

"You're ridiculous!"

"If necessary," I answered drily. Vavash was still up on the stairs, bending over awkwardly in an effort to see me under the glaring lights. Her feet seemed cemented to the step. I called, "Why don't you come down where we can talk more comfortably?"

"You come up here."

"Hmm," I said. "Now why would a grown woman be afraid to come into a well-lit basement?" I turned my back on her and began walking toward the area that was still dark.

"Mr. Scalpel!"

"Is she afraid of mice?" I continued. "No, there aren't any mice in your standard Straight-from-the-Package terraformed ecology. Dust? No, the air filters in the dome make sure all dust is hypoallergenic. Things that go bump in the night? No, that's just childish, and there've never been children on Crèche, have there?"

"Mr. Scalpel . . ."

Another bank of lights flashed on, and there before me slept a herd of stasis chests . . . row upon row of glimmery mirror cylinders, laid out with the care of a graveyard. The chests were less than half of normal adult size. In front of each was mounted a machine-lettered card. I walked among them in slow wonderment, picking up a card here and there to read: *Samandha Sunrise, April 23, 2168. Jubilo De Féliz, June 12, 2169. Tomas Vincent-Vavash, October 3, 2165.*

"So," said Vavash softly, "now you know."

She had approached silently. She stood like a statue among her artworks, her body limp, her face old.

"I don't know anything," I answered. "Are they dead?"

"They were alive when they were put in," she said. "That means they're alive now, right? Time doesn't pass in stasis. Not a fraction of a second. Not even over all the years . . ."

"They've been in stasis for sixty years?" I asked in disbelief.

"Some. We kept having them . . . no medical supplies, no birth control. We'd try celibacy, but it got so lonely . . ."

"You just kept dropping foals and stuffing them into stasis?"

"Oh, it's easy to be self-righteous, isn't it?" she said angrily. "Imagine yourself in our place. Imagine yourself with a world entirely to yourself, and being free, absolutely free, to follow your Art as you choose. No Philistines to question the value of what you're doing, no political system that feels threatened by your activities, no mundane responsibilities to weigh you down.

"And then the children come. In no time, you're up to your ankles in diapers, with this little howling *thing* bawling for your attention twenty-five hours a day . . . no time to work, not even a decent night's rest, the incessant crying . . . and finally, one night when you're groggy with lack of sleep, and desperate for anything to make it stop, you think of the stasis chests that you have by the hundreds, and it's like an answer to a prayer to tuck the baby away for the night. Just for a few hours of peace and quiet. And the baby isn't harmed—it doesn't even know it was ever . . . shut off. And you take to doing it every night—you get a good sleep, you rationalize the child will benefit from it too, you'll be more relaxed and attentive. And in the middle of the afternoon when you decide you want to get a bit of work done without interruption . . . after a while, you tell yourself it's all right, the baby's fine, if you take it out of stasis for an hour a day, that's enough. You can play with it happily, make that little bit of time, everything's fine . . . even if you miss a day once in a while when you're busy, when the work's going well. If you have a life of your own, you know you'll be a better mother . . .

"And you miss a day and a week and a month, and every time you think about it, you're filled with the most sickening dread, the most sickening paralyzing dread . . . you try to put it out of your mind but you can't, you want to make it right again but you can't, you tell yourself how simple it would be to plunge in and fix it, but you're just so paralyzed with the dread, you can't face it, you want it just to go away, and you scream at a bot to get the chest out of your sight, get it out, get it out . . .

"And when another baby's on the way, and you swear on everything you hold sacred you'll be *good* to this one, you'll never make the same mistake, you'll be so much stronger . . . and for a while it works. But then the others stare at you, they *shun* you, because they've put away babies too and they don't want to be reminded . . . and the sight of the baby in your arms reminds them, reminds you, makes you choke with the guilt . . . until finally you say all right, all right, to keep peace with everyone else, I'll shut this one away too . . . do you want to know something, Mr. Scalpel? I had five children. Five." She waved at the silent chests. "They're all out there. Sometimes I have nightmares that I lost count, that I really had six. Or seven. I don't know why that terrifies me. Losing count. What would be the difference? But the thought is chilling . . . I don't know why.

"But . . ." She straightened up a bit. "Stasis *is* stasis, isn't it? The children are still fine. No harm done."

"No harm done!" I roared. "You stupid bitch! Don't you realize what's happened here?"

"Nothing's happened!" she said. "The children haven't been hurt. When we're all dead and gone, someone will find them and let them out. They'll be fine. Famous even. They'll all be adopted into good homes . . ."

"Do you think I care about a pack of puking papooses?" I shouted. "What have these tabulae rasae ever produced but drool and stool? The harm was done to your Art! You're so obsessed with your little secret here, so wrapped up in your own culpability . . . Before you tied yourself in knots, you were capable of masterpieces like that rainbow tapestry. You could have produced a legacy a hundred times more important than Five-or-Six-or-Seven brats, but all you've given us is this facade of empty cradles and dolls and shit! At best, it's the product of plain old-fashioned guilt over abandoning your progeny. At worst, it's some shoddy con game begging for pity you don't deserve. 'O woe, we're so devastated at being childless, see how poignant our Art is, buy it.' What crap!"

"All right," she replied angrily, "I know it's had an effect on my Art. Don't you think I realize that? Do you have any idea how debilitating such a mess can be? Run away, lie about running away, cover up the lie, pressure others to do the same . . . God! The feeling there's no way out of a hopeless snarl. . . ."

"What you have here," I said, "is a Gordian knot." Which (for you culturally bereft swine who are only reading this column in the hope that I'll savage someone) was a knot from classical Greek history, a knot that was touted to be impossible to untie. "And," I went on, "the way to deal with such knots is always the same, isn't it?"

I pulled out my scalpel.

"What are you going to do?" she asked.

"Do you know why Art Critics exist?" I said. "Because every polite community needs barbarian assholes who aren't afraid to slice through the bullshit courtesies." And before she could stop me, I plunged my blade into the silvery static surface of the nearest chest.

My intention, Dear Reader, was to <BINK> open the chest, reveal the child within, and force a Reunion-Slash-Confrontation. Alas, stasis dynamics do not seem to be so clear-cut. In the time that has passed since the events I relate, I have discussed stasis fields with many learned physicists, and while they are apt to hem and haw about the point, they eventually confess we know little more about said fields now than when we were first given the technology by our chums from the League of Peoples. We know the fields will cooperatively <BINK> off when touched with a standard-issue dispeller wand; we know they will collapse under intense heat or pressure or magnetic fields; and we have recently discovered they put up one roaring pig of a fight when you attempt to cut them with a magnificent solidinum scalpel that can purportedly slice through anything short of White Dwarf material.

Fluid silver energy flowed up my blade like a mercury cobra on a rope, swallowing my hand with a blisteringly cold mouth. I jerked away fast and tried to let go of the knife, but the nerves and muscles had stopped talking to one another in the neighborhood of my wrist. The silver kept coming up my arm. A snowfall of ice crystals cracked out of clear air as the temperature plummeted . . . and it occurred to me that molecules in complete stasis would naturally gauge in at zero degrees Kelvin.

Oops.

Another moment and the zone of cold reached the concrete floor, riming it with frost. I couldn't believe a single stasis chest could freeze such a wide area . . . but it did, ice spreading like Fimbulwinter before a truly nasty Ragnarok. The concrete underfoot couldn't withstand the piercing chill of the cold—it shivered once, then groaned open in a wide cleft that snaked out beneath the field of silvery chests. Chests trembled on the edge; one began to tip in.

I called to Vavash but my throat wouldn't work. Slowly, ice in my veins, I turned her direction. She was coming toward me, but I couldn't tell if she was moving fast or slow. Something hissed behind my back and a fist of sulfurous steam punched its way from a fissure in the bedrock. Hot and cold met like two hands clapping together thunderously in preparation for a cyclonic arm wrestle. Then, just when things promised to get *really* interesting, something silver swept over my eyes and <BINK> I was in a clinic, surrounded by white-haired medical types who threw themselves on whatever wounds I possessed. Tongues clicking, they busied themselves with my knife hand. I couldn't feel anything from my shoulder down, and didn't want to.

"Don't move, Mr. Scalpel," Vavash said, her face looming into view above me.

"What happened?" I croaked.

"While I was showing you the basement of our retreat, we had a small geological tremor and a minor geyser broke through the floor. You were injured. I managed to preserve you in a stasis field and bring you to our Med-Center for treatment."

"I see. Was there much damage?" I asked carefully.

"Not very," she replied evenly. "Some minor works that had been sitting around for a long time fell into a crevice."

I stared at her. She met my gaze without flinching. The doctors murmured about tissue grafts. I asked, "Were all the works in that area destroyed?"

"Yes."

"You don't seem bothered by the loss."

"Mr. Scalpel, when one is forced to confront one's past . . . it's been forty years since I stopped doing that kind of work. I'm not the same woman—not at all. I realized I no longer had any feelings for . . . for the works themselves. My anxieties were just a pointless emotional residue that had accumulated over the years. Now that the situation is resolved, I feel cleansed. <BINK> and my stasis was dispelled. Isn't that what you wanted?"

My mind was clearing a little from the adrenaline rush, the fear that was still so recent for me. I wondered how much real time had passed since the stasis field swallowed my body. I wondered what had happened while I was silver-sleeping. I wondered if my abortive attempt at cutting open a chest had really killed all those children. "How do I know that all of those old works really fell into the crevice? And if they did, how do I know they weren't pushed?"

Vavash smiled without warmth. "If you want to be Art's barbarian asshole, Mr. Scalpel, you shouldn't concern yourself with irrelevant niceties. Neither swords nor palette knives can indulge in the luxury of a conscience. Or are you just a spoiled young dilettante who talks about devotion to Art but runs crying at the first little harshness?"

There was a bright fire in her eyes, a fire like none I'd ever seen before; but like all fires, it was terrible and awesome, powerful and pitiless.

Dear Reader, many before me have written about the first cave dweller to tame fire; but none, I think, have considered the man who next entered the tribal cave and saw the blaze leaping wildly toward the rocky ceiling. That man had to choose on behalf of the human race: whether to praise the Fire-Tamer's vision or denounce it as madness, whether to put out the fire or gaze at it in wonder.

In the end, perhaps all he could do was run to his fellows and tell what he had seen.

Kent State Descending the Gravity Well: An Analysis of the Observer

According to the Kerr-Newman model of a rotating black hole, there is a region just outside the event horizon where certain space and time vectors switch properties with each other. This is just mathematics, you understand, merely a quirk of the formulas—physically, nothing changes wildly until you get inside the black hole itself, and then who cares what happens? Double-deluxe chocolate-chip cookies could spontaneously spring into being and it wouldn't matter to the universe outside. Reality may break down inside a black hole, but the effects never percolate back into our familiar space.

Just outside the black hole, however, if it's rotating, if the model is correct, there is a region called the ergosphere where certain vector fields describing the flow of space and time do a flip-flop. When I was trying to understand what this meant, I told myself that places became moments and moments became places.

Think of that. Places became moments. Moments became places. Years and years ago, I did my master's thesis on black holes. In those days, I could have explained the math to you . . . but now I've forgotten it all. I look at the book containing my thesis and the only thing I remember is how hard it was to type all those equations. The meaning of the equations has dribbled out of my understanding a grain at a time, and now all I hold is this: just outside a spinning black hole, in a region called the ergosphere, places become moments and moments become places.

Think of that.

Kent State University entered the ergosphere at 12:24 P.M. on Monday, May 4, 1970. That was the moment the Ohio State National Guard opened fire on demonstrators protesting American involvement in Vietnam and Cambodia. Four students were killed; nine others were wounded.

Kent State ceased to be a place and became a moment. Like Hiroshima. Like Chernobyl. Kent State fell off the map and became thirteen seconds of gunfire on a warm spring day. And maybe it kept dropping down the gravity well, from the ergosphere straight into the black hole.

Here is an ugly truth: back in 1970, when I heard the news about the Kent State killings, I felt smug.

I was fifteen years old. I was Canadian. It pleased me in a spiteful way that the U.S. had so blatantly screwed up.

I was fifteen. I was self-righteous. I had never been to a funeral.

The vectors that flip-flop in the ergosphere indicate symmetries in the gravitational field. One vector is timelike; it indicates that the laws of gravity don't change over time. The other vector is spacelike; it describes the rotational symmetry of the black hole.

These vectors are called Killing vectors. Really. They're named after a Professor Wilhelm K. J. Killing of the University of Münster. He gave his name to such geometrical objects in 1892, many decades before Kerr and Newman used them in their model of a rotating black hole.

Killing vectors.

May 4, 1990, was a Friday, but all the local newspapers saved their Kent State retrospectives for the weekend editions. I bought three papers that Saturday—the *Globe & Mail* for its book reviews, the *Kitchener-Waterloo Record* for local movie listings, and the *Toronto Star* for *Doonesbury*.

I didn't realize it was the twentieth anniversary of Kent State until I saw a commemorative article in the first paper I read. That article was written by a Kent State journalism student who happened to be in the right place at the right time to get the greatest news story of his life. The reporter told about his day: the rumors that something bad had happened at the noon rally, his race to get his camera, his sneaking through bushes to reach the parking lot where the killings took place, many details about the aftermath . . . but strangely, the reporter omitted any information about the victims themselves. He didn't even give their names.

The article in the second paper talked about the effect of the killings on the American psyche. Was it really the turning point in the Vietnam War, the moment when public consciousness crossed some unerasable line? Or was it just another straw on the camel's bending back?

The victims weren't named in this article either. Just four dead students. Four dead in O-hi-o.

———

Kent State is about 270 kilometers from my living room. I've never been there; it feels like a very distant place.

My wife's parents live more than 450 kilometers away. We visit them several times a year.

It was only in the third paper that I found an actual list of who died. Four students, two women, two men:

Allison Krause
Jeff Miller
Sandy Lee Scheuer
Bill Schroeder

This was the only information given about the victims: just their names. The article in the third paper was about the back-room machinations that made sure no charges were successfully laid against the National Guard.

I sat in my living room, three thick newspapers on the floor around my chair, and I wondered why all three treated the victims as if they were irrelevant to the story. Certainly, the National Guard didn't specifically target those four students; the Guard could easily have killed four different people, or a dozen people, or none. But why should that matter? Randomness shouldn't mean irrelevance.

The papers bypassed the reality of the victims, their lives, the grief of their friends and family, as if those things had nothing to do with the "real" story.

As if the four dead students were only there for the body count.

As if the students had no reality either before or after the shootings, but only in the moments when they lay bleeding on the pavement of a parking lot.

FIRST SCRIBBLE: THE FUNERAL RUN

McGregor grimaced as he reached the door of the time chamber. Inside, the lights had been muted from their usual glare to a moody brown tint. Dimness meant a funeral run: the group going out this morning would not be coming back.

If he'd been in charge—McGregor spent much of his time dreaming how the Corrections Institute would change if he were in charge—if McGregor ever got to be in charge, he'd scrap the gloom and doom, maybe put in something extravagant like orange flashers or a circus-holo show. People going out on a funeral run were depressed enough already. They didn't need the brooding browns, and the staff talking in hushed tones. Why not throw a bash instead? Crack open the booze, crank up the music, give the poor bums some last good memories of the twenty-third century. But the Executive Board were all tight-collars, sending out memos about "good taste" and "appropriateness," and they never, ever had to push the button that sent people off to die.

McGregor passed an eye over the four people in the chamber— not lingering long enough to fix the faces in his memory because he had enough bad dreams already, thank you very much—but he wanted to see whom he was dealing with. His subjects. Two male, two female. Apparent ages somewhere between 18 and 24. No way to tell if they'd been sculpted for the run or if these were their actual faces. Some correction jobs had specific requirements, some just needed bodies.

None of the people, the subjects, looked familiar. McGregor prided himself on his knowledge of history. A good grasp of history was what distinguished a professional from a mere button-pusher. He'd recognize faces taken from history if they were important.

These weren't; they were just faces. And he'd spent far too long looking at them. Tonight in his dreams, he might remember that dimpled chin, those sleepy eyes. He didn't need that crap, especially not when Joanne already complained how restless he was in bed. Grunting, he turned away from the door and stalked to the control booth.

"You're in a hell of a mood," Tanya Ramirez said as McGregor threw himself into his chair. "Joanne on the rag?"

"Ha-ha," he replied. He had no intention of talking about his feelings to Ramirez. She didn't give a damn whether this was a funeral run or one of the truly upbeat correction jobs, like the times they inserted top-of-the-line medical teams to save important lives. Only jerks got involved with the subjects; she'd said that once. So now, out of pride, McGregor pretended to be as blasé as she was . . . and of course felt like a jerk for pretending.

"Who have we got today?" he asked, trying to sound breezy.

Ramirez waved her hand at McGregor's display screen, where separate windows showed the official correction authorization, temporal navigation charts, the latest chronal flux reports, and background data on the people in the time chamber. "We have your typical funeral-run volunteers," Ramirez said. "Afflicted with your usual grab bag of terminal conditions, none contagious, and also afflicted with your garden-variety burning need to do something meaningful before they sink down the gravity well. If you want more details, read the History Thanks notices in Corrections Daily.*"*

"Forget it," McGregor told her. He had his newsreader programmed to skip the History Thanks column. After he'd sent someone on a funeral run, he didn't need to know that the deceased did needlework or had once dreamed of being an architect. "What time are we trying to hit?" he asked.

"Early January 1970, late December 1969 if we have to," Ramirez replied. "The correction goes down May 4, 1970, but we have to insert them early enough to establish camouflage."

"They can establish camouflage in only four months?"

"Prep department says it pulled out all the stops building background this time. Birth certificates, employment records, vaccinations—that Prep creep Terry Ying was in just before you got here, trying to impress me. You wouldn't believe how bad he wants into my pants. Anyway, Ying said four months was the max for camouflage on this group because that's the most the doctors can guarantee. Wouldn't want the subjects to die of natural causes before their date with destiny."

You get the idea. Time travelers dropped onto the Kent State campus for the purpose of dying. Their deaths were necessary to shape the future properly—otherwise, opposition to the war in Vietnam wouldn't intensify fast enough and the future would go to hell. I could invent an appropriate description of such a hell if it became relevant.

I wrote the above passage on Saturday, May 5, 1990. The notion that sparked the story was, of course, that the four Kent State students *hadn't* really existed before they were shot; they were dispatched from the future.

Partway through the writing, in the passage where McGregor scans the faces of the people waiting for the funeral run, I needed to know what the victims looked like. I made a quick trip to the library (only two blocks away), picked up three books on Kent State, and hurried back to the computer so I could keep writing. One of the books (*The Truth About Kent State,* by Peter Davies) had pictures of the four students on a page close to the front. I made note of Sandy Lee Scheuer's dimpled chin, Bill Schroeder's sleepy eyes, and went back to writing.

Conscience didn't set in till later.

Look: the real students weren't terminal patients who nobly volunteered to die—they were simply people in the wrong place at the wrong time and they died by random chance.

And they weren't just characters of convenience, devoid of families, people with no personality apart from what I might need in a story. At the end of a day of writing, I thumbed through those books from the library and I read interviews with parents, friends, people who had known the victims all their lives. The students didn't come out of nowhere—they came from homes and neighborhoods that mourned, prayed, lost sleep, wept, all trying to come to grips with grief.

Reading those interviews I felt ashamed.

Consider what an observer sees when an object descends into a black hole. For convenience, assume that the object is a burning candle that's somehow tough enough to withstand the tidal forces of gravity around the hole.

As the candle falls, it takes longer and longer (from your point of view) for each particle of candlelight to climb the gravity well and reach your eye. Light particles emitted near the very edge of the black hole may take thousands of years to fight their way out to the universe at large. The result is that you perceive the candle falling for a potentially infinite length of time. Every now and then, another light particle struggles free of the black hole's pull and reminds you of the candle's descent.

It's an obvious metaphor for grief. Hot and burning at the start, dimming over time . . . but even after many years, memory particles surface now and then to remind you of a life that's gone.

I should point out that the candle's infinite fall is only in the eye of the outside observer. A trick of the light. From the candle's point of view, it drops straight down and crosses the event horizon without pause. Inside the black hole its flame may still be burning; it's just that the light doesn't reach the outside world anymore.

———

The next morning, Sunday, May 6, 1990, I reread what I'd written, wondering if there was anything that could be salvaged. I was struck by a new regret: I'd written about some guy named McGregor, not about the students.

I knew why I'd written it that way, of course. I didn't believe I had the right to put words in their mouths, thoughts in their heads. How could I presume to speak for the real people? I could only deal with characters.

But I'd gone too far into the fiction. In my story, like the newspaper articles, the victims were only there for the body count. Without thinking, I'd started to write the story of a button-pusher who was troubled by his conscience, but who went ahead and did what he had to do for the good of history.

Sound familiar?

SECOND SCRIBBLE: THE BUTTON-PUSHER

Bannister sat in the time chamber, cradling his gun. An M-1 carbine in pristine condition. According to the antiquities database there were only five M-1s still in existence, four in museums, one in the hands of a collector who'd bought hers on the open market. You could assume another twenty or thirty still in secret collections around the world . . . maybe even a few in the arsenals of the Quarantined states, since most of the Q's were too stupid to realize the black market price of a single twentieth-century firearm would buy a hundred twenty-third-century E-guns.

Call it a nice round number of forty M-1s on the entire planet. And Bannister had one.

Admittedly, this weapon could just be a replica; but he doubted it. The Corrections Institute disdained replicas. If they needed some antique, they sent back a Special Services team to steal one. Bannister had gone out on plenty of those runs himself—popping into foxholes to pull Lee-Enfields from the cold fingers of gas victims, or materializing in the cargo holds of boats shipping AK-47s to terrorist groups. But as of today, Bannister had graduated from such gruntwork. As of today, he was going to make history.

"You about ready in there?" he called to the two techies in the control booth.

The woman of the pair flicked a switch and said over the intercom, "What's your hurry? Got a hot date waiting?"

"You got it," Bannister answered. "The date's May 4, 1970."

The intercom clicked off loudly. He wondered if the woman was annoyed at his attitude. Maybe she'd been making a pass at him. Maybe he should have said, "No date yet, but when I get back I'll really be looking for action." The woman's lab coat hid her tits and her ass, but the way she moved when she walked, he could tell she was thinking of her body all the time. Feeling it move, tuned in to being sensuous. A night with a woman like that would leave a memory or two.

And all of the psych profiles said he'd be horny afterward. It was sick when you thought about it, but if horniness was natural, it was natural. You didn't lose sleep if your body wanted to fart after eating beans—you just farted, didn't you? So if Bannister's body wanted to get laid after pulling the trigger on four strangers who died three hundred years ago . . .

The intercom clicked again and the male techie said, "Departure in thirty seconds."

"Going to be a bumpy one?" Bannister asked. He was trying to sound cool, but the words came out too sharply. It was eagerness, only eagerness. He hoped the woman in the booth wouldn't interpret it as nerves.

"The sea's calm as glass all the way back to 2042," the male techie replied. "Turbulence there, of course, but you've got clearance for one of the calmest straits in the area. Someone's definitely pulled

strings on this run—smoothest route we've been authorized to navigate since the beginning of the year. The Executive Board must really want these kids dead."

"It's crucial to world peace," Bannister said.

"Yeah, right." The man clicked off the intercom again.

Bannister wanted to shout back some kind of self-justification. The mission was crucial. No one liked killing, not even when it was necessary, but trading four lives for several hundred million . . . it had to be done. The deaths were the catalyst for change; so someone had to be the catalyst for the deaths. Someone had to start the shooting up on Blanket Hill, had to spur the Ohio National Guard into putting Kent State University on the map.

Same setting as the piece I wrote the previous day, but someone different in the time chamber. Someone who would join the National Guard and instigate the tragedy. Someone who would have to face what he had done and eventually . . . well, I didn't know what would happen to Bannister. As the story unfolded, as I got to know him better, I'd discover whether he went mad, found wisdom, became a soulless killer, whatever. Sometimes the reason you write a story is to learn how it turns out.

I spent most of Sunday morning on the Bannister story, but as time went on my doubts grew. By lunch I had to admit that my second try was just as corrupt as the first one. I was trying to reassure myself there was an underlying purpose to the events, that someone somewhere knew the price and made a choice. But I didn't believe that. Furthermore, I didn't believe in letting the National Guard off the hook by suggesting they were spurred on by an outside provocateur. As I sat in my study and comfortably sipped mint tea twenty years after the fact, it wasn't my place to lay blame; but it wasn't my place to make excuses either.

———

The Kerr-Newman model of a rotating black hole can be mathe-matically extended by recoordinatizing, using a scheme suggested by the work of M. D. Kruskal (1960). The result is a model where the black hole has a white hole on its flip side. Just as a black hole is a phenomenon that no slower-than-light object can leave, a white hole is a phenomenon that no slower-than-light object can enter. Light and matter can flood out of a white hole, but nothing can get back inside. Beyond the white hole, the extended model shows an area of space whose physical characteristics are the same as our own familiar space—"another universe," if you want to look at it that way.

Extending mathematical models is a dicey business. I could, if I wanted, extend the mathematical model of temperature below absolute zero Kelvin and find that (wow!) there was a whole other universe down there where temperatures were negative instead of positive. Mathematically, I could argue the idea was valid; but physically, it's nonsense. One mustn't get carried away believing scribbles on paper.

But the black hole/white hole model is more satisfying than an unadorned black hole. The white hole completes the black hole's story. Things vanish into a black hole and it seems they are gone forever; but unbeknownst to us, they pass through the darkness, through crushing forces, through a moment of infinity at the very heart of the black hole, and then they flood out the other side into a new and brightly illuminated universe.

It could be the oldest story in the world. Ra in his sunboat. Jonah in the whale. Dying heroes and deities from every culture on the planet.

The journey into blackness. The dark night of the soul. The moment of trial and grace. Glorious liberation and rebirth into a new world.

Kerr-Newman has it all.

I've never heard anyone talk about the black hole/white hole model from a theological viewpoint. No one is comfortable with theology anymore. I know I'm not.

But I'm comfortable with ghost stories.

THIRD SCRIBBLE: THE KENT STATE JAMBOREE

Walpurgisnacht came a few days late in 1990. Blame it on precession of the equinox, global warming, or whatever your pet cause might be—Walpurgisnacht 1990 fell on the night of May 4.

The honor of the first sighting went to Benjamin Howe, third-year math student at Kent State University, Kent, Ohio. May 4, Howe spent an uncomfortable evening sitting on the floor in Taylor Hall, hoping to intercept one Catherine Weiss as she left a night class. For the past six months, Howe and Weiss had shared a relationship; but that afternoon a discussion of what they would do over the summer break had not gone well. It had, in fact, sucked rocks. Neither of them shouted; neither of them cried; but after they went their separate ways, both felt sick in the pits of their stomachs, wondering if this was it, if it was all over, if they had ruined the best chance at love they would ever get. By suppertime, both wanted to apologize as profusely as necessary. It was just a matter of finding each other before it was too late.

Howe knew that Weiss had a night class somewhere in Taylor Hall. He drove there and wandered the corridors, peeping into classrooms without spotting her. Eventually he settled down on the floor near the exit that Weiss was most likely to take on her way home . . . provided she didn't take a different door as she headed for a sleaze-up at the pub with some slimy classmate. (Unbeknownst to Howe, Weiss hadn't gone to class that night. She'd parked herself outside Howe's apartment building and was waiting for him to come home, thinking he had probably gone to the pub to get sloppy drunk with his buddies from differential geometry.)

Hours passed. Benjamin Howe watched the classes get out, tried to scan every woman who went by but not too closely, not threateningly for fear one of them would report him as a potential rapist. He stayed an hour after the last class went home, not because he believed Weiss was still in the building but because he had no idea what to do next. He considered going to the pub to see if she was there; he considered phoning her friends; he considered phoning the hospitals; he considered walking aimlessly around campus in the hope that fate would bring them together again, the way it did in the movies.

Finally he decided to go home.

When he got to the parking lot, his was the only car left. That made it easy to see the long dark smear trailing out from underneath. "Great," he muttered to himself, "the end of a perfect day. Must have spun up a stone through the oil pan."

He got down on his knees to look. It was after eleven o'clock, and even though the parking lot was well lit, he could see only darkness under the chassis. A deep darkness, a black lump blocking out the light that should have been visible on the other side of the car.

Jesus Christ, he thought, I hit something. A dog. I must have hit a dog. Nothing else could be that big except . . . no, it had to be a dog.

He looked again at the smear on the pavement. The parking lot's blue-white streetlamps bleached out most of the color, but he could convince himself the smear was red.

Howe didn't want to touch the body, but he couldn't drive off with something stuck under there. Standing up, he walked to the edge of the parking lot and back to build up his nerve, then squatted at the rear of his car and reached under.

It was like reaching into a freezer: cold and a bit clammy. The night was warm and he couldn't imagine how it could be so cold under there, but first things first. Pull the damned body out, then worry about thermodynamics. He swept his hand back and forth, trying to grab some part of the animal, trying to do it blind because he really didn't want to look at it any sooner than he had to.

Nothing, nothing but the cold. The dog must be farther under than he thought.

He went down on his knees again and looked. From this angle, the light was good enough that he could make out a running shoe.

For a moment, he couldn't breathe. He'd known all along, hadn't he? It had been too big for a dog, he just hadn't let himself that . . . that he'd killed someone. He'd killed someone. It wasn't possible, but he'd killed someone. Run a person over, dragged the corpse under his car. Almost without thinking, he reached out to touch the shoe.

His hand felt only cold air.

Darkness or not, he could see quite clearly. His hand reached straight through the foot.

And then, because this was Kent State, and because every student knew this was the parking lot, Benjamin Howe realized what he was seeing.

He got into the car, started it carefully, and backed up. There was no sound of dragging, no sound of flesh and bone crushing under the tires. When he'd backed up far enough, there was only the sight of a body bleeding on the pavement. A guy about Benjamin's age, wearing ratty jeans and a T-shirt.

There was another body not far off. A woman's. A third corpse farther along, and a fourth in the middle of the road out of the lot. He cranked the wheel hard, hopped over the curb onto the grass, and kept driving.

When Benjamin Howe got back to his apartment, Cathy Weiss was still there. She thought that he treated her coldly at first, but he seemed glad to see her.

Back on campus, more bodies were appearing. At 11:30 the village of My Lai materialized in the football practice field beside the Taylor Hall parking lot—the village was close to Kent State in spirit, if not geography.

This materialization was observed by chemistry grad student Rebecca Kendall, who'd been awake 36 hours studying for exams. The sight of the phantom village terrified her . . . not because she thought it was a ghost, but because she thought it was a hallucination. The prospect of her mind breaking down filled her with fear, cold and pure. Her brain was all she had—no friends, no easy social graces, no Playboy bunny face and flesh, just her brain. And now her brain saw a ragged clutter of huts and butchered bodies out in the middle of a football field.

Rebecca started shivering and couldn't stop. If someone had convinced her she was seeing a ghost she would have felt nothing but relief. As it was, she walked home in a cold sweat and went straight to bed. She didn't fall asleep for hours.

On campus at quarter to twelve, a crowd of martyrs flickered into existence atop Blanket Hill . . . not the usual martyrs celebrated for clinging to their beliefs in the face of death, but the ones who died meaninglessly, without the chance to take a stand. Innocent women accused of witchcraft, hanged and drowned and burned. Civilians whose homes lay in the path of marching armies. Tribespeople who succumbed to disease, starvation, and sorrow in the cargo holds of slave ships. Hundreds of unmoving bodies appeared on Blanket Hill, many of them touching or overlapping: a young widow cremated in suttee, lying with her head on the chest of a teenage boy who froze in Siberia because his uncle denounced Stalin; a drowned passenger from KAL 007 linking arms with one from the Iranian Airbus A300.

As midnight approached, more and more bodies accumulated: in the roadways, on the Commons, inside buildings. Fearing panic, university security evacuated an on-campus pub when Bhopal gas victims began piling up the dance floor. "Nothing to worry about," the security guards said as they hurried students out. "We'll take care of it."

"What are you going to do?" someone asked. "Call in the National Guard?"

That was my question too. What was I going to do? Call in the National Guard?

Look: ghosts appear because they have unfinished business. And if anyone has unfinished business, it must be those who were killed senselessly. But what can they do to finish their stories? Should the four Kent State students haunt the living National Guardsmen and torment them for their acts? That's so cheap: just crude revenge.

Should the bodies be brought back to life at midnight, where-upon they could have a single hour to come to terms with their deaths? Maybe the same thing happens twice a year like business conventions, Walpurgisnacht and Hallowe'en, each get-together hosted by different committees—the soccer fans at Hillsborough, say, or the Jews and gypsies and gays processed through Nazi death camps—and the goal is simply to purge anger and regret, a little bit more each meeting, until finally the soul is ready to let go and move on. I could envision the Kent State students wandering their old campus, talking to night-owl students, trying to find peace . . .

Students at Kent State were demonstrating for peace when the four victims died.

I broke off writing for supper. Sunday supper, traditional time in North America for family and conviviality. I don't remember how convivial I was. I could have been distracted because I wanted to get back to writing after dinner.

But when I went back, I realized I had trivialized my subject again. It wasn't just that the tone of voice was flippant; it was the *glibness* with which I tossed off references to tragedy. My Lai, for example—what did I know about the My Lai massacre except that a lot of Vietnamese civilians were killed? I could research and find more details, but that wasn't the point. I had used the name My Lai for its immediate guts'n'gore familiarity, not out of genuine feeling for the victims. The same for all the other ghosts—I had used them to give the story color, nothing more. They were only empty names. They were just body count.

I stared at the computer screen for a long time, wondering what to write . . . wondering if there was anything I *could* write that wasn't just exploiting someone else's pain.

Nothing came to mind.

A mathematical singularity is a place where a function, a formula, breaks down. Often the breakdown happens because the function "goes to infinity" at that point; for example, the formula for the function may try to divide by zero.

In the heart of a Kerr-Newman black hole there is a singularity in a function called $\underline{R}$, the Riemannian scalar curvature, a measurement of gravity. $\underline{R}$ goes to infinity. It cannot be measured.

For a long time, physicists wondered if the singularity was genuine. Maybe it was simply a result of their choice of coordinates: the way they wrote out the formula for $\underline{R}$. With the right choice of coordinates, one can extend the black hole model past the singularity into the white hole beyond. Perhaps with another choice of coordinates the singularity in the middle would go away. Perhaps it was only the ruler that broke down, not the universe that the ruler measured.

In the late 1960s, mathematicians proved that the singularity existed in all coordinates. All possible rulers broke at the same point. At the heart of the black hole's darkness, physicists could only throw away their rulers and stand back in blank contemplation.

———

Days and weeks passed. I kept thinking. Nothing more, just thinking. I didn't see the dead students in my dreams. To tell the truth, if I wanted to remember their faces I had to go back and look at their photos in the book.

Kent State didn't haunt me. It niggled at me.

The library books came due. I wrote the names of the books in my files and took them back. I also recorded the names:

Allison Krause
Jeff Miller
Sandy Lee Scheuer
Bill Schroeder

Those names hadn't appeared anywhere in my three story attempts. I had to write them down separately so I would remember them. Otherwise I'd lose the names and be left with three uncompleted story-scribbles that all missed the point.

Now and then I would open my "ideas" notebook and see my original jottings about Kent State. Time travel. Ghosts. But I couldn't travel backward in time. I couldn't summon ghosts or lay them to rest. I could stuff my stories into the empty spaces surrounding the tragedy, but the stories themselves walled off the reality, put it out of reach.

The situation reminded me of a white hole. A white hole floods its universe with light; but you can never touch it.

And so I began thinking of white holes, black holes, and a mathematics thesis whose math had leaked away, leaving behind only metaphors. The result wasn't a story about Kent State. But at least it was my story to tell.

———

Imagine an object falling into a black hole: something small like the body of a young man or woman, or perhaps something large like the campus of a university.

Imagine an outside observer, a distant spectator far removed from the immediate pull of the black hole. He shines a light toward the falling object—the object casts no light of its own, so if the observer wants to see it he must provide his own illumination. He waits for the light to strike the object, then return to his eye.

There are several possibilities for what happens next.

The light may strike the object as it falls through the ergosphere, a region where places become moments and moments become places. That close to the black hole itself, the returning light particles may take years to climb back out of the gravity well and reach the observer. But someday the light *will* return.

Or the light may not reach the falling object until the object has crossed the event horizon. If the object is inside the hole, the light may strike the object and bounce, but it cannot reach the observer outside. The light will only bounce deeper into the blackness. The observer will never see it.

Or perhaps, if the cosmos deigns to conform itself to mathematics, there is a third alternative. The falling object plunges through the heart of the black hole and out a white hole on the other side. By the time the observer's light enters the black hole, the object is gone. The light finds nothing but blackness. There is no contact. To the observer, the object has fallen into an impenetrable dark; but in another universe, perhaps the object tranquilly sails on.

The outside observer waits for his light to return. He wonders if the object has fallen so far he will never truly see it. There is no way to tell until the light actually comes back. If it ever does.

Other observers have given up and gone home.

The outside observer waits.

Withered Gold,

the Night, the Day

The vampire Rogasz had taken to carrying a knife when he walked the streets on his hunt. It was not for protection; it was to slash the faces of his victims as they lay drained of blood, to cut them for being so stupid. "Stupid, stupid, stupid!" he screamed at them . . . and sometimes witnesses heard his cries, drunks hidden under piles of trash or street kids waiting to turn tricks in darkened doorways. The witnesses sold their accounts to impatient Eyewitness News teams and so the story spread throughout the city. "STUPID, STUPID, STUPID!" ran the headlines, and in the coffee shops, reporters from all the media brainstormed what they would call this latest novelty. The Stupid Slasher? No. Not menacing enough. And menace was what sold newspapers.

Meanwhile, Rogasz stalked through the city like a jaded library goer who can't find any books he wants to read. Some rainy nights he would just stake out a territory, attacking anyone who violated the space: striking them down, cutting them with his knife, throwing them off his land without even drinking their blood. He couldn't bring himself to feed on such meager feasts; they would taste the same as all the others, back through the centuries. Besides, he hardly needed to drink these days—the city air was so full of blood and desperation, it seeped into his pores by osmosis. In a more lucid moment, he wrote in his notebook,

> *I have the feeling I do not drink blood, but rather karma—the personal richness of a human soul. This explains the poignant flavor of a virgin as opposed to sluts . . . and yet, in this bleak age, the difference is nearly imperceptible. The best wine is but a hairsbreadth from vinegar. The world has lost its saints.*

There came a steamy summer night when the city smelled of garbage—garbage rotting in Dumpsters as hot as ovens, garbage thrown into the streets by children whose mothers said, "Get this stink out of the house, I don't care what you do with it." Long ago, no one heaved decaying food onto someone else's sidewalk, nor did people sit in front of overloud TVs, too desensitized to realize they were bored. Rogasz prowled past fortress apartment buildings and screamed at the flickering television light reflected in every window. "Poisons, poisons, poisons!"

(Lately, he had taken to saying things three times. He knew he did it; he couldn't stop.)

On he walked, words pouring from his mouth and tears streaming from his eyes, until he reached a corner bus shelter, its glass thick with obscenities written in faded black marker. A man leaned against the doorway of the shelter; and as Rogasz drew nearer, he recognized the man as the Adversary—the Fallen One, the Lost One, the Morning Star Eclipsed.

"Good evening, little brother," the Adversary said.

"Lord of Pus, Lord of Pus, Lord of Pus," Rogasz replied. "I am drowned in the depths of your ocean."

"Then it's time you learned to swim, isn't it? Whatever you're doing now, try something different."

"Different?"

"Yes, change your ways." The Adversary paused a moment.

"I've heard it can be pleasant to do good. Why not give that a stab?"

The Adversary smiled. His teeth were white and even. He had no fangs.

Rogasz thought how soothing it would be, to walk through the world so pure and clean.

That night, he killed a hundred pushers.

They died firing their guns at blackness, and their backup men, hidden in doorways or parked Cadillacs, also emptied their pistols into the dark executioner who seeped out of the night's shadows. Seven innocents were injured in the panicked gunplay, one fatally . . . if you can use the word *innocent* for someone who has come to the Zone in search of a fix.

Police talked of gang wars and gritted their teeth—not that most of them cared about the scum who got killed, but they dreaded the media circus that would follow. Besides, the streets got jittery with so much death in the air. Teenage kids necking in stairwells might suddenly catch the blast of a shotgun, fired by some righteous citizen terrified at the sound of a kiss. People might park their cars in their own garage, then find they'd lost the nerve to step outside, to walk the dozen paces to their dark back doors; and maybe come morning, their blue-lipped corpses would be found by paperboys or postmen, once-living mothers or fathers reduced to inert depositories of carbon monoxide.

That's what happened when death went on a spree: it was too contagious to be constrained by the hands of one person, even if that person had the ancient strength of a vampire. Rogasz killed a hundred pushers. Those higher up in the drug-peddling chain gunned down hundreds more, every rival or potential rival, every employee whose loyalty could be questioned, every wino or panhandler who sat too long across the street.

"I am cleaning up the city," Rogasz told himself. "Cleaning up the city. Cleaning up the city. I am changing my ways by doing good."

But when he killed a pusher, he never bothered to take the pusher's stash. The next customers to come along usually ripped off whatever they could find, unless the drugs had already been picked up by dogs or rats or street kids woken by the noise of gunfire.

So a few more deaths got added to the tally, this time from clumsy overdoses. Coke-ravaged nostrils poured out blood. Junkies sat dead on the toilets of all-night doughnut shops, infinitely reused needles still dangling from their arms.

"STUPID, STUPID, STUPID" read one paper's headline the next morning. The editor had seen no reason to change it from the previous day.

Rogasz stood in front of his soot-stained mausoleum and watched the eastern sky brighten before dawn. The weather looked like it would be lovely and clear. He felt changed, the claws of insanity easing their grip on his skull. Colors seemed more vivid—a dandelion growing beside his tomb had tiny yellow petals so sharply distinct, he could stare at them for hours. It took every drop of his strength to pull himself away, to retreat to his coffin before the sun's corona inched a blazing bead above the horizon.

Yet the promising daybreak faded quickly to gray overcast. Cops, ambulance drivers, waitresses snatching sips from their own cups of coffee whenever they picked up orders in the kitchen . . . many of those awake to see the dawn were struck by the way its initial brightness soon bleached out of the sky, leaving a hot muggy gloom no forecaster had predicted. Thunder rumbled softly as parents laid out their breakfast tables in the muted light of morning; and a troubled few who had somehow freed themselves from the compunction to explain things rationally whispered that the city itself had created the clouds—that the pall of death simmering in the streets had ascended on its own convection currents to block out the sun.

Near noon, a riot broke out in Shantytown. Every TV station gave a different reason for how it started, but their footage was identical: the broken windows, the angry accusations, the weeping faces, all interchangeable.

In response, middle-aged men wearing business suits sat in air-conditioned conference rooms and discussed the possibility of martial law; but they only dithered and delayed. Perhaps it was the dispiriting gray overcast seeping down from the sky. Perhaps even middle-aged men wearing business suits could feel weighed down by the overwhelming sadness, the hopeless, restless sense of damnation that smoldered in the streets.

Rogasz felt it as soon as he woke: the crushing sameness, the sense that any change had only been for the worse. "Stupid, stupid, stupid," he hissed, not knowing whom he meant. "Stupid, stupid, stupid . . . stupid, stupid, stupid." Like steam, he gushed from his tomb and flowed through the open window of the first car to pass the cemetery. Death to the driver; then Rogasz sped through the growing twilight, never slowing for stop signs or traffic lights, seizing a new car whenever the one he was driving got T-boned at an intersection.

Once he heard the yip of a police siren. Just once. The city was somehow thinning out, as if all the forces that tried to keep it working were shrinking to wisps of thread, laced on a wide, wide loom with giant holes in the weave. A crazy man could drive straight up the middle and never be touched by anyone who cared about saving the last scraps of the city's sanity.

At the end of a trail of wreckage, he reached a certain bus shelter. Abandoning his most recent car in the middle of the road, Rogasz stormed up to the Adversary.

"It didn't work," the vampire said. "I tried to do good, but it didn't work. I failed, I failed, I failed."

"Of course you did," the Adversary replied. "You can't do good if you don't know what good is."

"How do I learn what good is?"

"Not my department, little brother. I give tests, not answers. You have to find your own teacher."

The Adversary disappeared. Rogasz looked back at the street, thinking he might return to his vehicle; but a twelve-year-old boy had already shinnied through the open window and driven the car away to a chop shop.

Fifty years ago, Rogasz would not have been able to enter a church . . . or a mosque or a synagogue or even a museum displaying sacred Egyptian antiquities. Something had changed since then: a weakening, a diminishment. Holy water was merely wet. The Bible, the Koran, the Bhagavad Gita—just paper and ink, with no more power to harm him than the Sunday funnies. One night, only a few months past, he had choked a nun to death by making her swallow her crucifix.

He knew he was not sane.

The church he chose to enter was normally lit with huge floodlights, bright enough to discourage graffiti artists and drug deals on the front steps. Tonight, however, the street was dark: the deep guilty darkness of shadows who know they shouldn't be there. Something had cut the electricity on this block, whether the riot, or the drug war, or even one of the car accidents Rogasz had produced with his reckless driving. It didn't matter; whatever the reason, night had closed in on the church like a hungry dog that had been waiting for a sign of weakness.

Every door was locked, dead-bolted and chained. Rogasz chose the one he wanted to enter and it flew open before him, the locks shattering on their own rather than waiting for him to use force. Within, there sounded a brief chitter of bats reacting to the vampire's presence; then the little animals squeezed themselves out through chinks in the roof and walls, letting silence descend on the sanctuary.

Rogasz walked through the vestibule and advanced down the aisle, his ears and eyes scanning for . . . whatever one could learn from churches. Despite the darkness outside, the vampire's preternatural vision could catch the background glimmer of the city filtering through the stained-glass windows. Time-bleached images of Christ and the disciples alternated with newer ones that appealed to urbanite longings—doves, and sheaves of grain, and grape-laden vines.

"Teach me!" screamed the vampire. He stood on the altar, arms stretched wide to the vaulted ceiling. His shoes left smears of dirt on the white altar cloth, gritty footprints tracked across the words I AM THE RESURRECTION AND THE LIFE.

"Teach me, teach me, teach me!" he cried into the darkness. "Change me into something different!"

No answer but silence.

"Make me better! Make me good! Make it stop being *stale*."

He pulled out his knife and slashed it viciously across his own face. "See?" he shouted . . . but the cuts only oozed jellied blackness and shut themselves sluggishly. "See? See? Stupid, stupid, stupid."

Outside the church, things began to burn.

A few of the fires were started by deliberate arson—old scores being settled in a city stretched so thin it was flammable as paper. Other fires simply happened: people sitting in front of their television sets suddenly found themselves poised with a matchbook in one hand and a lit match in the other, seeing how long they could hold the match before its heat made them let go. Maybe the flame would go out as it fell, or the match would gutter on a dirty plate left over from supper and set on the floor beside the TV chair. In some households, however, the match landed on a rag rug, or in a basket of never-finished knitting that had long outlived the need for baby sweaters or booties. The burgeoning flames gave off an incense of paralyzed sadness, holding viewers in a melancholy trance until they quietly conceded it was too late.

The sound of fire sirens seemed so weak in the deepening night . . . like an infant's last cry of starvation.

Rogasz sat at the church's grand piano, softly playing one minor chord after another. He couldn't remember how he'd moved from the altar to the piano bench. Any key higher than middle C buzzed unpleasantly; when he looked into the open piano, he saw his knife lying across the strings of the upper octaves, rattling with the vibration of the notes.

He pulled out the knife and jammed the blade into his thigh. After that, the piano sounded better.

One soft chord after another—it had been years since he had played. Long ago, when the sun still shone, every civilized man could read Latin, dance the minuet, and play Bach by memory. Rogasz had been doing precisely that, mere minutes before his tryst with a woman who called herself Juliet. He'd considered her a casual indulgence, the amusement of a moment . . . but that amusing, indulgent moment led to the short, sharp violation and centuries of night-bound withering.

"Juliet," Rogasz called to the empty darkness. "I forgive you." He said it mostly to curry favor with the god who was supposed to inhabit this church; yet he found that at this second, his heart held no hatred for the long-lost woman. She had drunk his blood and stolen his sunrise, but even rage could burn itself out. "I forgive you, I forgive you, I forgive you," he said aloud, striking a chord with each phrase.

A tiny rustle came in response . . . *Hallucination,* he thought at first, but his keen eyes soon picked out a shabby figure sitting in the darkness. A teenage girl, a street kid, sat in a back pew and silently tried to shift her weight to a more comfortable position. Of course it wasn't Juliet—Rogasz had tracked that bitch down less than a century after she created him, and now she was dust on the boots of Prague—but this girl had something of the same look. Tired. Controlled.

"Is there anything you'd like me to play?" he asked, staring directly at her.

She jumped, apparently startled he could see her in the darkness. Then she shrugged and said, "Whatever."

"Is that the name of a song?"

"Play what you want. Just keep your distance."

He wanted to tell her what a fool she was—he could bolt from one end of the sanctuary to the other and sink his teeth into her throat before her brain had a chance to react. The words *Stupid, stupid, stupid* quivered on his lips.

But . . .

But . . .

After a few experimental notes, he knew his fingers could no longer manage Bach. Too many centuries had passed without practice . . . and his daggerlike fingernails clicked unpleasantly on the keys. He went back to slow minor chords, improvising a bittersweet tune to fit against them.

The next time Rogasz looked at the girl, her eyes were half closed.

Outside, the fires spread through the night—fires without noise, without fire chiefs yelling through bullhorns or alarms clanging into the darkness. To be sure, every fire crew in the city was making a stand, staked out around propane tanks, ammonia dumps, chemical manufacturing plants; but that left everything else to burn, spreading the flames unchecked from each building to its neighbors. Dispossessed families simply fled into the night . . . and none of them could say whether they intended to return, whether they would even file insurance claims on their homes or just wipe the ashes off their shoes and move on.

The stained-glass windows of the church grew brighter as the fires approached. Flickering light wavered behind the faces of saints; the dove of peace shimmered. One window read BEHOLD I STAND AT THE DOOR AND KNOCK . . . and the light in Christ's stained-glass lantern glinted with a beam that shone goldenly across the pews.

The light showed a legion of rats, streaming into the church.

They were, of course, fleeing the fires: running from nests behind ancient basement furnaces or dashing from summer lairs inside the garbage heaps that cooked in every alley. Some had flooded up from the sewers—climbing through gratings and road-work sites as the sewer water began to steam from nearby flames. In other parts of the city the animals soon headed for water again, diving into cooler sewers, into the harbor, or even into backyard swimming pools, snorting against the sting of chlorine. But here, in the blocks around the church, they were drawn by the presence of Rogasz, diverted by the vampire's aura to gather at his side.

Hundreds of rats poured silently into the sanctuary. They did not squeak. Their claws scarcely made a sound on the hardwood floor. Like an audience filing in for a concert, they congregated in a circle around the piano.

And the circle grew.

"Shit!" squealed the girl in the back of the church. Dozing with the soft music, she had just woken to find a rodent army surging through every door. In an instant, she had scrambled up to stand on the pew, climbing as high as she could above the invading horde . . . not that she was a timid little kid afraid of mice, but a thousand full-grown sewer rats, their fur matted with urine and feces, were enough to daunt any human.

"What the hell's going on?" she shouted.

"It's the fire," Rogasz replied. "They've come to the church seeking sanctuary."

"Rats? Are you crazy?"

"I expect so."

"Fine," the girl said. "You be crazy. I'm getting out of here."

"You wouldn't survive," Rogasz told her, putting a hard edge into his voice. "Can't you see we're surrounded by flame?"

He nodded toward the stained-glass images. Firelight raged outside now, blazing fiercely through the windows on both sides of the church. "If you went outside," Rogasz said, "you'd suffocate from the smoke."

"So I should stay and burn instead?"

"Have faith," he told her. He said the words because good people said such things, and because he wanted to win the approval of any deity who might be listening. "Have faith, have faith, have faith. Haaaaaave faith. Haaaaaaaaaave faith."

The girl died an hour before sunrise. Some of the rats survived, though.

Fires on the horizon brought a false dawn to the city; but the vampire could feel true sunup only minutes away as he approached the Adversary's bus shelter once more. Rogasz had not escaped the church unscathed—he had played the piano till it burst into flame, its strings snapping one by one with enough tension to drive the broken ends through the burning wood around them. One side of the vampire's face was baked raw, oozing fluids. He had stopped playing because his right hand no longer worked.

The gray predawn streets were mostly empty, except for jeeps of uniformed men driving grimly through the smoke. Three hours ago martial law had been imposed at last, and already the soldiers had fallen under the city's spell: an urge to scurry from one safe place to another, a willingness to blind themselves to everything in between. No patrols stopped the vampire. None even glanced in his direction . . . not because he had invoked some supernatural concealment but because the patrols had become their own islands of consciousness, turned inward and brooding.

Unchallenged, Rogasz made his way to the bus shelter. He walked with a limp; for some reason, he'd never removed the knife from his thigh. The Adversary was once more leaning in the shelter's doorway, his face smudged with soot. "Busy night, little brother," he said.

"I went looking for God, but I haven't changed," the vampire replied. "People die and I have no grief."

"You can't mourn for everyone." The Adversary shrugged. "Only heaven has enough tears for that."

"But I want to *feel* something. I want to be moved. Moved! Pushed away from wherever I am and over the line."

"What line?"

"The dawn," Rogasz said. "Over the edge of dawn into the light."

"The sun rises every day, little brother. Don't blame me if you decide to hide from it."

"But it will kill me."

"There, you've seen through my plan." The Adversary laughed. "All this time, I've been secretly tempting you to suicide. That's a big bad mortal sin." His face abruptly turned grim and he looked at Rogasz in disgust. "Do you think redemption is free? Stupid, stupid, stupid."

"But I tried—"

"Listen," the Adversary snapped, "whatever price you've always avoided paying, that's precisely what it costs. Understand? If you want things to be different, you have to let go of the thing you're trying to keep the same. Simple logic."

"I could think of a hundred counterexamples . . ." Rogasz began.

"Then I'll see you back here a hundred more times." The Adversary disappeared in a puff of smoke that smelled of burned rat hair and the screams of children.

Dawn came. The dark day of the soul. Rogasz greeted it.

In the first hour, there were still too many cinders in the air to admit more than a ghost of sun. The vampire felt his hair smolder, but that was all.

In the second hour, people began to come out of hiding. Some wept; some had faces of stone. One man walked through the ruins of a tenement, calling for his dog. Rogasz helped him shout, "Skeeters! Skeeters! Skeeters!" The vampire knew there was no life left under the debris, but he liked having something he could yell over and over, hearing his voice echo off the scorched masonry.

By the third hour, the ash was finally settling out of the air. Fires still burned in some neighborhoods, but a day fire is a sheepish thing compared to a night one. As the haze cleared, the sun broke through. Rogasz spent a few minutes dodging it, then gave up. The good side of his face burned to match the other, but it was a dry burn, like a piece of leather curing in the desert.

Sometime in the fourth hour, a beagle came in response to the vampire's calls. By that time, the man looking for Skeeters had gone away, so Rogasz had no idea whether this was the right dog. "Skeeters, Skeeters, Skeeters," Rogasz said, and the dog wagged its tail.

For much of the fifth hour, the vampire lay on a stone bench in

front of a law office. A sign on the office door read CLOSED WHILE
EMERGENCY CONTINUES. No emergency was visible. The dog lay
on the ground beside the bench, sleeping in the sun. Rogasz didn't
sleep, but he closed his eyes, feeling daylight sear into him like a
welding torch. "I am being purified," he told the dog. "This is
what redemption feels like."

In the sixth hour, a policeman yelled at him, "You can't sleep
there, fella." But when the officer got closer, he said, "Holy shit!
Just stay put, don't try to get up. I'll call an ambulance." No ambulance ever came—not in this city, on this day—and at some
point the policeman left, too.

As afternoon drew on, the shadow of the law office fell across the
bench where Rogasz lay, and after a while he felt strong enough to
sit up. The dog followed him down the street, past an army check-
point that waved him through with directions to the nearest hospital. When Rogasz turned the opposite way, none of the soldiers
bothered to correct him.

In time, vampire and dog reached the church where Rogasz had
spent the previous night. The walls had toppled in, but by some
quirk of combustion, the massive pipes of the organ had survived
the fire. They stood side by side, towering over the rubble like a
stockade wall, their false gold paint leprous with blisters.

Rogasz searched until he found the body of the girl: peaceful
looking, he thought, once he had arranged her limbs properly. He
wrenched the metal frame from the grand piano's skeleton and
propped it, harp-shaped, over the girl's head. With a blackened
stick of wood, he wrote

JULIET

JULIET

JULIET

on the frame, then called the dog to see what he'd done. "This is Juliet," he told the dog; then he remembered Juliet was someone from long ago, and this was just a dead street kid whose name he'd never known.

"Stupid, stupid, stupid," he murmured. "I should have asked her name. That's what clean people do—they ask each other's name." He leaned over the corpse and shouted, "Why didn't you tell me your name? Stupid!"

The dead girl answered with silence . . . not a profound silence, just the flat silence of death. When the living don't speak, they're always saying something with their silence; but a lifeless body has no implied message, no secret it might whisper if coaxed or intimidated. The corpse was now an "it," not a "she"—a thing lying on rubble, as meaningless as air.

"Oh, Juliet," he said. "Where did you go?"

He bent down, and the dog came forward, too, snuffling at the corpse. For a moment Rogasz watched, wondering what the dog would do . . . if the smell of cooked flesh would stir its appetite. But then he thought he didn't want the dog to do anything to Juliet, so he took a burned chunk of pew and threw it off some distance so the dog would have something else to occupy its attention.

The dog ran to fetch, although it was a small dog and a big piece of wood. Growling happily, the dog began to drag the burned lump back toward the vampire.

Rogasz turned toward the organ pipes rising at the front of the church: a wall of pipes, a barricade that must be hiding something—the god who lurked in this place. "I'd like to mourn," he called to the god. "I really want to feel that something has happened here. That something important has changed. I knew her, I played music for her, and she died. That should change me. What was it all for, if it didn't change me?"

The god gave no answer.

"I have a dog now," Rogasz told the god behind the pipes. "I have a dog named Skeeters and I'll take good care of him. He'll love me and I'll love him, and we'll play together all day long . . . in the sun. I've spent a day in the sun and I have a dog who loves me. What else do you want?" He grabbed a blackened chunk of brick and stood up suddenly. "What else could you want?"

With all his strength, he heaved the brick at the organ pipes, striking the largest pipe dead center. Metal clanged and crumpled, leaving a teardrop-shaped dent.

"What else do you want?" the vampire screamed. "Isn't this enough? Juliet's dead. Isn't that enough? I'm burned and I have a dog. Isn't that fucking enough?"

He pulled the knife from his thigh, loosing a spray of burned red blood. With a roar of fury he scrambled over the ruins of the church—nuggets of stained glass, the altar with its charred swath of linen, the roof beams fallen on top of the pulpit—and he propelled himself in a frenzied leap onto the organ's remains . . . a palisade of sooty, paint-blistered pipes, barring him from God on the other side. He could hang there by jamming his hand into the mouth of one of the pipes, sharp metal cutting into his fingers; and with the other hand, his right hand, too burned to play piano but still strong enough to hold a knife, he slashed at the pipe barrier and howled, "Stupid!

"Stupid!

"Stupid!"

Rain fell soon after sunset . . . just a light shower, but enough to bring Rogasz back to consciousness.

He hung, arms outstretched on the rack of pipes, both hands thrust into mouth holes in the flues. His knife had fallen some time ago, after failing to do more than damage the false gold paint.

The dog had run off, upset by the vampire's shouting.

Rogasz released his grip and dropped to the ground, landing heavily on the scattered debris. It was slick with the rain; he slipped and went sprawling. If he injured anything, if he broke bones in the tumble, he was no longer able to feel such insignificant pain.

Juliet's face was wet in the twilight, her clothes lightly soaked. He didn't like seeing her that way, but he didn't want to cover her up. The rain had made the charcoal letters of her name bleed down the frame where he'd written them. Rogasz stared at them for a time, wondering if he should wipe the words away and write them again. No. The frame was wet, all the charcoal, too; he might not be able to write anything this time, and a streaky epitaph was better than nothing.

"I could have saved you," he said. Gently, the vampire laid his hand on her cheek. "I could have made you like me; then you would have survived . . . like me. You wouldn't thank me for that, not in the long run. Still, maybe I should have given you the choice. I don't know. I don't know."

He bent over and kissed her cracked crusty lips. "You died in a church," he whispered to her silent face. "You'll be all right. And here . . ." His knife was lying atop the rubble a short distance away. He retrieved it and folded the girl's limp hands around it, laying it across her chest. "This will keep you safe." He was tempted to add, *You need the knife more than I do;* but he recognized the words were empty. Just said to prove something to someone. Rogasz had no need for such words—not in this quiet twilight.

Instead, he said, "I don't know." He kissed her again. "I don't know, I don't know, I don't know."

He smiled and patted her hands, making sure they held the knife firmly.

———

When he lifted his head from Juliet's corpse, the Adversary was leaning against the ruined piano. "So," the Lost One said, "how are you feeling tonight?"

"I don't know."

"Redeemed?"

Rogasz let himself take a deep breath. "Unlikely—I haven't done anything to deserve it."

"What did you want to do? Slay a dragon? Heal a leper?" The Adversary waved his hand dismissively. "Melodramatic crap. A childish need for flashy resolutions. Same as if you dropped to your knees and wailed that you were finally embracing God. That's not salvation; that's just trying to be the star in some grandiose show. Trust me, I know what salvation isn't." He laughed. "Still, you survived the whole day."

Rogasz shrugged. "I've survived a lot of things."

"True." The Adversary pushed himself away from the piano and sidled forward over the debris. "Who's the girl?" he asked, nodding toward the ground.

Rogasz opened his mouth, then closed it again. "Just a street kid," he said at last. "I've been calling her Juliet."

The Adversary raised his eyebrows. "And you're Romeo?"

"No. I'm not Romeo and she's not Juliet. She's just dead."

The Adversary stared at Rogasz silently. "You sound calmer," he said. "More at peace than when we last spoke."

"Just too burned out for rage. A day of shock therapy. Don't expect it to last."

"Nothing lasts, little brother. Things fall apart; the center cannot hold. Everything changes in time."

"Have *I* changed?" He looked down at the dead girl. "She's changed. She has definitely changed. But I'm still here. My injuries will heal like always, and then what? The same old thing?"

"That's up to you," the Adversary replied. "But if a vampire can find a moment of grace . . . who knows who might be next?"

He gave the ghost of a bow. "Stay sane, little brother; I look to you as my inspiration. Stay sane, stay sane, stay sane."

With a backward wave of his hand, the Adversary walked into the darkness. Full night had fallen: a night rinsed with soft rain.

Rogasz decided to wait beside the corpse a while longer—maybe the dog would come back.

The Last Day of the War,

with Parrots

It was a sprawl-shot, and this time I was sprawling hips-down on top of a bunker, just behind a hole where something had disintegrated a corner of the roof.

When the cameras turned in my direction, I was supposed to lift on my forearms, with my shoulders high enough that every lens got an ample view down my cleavage. I wore a deep scoop-neck blouse, of course, ripped and ragged and thinner than gauze. I wondered if I should make up business cards—*Lyra Dene, singer: backup and boobs*. But tape wasn't rolling at the moment, and I'd scrunched up rump-high, because if I stayed in the rehearsed cheesecake pose, the navel battery-pack for my microphone dug sharply into my stomach.

The cameras were scattered all over the battlefield, some on the ground, some hovering on chunky anti-grav platforms. Each had its ready light glowing green, but the operator who ran them all was sitting in a lawn chair beside the control console, reading a book. His hand rested on the fog machine beside the console; occasionally, he had to sweep away threads of mist that dribbled from the machine's nozzle and trickled across his reading screen.

In front of the console loomed the remains of a giant subterranean battle-tank. The most visible part was its drill-like snout, jutting up at a 45-degree angle and reaching five or six stories above the ground. The tank must have been ambushed just as it surfaced. Enemy lasers had drilled a dozen clean-edged holes in its hull, and something had blasted its caterpillar treads off their sprockets, splaying them over the ground like black lasagna noodles.

Three people stood at the base of the drill-snout: Helena Howe, director of the video we were supposed to be shooting; our songwriter, Roland Simard; and Alex Kilgoorlie, probably the only one you care about.

Soon after I got hired as Alex's backup vocalist, I read an article claiming that 63 percent of all human households had downloaded his debut album, *Ghost of the Tattered Heart*. One review said: "His songs are compelling dreams . . . or nightmares." I don't mind admitting I'd dreamed about him myself. The dreams centered on a gaunt, disquieting man walking moodily over a bleak landscape . . . and like on the *Ghost* album cover, he wore a loose white shirt that billowed in the wind.

In my dreams, the front of Alex's shirt hung open to the waist; but it was still buttoned to the throat that day around the battle-tank. While Helena and Roland stood irritably over him, Alex crouched, making kissing sounds with his lips and holding out a cracker in his hand.

"People are *waiting*, Alex dear," Helena said. I could hear her voice through the tiny receiver tucked into my ear and hidden by my hair. All of us wore such earphones; when she gave an order, she wanted everyone's undivided attention.

"Just another sec," Alex whispered. A concealed mike amplified his whisper clearly. He made more kissing sounds.

In front of him was an animal about the size of a mouse, part of the local wildlife. I could see the beast was brightly colored, a splash of green and crimson stripes against the drab dirt back-ground; but it was too far away for me to make out much else. It inched toward the cracker Alex held out, its head wobbling back and forth slightly. I guessed it was sniffing, trying to make up its mind about the food and the human that held it. The animal seemed just about to nibble when a voice yelled, "Don't!"

Every head jerked up, including the little beastie's. Scrambling over the partly buried tank came Jerith, our archeologist and resi-dent expert on the planet of Caproche. He'd lived on these aban-doned battlefields for years, alone except for his robots, excavating dozens of sites as he tried to determine who had fought here and why.

I flattened down on the bunker roof. In the two days our group had been on Caproche, Jerith had already passed his quota for peeks down my blouse. I didn't fuss about it—he seemed harm-less, just a guy who hadn't seen a woman in a long, long time—but I refused to give him the ogling opportunities provided by a sprawl-shot.

"What's wrong?" Helena asked. "Is the animal dangerous?" She put a hand on Alex's arm and tried to pull him away from the creature.

"No, no, they're harmless," Jerith said, scooping up the little beast with a sweep of his hand. He cradled it against his chest and began stroking it the way you'd pet a hamster. "I call them par-rots."

"It doesn't look like a parrot," our songwriter Roland said. "More like a lizard."

"It's brightly colored like a parrot," Jerith answered. "Anyway, the point is, everyone should leave them alone."

"I wasn't going to hurt it," Alex said in a wounded tone.

"You never know," Jerith told him. "Earth food can be poison-ous to aliens. The tiniest nibble might kill this little guy."

"Polly doesn't want a cracker," Roland smirked to Alex.

"And even if Polly does, we have work to do," Helena said briskly. "Come along, Alex. Recording time."

"Can I pet the parrot for a sec?" Alex asked, reaching out his fingers. Jerith shied away and Helena grabbed Alex's arm with both hands.

"We're going to work now," she said, "and I mean *right* now. Jerith, take that animal away. Roland, get off the set. Alex, I want the Singer, and no more putting it off. You aren't fooling anyone with these delaying tactics; I want the Singer *now*."

She turned her back on him and marched to the control console. The console operator quickly shut off his book and tried to look busy. Helena glared but said nothing.

Back in front of the tank, Jerith turned to walk away, still caressing the parrot. Roland patted Alex on the back, said, "Break a leg," and sauntered toward the control console too.

Alone, Alex stood dejectedly for a moment, his eyes moving aimlessly around the battlefield. I smiled when he looked in my direction, but I don't think he saw. He sighed an amplified sigh that echoed through the surrounding ruins: a litter of shattered warmachines that stretched as far as the eye could see. Then he reached up and undid the top button of his shirt.

He stood straighter.

Another button. His hands took on some flourish, like the hands of a concert keyboardist.

"Cue the fog," Helena's voice whispered in my earphone. The nozzle of the fog machine gushed a cataract of mist, flowing along the ground and pooling at Alex's feet.

Another shirt button. He shook out his ringleted brown hair and flicked it off his shoulders.

"Cue the wind," whispered Helena, and massive fans on antigrav platforms began to turn, slowly at first, then faster and faster until they were silent blurs. The anti-grav platforms banked slightly to resist the force of the wind. Alex's hair caught the breeze and grew wild.

The final button. His head lifted. His cheeks were gaunt, his eyes feral and glittering. A dangerous face: a striking, compelling danger.

"Cue cameras," whispered Helena.

Time for work, I said to myself. But I found I was already in my pose, sprawled and primed; roused without thinking when Alex became the Singer. Sure, I'd rehearsed this scene till it all came naturally, but there was no feeling of rehearsal—just pure reaction to the Singer's presence. I was panting, budding with prickles of sweat.

"Cue music," came a far-off whisper.

The ground rumbled with a heavy bass riff. Wind washed across me, whipping my hair against my shoulders; I screamed into the gale, and no rehearsal had taught me to scream with such fear and desire.

Then silence. The eye of the storm. And the Singer stepped forward through swirls of mist to whisper,

> *You have entered my heart, milady;*
> *Now I shall enter your mind . . .*

He swiveled sharply and pointed his finger directly at me.

> *Betray me not, milady,*
> *For then I shall be . . . unkind.*

I'd laughed at the lyrics in rehearsal as Alex good-naturedly waved a finger in my direction. Now the words came from the Singer, skeletal, ominous; and the threat in his voice chilled me. He blazed with danger . . . and I, in ripped and ragged clothes, shuddered at my vulnerability.

"Close-up on Lyra," I heard Helena whisper.

I screamed again. On cue.

"That Kilgoorlie is a spooky guy," Jerith said.

It was after supper and we were in a Quonset hut in Jerith's camp. Three of us, Jerith, Roland, and I, stood at a workbench where we brushed dirt off chunks of metal that Jerith claimed were archeological artifacts. The piece I had to clean was slightly bigger than my hand, fairly solid, and heavier than it looked. It was mostly copper-rust green, but a trumpet-like mouth at one end had its interior streaked with bronze. Like most of the artifacts on Caproche, this was probably a broken weapon.

We were dusting off the past because we had become archaeologists-in-training. Technically speaking, the planet Caproche was classified SIO, Scientific Investigation Only; but seven hundred years ago, unknown alien races had warred here from tropics to tundra, and the resulting devastation fit Alex Kilgoorlie's music like a chain mail glove. Helena had decided she *must* shoot Alex's next album on Caproche. To get around the Planet Protection Agency, she paid Jerith a great deal of money to claim our party was helping him in his studies; so when we weren't in recording sessions, we made a show of devotion to the digs. Well . . . most of us made such a show—Helena had yet to touch a shovel. And Alex got so enthusiastic the first time he came to the work hut, he'd somehow smashed the lens of a heavy-duty battle laser; so Jerith excused him from future duty.

"Alex isn't spooky," Roland said. "He's the most normal person here."

"Don't give me that," Jerith replied. "I saw him this afternoon. When he was singing . . . it was like he was some kind of wraith. That's exactly the word, a wraith."

"You're confusing Alex with the Singer," Roland answered

calmly. "Alex is a regular guy; the Singer is something else." He busied himself with dabbing at a clot of mud that clung to the snarl of wires he was cleaning, then added, "The Singer is spooky as hell."

Jerith stared at Roland for a long moment. "Are you talking split personality?"

"I asked a psych-tech about that once," Roland answered. "She laughed at me. Everyone knows split personalities only exist in low-budget grislies. These days, potential splits are detected in childhood and sewn right back up. Oh yes, that perky little psych-tech had herself a real giggle over my naïveté."

"Sorry," Jerith said. From the tone in his voice, I guessed that our resident archaeologist had also been laughed at by women sometime in the past.

"I went to school with Alex," Roland said, making a show of attention to his work. "Good guy. Everybody's friend. Not too bright . . . not very bright at all . . ." Roland slapped his brush roughly at the dirt. "But he was everybody's friend. Women loved him." He looked up at me accusingly. "What do you think of Alex, Lyra? Not the Singer, but Alex. Kind of cute, kind of helpless, right? Sweet lovable guy?"

"I like Alex," I replied, trying not to sound defensive. "What's wrong with that?"

Both men looked at me silently. Neither one came close to Alex's easy charm. Roland, overweight, his hair thinning though he was only twenty-five, and his lips too red and blubbery. Jerith, with his droopy face and weak chin unsuccessfully hidden by a patchy blond beard, uncombed and scraggly . . . no doubt he'd known people like Alex too, and . . .

Jerith turned quickly away from me. His hand went reflexively to his beard. I told myself I must have been staring and I felt like shit.

"There's nothing wrong with Alex," Roland said quietly as he went back to cleaning his artifact. "I admit, the problem was mine. I envied him like hell. Especially back when we were starting our band. Eighteen years old, both of us, playing school dances and grotty little booze bins. Me playing keyboards, writing all the songs, doing the *work*!" He dug the brush into the gap between two metal tubes and twisted it hard. "Alex sang my songs, *my* songs, every word mine, not his . . . but who did the women steam for? Pissed me off, pissed me right . . ." He stopped and calmed himself. After a moment he said, "These days I can handle it. I'm not writing to impress people, I'm not writing to get *laid*." He gave me a pointed look. "I'm writing to say something and the message is what counts. If the only way to be heard is putting my words in the Singer's mouth, so be it."

There was a lengthy silence, a painful one. I felt guilty without knowing why, like I'd been accused of some crime . . . as if I were a slut waiting to fall at Alex's feet just to spite Roland. I wished Jerith would say something, anything to ease the tension.

And he did.

"You still haven't talked about Alex and the Singer," Jerith said, sounding like the words came awkwardly to him, but clearly doing his best to break the silence.

"Oh, that," said Roland. "Do you believe in possession?"

"No," I answered, though the question was directed at Jerith.

Roland laughed without humor. "I don't believe in it either. But I'll tell you, when Alex and I first started performing, we stank. I have no idea why—he had a decent voice, and I knew the songs were brilliant . . ." He laughed again. "We just didn't have the chemistry, that's all. Then one night in this ratty blow-bar called Juicy's . . . one night this woman came to see us backstage between sets. An older woman, maybe as old as thirty. Hey, I was eighteen, she was ancient. I thought she was a hooker and I was prime self-righteous the way only teenagers can be, so I made some cutting remarks and stomped out for some air. What you'd call a very pointed exit.

"By the time I got back, she was nose-to-nose with Alex, talking about ways to improve the act. That pissed me off, this woman telling us our jobs. I grabbed Alex by the arm and dragged him off toward the stage, but she called to Alex's back, 'And undo your shirt. Strut the flesh, for Christ's sake. Put some groin into it. When people watch the stage, they don't want the boy next door. They want a goddamned *performer*.'

"Well. We hit the stage for the next set, and Alex started trying stuff. Rolling his eyes, swiveling his hips . . . completely forced, and embarrassing. He wasn't that kind of guy—not a drop of sleaze in him. When he tried it, I'm telling you, he just had no clue! I told him to smarten up, but that woman was watching from a front row table, and Alex must have figured he could get lucky if he played up to her.

"The mood of the bar shifted from bored to hostile; we'd been mediocre before, but now the act positively turned your stomach. Even Alex sensed how ugly the crowd was getting. One guy, built like a tank, dressed in leather from head to toe, this guy pulled out a switchblade and started clicking it in, out, click, click, making sure we saw him. I broke into a cold sweat, and Alex, he panicked completely. Panic was the only thing that could have made him unbutton his shirt, because believe it or not, he was shy about his body, showing it in public.

"He started unbuttoning in the middle of this long instrumental break, after the chorus of 'A Short Spell of Rain'—first cut on our first album, you should know it. And with every button he undid, it was like something rewiring itself in his head. Like a puppy changing into a wolf. When the instrumental break was over and he started singing the next verse . . . God, my hands were shaking so bad I could hardly play. The room fell absolutely still—not a whisper, not a glass tinkling. The bouncer outside the front door came running in, pulling on his brass knuckles like he expected real trouble; but he stopped in the entranceway, just froze there, with the brass knucks dangling on his fingertips, and he listened to the rest of the song. And the next song. And the next. Until we'd run through our whole repertoire. We left the stage, we went to the dressing room, and I buttoned up Alex's shirt without looking into his eyes. Then we both had terror-fits for a few hours."

Silence. Nothing but the swish of our three brushes sweeping old grit and dirt.

"I take it the woman in the audience was Helena Howe?" Jerith asked at last.

"You got it," Roland nodded, setting down his brush. "Our very own manager, director, and ballbreaker. And yes, Alex did get lucky that night. Or unlucky, depending on your point of view. He says they're in love." Roland wiped his dusty hands fiercely on a rag he picked up from the workbench. "I've never found out whether Helena makes him unbutton his shirt in bed. Interesting question, don't you think? Alex is easier to control, but the Singer would be more . . . volcanic."

He threw the rag down on the workbench and strode out into the gathering twilight. He didn't look back at either of us as he let the door click shut behind him.

Jerith let his breath out slowly. "I think I need a walk," he said. "How about you?"

My first reflex was to say no—too much potential for complications. Jerith had lived alone so long, he was ripe to get soppy about the first woman to happen by. Me, I have a policy against getting soppy. Walking with Jerith, giving him hope, would only be cruel. On the other hand, I still felt bad for making him self-conscious about his beard, and he was so desperate for company . . . what harm could there be in a friendly stroll, if I didn't lead him on?

"Sure," I said, "let's get some air. You can show me the sights."

The dusk was already full of stars, thousands more than you see on New Earth—Caproche is a lot closer to galactic center. A few ribbons of purpling cloud streaked the sky, but all were scudding off rapidly toward the horizon. It would soon be a clear, cool evening, with plenty of starlight to see by.

"It might turn cold," Jerith said, looking at the sky too. "I can get you a sweater if you like."

"I'm fine," I said.

Jerith led me around the base of a small hill and immediately the sounds of the camp were cut off, leaving only empty stillness—the stillness of starlit hills decorated with nothing but ruined bunkers and the scars of energy blasts. A desolate silence. "Don't you ever worry about being out here?" I asked Jerith. "All alone on a planet like this?"

"What would I worry about?" He sounded surprised at my question. "Alien ghosts?"

"Not ghosts," I answered, trying to sound like a woman who never gets the creeps. "But with so much junk left over from the war . . . what if you stumbled onto an old minefield? Or some robot weapon that's still active?"

He shook his head. "By the time humans arrived on Caproche, every battle site had been picked through a dozen times. The Myriapods surveyed the planet only two hundred years after the war, and you know how thorough they are. Even with their best sensing equipment, they didn't find a single functional weapon, nor a working vehicle, not even a battery pack that still held its charge. No bodies either . . . well, nothing they recognized as bodies. Other groups came after the Myriapods—the Cashlings, the Fasskisters, five or six others—but they didn't find anything either. The races who fought here stripped the place clean when they pulled out. Nothing left but trash." He smiled. "That's why Caproche only has one loony archeologist instead of a horde of prospectors looking for alien tech."

I expected him to make one of the classic moves at that moment: casually bumping against me, or touching my shoulder to direct my attention toward something, or taking my hand to lead me across a rough patch of ground . . . but he kept both hands thrust firmly into the deep pockets of his work pants, and as we started walking again, he scrupulously avoided accidental contact.

That irked me.

I mean, he'd been alone and celibate on Caproche for several years. In many circles, I'm considered sexy; when I sang with the Mootikki Spiders on *Trash and Thrash,* the reviewer from *Mind Spurs Weekly* singled out "the hot brunette on the bicycle" as the high point of the album. It was insulting that this desperate man didn't even *try* to . . .

He touched my shoulder.

I turned to look at him, relieved and preparing my "thanks but no thanks" speech.

He looked away. A moment later, he mumbled, "Over here. There's something you might like."

I followed him to a low wall built from fat bricks. Once upon a time those bricks might have been sandbags, but the bags had rotted and the sand left behind had hardened like concrete.

Splayed over the wall grew a mat of snarled threads, each thread porcelain-white under the stars. I could see more patches of the stuff beyond the wall, on rocks, on the grass, even streaked up the trunks of trees.

"I call it the Silk," Jerith said.

"Some sort of fungus?" I asked.

"No, it photosynthesizes," he answered. "It lives on UV light— I had it analyzed. Now watch this."

He poked at a strand with his finger. A moment later, the Silk made a sharp <SPLINK> sound and shattered with a forceful eruption that sent a cloud of powder into the air. I'd been watching so closely, the dust sprayed all over my face. It had a grimy feel, a little moist and gluey. I rubbed at it vigorously, trying to wipe it off.

"Oh, God, Lyra, I'm sorry," Jerith said. "Let me. . . ." He reached out to help.

I ducked back from his outstretched hand. "Is this some gag?" I asked. "Like a squirting flower? Get me all gooey?" I gave my nose another rub.

"No, I just wasn't thinking," Jerith said. "I'm sorry. It's, uhh . . . I wanted to show you the Silk because it's my big discovery."

"Oh, yes?" I'd got most of the gunk off my face, but now my hands were sticky. I looked around for some Silkless terrain where I could wipe them off.

"Yes, the Silk," Jerith said. "My theory is it's a biological weapon. From the war."

I looked at my hands, covered with powder. Very quickly, I wiped them on my dungarees.

"You don't have to worry," Jerith went on hurriedly. "It's harmless to humans. The best labs on New Earth have checked it out. Biological weapons are usually species-specific, especially in a war like this, between different alien races. This dust probably shriveled one side but left the other side untouched." He poked another strand. <SPLINK> "It's funny when you think about it. This is probably lethal to some mysterious aliens, but to us little old humans . . ." He poked again. <SPLINK>

It didn't seem so funny to me, and I didn't like biological weapons going off in my face even if I was the wrong species; but Jerith looked so forlorn there, going <SPLINK>, <SPLINK>, <SPLINK> with his big discovery, that I didn't have the heart to stay mad at him. He smiled at me, I grudgingly smiled back, and in a few moments, we were both <SPLINK>ing away. You could get different pitches depending how hard you struck each thread, and I started trying to <SPLINK> out "Betray Me Not," the song we'd recorded that afternoon. Jerith was using both hands to <SPLINK> out a background rhythm and we were having a great time until a Caprochian parrot climbed out of Jerith's pants pocket.

I didn't shriek, just made a choked "ungh" sound as I jumped back. When I'd watched Alex try to feed the same kind of animal at the recording session, I hadn't been close enough to see how ugly the little beasts were. This one was small and flat, like a mouse-size Gila monster, but with a topknot of three antennae, each undulating like weeds in water. The animal didn't scare me—it wasn't even repulsive after I'd got over my initial shock—but it definitely wasn't the sort of thing I'd keep in my pocket.

Jerith saw my reaction, looked down at the brightly colored creature crawling up his clothing, and immediately detached it from his waistband. He winced slightly when he touched it, but held it gently, caressing it. "It's only my pet," he said. "It's very tame."

"Why did you have it in your pocket?"

"They like warm, dark places. They just curl up and go to sleep. When it heard us popping the Silk, it must have woken up and felt hungry."

"Hungry?" I said, uneasy with the way Jerith fondled the little beast.

"They eat the Silk," Jerith answered, holding the animal close to a patch of strands on the wall. The parrot pushed its snout forward; gingerly it tugged loose the end of a thread and sucked up the Silk like spaghetti. "Very delicate mouths," Jerith added. "They can gobble the stuff without popping it."

For a while, I watched the tiny animal eat. I wouldn't say it was cute, but its determined slurping did have an endearing quality. I put out my hand to rub its nose, but Jerith immediately jerked the parrot out of reach.

"What's wrong?" I asked.

"They don't like to be touched by strangers," he said, backing away from me.

"Do you know how suspicious you're acting?" I wasn't one for melodrama, but who hasn't seen a dozen shows where an archaeologist on some isolated planet fixates on an alien species? And nine times out of ten in those shows, someone gets her brains eaten before the closing credits.

"It's not what you're thinking," Jerith blurted out.

"How do you know what I'm thinking?"

His face blanched. Turning away from me, he hurriedly slid the parrot back into his pocket. The animal didn't put up any fight at all. When he turned back to face me, Jerith kept his hand in that pocket.

"Look," he said, "I know I've developed some quirks out here. Being alone . . . knowing there isn't another human being within seven light years . . . I'm a little obsessed about the parrots, I know that. But they've been my only company . . . Caproche doesn't have any other land animals, not really, you can't make friends with insects . . . and the parrots are these sweet-natured, gentle little animals. . . ."

"I was only going to pet it," I said.

"I know, I just . . . I'm possessive, it's wrong, I know, I'll work on it. I have to get used to dealing with people again. To tell the truth, Lyra, I've never been good at dealing with people, certainly not beautiful women . . . damn, you're defensive again, I'm sorry." He closed his eyes in pain. "Look," he said at last, "you can find your way back to camp, right?"

"Yes . . ."

"I really have to be alone for a while. To think. I'm sorry." He took a few steps into the darkness, then turned back. "I know I'm odd," he said, "but I'm harmless, you said so yourself. I won't hurt you or embarrass you . . . oh, good-bye."

He hurried away, around the Silk-covered wall and off into the night. I watched him till he disappeared behind a charred stockade fence.

Once again, I felt like shit. Maybe it was something in the Caproche air—I hadn't done anything, I hadn't said anything, and still I felt guilty. Angrily, I punched at a thick patch of Silk on the wall beside me. It exploded with a double-bass <SPLINK> that coated my hand with gunk. I bent to wipe off the goo on the ground and saw a small nose emerge from a hole under a stone.

"Hello," I said softly. "You just heard the dinner bell, didn't you?" I nudged a nearby thread. <SPLINK> The nose came out a little farther. Another <SPLINK>, and the parrot under the stone waddled into the starlight, its crimson head swaying slowly back and forth.

Hesitantly, I reached out my hand. It actually moved slightly toward me, extending its neck. "Going to bite me?" I asked. But it made no further movement, so I bent my finger and rubbed its nose.

"Going to bite me, to bite me, bite me?" I heard my own voice say.

I pulled back from the parrot and looked sharply around. Had someone recorded me, putting my voice through an echo synth? It wouldn't be the first time a smartass roadie targeted me for a practical joke. But when I thought about it, the sound wasn't my recorded voice, the one I heard on playbacks and barely recognized as my own. It was my head voice, the one I heard when I talked—fuller than my recorded voice, less shrill.

It was me.

Oh, shit, I thought, and reached out to touch the parrot again. "Oh, shit, oh, shit, oh, shit . . ."

Except I hadn't said anything this time. I just thought it.

"Thought it, thought it, thought . . ."

Parrots.

"Parrots, parrots, parrots . . ."

I lifted my finger and the sound stopped instantly. I touched the little animal lightly and the sound kicked in again . . . but I knew it wasn't a sound, not a real one.

I tried to think things through; and as I did, every chance thought, every tiny notion echoed back to me a fraction of a second after passing through my mind . . . disorienting at first, but I was used to singing in concert halls with a tiny delay between hitting a note and hearing it over your headphones. I could handle the telepathic equivalent.

First question: did the parrot only echo the thoughts of the person touching it? Or did the parrot echo every thought nearby?

I remembered how Jerith had responded to my thoughts all evening, like touching me when I was annoyed that he hadn't tried anything yet. His hand had been in his pocket most of the night, the pocket that held the parrot.

The parrot must echo everyone's thoughts. And not just the unspoken words; I could sense it broadcasting my emotions too, the outrage growing in me as I realized how Jerith had eavesdropped on my mind. I felt violated. He'd seen me more naked than naked. Hell, who cared about being naked anymore? I'd bared my all three times on *Trash and Thrash;* by now, half the galaxy had had the chance to count my freckles.

But this . . . I tried to remember all the thoughts I'd had in Jerith's company. I tried to recall what shameful things might have passed through my mind . . .

Jerith had said, "That Kilgoorlie is a spooky guy."

I wondered what thoughts the Singer had. About me.

I wondered what thoughts Alex had. About me.

And Roland. And Helena. And the roadies and everyone.

But of course it was wrong to eavesdrop on them.

The parrot didn't resist as I picked it up and stroked its nose. The little animal seemed perfectly content to be held. It nestled into my palm and gave a tiny yawn.

I told myself I would take it back to camp, to prove to the others what the animals could do. Telepathic parrots that echoed people's thoughts—no one would believe that without proof. Well, Alex probably would; but that was a mean thing to say. The parrot repeated the thought over and over, "Alex would believe it" . . . and under that phrase other thoughts chorused like backup singers, copies of my own voice whispering things I hadn't put into words: Alex is gullible, Alex is a child, I want to know what he thinks, I want to know what he thinks *of me.*

I barely recognized I'd had those thoughts, but they echoed back clearly.

"I won't use the parrot," I said aloud. "I'm just taking it to camp as proof."

The backup singers in my brain said, *I'm lying to myself, I'll probably eavesdrop, I don't know what I'll do.*

I stuffed the parrot into the pocket of my dungarees and hastily pulled out my hand. The voices cut off instantly and the silence of the night flooded in. I breathed a sigh of relief and began walking back to the camp, trying to fill my heart with good intentions.

I touched the parrot several times as I walked, just to see that it was still working. The parrot didn't react. It seemed to be asleep, but it still broadcast my thoughts loud and clear. Some creatures give off body temperatures; others give off mental echoes.

What did I hear from the parrot? Excitement mostly, the feeling of power. Qualms too—using the parrot to spy on others was wrong, but could I resist? And a memory of facing a similar conflict when I discovered masturbation at the age of thirteen: an exciting power, an irresistible compulsion, yet an act I'd been told was dirty. Secret vice. Is that a parrot in your pocket or are you just glad to see me? "How far do I have to dig this damned hole?"

I jerked my head around. That last thought wasn't mine.

There was no one in sight . . . but I stood on barren ground between two flat-topped hills. Someone could be on one of the hills, within range of the parrot's hearing, whatever that range was. I took a few steps toward the hill on my left, then stopped and touched the parrot: nothing but my own thoughts, racing, trying to figure out whose voice it had been. Male. Alex? Roland? I hadn't paid enough attention.

I wanted it to be Alex. The thought of eavesdropping on Alex was so tantalizing . . .

As quietly as I could, I moved back toward the other hill, stopped, and listened again. "Damned stone. Why are there so many damned stones?"

Alex.

Taking a deep breath, I pulled my hand from my pocket. I would resist. I would be good.

One last touch. The echoes of my thoughts told me I was only delaying the moment of eavesdropping on Alex. I was intent on doing it, and simply holding off a few seconds to excite myself more, the way you sometimes hold off on a kiss: you know it's going to happen, but you wait an extra second to make it sweeter.

The hill was too steep to climb with my hand in my pocket.

Alex stood a short distance away, stabbing a shovel into the ground and wrestling up a load of dirt. His body was soft with starlight. He still wore the billowing white shirt and tight leather pants from the recording session, but his shirt was buttoned to the throat. With each thrust of the shovel, he grunted. At his feet lay a knapsack and a growing pile of dirt.

I walked quickly up to him before I could be tempted to reach for the parrot. When he heard my footsteps and turned around, I asked, "Digging a grave? Or just robbing one?"

Alex laughed. "I'm excavating an archaeological site," he said. "We're an archaeological expedition, you know."

"And this excavation couldn't wait till morning?"

"I'm not in Jerith's good books right now," Alex said. "I broke something—something glass, I don't know what it was. It could have happened to anyone, but Jerith told me I wasn't careful enough to be an archaeologist." Alex plunged the shovel into the hole with all his strength. "So I decided to head out when no one was looking and find something so important Jerith would have to let me help again."

"Why here?" I asked, looking around. The top of the hill showed almost no signs of the war, except for a rain-filled bomb crater twenty meters away. The area had none of the markers Jerith usually set up at sites he planned to excavate. "Is there some reason to dig here, or did you just pick a place at random?"

Alex looked sly. "Can you keep a secret?" He picked up the knapsack that lay on the ground beside him. When he lifted the flap, I saw some kind of electronic apparatus topped by a cylindrical holo-tank. "Metal detector," Alex said in a stage whisper. "Absolute state of the art. I can afford it, Jerith can't." Immediately, he looked guilty. "I'm going to give it to Jerith before we go. As a token of appreciation for how he's helped us. But first, I'm going to find something important."

"Down this hole?"

"If I'm lucky. There's something big down here; and deep enough that Jerith's cheap detectors don't pick it up."

"Do you want help digging?" I asked.

"I only have the one shovel. But if you stick around, I may need a hand lifting out whatever I find."

I stuck around—found a stone that wasn't quite as damp as the ground and sat on it. Now and then, I offered to dig for a while to let Alex rest. He turned me down each time, and speared his shovel in harder to prove he wasn't tired. I just sat there and inhaled the damp smell of freshly turned soil.

Rather than mope in silence we told each other stories, the kind of stories that people in the industry share when they get together: disastrous concerts, botched bookings, fans from hell. Many, many stories. We laughed, we talked, I put my hand in my pocket.

"I wish she were wearing a tighter shirt," he said in his thoughts. "She's got such a body . . . Helena's crazy to say she's fat."

I didn't react. Well, yes, of course I reacted and the noise of my thoughts screaming, "I'll kill her!" drowned whatever Alex thought next. But outwardly I didn't move. I tried to force myself to calm down, but that just turned out to be my brain shrieking at my body, "Get calm! Relax! Loosen up, loosen up!"

Too bad I'd never studied meditation.

Taking a deep breath, I tried to relax for real instead of just going through the motions. It would have been easier if I could take my hand out of my pocket and shake myself loose; but that hand was staying put.

By the time my thoughts stilled enough to hear Alex again, he was fantasizing about kissing me. No technical details, not even a feeling of passion, just lips touching. In his mind my lips were very soft. And I responded, in my own imagination and in the dream Alex dreamed. My arousal doubled itself in a feedback loop, as I felt the desire, responded to the desire, felt my response echoing back and succumbed more deeply, desire feeding on its own echoes . . .

"What's this?" a voice whispered. A chill voice with a sharp edge that stabbed through all the fantasies.

Alex was still digging, glancing over at me from time to time. No one else was in sight.

"Have we got a visitor then?" the thready voice went on. "Someone peeking through the basement window?"

My own thoughts asked who is it, who? I could hear the chatter of my questions, even though other voices in my brain pleaded for silence, not to draw attention to myself.

"Ah, one of Alex's friends come to call," the voice whispered. "But he hasn't thought your name yet. . . ."

Reflexively, I thought "Lyra." Horrified copies of my voice screamed, "No!"

"Lyra," whispered the voice. "I saw you this afternoon, milady. We sang together. Yes. Your beauty entices me. You have entered my heart, milady. Now I have entered your mind."

That's just a song, I thought wildly.

"There's no such thing as 'just a song,' milady. Song is a realm unto itself, separated from your world by the tiny thickness of an eighth note. Strange things live in this realm, milady. Wraiths. Ghosts with tattered hearts." The voice laughed, a laugh with claws of ice. "It's dangerous to enter this realm, milady. Once a song gets into your head, sometimes it's impossible to get out."

The thing's laugh gushed over me like glacier spill water. Blackness pooled in front of my eyes; the real world began to dissolve. Beneath the laughter, I could just make out a tiny voice, my own voice, murmuring, "Let go of the parrot, let go, let go." But my body was freezing up, heavy with ice. I couldn't remember what it felt like to move. Try to move, think of moving, focus on motion, any motion, the spasming dance I did for that cut on *Trash and Thrash,* sing the song: "Damn it, slam it, break it; don't give me your repercussions . . ."

Forcing myself against the stony cold, I moved my hand a hairsbreadth. I let go of the parrot.

My eyes snapped into focus: the hilltop, the stars, the silence. Shivering, shuddering, the memory of ice.

Then Alex touched my shoulder and pointed to the hole. "I've found something," he said.

I could barely keep my teeth from chattering. I wanted to scramble away screaming but could barely move—I felt divorced from my body, like waking up from a nightmare. Alex's grin melted to a frown. "Are you all right?"

"Uhh. Hmm." My mouth wouldn't work. "I just, uhh . . . I must have drifted off. Weird dream." I eyed Alex closely, searching for any sign of the Singer; but this was good old amiable Alex, sweet, even innocent. Maybe I *had* just been dreaming.

"Come see what I found," Alex said, holding out his hand. I took it without thinking. He pulled me up to my feet and didn't let go as he led me to the hole. I didn't let go either—I was grateful for human contact. I considered sliding closer to him and stealing a hug, but didn't know what he'd think of it. (I could use the parrot to find out . . . but no, I couldn't do that again. Never. Never. Not yet.)

At the bottom of the hole lay a rusty expanse of sheet metal, about a meter square. One edge showed a set of hinges and the opposite edge had a handle. "I think it's a lid," Alex said eagerly.

"I think so too." I leaned against him. His body was warm and solid.

"Can we open it?" he asked.

"We probably shouldn't," I told him. "Jerith would want to document everything first. The position of this thing in the hole, the depth, all that. And we don't want to damage whatever's inside. Didn't most of those Egyptian mummies crumble to dust when people opened the sarcophagus?"

Alex's face fell. "You mean I make a major discovery and I can't even see what it is?"

"It's up to you," I answered. "You wanted to impress Jerith, right? For that, you have to be meticulous." I squeezed his waist tightly. Very tightly. But I tried to make my voice sound playful. "If you open it, I won't tell anyone."

He whooped with elation and leapt, sliding down the loose dirt to the bottom of the hole. I knew Jerith would be appalled at what Alex was up to, but it certainly wouldn't be a serious blow to science. You couldn't walk thirty seconds in a straight line without tripping over debris from Caproche's war—the entire surface of the planet was heaped with the stuff. Given so much material to draw upon, Jerith's investigation would scarcely suffer if one artifact wasn't dug up with full pomp and circumstance. Besides, after my recent experience, my dream, whatever it was, I loved Alex's high spirits and didn't want to dampen them.

The box's handle was set too tightly against the lid, at least by human standards—it must have been built for an alien race with thinner hands, or tentacles—but Alex eventually wiggled his fingers under the bar. Down at the bottom of the hole, standing on loose dirt, he wasn't in a good position for lifting, so I got the shovel and slid down to help, jamming the shovel blade under the lip of the lid and levering upward. Together, we managed to break the grip of the rust holding the lid shut, and with protests from the hinges, the lid groaned open.

There was nothing inside: just an empty canister, divided into two compartments by a metal partition down the middle. Whatever the box once held, it was long gone.

I started to laugh—a bit too hysterically, but still, all that work for an empty box. Alex started to laugh too, and suddenly we were kissing, twining together. The kisses were hungry; I'd never felt so desperate. I'd been terrified by the Singer and now I was plunging for safety into the same arms . . . but they were Alex's arms, and Alex seemed like the only comfort on the planet.

Soon we were out on level ground again, stretched body to body beside the hole. For the flicker of an instant, I considered reaching for the parrot, to see what was going through Alex's mind. But I didn't want to let go of him; and I realized I didn't *want* to know what he was thinking. I wanted to kiss him, I wanted to hold him. Everything else could wait.

We agreed we shouldn't go back to camp together. Cool reason had replaced heat, and second thoughts were piling up in my mind. Helena. The complications of working side by side. Doubts and apprehension.

"You go on ahead," I told Alex. "I'll wait out here a while longer. Go on."

We kissed awkwardly. He gave me a smile, a sweet confused smile, and said good night. As he vanished down the side of the hill, he began whistling.

I laughed in disbelief. Was he happy, was he sad, was he just whistling because men get the urge to whistle? It was tempting to reach for the parrot. So I did.

"Do I confront her? Talk to her, woman to woman? Threaten her? Or just ignore everything?"

The voice I heard didn't belong to Alex. It was Helena, and she was close by. Close enough for her thoughts to drown out whatever Alex was thinking as he walked back to camp. Close enough that she must have seen whatever there'd been to see.

Shit. The whole damned planet was practically empty, and everyone wanted to crowd up on my little hill.

"I could fire her," Helena's thoughts went on. "Slit her throat. No, there isn't another decent backup singer within a dozen parsecs. Not with perfect tits. Damned perfect tits. Alex, there's more to life than tits, isn't there? After everything I've . . . but it isn't Alex's fault. He's just this big simple . . ." The next thought wasn't a single word, but a montage: man, child, baby, bumpkin, son, lover. And there were images too—Alex grinning, with spaghetti sauce dribbling down his chin; Alex looking up as Helena's hand brushed hair from his eyes, Alex's face looming close in a darkened room. Underneath was Helena's soft fear that she was losing him, that she couldn't compete with younger women, that she was growing old.

Suddenly, like Silk going <SPLINK>, her thoughts grew sharp and hard. "It's Lyra who should know better," she thought. "Hateful bitch." And then Helena was walking toward me, planning how to browbeat and sweet-talk me into giving Alex up.

She'd taken a flashlight with her when she'd set out to look for Alex. Now she waited till the last moment to turn it on, hoping the sudden light would startle me. I stared up calmly as she shone it into my eyes.

"Hello, Lyra."

I nodded. "Helena."

"Doing some impromptu excavation?" she asked, making a show of looking at the freshly turned dirt.

"The search for knowledge never sleeps," I answered.

She shone the light into the hole. It lit the unearthed box more distinctly than the starlight. I could see that one of the compartments was completely lined with sticky white powder from exploding Silk. The other compartment wasn't as empty as I'd thought. Tiny bones littered the floor, with one skeleton intact enough to recognize as the remains of a Caprochian parrot.

"Looks like an important artifact," Helena said. "A trash bin."

"The search for knowledge sometimes craps out." I shrugged.

"What about you and Alex?" she asked. "Was that a search for knowledge too?"

She wanted me to be surprised by the question. Thanks to the parrot, I wasn't. "I don't know what it was with Alex," I answered honestly. "Just one of those things. I was feeling pretty needy at the time."

Her thoughts shouted, "Selfish bitch!" but aloud she said, "Your needs aren't Alex's needs."

"I didn't hear him protesting," I replied. But my background chorus told me I knew that was no excuse.

"Alex is a sixteen-year-old in a twenty-five-year-old's body," Helena said. "He's not going to fight off *any* woman. He may even initiate the . . . festivities. He may have initiated things with you, I don't know—the starlight wasn't quite bright enough for me to see."

"I don't know who initiated what," I told her.

"The point is, Alex is a little boy who never grew up." She faked a laugh. "Do you realize that he proposed to me after our first night together? He thought it was *required*, the only gentlemanly thing to do after *ravishing* me. He has this terribly constricted background . . . I bet he was too shy to take off his shirt, right?"

"True." And I was glad he didn't. If unbuttoning his shirt released the Singer . . .

"He's so unsophisticated," Helena said, nodding, "and that's why there's a problem. I'm a broad-minded woman, I don't own him . . ." Her thoughts yelled, "He's mine!" and added softly, "Why can't he just be mine?" She put on a brittle smile and said, "Alex can't handle the complications of dealing with both of us. Someone like Roland . . ." I picked up a snap memory of Helena in bed with Roland. Well, well. "Roland wouldn't get hung up about an idle one-night stand. He's not one to confuse sex with *loyalty*. But Alex . . . he confuses easily. You see?"

"See what?"

"That someone is going to get hurt. Certainly Alex, and maybe you. Not me," she added airily. "I don't get hurt. I just have to pick up the pieces."

"Noble you."

"Noble me." Internally she debated whether to threaten me. She could fire me, and could probably arrange that the major recording labels wouldn't let me into their studios; but backing me into a corner held too many risks. Especially when she believed I could steal Alex with one nudge of my nipples. So keep it cool, keep it sophisticated, woman to woman, one tuck-and-tumble doesn't have to mean anything.

"If I were you," she said, "I'd tell him this was just a brief . . . *weakness* on your part. You could say you were under the influence of some fiendish psychological weapon still at work on the battlefield. A lust gun. Makes you rut like a mink in heat no matter how ridiculous you look. No matter how damaging it might be for your career. Lust grenades. Lust *lasers*. Alex would believe that."

"You don't give Alex enough credit."

"I give Alex *all* the credit," she replied. "I do the work, he gets the credit. If you want to start a tug-of-war, Lyra, you may pull Alex away from me. But without me, he's no star. He's just a not-too-bright guy with a so-so voice. Not a great catch, believe me."

"What about the Singer?" I asked.

Her thoughts shriveled. Fear. Cold fear so sharp and similar to mine I jerked my hand away from the parrot. "You can have the Singer," she said, her voice trembling slightly. "If you can catch the Singer, he's yours."

She turned abruptly away and started walking toward the edge of the hill. Without turning, she called back, "I'm sure you'll do the right thing, Lyra. The smart thing."

I watched till she was gone. At the last second, I brushed my finger across the parrot. On the surface, Helena fretted about me watching her walk away—she was sure I was laughing at her, at her hips and ass thickening with middle age. But deeper down ran a current of terror: wordless, imageless fear of the Singer.

Her thoughts echoed my own.

———

When she was gone, I made my way in the same direction, keeping my hands off the parrot. Even so, the parrot dominated my attention . . . like when you meet someone who's completely wrong for you and you know he'll screw up your life, but every minute of the day you find yourself thinking about him. Not love, not lust, and you know you're too sensible for *obsession;* but you still keep turning it over and over in your mind. I could laugh at how I was getting in so deep with the parrot, I could tell myself it would only take a tiny effort of will to set my parrot free . . .

But I didn't do it. Fixations can be sweet.

Following Helena's footsteps through the dew soon brought me back to camp. Music played in the main Quonset hut, the timeworn feel-good classic "Orange Puppy," recorded by "Vivaldi's Love-Child." That meant the hut had been taken over by roadies—only they were old enough to play such a rusty dusty nostalgia number. I could imagine them sitting around, wearing sloppy T-shirts from old groups like "Madrigal Canyon" or "Freckles on a Green-Eyed Girl," and saying spiteful things about the music scene today.

I considered joining them, but didn't think I'd be up to eavesdropping on a crowd. Besides, what could the parrot tell me that I couldn't guess myself? The roadies all said exactly what they thought the moment it crossed their minds . . . except for the wet-dream fantasies a few of the guys had when they looked in my direction, and who needed telepathy to pick up those?

Instead, I turned toward the huts that served as sleeping quarters. The nearest belonged to Alex and Helena, but I didn't want to see either of them again tonight. A few meters farther was the hut that songwriter Roland shared with our equipment manager. The equipment manager would surely be keeping company with the rest of the roadies, and Roland would be alone.

I knocked on the door.

"What?" The question sounded angry, but Roland always sounded angry.

"It's Lyra," I said. "Are you busy?"

"Yes." The door opened and there was Roland, a towel draped over one hand but still fully dressed in his usual black. "I was just going to take a shower." He snorted an unpleasant laugh. "Unless you'd care to join me?"

"I have a shower in my own hut," I answered.

"Once you've had the best, don't settle for the rest," he muttered.

"What's that supposed to mean?" I wanted to reach for my parrot, but he was staring at me so intently there was no way I could make the gesture look natural.

"Alex doesn't keep secrets," Roland said, still blocking the doorway. "Even if he doesn't blurt it right out, it's written all over his face. I guarantee Helena will know about you and Alex within the hour."

"She knows already."

"And?"

"No 'and,'" I told him. "We're both being civilized. Sophisticated women of the world. Although it would *obviously* be best for all concerned if I dropped Alex immediately."

"She's right," Roland said. "Not that I expect common sense to prevail. You still haven't mentioned why you're here."

"Just to chat," I replied, stretching as if my shoulders were stiff and casually reaching toward my pocket. "I thought maybe I could talk to you about Alex and . . ."

His hand snapped out and grabbed my wrist. He pulled it tight to his chest and dragged me closer, eye to eye. "No games, Lyra," he said, his breath hot on my face. "No casual little chats. I know."

He held up his other hand, the one that had been covered with the towel. The towel slid down his arm to reveal a parrot squeezed between his fingers.

"I wondered why Jerith was so possessive of his damned parrots," Roland said. "I found out. And if you ever try to eavesdrop on me, I'll know it. If you can hear my thoughts, I can hear yours. Toy with me, and I won't act *civilized* like Helena."

I opened my mouth to say something, but he interrupted. "You think I'm bluffing? That I don't have the balls to play vicious?" He put his fist against my face and roughly dragged the parrot's snout along my cheek. The moment the parrot touched me, Roland's fury screamed in my ears like a howl of feedback from an amplifier; then he pulled back the parrot and the noise cut off. "Now you know it's no bluff," he said. "No one gets into my head but me."

"The same goes for me." I tried to snatch the parrot from his hand, but he swung it back out of my reach. His grip on my wrist tightened.

"I don't need a parrot to get into your head," he snapped. "I know exactly what women like you think. 'Creepy Roland, ugly Roland,' that's always the attitude. With a pinch of pity thrown in, just to make it hurt more."

"I'm not—"

He twisted my arm and jerked it down hard. "Shut up!" he screamed. "I can hear you. I can hear you trying to decide which lie will pacify me. I can hear you wonder if you should come on to me, if you can stomach giving Roland a press of the flesh, ugly Roland will be so *overcome* . . . God damn you!"

In blind rage, he swung his fist at my jaw. I managed to block with my free arm and took the blow above my elbow. The crunching impact hurt like hell, his knuckles hammering into me deep as the bone. Then he whispered, "Oh, shit," and his grip on my other arm went slack.

I writhed away from him. He fell over facedown and stopped moving.

For several seconds, I kept my distance, panting and rubbing my arm. He still didn't move. Had he fainted? Or was he just faking? But why? I thought of reaching for my parrot to see what was in his mind; but if he was just faking, that would infuriate him.

I stretched out my foot and nudged him. No response.

Harder. Still nothing.

At last I bent beside his body and rolled him over. The exertion hurt my bruised arm but I gritted my teeth. Roland's breathing was very shallow. There was an odd smell in the air too, a thin, metallic smell. I sniffed more closely, his body, his clothes, trying to find the source of the odor.

It came from his fist—still clenched tightly around the parrot.

The parrot had been crushed like a handful of grapes when Roland's punch landed on my arm. Bits of its flesh bulged out between Roland's fingers and a dark fluid spilled over his knuckles.

I pried his fist open, using a stick to lever the fingers so I wouldn't have to touch the blood. The smell grew stronger. The parrot looked like a squeezed rag. Indentations shaped like Roland's fingers had crushed into its body.

The parrot had died and Roland collapsed. I wondered what he'd heard in the moment of the parrot's death.

I dragged the roadies away from "Orange Puppy" and told them to hoist Roland into his bed while I got Jerith's medical robot out of storage. The bot was decades old, scratched in places, and tarnished around the sampling mouths, but it moved easily over the rough terrain and its voice was free of static as it asked me to describe the nature of Roland's problem. Jerith obviously maintained the bot with great care . . . which only made sense when the closest doctor was seven light-years away.

I considered keeping mum on the circumstances of Roland's collapse, then decided to tell the bot everything. Medi-bots are programmed for confidentiality. Besides, no matter how furious I was that Roland hit me, I didn't want him to die.

By the time the bot and I got back to Roland's hut, a crowd of people had gathered around the bed. Teary-eyed Alex knelt on the floor, holding Roland's hands in his. Helena stood behind him, her hand patting Alex's shoulder over and over again. I was reaching for my parrot to see what was going through their minds when a roadie spotted the bot and me. He raised a fuss, making such a show of dragging us over to the bed that I didn't have a chance to touch the parrot. A moment later, Helena drove the roadies and me out of the hut, saying the "doctor" needed room to work. Yeah, right.

I headed off to my own hut. I shared it with Violette who did makeup, but she and the other roadies went back to the main hut, so I had the place to myself. Good—peace and quiet. I took the parrot out of my pocket and set it down on the dressing table. The others weren't close enough for me to hear their thoughts distinctly. When I touched the parrot, I only picked up myself and a background mumble from everyone else in camp.

The parrot yawned itself awake, stretched, and decided to walk around the table a bit, sniffing at the powders and perfumes Violette and I left lying about. I wondered if the little animal was hungry. I got out some bean sprouts I keep for snacking, but the parrot just snuffled at the sprouts, then lay down on top of them.

"Probably bad for you anyway," I said. I went outside for a moment, pulled a few blades of the local grass, and laid them down under the parrot's nose. One of its antennae waved above the grass briefly, but then the parrot pointedly turned away.

"Not good enough for you?" I asked. "Won't eat anything but Silk?"

The parrot stared at me without blinking.

"There must be something else you'll eat. If the Silk came here as a weapon in the war, that was only seven hundred years ago. What did your species eat before then?"

The parrot closed its eyes and went to sleep.

I laughed softly. "You don't care what kind of garbage your barbarian ancestors chucked down their gullets. Only modern cuisine for you. I don't blame you—*I* probably couldn't stomach what my ancestors ate either."

The door opened without warning and for a few fearful moments I thought it was the Singer. No. The shirt was buttoned and it was only Alex, but Alex looking grim and worried. "Roland wants to speak to you," he said. He didn't look me in the eye.

"Roland is awake?" I asked.

"He's awake, but he's not . . ." Alex's voice trailed off and he looked down at his hands. One palm had a brown stain on it. "He's not very good, Lyra. Maybe seeing you will calm him down."

"I don't know," I said, wondering how obvious it would be if I just picked up my parrot from the dressing table and put it into my pocket. "Seeing me might only upset him."

"He's asking for you," Alex replied. "He says it's important. Roland, he's . . . Women *affect* him strongly, you know? That's why he writes such good songs. Women affect him. Sometimes they make him mad and sometimes he just burns himself up wanting them. Most guys . . . this is hard to say, Lyra, but for most guys, being with a woman is nice and all, but it's not *everything*. Not to live and die for. But with Roland, it *is*. And whatever happened between you and him before he got all keyed up . . . I don't know. It's just, the only thing that calms him down when he's upset is attention from a woman. Talk, I just mean talk. But you have to go see him."

Sighing, I stood and reached toward the dressing table.

"Don't take the parrot," he said. "That will only complicate things."

He took me gently by the arm and guided me away from the parrot on the table, toward the door. I tried not to wince—he'd taken the arm that Roland punched and it throbbed with pain when Alex touched me.

Alex immediately switched his grip to my other arm. I thought, Oh, shit, but he said, "Shhh, shhh."

As we crossed the compound I tried not to think of anything. In my head I sang that *Trash and Thrash* song, "Damn it, slam it, break it; I don't want your repercussions." I sang it over and over again, hoping it would fill my thoughts, drown out everything.

At the door to Roland's hut, Alex whispered, "Songs make flimsy shields, milady. I *live* in songs." He closed the door between us. I was left alone in the hut with Roland, and I was trembling in cold, cold terror.

Roland groaned, "Lyra?" I didn't answer. I desperately hoped I would faint, shut down my mind . . . but I wasn't the fainting type. Had it been Alex? Or was it the Singer? His shirt was buttoned. And back in my hut he'd talked like Alex, fumbling for words, shying away from unpleasantness. But he'd told me not to take the parrot, and he'd known about my sore arm, about singing that song in my head.

"Lyra!" Roland's voice was louder. The medi-bot whirred briefly but did nothing. "Lyra!"

"What?" My voice was hoarse.

"Lyra?"

"Yes. What do you want?"

"Come here."

I stirred myself and approached the bed. Roland's face was pale but with flushes of pink on both cheeks. "I look worse than usual, don't I?" he said with a weak smile. "I know what you're thinking."

"I thought your parrot died."

"Oh, yeah. It died."

"Looked like a traumatic experience for both of you."

He gave a small snort of a laugh. "You know that phrase 'My life flashed before my eyes'? Not a completely accurate description, but it will do. I think my entire subconscious uploaded into my consciousness for a second."

"Instant self-knowledge," I said. "If word gets out, Caproche will be crawling with mystics."

"I think not," he replied, closing his eyes with a shudder. "It's not an entertaining experience. I'll probably kill myself soon."

The medi-bot whirred through a long silence.

"You think I'm bluffing," Roland said after a while, his eyes still closed. "Pleading for attention from a beautiful woman. No. Suicide is definitely an attractive proposition."

"Because of instant self-knowledge?"

"Because I have the parrot's blood on my hands."

"Come on, Roland," I said, "it's a shame you killed the poor little thing, but it was only one small animal. It's not worth—"

"Lyra," he interrupted me. "I have the parrot's *blood* on my hands."

He held up his palm for me to see, the hand he'd punched me with, the hand that had crushed the parrot. It was streaked with rusty brown stains reaching down as far as his wrist. He turned the hand slowly and stared at his palm. I could see more stains on the back of his hand, where blood had squirted between his fingers.

"It's in their blood," he said calmly. "Whatever *it* is. The telepathy. And now it's in me. The bot tried to wash the blood off, but my hand won't come clean. I wish I could remember that passage from *Macbeth*."

Out, out, damned spot, I thought.

"Yes, that's the one," he agreed as if I'd spoken aloud. "I'll wait a few days to see if it wears off. But I'm not optimistic." He lifted his head and looked straight into my eyes. "Instant self-knowledge conveys a certain amount of wisdom, Lyra. Wisdom says I can't handle knowing what other people think. Let alone myself. You saw it—two minutes talking to you while I was holding the parrot, and I went berserk. Ugly. Very ugly.

"No," he said loudly, interrupting what I was going to say. "Don't, please. You were about to forgive me for hitting you. I'm in bad shape, and you feel guilty. Don't. Just don't. It's stupid. If you want to do something, stop using the parrot. That's why I asked you here. To warn you. Just stop."

"Okay, I'll stop."

He shook his head sadly. "You don't mean that. Deep down, you think I'm an unstable asshole. You think I can't handle telepathy, but you can. Well, you're half right. I can't handle it. It's too bleak. A while ago, when Alex and Helena were hovering over me, wondering if I'd had a heart attack or something . . . they're supposedly my two best friends in the world, and you know what they were thinking? Helena was going over names of other songwriters, trying to choose a replacement for me if I died. And Alex, he was scarcely *there*. I don't know where his mind was, but I couldn't pick it up. Stupid me, I expected some kind of *sympathy* . . ."

"You can't tell me Alex didn't care," I said. "I saw him, Roland. He was crying . . . he was truly worried."

"That's not what the parrot was broadcasting."

"Then maybe parrots don't broadcast everything. I saw Alex right there beside you while you were unconscious, and he was crying, holding your hands . . ."

I stopped suddenly.

"He was holding my hands?" Roland asked. "While they were still bloody?"

I remembered the brown stain I'd seen on Alex's hand when he'd come to get me in my hut.

"God, no," Roland murmured. "Not Alex."

I shivered. "No. It's not Alex."

Outside, hurrying across the compound, I asked myself, So what? Alex or the Singer, he was just a person who recorded songs. He might come across like a lunatic, but so did half the other acts in the music industry. And even if he *was* dangerous, I was no delicate flower. Back when I was getting started, I'd sung in bars filled with street scum and run by organized crime. If the going got rough, I could handle myself.

So why was I terrified?

No time for terror—I had to tell Helena what was going on. How she dealt with the Singer I didn't know, but she'd kept him on a leash for years. If anyone could control the situation, she could.

Before I knocked on the door of her hut, I took a deep breath. It wouldn't be fun to confess I'd eavesdropped on her thoughts back earlier.

"Hello," I called. "Helena?"

"Come in . . ." Her voice sounded soft and uncertain. I opened the door slowly.

She was alone, sitting on the edge of the bed and looking at her hands. They dripped with brown blood.

"Alex was just in here," she said quietly. "He had one of those little animals, you know, the parrots? Only it was dead. Crushed. Someone had stepped on it; I could see boot treads on its body. The poor thing was all broken bones and blood, and Alex . . . he *smeared* it on my hands. Just wiped it all over . . ."

Her voice trailed off.

I shuddered.

She looked up at me sharply. "Did you say something?"

"Clean the blood off," I said quickly, grabbing her by the elbow and moving her toward the sink. Our camp was supposed to ration water, but I turned the hot tap on full and pushed her hands into the flow, keeping myself clear of the splash. Stringy bits of parrot meat washed down the drain, and the basin turned brown, with the blood rinsing off her fingers. Even so, her palms stayed discolored with dark stains. I poured soap onto her hands and said, "Scrub. Scrub."

"How can you be saying two things at once?" She made no effort to use the soap. "You're saying scrub but you're also afraid I'm going to hear . . ." She looked at my face, and her eyes focused on my mouth. "You aren't talking," she said in surprise.

I stared back at her for a moment, then turned off the water and quietly walked out of the hut. I really couldn't say what I was thinking or feeling at that moment; but I was sure Helena knew.

The parrot was no longer on the dressing table in my hut, but there was an ugly wet smear on the floor. I could guess where the Singer found the parrot that he'd used on Helena. He must have come back after taking me to Roland, then ground the poor beast under his heel.

A nasty way to kill the little animal . . . but a safe one too. The Singer's boot protected him from the brain-flash that stunned Roland when the other parrot died. Even the Singer must fear instant self-knowledge.

But why kill the parrot at all? And why wipe the blood on Helena? A prank? Or an attack? Roland said the onslaught of voices made him want to commit suicide. Did the Singer want to drive Helena mad too?

And what about the other people in the camp?

Out into the night again—I rushed across the compound toward the main hut. I found myself trying to move quietly, hoping the Singer wouldn't hear me . . . as if the sound of my footsteps mattered when my thoughts were howling with fear. Bright girl, Lyra; but it was still a comfort to be stealthy.

The main hut was lit brightly and I could see in through the windows. Music still played, but not "Orange Puppy"—something much softer, the volume so low I couldn't identify the tune from outside the building.

The roadies had gathered in a circle to watch something in their midst, the way onlookers might surround two people arm-wrestling at a table. A few nights ago I'd seen the same thing, when our stage manager and my roommate Violette had challenged each other to a drinking contest: rum for rum, gin for gin, beer for beer, then back to rum again. We'd all crowded around, cheering and applauding. No one cheered tonight, but it was still comforting to see them together, up to their usual antics, and I was eager to join them . . . until I recognized the music.

"Ghost of the Tattered Heart." The title track.

I stopped cold, just outside the door. No roadie on the crew would ever admit to playing Alex's music for pleasure. Call it roadie pride—playing the boss's music is sucking up. Unprofessional. Not cool.

As I stood there, frozen with my hand stretched toward the door latch, every head in the hut turned in my direction. All of them, like puppets in a show. Each had a smear of brown parrot blood on the forehead.

The Singer stepped out from the middle of the group. He held up his hand and waved to me. A teardrop of brown trickled down his palm and dripped off his wrist.

I ran.

I ran through the night, wondering if they would chase me. Ugly images danced through my mind, all the roadies possessed by demons who were exactly like the Singer, howling after me in pursuit. "Lyra, you've been watching too many late-night broadcasts," I muttered, and kept running.

In time I had to slow to a hard-breathing trot. No one was following me, not the roadies, not the Singer. If the Singer wanted to blood me like the roadies, he didn't have to track me in the dark; he could just wait for me to return to camp. I'd go back eventually. I had no choice—Jerith's protein synthesizers made the only human-edible food on the planet.

And when I went back, the Singer would hear my thoughts coming.

Maybe it didn't matter, I tried to tell myself. If I got smeared with blood and started to hear people's thoughts, was that so bad?

Yes . . . when the thoughts belonged to the Singer. If his voice invaded my mind again, I truly might kill myself to get away.

Passing through a narrow gully between two hills, I heard a voice call, "Lyra?"

I looked up to the hill on my left and saw Jerith. Sweet, unintimidating man. "Jerith!" I cried. "Jerith!" I scrambled up the hillside and wrapped my arms around his neck. Awkwardly he put one arm around me. The other was thrust deep into his pocket.

A moment later he took his hand out of the pocket and pushed me away. "You know about the parrots."

"Don't worry," I said. "I was mad at you for a while, but I got over it."

"Don't lie to me."

I took his hand and pushed it back into his pocket. Then I put my arms around his neck again, stared him straight in the eye, and said, "Jerith, I am really, truly glad to see you. Okay?"

He looked away. "You're annoyed I don't believe you. That's all I hear."

"Then your goddamned parrot is *broken,* Jerith! The stupid thing broadcasts a tiny bit of annoyance and completely ignores the relief I feel . . ."

I stopped shouting, started thinking.

"Whoa, slow down," Jerith said. "Your thoughts are all jumbling together—"

I interrupted him. "After Roland collapsed, Alex felt sorry for him, but Roland couldn't hear it. And *you* can't hear how glad I am to see you. They don't broadcast good thoughts, Jerith! Little irritations come through loud and clear, but not the positive stuff."

"Lyra, that doesn't make sense," he replied, shaking his head. "It's hard enough to believe parrots evolved the ability to broadcast thoughts. I mean, there's no evolutionary advantage to their kind of telepathy, is there? Caproche's animal life is so primitive, other species scarcely *have* thoughts. So don't ask me to make another leap of faith and believe parrot telepathy is selective. Evolution is strained to the breaking point as it is."

"Then screw evolution," I said. "The little buggers didn't evolve. They were summoned from hell."

"Come on . . ."

"Don't *dismiss* me! The things only eat Silk, right? Silk is a *weapon,* Jerith, you said so yourself. Eating Silk is like dining on dynamite. If they were normal animals, they'd eat grass or something."

Jerith sighed. "Yes, it's unusual they only eat alien plant matter. But that scarcely means they're demons."

"Okay, they're aliens then," I said. "They're aliens brought in during the war, the same time as the Silk. Come to think of it, Alex and I found a carrying crate for them earlier in the evening. One side for Silk, the other side for the parrots. A one-two punch: a biological weapon and a psychological one."

"What do you mean, a carrying crate?"

I described the box Alex and I had found: one compartment lined with Silk dust, the other littered with parrot bones. It was easy to imagine the box being parachuted in and crashing down harder than expected, killing a few parrots, <SPLINK>ing a little Silk, then getting buried later in some artillery barrage. Who knew how many other boxes were still out there?

Of course Jerith wanted to see the box immediately, but after my flight from camp I wasn't sure where I was now, let alone how to get back to where Alex had dug up the box. "You can find it eventually," I told Jerith. "If we get out of this with our brains in one piece, I'll help you look."

"You really think we're in danger?"

"Remember how I worried that some weapons from the war might still be active? Well, they are. The parrots."

"Other races studied the debris of the war before humans got to Caproche," Jerith pointed out. "If parrots are weapons, why didn't the other survey teams notice?"

"Maybe telepathy has different wavelengths, I don't know. The other races didn't pick up anything from the parrots, but humans just happen to match the wavelength of the original targets."

"Maybe," Jerith admitted. "Telepathic races like the Laysens say they can read some species but not others. Still, the idea that parrots might be weapons . . ."

I grabbed his arm and said, "Think about it. They're all over the place, they're brightly colored, they're happy to be picked up and kept in your pocket . . . I bet they even looked cute to whatever species fought here. They were bioengineered to attract attention and be adopted as pets. So the troops picked them up, and suddenly they could hear what their fellow soldiers were thinking: all the angry stuff, all the bland stuff, but nothing good. Can you imagine what that would do to morale?"

Slowly, Jerith nodded. "If they heard all the bad stuff . . . the anger without the friendship, the lust without the affection . . . in a day or two, the soldiers would forget the enemy and start shooting each other."

"Damned right they would," I said.

With a thoughtful expression on his face, Jerith pulled his hand from his pocket. For almost a minute he stared off into the darkness. Finally he turned back to me. "Want to coauthor a paper?"

"I want to live to a ripe old age," I said.

"Why wouldn't you?"

I gave him a quick summary of what had happened back in the camp . . . no, to be honest, I started a quick summary, a quick clinical summary, but somehow it got away from me. The stress, the terror, everything began blubbering out in half-sentences and tears, until he was holding me in that gingerly awkward way men have when they don't know what to do, while I was apologizing for getting emotional and wishing he were taller so I could bury my face in his shirt. "I shouldn't be crying," I said over and over again. "This is really stupid." And watching myself, angry with myself, I started crying again.

In time, the force of my outburst drained away. I pulled out of his arms, turned my back on him, and desperately wished for something to wipe my nose. Jerith offered me a handkerchief. I whirled to face him, expecting to see his hand in his pocket, using the parrot to read my thoughts; but no, he was just volunteering the handkerchief because I needed it. I smiled with chagrin, then turned away again to give my nose a good blow.

"Sounds to me like the Singer is just being a shit," Jerith said to my back. Maybe he was trying to comfort me, maybe he was only talking to avoid an embarrassing silence. "This 'come into my realm' stuff," Jerith went on, "that's pure stage show. Popular music often dresses up in demon clothes. I mean, Paganini in the 1800s, he encouraged the public to think he'd sold his soul to the devil. And farther back, in almost every shamanistic tradition, music was associated with otherworldly—"

"Jerith?"

"What?"

"Stop being an archaeologist."

"Sorry." He was quiet for five seconds at most, then hurtled on. "My point is, you talk about the Singer as if he's some malevolent supernatural force. As if he's got some sinister master plan. I think you're overdramatizing. This stuff back at the camp . . . *toying* with people is just what the Singer always does. That's his act, isn't it, when he's onstage. He spooks people. He gets under your skin."

I had to admit Jerith was right.

"So what he's doing with the parrots is more of the same," Jerith went on. "Smearing people with blood . . . it's all theatrics. Harassing people, making them sweat."

"If the effects of the blood are permanent—"

"I'm not denying he's dangerous," Jerith interrupted. "I don't want him smearing blood on me; I don't want to hear everyone being hateful for the rest of my life. I'm just saying he's not some demonic evil—the Singer is an ordinary punk getting his kicks by making a mess. A petty vandal, nothing more."

My only reply was a shrug. If Jerith wanted to believe the Singer was an ordinary punk, I wouldn't waste breath arguing. I knew better. Nothing about the Singer was ordinary.

"The immediate question," I said, "is what do we do now?"

"Sooner or later, we have to go back to camp," Jerith replied. "You knew that, right? But we can wait till morning if you like. It's not raining, and it won't get too cold; spending the night outside won't kill us."

The longer I went without facing the Singer, the happier I'd be. And sunlight would give me courage . . . a little bit, anyway. "All right," I told Jerith. "A night in the great outdoors, huddled together for warmth. But I doubt if I'll get much sleep."

He looked at me, obviously trying to figure out if I had intended any sexual overtones. I liked that look of uncertainty. It was refreshing that someone didn't know exactly what was on my mind.

Sleep. Not comfortable sleep—the patch of grass Jerith led me to wasn't as soft as advertised—but I did sleep, deeply and with ugly dreams.

The dreams were broken by a voice: "Are you awake? Are you awake?" whispered over and over again, until I surfaced from confusion and opened my eyes. I closed them again immediately, appalled by the brightness around me. Even with the light red-filtered through my eyelids, it was bright enough to be painful. I tried to scrunch my eyes shut more tightly.

"I take it the damned sun has risen," I growled. "Top of the morning to you, Jerith, but if you don't want a punch in the nose, you'll let me go back to sleep."

"Ah, milady," whispered a voice in my ear, "yond light is not daylight; I know it, I. It is some meteor that the sun exhales to be to thee this night a torchbearer and light thee on thy way to . . . well, let thy destination remain unspoken."

Chilled, I opened my eyes again. The Singer was there, kneeling beside me. "A passage from *Romeo and Juliet*," he said. "Their last scene together. Or more precisely, the last scene with both of them alive." He smiled.

The sky above his head was still black, flecked with stars. Off to one side, several anti-grav platforms floated in the air, holding the huge beam-lamps we had brought for recording at night. The lights all aimed at me, as if I were a surgery patient on an operating table.

I jerked up to a sitting position and looked around for Jerith. He was gone. The grass he'd slept on still showed the imprint of his body.

"What did you do with him?" I asked.

"I anointed him," the Singer said, "rather forcibly. Specifically, I tucked a pretty little parrot under his hand while he slept, then crushed hand and parrot under my heel. The pain woke him briefly, but with the lovely jumble of thoughts that rose in his mind as the parrot died . . . ah, well, he passed out again. I kindly instructed one of Jerith's robots to carry his body back to camp. Very cooperative machines, those robots."

Another robot picked its way through the grass toward us, the blue lights from its eyes sweeping the ground for safe places to plant its feet. "Grab this man!" I shouted to the bot. "He wants to hurt me."

The bot's attention remained fixed on the ground.

"Alas, milady," said the Singer, "some petty vandal damaged its direct audio input with a laser drill. Now it can only respond to radio instructions." He drew a tiny radio transmitter from his pocket and spoke into it. "Please carry the lovely Lyra to that bunker over there." His finger pointed to a squat concrete building set into a nearby hill. Turning back to me, he said, "Worry not, milady. This machine is programmed for transporting archaeological artifacts, so it will bear you quite gently . . . unless you force it to exert its strength."

I didn't have time to get away. Before I could twitch a muscle, the bot had snared my ankle with one of its steel cable tentacles. I tried one desperate yank with my leg, hoping to catch it off balance and topple it forward to the grass; but the bot was firmly planted and far too heavy for me to dislodge. Patiently, it stretched out more tentacles and I couldn't avoid them all. In a matter of seconds, I was well and truly webbed in.

"A pity we had no tape rolling," the Singer said, gazing down on my trussed-up body. "Your struggles would have made good footage."

"Footage for what?"

"A song we'll be recording in just a few minutes. A ballad named "Parrot Blood Baptism." And you have a starring role."

I assume he wanted to scare me; but I was lying wrapped in steel cable, with a robot whirring above me as it calculated how to heave me about like a sack of potatoes, and suddenly my fear hardened into anger. I met the Singer's stare and asked, "What kind of melodramatic bullshit are you trying to pull?"

His eyes narrowed. He lifted the radio transmitter and told the robot, "Please hold for a moment." The robot whirred as the Singer turned back to me.

"We're going to record a song," he said. "Just you and I, milady. I'm afraid our colleagues back at camp are indisposed—it seems they took poorly to telepathy. Fights broke out, a number of people locked themselves in their huts, others were grabbed by robots . . . suffice it to say, no one is in any condition to help us or disturb us."

"What are we going to record?" I asked.

"A song, milady, a *real* song. I cannot tell you how tired I've grown of the juvenile pap that passes for music these days. All the world adores my album . . . but what is that album but shallow artifice? Fog from machines. Women screaming on cue. I am reduced to a puppet, prancing amidst hackneyed symbolism, to portray a dangerous man. A sanitized danger. A packaged little danger to delight complacent adolescents who fancy themselves rebels.

"Well . . . not tonight, milady. Tonight we shall have no special effects or stunt doubles. Tonight the script calls for unflinching reality."

I snorted in derision. "So you're going to baptize me with parrot blood? Yeah, sure, that's a brilliant departure from hackneyed symbolism. I haven't seen a blood baptism since . . . oh, that one Lew Jackell did on 'Bad Night for a Burning.' And the Black Sabbath sequence from the latest album by Chocolate Oracle. And Oiled Heat did a blood baptism too, if I recall correctly, in that terrible little number they recorded on those mud flats . . . what was its name? 'Sweet Soulless Machine'?"

The Singer put a single finger under my chin and pressed it sharply into the softness of my throat. "Milady," he said, "remember that I can hear your thoughts. You are simply trying to make me angry."

"I'm trying to tell you, you're not as smart as you think you are," I replied. "Alex only trots you out for concerts and recording sessions; you can't know dick about the industry at large or how things really come together. You've never been to a rehearsal or a sound check . . . and as for creating songs, you do *nothing*. Roland writes the tunes and lyrics, Helena storyboards the visuals, Alex walks through it all and helps refine things till they click. Oh, sure, when the tape starts rolling you're the spark that adds the magic, there's no question you're the spark . . . but a spark isn't worth squat if someone doesn't chop the firewood first. And now you're going to show us how to cut a *real* song? I can't wait to see it."

Half my outburst was genuine anger, half was trying to pierce him, deflate him any way I could. But he simply removed his finger from my chin and patted my cheek gently. "Through long afternoons in Roland's basement, while Alex lay on the couch and read comic books, I listened to Roland poke at his piano and I learned how songs were born. Late nights in hotel rooms, as Helena muttered to herself about camera angles and lighting effects, Alex may have slept but I didn't. And at rehearsals, who kept Alex working when he was bored and hated the thought of one more run-through? Who's held him together all these years? Who grew up while Alex stayed a child?

"When Alex and I were young, milady, we were two souls in one body. Ah"—he smiled thinly—"your mind says, 'Split personality.' A number of psych-techs reached the same conclusion many years ago and salivated at the chance to handle such an exotic condition. They plied us with drugs, hypnotherapy, symlinks, and eventually announced Alex cured. As if I were an appendix they could casually snip off. Their efforts only drove me into hiding, down to the depths of our shared unconscious, and I grew up there, wary and sly.

"Let me tell you," he went on, "Alex does not 'trot me out.' I come when I'm needed. The hero arriving in the nick of time. I believe Roland told you about that night at Juicy's? Alex playing the fool to impress Helena, angering the rest of the audience . . . until suddenly he realized he was in desperate trouble, that people could actually hate him enough to hurt him. It's hard to say which frightened him more, the physical threat or the hatred. Alex had never been hated before. He fell to pieces . . . and I came to the rescue. Helena had nothing to do with my emergence, you understand? Nothing. Alex got into a scrape he couldn't handle and my presence was required.

"The same thing happened earlier tonight, when the blood on his hands assailed him with strange unsettling voices; Alex retreated in confusion, and lo, I was there. I'm always backstage, milady, waiting in the wings. Biding my time for the show.

"And now it's showtime again."

He held the radio transmitter to his lips and murmured, "Resume. Take her to the bunker." Immediately the robot hoisted me off the ground . . . not roughly, but it clearly hadn't been programmed to maintain a woman's dignity. Its gripping arms didn't care where they gripped, and it held me on a slight downward angle—I could feel my blood draining into my head. When it started to walk, each step was spring-loaded: not jarring, but a big upward movement, then a sudden dip down as the bot shifted its weight to the next leg. Up, down, up, down, very smoothly, and if I'd been an archeological artifact, I wouldn't have felt jostled a bit. Being human, however, I got seasick after the first three steps.

The Singer walked beside the bot for a few moments, watching me surge up and down with the bot's motion. Then he tossed something light onto my pinioned body. "That is your costume for the song," he said. "Please do me the honor of donning the outfit when you reach the bunker."

I craned my neck to get a better look at the clothes. Scanty and gossamer, of course. "Are you going to tell me what I do in this song?" I asked.

He shook his head. "I prefer it to be a surprise."

"No rehearsal, no direction, a brand-new song and I don't know the words or the tune . . ."

He caressed my hair with his long, cold fingers. "You'll be superb, milady. I have faith in your professionalism."

The bunker smelled of mildew and cement; its only illumination was a gun slit that let in a strip of light from the beam-lamps outside. The robot lowered me carefully to the floor, withdrew the cable tentacles wrapped around me, and took up a position blocking the exit.

Queasily, I got to my feet. "Let me leave," I ordered the bot, and stepped toward the door. It couldn't hurt me, could it? Robots are programmed not to injure humans. But the moment I moved, the bot spread its cables wide, closing off the doorway like a spider-web, with a big bot spider in the middle. I wasted a minute trying to pry free enough cables to give me room to escape; but steel is stronger than fingernails, and at last I gave up. I wasn't getting through that door till the Singer ordered the bot to let me out.

Sighing, I turned away and looked over the rest of the bunker's interior. It would cheer me no end to discover some functional weapon left from the war, a snare rifle, a jelly pistol, or whatever alien armament once fired through the gun slit; but the bunker had been emptied as meticulously as the rest of the planet. All I could make out in the shadows were cobwebs, dirt, and weeds sprouting from cracks in the concrete.

I began to pace, idly fingering the flimsy costume I was supposed to put on. One strong pull could rip the fabric to swatches, but that wouldn't help—the Singer would just drag me out naked. Angry at the thought, I gave the wall a good solid kick.

<SPLINK>

"That damned Silk sure gets around," I grumbled. But if it really was a biological weapon, I shouldn't be surprised it could take root in enemy strongholds. During the day, enough light would come through the bunker's doorway for the Silk to keep growing.

I tapped the wall with my foot.

<SPLINK>

<SPLINK>

<SPLINK>

Tiny feet scuttled across the floor toward the sound.

"Hello," I said. "Rotten little beasts."

A few minutes later, I was dressed in sheer see-through and making final adjustments on the sash about my waist. The sash wasn't part of the original costume—I'd made it from folding and twisting the blouse I'd been wearing—but I needed the sash to hide my hitchhikers: two parrots that had come scurrying at the sound of popping Silk. I'd slung them at my hips like six-guns, tucked under the sash and sleeping placidly after a full meal. Their small bodies pressed lightly against me, just inside the ridges of my pelvis, on either side of the flat of my stomach. Even under the bright beam-lamps outside, they'd be completely hidden.

The parrots weren't touching my skin—with stockings wrapped around my hands, I'd picked up the parrots and nestled them between my costume and the outer sash. It was hard to resist touching the little beasts just once, just the brush of a finger to hear if other minds were nearby. But now was not the time for pointless voyeurism; I had a different plan.

Once before I'd tried to close my mind to the Singer, trying to drown out all thought with the *Trash and Thrash* song. It didn't work. As the Singer said, he lived in songs, especially songs that were hard-edged and troubled . . . not to mention that the parrots were designed to broadcast trouble loud and clear. To hide, I had to lose myself in gentleness, restrict my thoughts to the kind of caring and concern where the parrots were mute.

I had to fall in love.

Concentrate on Alex: his face, his smile. I'd made love with him on the hill, clumsily, tenderly. No, to be honest it wasn't making love, it was just running away from my fear of the Singer, and the jangle of emotions aroused by using the parrots; but it could turn into love, couldn't it? Alex, beautiful, gentle child. In need of protection from himself and the world. Alex, who had tears in his eyes as he held unconscious Roland's hand. And Alex, coming to me in my own hut, stumbling over his words as he talked about his concern for Roland . . . if that really was Alex, and not just the Singer pretending to be Alex. No, it was Alex, it was Alex, even if he was feeling the Singer creep up inside his mind as the parrot blood took effect. It was appalling to imagine that: Alex hearing an icy other voice lurking beneath the surface of his thoughts, a second personality slowly gripping . . .

Damn. Concentrate, Lyra.

Deep breath. Falling in love with Alex. Who was kind and eager and vulnerable. A handsome prince held prisoner by his evil twin and now desperately yearning for a loving minstrel-girl to save him.

Alex's smile. His eyes. His need.

When it flows, it flows.

The lights bake the stage, the beat is driving hard, the music stabs you like a grimy finger. Your heart pounds, and if you don't kiss the first face you see, you'll grab the throat and squeeze. You feel hot style. You want to put on a show.

And if you're in love, the flow is creamy juicy lightning.

The music starts and you're on. Cue the backup singer. Showtime.

Thunk thunk thunk-ah thunk. Thunk thunk thunk-ah thunk . . . a heavy tenor drum, stomped full force, began pounding the night outside the bunker. I recognized the beat as the intro for "Moth Metamorphism," a cut that we'd scheduled to record later in the week. I should have known. All on his own, the Singer couldn't lay down instrumental tracks; for his new song, he must have written new lyrics to existing music.

The flow inside me clicked a notch higher. I knew this music, knew the through-line, the harmonies. I could kick the hell out of it.

When it flows, it flows.

The robot in the doorway began to whir, receiving radio orders from the Singer. I didn't resist as it wrapped a tentacle around my wrist and led me from the bunker; the bot could barely keep up with me as I strode out into the night, up to the plateau where the beam-lamps shone. A second bot appeared, carrying a microphone. I grabbed the mike, no time to wait, the music still booming. One slap to stick on the throat patch, a second slap for the battery pack, check the adhesive on both, and then I was surging forward, into the heat of the lights.

I stepped onto a green expanse of meadow, showing only one sign of the war: a glistening patch where the soil had been seared to black glass by some energy weapon. In the middle of the glassy surface stood a stone altar, a prop made for the recording of "Dead Man's Prayer"; and just back from the altar lurked the fog machine, hooked up with an extra hopper of dry ice.

The mist would really roll tonight.

All right, all right, keep going. The Singer wasn't here, but keep going. Set up for a sprawl-shot on the altar. What else could the Singer want? I slid up on top, sprawling, waiting, shaking, THUNK THUNK THUNK-AH THUNK.

And Alex appeared.

He came over a rise, just a silhouette, sharply backlit with sprays of yellow sparks—nothing more than a black outline against a fountain of fire, but I knew it was Alex. The Singer moved more gracefully, more intentionally, like he was trying to prove a point; Alex just moved. I lifted myself higher, hands and knees, truly believing I could simmer Alex's blood just by staring.

THUNK THUNK THUNK-AH THUNK.

Alex picked his way down to the plateau, trying to hurry but slowed by clumps of weeds on the hillside. Once he lifted his head and maybe he called to me, but the drumbeat drowned that out.

THUNK THUNK THUNK-AH THUNK.

Now Alex hurried into the light of the beam-lamps. His shirt was buttoned and he was shouting, "Get out of here, Lyra! Get out!"

I simply shook my head.

"I pushed him down for a minute," Alex said as he ran to me, panting. "He'd been outside for a long time, he was tired. But he'll be back, he will, and you can't . . ." Alex held out his hands, showing the brown bloodstains. "This will drive you crazy, it really will. The noise gets so loud, it deafens you. And it's all so *an-gry*. I never knew people were so *angry*. Back at camp it was like a chain reaction, a little hostility, people getting angry in return, then everyone going *furious* . . . in five minutes, they were honestly trying to kill each other. And *him,* the Singer—he was in the middle of it, egging them on . . ."

I took Alex's hand. The blood on his skin was dry, textured like satin. "It will be all right," I said. "Don't worry, it will be all right."

"It won't, it won't. He loves the anger, he thrives on it, but it'll rip you apart. He wants to *see* it rip you apart. He wants to see you snarl like an animal."

"Alex," I said again, threading my fingers through his, "it will be all right." I squeezed his hand tightly, wanting to squeeze my strength into him.

"You don't . . ." He pulled his hand from my grip and pressed it against his forehead. "You aren't . . ." His head snapped down, then up again, and he roared, "Where are you, milady?"

The Singer emerged in gentle Alex's face like ice crystallizing in water. His eyes narrowed; his mouth grew hard. "Damn the fool!" he screamed, and with both hands, he grabbed the collar of his shirt and ripped downward, tearing fabric and scattering buttons onto the ground. Gasping, he lunged forward to support himself unsteadily on the altar. "He caught me by surprise. What has he done with milady? Milady! Milady!"

The man was staring straight at me, blind to my presence. All the rehearsal I'd done before, trying to make myself love Alex— that was pure nonsense, just priming myself to put on a good show. But in the moment of transition, when simple well-meaning Alex was crushed away by the Singer's rage, something sparked in my heart and made the love real. The love didn't feel like *Romeo and Juliet* or *Trash and Thrash.* It probably wasn't woman/man love . . . mother/son maybe, or big sister/kid brother. So what? My heart and brain filled with compassion, and to the Singer, I was invisible.

I rocked back onto my knees and thrust both hands into my

sash. Two parrots, the last weapons to be drawn in Caproche's long war. As I touched them, the blare of the Singer's thoughts struck my brain like thunder, hate mixed with fear mixed with anger; but I was moving and mere noise couldn't stop me.

At the last instant, the Singer's head jerked up and his eyes met mine.

With all my strength, I clapped the parrots against his temples, slam, both sides of his head. The parrots burst in my hands like rupturing bags of blood, gushing across the Singer's face in brown spatters. For a split second, I could hear the echoes of fragmented thoughts outside me: the roadies, Helena, Roland, screeching far away. Then a jagged ripping sound split inside my head and my brain shattered.

Two parrots had died in my bare hands.

Imagine reliving your life through a black filter.

You get to remember that first kiss: two hours of standing in front of the house on a cold winter night as your boyfriend worked up the courage to go through with it. You can remember how you shifted back and forth from one leg to the other, shivering because you were only wearing a short skirt and stockings, and you can remember how many times you almost gave up hope, how you hated him for being so stupid, how you hated yourself for being too scared to grab him and kiss him before you died of frostbite. But do you remember the elation when it finally happened? Do you remember how you lay awake for hours with a huge smile on your face, as you counted the ways your life had changed? No—your memory is too busy skipping ahead eight months, when suddenly you and your boyfriend can't agree on anything, you know he makes up excuses to avoid seeing you, and when the two of you *do* get together it's only because you're hooked on those hour-long petting sessions on that couch in your basement. You get clean, clear memories of all the people you hated or feared, but the people you loved? Only the times they annoyed you.

Imagine reliving your life through a black filter.

Then imagine doing the same thing with two men watching.

One of the men is a lunatic. The other is so innocent you can't bear him to see your life, the many petty ugly things you've done.

But that's not the end. Imagine reliving someone else's life while you're reliving yours. A life with two strands, lunacy and naïveté. Oh, yes, relive a childhood so tormented that your personality crumbles to fragments, then a dozen harsh psychological treatments intended to heal you, then the blood-red fury of the Singer suppressed but not extinguished. Every memory from infancy to adulthood seen through two sets of eyes that never agree, every tenderness seen as weakness, every love dismissed as infatuation.

Reliving everything through a black filter.

Imagine doing all that in the time it takes a parrot to die.

My eyes met the Singer's at the moment I smashed the parrots against his head. We shared the parrots' deaths. We shared our own lives.

Then white noise. Static. The Singer screeched and reeled blindly away from me, staggering backward toward the fog machine. He collided with the nozzle and grabbed at it, seizing it with both hands. Maybe he was just catching his balance, maybe he was trying to break something, I don't know; but he gave another scream and wrenched the nozzle loose from the machine, setting free a bloom of fog that had built up inside. Berserk, he began to smash the broken nozzle down on the machine, over and over, howling all the while.

The Singer wrapped in fog—a gaunt silhouette in the night, backlit by beam-lamps. THUNK THUNK THUNK-AH THUNK.

Then the noise changed, the sound of his howls. I had parrot blood on my hands and maybe the sound I heard was only in my mind, but the explosive fury was overlaid with louder moans of pain: not from the Singer, but from Alex.

All this time I hadn't moved. My head was swimming, and like Roland after the parrot died in his hands, I was on the verge of passing out. But when I heard Alex's cries, his pain and terror, I forced back the edge of my dizziness and clumsily crawled off the altar. Fog was billowing everywhere, spreading fluidly over the grass. I staggered into it, the cold, dusty-smelling CO_2 fog, trying to stay on my feet long enough to reach Alex.

I found him in the heart of the fog bank, sprawled across something my muddled mind didn't recognize at first—a box, some kind of open box, like the one Alex and I had found on the hill. But as I stumbled closer, I saw it was the hopper for the fog machine, its lid smashed off in the Singer's rage. Steam boiled off the dry ice inside, curling and churning around Alex's prone body. He lay flat across the exposed ice, his bare chest pressed against it.

He screamed as the intense cold burned him like fire.

I grabbed his ankles and pulled weakly, trying to drag him off the ice pile. He didn't budge; I wondered if he'd actually frozen in place, like flesh bonding to sticky-cold metal. Then his legs kicked feebly out of my grip and I heard the voice of the Singer in my mind. "No, milady. I have sought the cold and found it. Cold, true cold, bright cold."

Alex howled.

"You're killing yourself," I shouted to the Singer. "You can't survive in there. God only knows what it's doing to your heart."

The Singer just laughed.

"Lyra?" Alex whispered. A real voice, forced through his lips by lungs that could scarcely breathe.

"Yes, it's me." I fumbled around to the other side of the hopper, only managing to stay on my feet by clinging to the edge of the bin. "Yes, Alex, I'm here."

His hand moved slightly, but his palm seemed stuck to the ice. I could feel him steeling himself, Alex's voice in my mind muttering, Do it, do it. Then he heaved the hand upward, ripping off most of the skin as he freed it from the ice's grip. Bleeding, he held it out to me. "Lyra."

I took his hand, holding it high above the ice. My fingers still dripped with parrot blood; Alex's blood mingled with it, in the fog and the cold.

The Singer's thoughts crooned with the cold, but I could hear nothing from Alex. Whatever went through his mind was too gentle for parrot blood to transmit.

"Alex," I said. Then a fresh surge of dizziness washed over me and I sank into its blackness.

I woke groggily, roused by burning pain. When I had fainted, my arms slumped across the dry ice, still holding Alex's hand.

His hand was as cold as the ice. Fog filled the hopper and dribbled out over the sides.

I looked down at my hands, still lying against the ice. Their skin was white and puckered, and they didn't ache much; the serious pain was higher up, near my elbows. I knew that was a bad sign—so much nerve damage in my hands, I couldn't feel how badly I was hurt.

That was when I realized the night was silent—no sound of thoughts. Not Alex's, not the Singer's, not mine. Parrot blood glistened on my fingers, parrot blood crystallized to ice; but my hands were too injured for the blood to work.

Pulling my hands off the ice left strips of skin behind. I scarcely felt it. For a moment, I considered pulling Alex's body out of the hopper, but I couldn't move my fingers. I couldn't grab him, I couldn't hold him; and it wouldn't make a difference if I could. It was far too late for anything to make a difference.

I took one last look at him lying there, burned and blue, silent on a bed of fog. Then I began plodding back to camp.

My hands will never move again. Jerith's medi-bot works on them daily to stave off gangrene, but repair is out of the question; that has to wait till I get to a populated planet. The bot says a good med center might be able to cut off my arms at the elbows and put me in a tank till they grow back.

No one knows what to do with the others in our party, still marked by parrot blood. A week has passed, and the telepathy shows no signs of wearing off. One of the roadies tried to cut away his bloodstained skin with a knife, but he passed out before finishing the job. Now the medi-bot keeps him under sedation.

Sedatives are handed out freely these days—the bot can synthesize enough to keep everyone subdued until the rescue ship arrives. The ship is scheduled to land an hour after sunset tonight, and the Planet Protection Agency has a good record for punctuality.

They've reclassified Caproche as TPI: Total Permanent Interdiction. Jerith will have to start over, another dig, another planet. He says he doesn't mind.

Jerith spends a few minutes with me every day . . . but with blood on his hands like everyone else, he mostly stays out in the wilds—a long way out, where he can't hear anyone else's thoughts.

I stay in camp, close to the medi-bot. It watches me and feeds me.

From time to time I catch sight of parrots, bright green and crimson, waddling across the dirt of the camp compound. I like to stroke their noses with my bandaged hands. When I do, the medi-bot stands beside me and whirs in disapproval.

It's decided the parrots are dangerous.

A Changeable Market in Slaves

n the first day of the Month of the Quill, Slavemonger T'Prin finally admitted to himself he was bankrupt.

On the first day of the Month of the Quill, Slavemonger T'Prin finally admitted to herself she was bankrupt.

On the first day of the Festival of Galactic Harmony, Slavemonger T'Prin finally admitted to himself that the Avatar of Financial Abundance had not accepted his sacrifice.

On the first day of the Month of Joyous Struggle, Mother Machine awoke Slavemonger T'Prin with the cheery message, "Good morning, Citizen. In order to serve you better, your credit chip has been reduced to scrap plastic."

On the first day of the Month of Desolation, Slavemonger T'Prin found no cup of blood by the coffin when he rose at sunset. The

servants were dead, the chapel had been desecrated, and his pos-
sessions were gone, down to the last gold candlestick.

On the day after the orcs had been driven across the river for another winter, Slavemonger T'Prin discovered the contents of his
storehouse had gone with them.

On the day after his revivification, Slavemonger T'Prin was informed by an embarrassed Integration Counselor that he had been
reclassified as Financially Bereft, Category III (Organ Donor).

On the third day of Ragnarok, Slavemonger T'Prin finally admitted to himself that business would not improve.

On the day after Judgment, Lucifer informed Slavemonger T'Prin
of a universal truth: you really can't take it with you.

On the day after his reincarnation, Slavemonger T'Prin realized
money is useless to those without opposable thumbs.

It was the first day of the Month of the Quill, a cold gray day with
the wind blowing down from the hills like a banshee looking for
fun, a day when the whores on Galadriel Boulevard were lowering
their prices to get indoors faster and the thieves from Rudyard Alley stole gloves instead of gold; the sort of day when you long to
be inside with someone who'll say she loves you and maybe for a

while you'll even let yourself believe it because you want to think there's such a thing in the world as warmth. Not the sort of day for sitting in your office and going over bank statements again and again, looking for anything that will tell you it's all a mistake, that the money isn't really gone like a woman who's decided she needs time to find herself.

My name's T'Prin. I sell slaves.

He awoke, remembering nothing. They told him his name was T'Prin, that he'd been a slavemonger, that he was now bankrupt. They thought he'd want to know what date it was and kept repeating it to him.

He'd never heard of the Month of the Quill—he knew the months by other names. But he'd call it Quill if they did. He'd play along with everything they said until he found out who he was this time and what the hell they'd done to his eyes.

"I say, fellows," said Waddams after the sherry had been poured and the esteemed members of the Zambezi Club were settled into their accustomed postprandial positions, "did you hear about old T'Prinzy?"

Slavemonger T'Prin thought his worst problem was impending bankruptcy. Had he but known of the gibbering horror that was even now slithering from the well behind his isolated country home, had he caught the merest glimpse of its fetid claws dripping with noisome ichor or its thousands of facial tentacles blasphemously quivering with subliminal phallic intent, had he suspected for a single moment that before the night was through he would come face-to-face with the malevolent forces that wait in a place beyond darkness for the call that will summon them into our blindly unsuspecting world . . . perhaps the demands of his creditors would have occupied less of his mind.

As she drove along the yew-lined driveway toward the imposing Jacobean manor where she was to serve as governess to the T'Prin offspring, Harmony Bellancourt thought back to the unsettling interview where she met the broodingly handsome master of the house and said to herself, "I suppose it doesn't matter that he's a notorious slavemonger, as long as he pays *me*."

Month of the Quill. Day one. Slaves restive. Hungry. Told them I was bankrupt. They thought I was lying.

Those muties will have to learn to believe me.

Slavemonger T'Prin came onstage wearing his trademark leather and leopard skins and immediately broke into his hit single "Month of the Quill." The throbbing beat reached into the audience like a grimy fist, grabbed every blood-meat heart, and squeezed with a grip that tore away candy-assed restraints. It was a sonic drug, an injection of Primo Primeval that mixed with the other chemicals in the mob's bloodstream to make a groin-grinding stew. Maybe the preachers were right when they said T'Prin was morally bankrupt; but bankrupt boys could still kick ass and the preachers shouldn't forget it. When Slavemonger played, the audience *demanded* to be slaves; and they were, by God, they were.

How many times had T'Prin walked down this narrow lane? How many times had he slunk away from the law courts, avoiding the high street for fear of meeting someone he knew, someone who would ask about the proceedings against him? How many times had he come this way with his head reeling, wondering what tricks he could use when the bailiffs served him with another summons? Yet in all those times, he'd never before noticed the little shop tucked between the out-of-business bakery and the run-down travel agency: a little shop with its window caked in dirt and a door sign reading EXOTIC CURIOS.

In the land of Ithlandril, at the confluence of the rivers Udalanar and Surandimir, not far from the Plains of Occlanoue where Garth One-Finger fought the Battle of Kennings Mill against Malevon Darkstrider and the forces of Hnurn, a day's march from the Jhallawel Forest so famous for Ba'ullahnut berries and the no-madic Quinquopel horses, there was a village named Fe'Huulin's Rest, not named after Fe'Huulin the Gray, as you might expect, but after his son by the beauteous Ellandewollinir, Fe'Huulin d'El-landewollinir, sometimes called Fe'Huulin Vallamarn or more simply Fe'Huulin of the Seven Dancing Servants of R'ynnhwn; and though the village had the reputation throughout the length and breadth of Adragharzh as a place of wealth and prosperity, second only to the cities of the Diacrectic League in the Archipel-ago Isles of Dragon Longing, it happened that a certain slavemon-ger named T'Prin, on the first day of the Month of the Quill (or more fully, Quillaamer'xhanderzjee), discovered that, though filled with rue, he must file a writ of surrendered suzerainty before the Judges of Ulm.

One ducat and eighty-seven pence. That was all. And sixty pence of it was in coppers. Coppers saved one and two at a time by haggling with the meatmonger and the wine merchant and the temple prostitutes until one's cheeks burned with the silent imputation of parsimony that such close dealing implied. Three times T'Prin counted it. One ducat and eighty-seven pence. And the next day was the slave auction.

Listen. T'Prin was a slavemonger in the last days of slaves, when everybody owned them and made excuses. Owners said they couldn't just free the slaves because they were like children in adult bodies, too naïve to get along in the world. And it wasn't a good time to start paying them as hired hands, because crop prices were down. And slaves really were happier with someone else taking all the responsibilities.

T'Prin was a slavemonger in the last days of slaves, when shipping embargoes by emancipated countries reduced incoming supplies, when local slave owners felt guilty about buying new slaves, when the market fell through. He had been an honest businessman in a trade that people once said was necessary. He kept his stock healthy and always gave customers good value.

Still, through no fault of his own, he found he was bankrupt. And he had no idea what to tell his family.

A man sits beside a pond. It is night. The sky is full of stars, but he does not see them.

He throws pebbles into the water one by one. Each one gives a blooping splash, and rippling circles glide outward from the point of impact. When the ripples have died down enough that he cannot see them in the starlight, he throws another pebble.

His name is T'Prin. This afternoon, creditors came to his dirty shop on the edge of town and told him to get out. They had a written order from the Tribunal. They refused to let him remove a single thing from the premises, not even his father's small library of books.

He had hated his job. He had hated treating people like animals. But as his father lay dying, the old man made T'Prin swear to keep the business going. It was the only thing his father had to leave the world. His mark. His legacy. T'Prin couldn't find the courage to say what a shabby little legacy it was, so he made the oath his father demanded.

Tonight the business is gone, the oath broken. A friend told T'Prin he should be glad to get out of that squalid place. And so he should be.

He throws another pebble. It disappears beneath the water. Its ripples disappear slowly. The surface of the pond becomes clear as if the pebble had never been thrown.

T'Prin throws another pebble.

"Mistah T'Prin—he broke."

Reaper

I could tell this Call would be a traffic fatality. It was a Friday evening in early March, the pavement was icy, and the sun was low on the horizon, at the precise spot to strike drivers' eyes as cars came around the curve. My compass pointed to that curve and my hourglass was almost empty.

A dozen of my fellow Reapers were already there—we were certainly going to make network news tonight. Most of the other Reapers sprawled indolently on the snow of the embankment beside the road; one boy who looked fourteen years old was showing off by pretending to make angels in the snow. (Of course, his ethereal body left no mark.) He thought making angels was very funny. I was about to instruct him on the way that sacrilegious flippancy can extend a soul's period of penance when my eye was caught by another Reaper pacing anxiously on the highway's median.

She appeared to be in her twenties, her eyes as clear as the eyes of doves, her body glorious in a Reaper's celestial raiment. (Praise God I am no longer tormented by the hormones that inflame a man's physical body.) Her gaze was fixed on the traffic speeding down from the north; from time to time, she leaned out over the lanes of cars for a better view, like a woman waiting for her lover to appear. Her scythe lay abandoned on the muddy snow behind her.

I thought to myself she must be a newcomer to our Calling, anxious to do it correctly. I do not wish to belittle the angels who supervised us, but they were not good at talking to mortals. They didn't give clear and specific instructions; they failed to provide the firm guidance that most of my fellow humans needed. As in so many cases where Heaven spoke ambiguously, I was forced to step in and declare the truth more plainly.

"Greetings, sister," I said in my most comforting voice. "Are you troubled?"

She threw a distracted glance my way, then turned back toward the cars. "I'm fine."

"You don't look fine," I said. "You look like a woman who's worried she'll make a mistake."

She gave me another look, but this time surprised.

"There's no cause for worry, sister," I went on. "Heaven has made our jobs very simple. The compass leads us to our Charges. The hourglass tells us when to act. The scythe cuts the cord that binds spirit to flesh. Then we may joyously greet the freed soul in the Name of our Lord Jesus Christ who judges most . . ."

I had lost her attention. She took a few impatient steps away from me and peered out over the traffic again.

I was not upset. I have been ignored before. Human nature is devilishly proud and often spurns those who try to help.

"Are you worried about the violence?" I asked. She moved away from my voice, but I followed her. Many try to flee from unpleasantness when they would be happier facing it. "I realize most new Reapers are sickened by the blood," I said. "I would guess you come from genteel society and have never seen the horrors of mutilation and disease. I promise you, though, you'll get used to the ugliness. Everyone does. We may still find it distasteful but not intolerably repugnant. We—"

"Shut up!" she snapped, wheeling to face me. "I'm finding *you* intolerably repugnant. Blood is just blood. You, you're—"

A truck horn trumpeted up the road, like Gabriel signaling all Reapers of Souls to their preordained missions. A tractor-trailer had been cut off by a lane-hopping sports car; then there was a chaos of brakes, ice, sun, the trailer jackknifing, the truck heeling over on one side as the driver tried to regain the road. The front grill of the truck passed through my insubstantial body as eighteen wheels of death crossed the median into oncoming traffic.

I forced my eyes to stay open. It was an exercise of discipline. I didn't want to watch, so I did. The destruction had a brutal sort of grandeur, like a dance of giants: some parts dizzyingly swift, others slow but inexorable. Brakes squealed and horns blared a musical accompaniment on top of an ongoing percussion of metal on metal.

The spectacle was so dazzling, I came close to forgetting my purpose . . . but then I saw the fourteen-year-old Reaper scrambling into the overturned tractor-trailer and I remembered my duty.

The Reaping was routine—my Charge was a mousy sort of man in his forties, impaled on the shaft of his steering wheel. The sand in my hourglass was down to the last few grains even as I arrived, but I had been a Reaper for nearly a decade and was adept at my work. Reaching into his solar plexus, I found his silver cord, pulled it out, and levered my scythe under it. As the last grain ran out, a sharp clean jerk severed the cord.

I sang a hymn of thanksgiving, as an example to the other Reapers. I tried to raise my voice loud enough for them to hear over the thundering din around me.

The moment the mousy man's soul slid from his body, he began apologizing. He assumed full blame for the accident . . . an example of self-centered pride, since he was not the cause, merely the effect. He also assumed blame for unhappiness in his own life and the lives of those he loved, and blame for various future miseries that would result from his death. In short, he was hysterical, and his remorse wasn't worth a cinder. I left him to babble and went in search of the young woman I'd been trying to instruct.

I found her on the embankment, sitting beside the body of a sixteen-year-old boy. Apparently he'd been thrown from one of the cars in the pileup below us. (Boys his age defy seat-belt laws . . . more self-centered pride.) His head was bloody, his hair spangled with beads of safety glass glinting red in the sunset. The Reaper woman rested her hand on his arm in a tender way I thought ill advised. "It doesn't do to become too attached," I told her as I drew near. "It can only interfere with doing your duty. You aren't even watching your hourglass. How will you know when his time runs out?"

"It already did," she said. She reached around behind her back and produced the hourglass for my inspection. It was as full as a newborn baby's. "I saved him," she said, looking at the hourglass as if she could hardly believe it herself.

"I don't understand."

"I didn't take him. The time came and I didn't cut his cord. After a while, the hourglass filled up again."

"Do you know what you've done?" I shouted at her.

"I've saved him. He's already stopped bleeding." The boy stirred under her hand. "He's going to be all right."

"Nothing is going to be all right! You've committed a monstrous sin, don't you see that? You're supposed to do penance; you're supposed to *do as you're told*. You've defied the will of Heaven. You've spit on our Savior's mercy!"

"He reminds me of my brother," she said, stroking the boy's cheek. I turned my head away, sickened. "I've been following him for weeks," she went on. "His name's John. He hates being called Johnny, but his mother still does it to tease him. He plays hockey . . . tries different ways to comb his hair to impress girls . . ."

"He's an ordinary teenager, nothing more," I said, grabbing her arm and yanking her smartly to her feet. "You've jeopardized your immortal soul on a whim I can't begin to understand. Don't you hold your soul precious? Don't you understand the risks? *I* had a sister . . . should I damn myself forever for some woman who merely *reminds* me of her?"

But it was too late to reason with her. The air around us grew suddenly warm and clean, scented with the breath of roses. I pushed the woman away from me and rushed a few steps down the embankment. For a moment, I glimpsed the radiant hand of an angel reaching out of nothingness to touch the woman's shoulder. Then she was gone.

At my feet, the boy lifted himself groggily on one elbow. Slowly shaking his head, he took the Name of our Lord in vain.

That was the kind of boy she had chosen to save.

For weeks afterward, I tried to put the incident out of my mind, but it repeatedly ambushed my thoughts. If I had one complaint about my role as a Reaper, it was my inability to affect the living world and guide it toward the path of righteousness. Now I had seen a way to have such an effect, but one I dared not use. Still, it fascinated me.

Standing at the bedside of a ninety-five-year-old woman, I suddenly wondered what would happen if I just walked away. Would her hourglass refill itself, her cancer vanish, her senility uncloud? Or would she remain a near-empty husk requiring a few more years of feeding and bathing? What sort of change would either alternative make in God's divine plan?

Watching a fool and his snowmobile crash through thin ice in the middle of a lake, I asked what would happen if I left him. Would he be rescued in some unforeseen way? Would he make medical headlines: Man Survives Hours of Icy Immersion. Would his doctors believe they could work marvels, when in fact it was *my* doing?

As I kept vigil with a family around the crib of a fevered infant, I thought of how easy it would be to answer their prayers, to give them their miracle. I imagined their jubilation, their relief, their effusive gratitude. With scarcely an effort, I could change their lives profoundly. I could grant them joy.

Oh, it was hard to cut that tiny cord.

In late June, I was relieved to gain a respite from the torment that lured me toward disobedience. I arrived on a Call in a quiet tree-shaded neighborhood, only to find my hourglass still gave my Charge abundant time to live. Three weeks, perhaps? A month? It was possible. Heaven sometimes arranged such interludes as vacations from the stresses of Reaping. Or perhaps it was simply a reward for me, recognizing my faithful ministry in death as in life. In the meantime, I would not be forced to choose between death and life. For a while, I had no tempting decisions to make.

My Charge was one Louis Gerard, a man who lived with his sister Anne in a grand house more than a century old. I already knew Louis by reputation: he was a celebrated pornographer whose photos of naked women sold as High Art because he used black and white film and cropped their heads from the picture. Sometimes he used Anne as his model—she was unflamboyantly lovely and worshipped Louis as a genius. More often, he would bring home sleek young bundles of ambition who were only too eager to flaunt their flesh if it would look good on their résumés.

I say I knew Louis Gerard by reputation, but in a few days, I knew him by his very stench. I sat in on his photo sessions and watched him exhort his women to caper for the camera. The foolish ones let him have his way with them afterward; the more astute did the same, but extracted letters of recommendation first. I watched his insatiable animal rutting and was appalled to the core of my soul.

I watched Anne too: Anne cooking, Anne cleaning, Anne listening to the giggles coming from the studio and keeping her face blank. She developed all of her brother's photos, making print after painstaking print until she was satisfied with the result. For hours, I watched her working under the red developing light, its glow softening the intensity of concentration on her face.

She worked diligently on her brother's lurid photographs, but more happily on her own. Her subjects were simple: melancholy landscapes, rusted machinery, sometimes gravestones. She never showed them to Louis—he would certainly have mocked her for wasting film on such sterile material. She showed them to me, though, even if she never knew it; and I saw more worth in one of them than in her brother's entire portfolio.

I often contemplated the gift I would be giving Anne when I Reaped Louis. She would inherit his wealth and build a life of her own. I fancied her as a cherished protégée whom I would launch on a photography career more wholesome than her brother's. There was justice in that; and it led me to see justice in all acts of the Almighty. Could I interfere with that justice by refusing my duty? No. I would Reap those who must be Reaped, without questioning. That was the way of the righteous man. That was the path of faith.

Thus I reflected to myself as Anne quietly read photography magazines and I watched her lovely face. But I had forgotten it is a law of Heaven that every faith must be put to the test.

One sunny morning, as I sat on the patio and Anne pulled up weeds from the garden at my feet, a Reaper walked nonchalantly through the back hedge. It was the snow-angel boy from the highway, and he gave me an impudent wave as he sauntered up. "Hey, Reap! How's the scythe hanging?"

"Do you have business here?" I asked.

"Give me a sec to check my bearings," he said. With a great show of rummaging through the pockets of his raiment, he located his compass and flicked the case open. "And our next contestant is . . . the little lady crawling around here in the dirt! Let's have a big hand for her from the celestial audience. Yay!"

He applauded derisively under Anne's nose. She continued to pull weeds calmly.

Inwardly, I shuddered.

The boy called himself Hooch and he would not go away. I demanded to check his instruments, of course, but he was telling the truth. From all angles, his compass pointed directly at Anne. The hourglass for her seemed to have precisely the same amount of sand as her brother's.

"Mutual suicide pact?" Hooch suggested. I tried to slap him, but he skipped away, laughing.

The serenity of my past few weeks quickly shattered into nightmare. Hooch proved inescapable. If I chose to watch Louis and his obscene photo sessions, Hooch was there, shouting, "Grind that pelvis, woman! Make it wet!" If I slipped into Anne's bedroom to savor her quiet breathing as she slept, Hooch would barge through the wall and shout, "Hot damn, she sleeps in the raw!" He lewdly intruded into her most private moments; he mocked her face, her voice, her clothes, her walk; and when he saw her photographs, he burst into laughter. To his crass intellect, they were "stupid, ugly, and boring."

In my heart, I cried, Where is justice? Why was Hooch not burning in hell? Why was he, of all Reapers, called to Reap Anne?

And why did Anne have to die now, when the death of her brother would free her for a new and better life?

Then, in the depth of my despair, the answer came to me. Justice does not merely happen. Justice is made.

The morning came when my hourglass showed Louis had less than a day to live. He was not making the best of his brief time— he sat at the breakfast table, holding his head in his hands and staring blankly at his coffee mug. His eyes were bloodshot, his face flushed and unshaven; if his woman from the night before could see him now, she would have laughed and shouted just to cause him pain.

Anne was at the stove, making French toast. I had watched similar scenes before and knew Louis would refuse to eat what she served; nevertheless, she always made the effort.

Hooch sat on the edge of the stove and watched Anne work, her hand occasionally passing through his body. "She's burning this toast, you know," he told me. "She's standing right here, she's watching it all the time, and she's letting it burn."

"Hooch," I said, "let's trade."

"Trade what?"

"People. Just for fun. You Reap Louis. I'll Reap Anne."

"You have the most colossal hard-on for this broad, don't you?"

"I merely think it would be interesting," I said, pleased how I kept the anger out of my voice. "Doesn't it bother you we Reapers have to toe the line all the time? We have to Reap *who* we're told *when* we're told. That certainly annoys *me*."

"Don't try to con me." He laughed. "You've got the salami blues for Little Arfing Annie, and you want to be there to sweep her into your big strong arms when she croaks. That's cool, I don't mind. She's yours."

I had my mouth open to protest, but I closed it quickly. Let him believe what he wanted; I knew the truth.

The day continued badly for Louis. His model for the afternoon shooting session had too many ideas of her own. The two of them quarreled about poses, lighting, and the use of props. He finally threw the woman out of the studio, then spent an hour venting his anger on Anne: Anne couldn't cook, he said; Anne had botched developing the latest batch of prints; Anne should go get a real life instead of sponging off him. Of course, she made no effort to argue—she let him rage for a time, then left him alone.

Without a target to strike at, Louis struck at himself. To be precise, he began to drink. Hooch egged him on. "Come on, Louis, belt back that gin. Be a man, make it a double. Yeah, a beer chaser, go for it!" As Hooch cheered, he stood with his scythe pressed to his cheek, his fingers avidly fondling the handle.

Near midnight, Louis got the urge to work in the darkroom. "I'll show that bitch how to develop photographs," he muttered. I looked at the sand in the hourglass; it had almost run out.

Inside the darkroom, Louis fumbled with the chemicals and spilled them several times. His hands were shaking and clumsy. When he lit a cigarette to calm his nerves, Hooch and I exchanged smiles.

"Gonna have a hot time in the old town tonight," said Hooch.

"I'll see to the lady," I told him, and started up to her bedroom.

The explosion was less violent than I expected—we have all grown too accustomed to Hollywood's excess. From Anne's bedroom, the noise was barely audible: an airy whump that didn't disturb her sleep. When I stuck my head out the door, however, I could see flames racing down the hall like unruly children, tearing through the aged building with hot glee. It was easy to see that brother and sister might well have died simultaneously.

I went back to Anne and sat on the edge of her bed. As the wood of the door frame began to smolder, I fondly stroked her hair. "Behold, I am with you," I told her. "While I am here, you shall not perish but have eternal life."

Before the end, the roaring of the fire awoke her. She reacted unwisely: stood up, tried to run to the door. The smoke filled her lungs almost immediately and doubled her over with a wrenching spasm of coughing. She felt very dear to me then: so human and vulnerable, with the desperation of a lost child. When she succumbed to the fumes and crumpled to the ground, she looked as innocent as a baby waiting for my baptism.

Her hourglass emptied. I did not Reap her.

Her body burned with fire, yet she was not consumed.

In the course of time, the fire department arrived. Looking at her, they could not understand how she still lived. They sped her away in an ambulance.

Soon after, Louis's now-dead spirit burst into the room with Hooch on his heels. When the boy caught sight of me, he began to sing, "Fire's burning, fire's burning, draw nearer, draw nearer . . ."

Louis grabbed my elbow and shouted over the crackling and hissing, "Where's my sister?"

"She's been taken to hospital."

"Thank God," he said. "Thank God."

I didn't correct him.

Suddenly Louis howled and began dragging me toward the door. "My negatives! We have to save them!"

"He still hasn't figured out he's dead." Hooch laughed, prancing in the flames. I caught sight of the hourglass bouncing where it was tethered to his belt. Anne's hourglass. It was full. I felt a surge of triumph.

Hooch noticed the direction of my gaze and looked at his hourglass in surprise. "That's weird, isn't it? Hey, what did you do with the bimbo's soul?"

"I didn't Reap her."

He gave a low whistle and backed away from me. "You're in trouble, man."

"I'm not in trouble. She was your Charge."

"Help me get the damned negatives!" Louis shouted, but neither Hooch nor I paid attention. Reapers are Reapers; Louis was merely another dead man.

With narrowed eyes, Hooch raised his scythe high, holding it as a weapon. He came slowly toward me. "You suck, man. You really suck."

I laughed at his monumental arrogance.

Whether he would have struck me, whether it would have hurt, I do not know. I could feel sudden warmth in the air, smell the breath of roses. The glorious hand of an angel materialized between us and Hooch lowered his scythe slowly.

"Good-bye, Hooch," I said. "Enjoy the wailing and gnashing of teeth."

But the hand reached out for me.

In a place of darkness, I asked, "Am I in hell?"

A voice said, "Should you be?"

I didn't answer.

———

After a while, I said, "I did it for Anne."

The voice asked, "Did you?"

I didn't answer.

Much later I said, "I understand now. You make people Reapers to test them. We're *supposed* to care so much for a Charge that we risk our own souls for their lives."

The voice asked, "Did you risk your own soul?"

I didn't answer.

Lesser Figures of
the Greater Trumps

The "Greater Trumps" are the major Arcana of the tarot. This piece is based on pictures from the classic Rider-Waite deck.

o. **The Fool's Dog:** He smells interesting. Like a long walk and sweaty. Like sex too. His crotch smells like sex.

I like the smell. I push up against him to remind myself of the fragrance. A little while later I'm not sure I still remember it exactly, so I push up against him again.

I wonder who the woman was.

I wonder what she smells like now.

1. **The Tree Above the Magus:** The sun is warm. The sun is tasty.

The wind whispers that fall is coming. She tests my leaves to see if they will come loose.

I am perfectly aware that fall is coming. But today, the sun is delicious.

The man below me poses as if he is someone special.

But he's in *my* shade.

2. *The Scroll in the High Priestess's Hand:* She holds me gingerly as if I am fragile; but I am parchment. Decades ago, I was the skin of a sheep. When the sheep was shorn, I was all that protected it from the elements. Rain made me slick. Snow melted slowly against me. I wasn't fragile then.

The sheep died, but I was rescued. Humans blessed me and scraped me clean. They scratched me with quills; it stung, but it made me special in their eyes.

I don't know what they wrote.

The woman's hand is warm and gentle. It reminds me of my sheep.

3. *The Dress of the Empress:* Am I not of *regal* cloth? Am I not elegant? Am I not *luxuriant* with color?

I was designed by a man from across the sea. I was sewn by imperial seamstresses. One seamstress was whipped because her hems were uneven. Right in the palace workrooms: the woman was *whipped* in front of me. A speck of her blood sprayed onto the cloth, where it falls across the Empress's breast. No one noticed. It blended right in.

Isn't that *delightful*?

Each morning, the Empress rises from her bed and puts me on. Three maids help with her hair and makeup and perfumes, but she puts me on by herself. I drape her body; she *basks* in my caresses.

If she did not surround herself with my finery, she would not feel like an Empress.

Without me, she is *nothing*.

4. *The Emperor's Crown:* For five hundred years, I have watched this family. This boy, his father, his grandfather . . . so many generations I've lost count. Some were good rulers; some were tyrants; some were mad.

This boy is the best of the line. He's rather stupid, but he keeps his hair clean.

5. *The Two Monks Who Kneel Before the Hierophant:* One of us will replace the Old Man soon. He can't live much longer. His mind wanders. He mumbles when he's giving an audience, and he mumbles when he's alone.

At one time, he was the voice of the gods on Earth. They possessed him and spoke through him.

Now he mumbles.

I wonder what it feels like when the gods speak through you. It's frightening to imagine. In all the pantheon, there isn't a single god you'd want to turn your back on. If you lent your coat to a god, you'd never get it back again. Not in one piece. So why is it such an honor to lend them your tongue?

Stop mumbling, old man. Pull yourself together.

6. *The Snake Who Watches the Lovers:* Humans know nothing about love. They stand beside each other naked and think nakedness is love.

A snake knows love.

Love is the smell that drags you away from everything that is safe, across fields, over roads, into villages, while in the back of your mind a voice tells you truly, "If humans see you, you'll die." Not death by languishing, but death by crushing, feet trampling you as bones snap and guts rupture. And you continue anyway, not because you want anything but you are incapable of seeing anything but the path toward passion.

Humans think that lovers are star-crossed if their families disapprove.

At their most ardent, humans still take a moment to find a soft place to lie down.

7. *The Black Sphinx Who Pulls the Chariot:* The conquering hero rides through the city, believing he is the terror and envy of all who see him. With his helmet stuffed down around his ears, he can't hear the muttering of the people in the street.

"Can't he afford a horse?"

"I knew him when he was a brat who threw stones at old women."

"Putting on weight, isn't he?"

When he parks this chariot outside the Ministry of War, children come and scratch my ears. They call me kitty.

8. *The Flowers That Girdle the Woman of Strength:* What is the nature of strength?

Nothing fights with us flowers. Nothing eats us, except for the occasional budworm. People don't try to make their reputation by conquering us.

The woman of strength strives to close the lion's mouth, and this time she succeeds. Or maybe it's just that this time, the lion allows himself to be subdued.

If the lion wins the next time and tears her apart, we flowers will certainly be damaged too. But the lion won't go out of his way to hurt us. He won't resent us. He won't want revenge on a bunch of flowers.

What is the nature of strength?

9. *The Hermit's Staff:* Straighter than any tree that ever grew . . . I was a tree once, a sapling. Cut down by a woodcutter, because it was his nature to cut wood. Selected by an artisan, because I stood straighter than my fellows. Whittled and trimmed, planed and sanded . . . shaved down to some human's idea of how trees should really grow.

I am half the diameter I once was. A spindly weakling. If this hermit put his full weight on me, I would snap.

But I am very straight.

I am here for symbolism, not support.

10. *The Creature That Bears the Wheel of Fortune:* The wheel doesn't float in midair; I hold it up.

The crowd watching the wheel thinks that it turns on its own. I like to foster that illusion.

"Oh, no!" I shout. "It's turning, it's turning, oh, no! Harvests will be bad, winter will be hard, infants will be born sickly." And people of the celestial audience shake their heads gravely as if the universe has revealed its callousness.

"At last!" I shout. "It's turning, it's turning at last! Crops will ripen, summer will be kind, children will laugh and see the world with wondering eyes." And people of the celestial audience sing hymns to laud the banishment of evil.

The spectators think the wheel turns on its own.

They think it really has an effect.

When I grow bored of this game, I'm going to drop the wheel and watch the looks on their faces.

11. *The King Who Bears the Scales of Justice:* Visitors to my court wonder why I'm not wearing a blindfold. But if I wore a blindfold, how could I read the scales? Put my finger on one side or the other? That would give a fair reading, wouldn't it?

I'm not being cynical.

I know that if I were wearing a blindfold, I'd peek. People wearing blindfolds always peek. Stage magicians. Knife-throwers. Children pinning the tail on the donkey.

I'm not being cynical.

It wouldn't matter. The scales still work. Justice is served.

But a blindfold would be pure showmanship.

Not that I have any complaint with showmanship. I've thought of getting a blindfold so people would believe I'm impartial.

"It's not enough for justice to be done; people must *believe* justice has been done." People always repeat that maxim after the scales make an unpopular judgment. What they mean is that the truth is not good enough if the truth is unappealing. They don't want the scales to reveal the truth, they want the scales to confirm majority opinion.

I'm not being cynical.

12. **The Tree That Bears the Hanged Man:** Other trees get normal lynchings. On me, they hang the guy upside down.

I feel ridiculous.

The lynch mob strung him up last night. There was a lot of shouting, a lot of hysterics. No one mentioned what this guy's crimes were. If any. The mob laughed and cursed loud enough to frighten the squirrels out of my branches.

At one point, I thought two of the vigilantes were going to get into a fight, but the others stopped them. I don't know what it was all about.

Then they hung up this guy by his foot.

What morons.

It hasn't hurt him. He's humming to himself. Humming, for God's sake! He sounds quite cheerful.

What morons.

The elm across the road has been sniggering for the last two hours.

It'll be the talk of the county.

I'll never live this down.

13. **The Bishop Who Follows the Specter of Death:** Some criticize me. Some say I give the murderer legitimacy.

No. Not true.

I have never condoned death. Nor war. Nor famine. Nor pestilence.

I march in the parade of destruction because I have vowed to attend those who suffer misfortune. I am *in* the parade, but not *of* the parade.

I have no vested interest in suffering. But when suffering happens, a righteous man must face the problems head-on. He must take action.

Bless you. Bless you. Bless you.

14. *The Pool of Temperance:* I'm working on a stone.

Millennia ago, a lizard of a now-extinct species knocked a stone off the bank. The stone was red and sharp-edged. Quartz, I think.

I was looking for a project at the time. Something to keep me busy. Something to occupy my mind in the dry days of summer. Something I could look at and think, "I made this. It's mine."

The stone is my project. It's almost smooth now. A smooth, speckled red.

It's pretty. I think so, anyway.

The angel above me has his foot on the stone and seems to find it comfortable. My stone is clean and polished. I'm proud of that.

I know it's not much. It's just a stone. But it's mine, it's mine, it's mine.

I made it. Me.

15. *The Devil's Pedestal:* Day 2,189,345 in Hell. Noon. Greenwich Mean Time.

Satan lifts a claw and gores another notch in my side. Two witnesses stand by to watch, to make sure all the legal formalities are observed. This is Hell; we believe in legal formalities.

There are now 2,189,345 notches in my side. I am zebraed with notches, tigered with notches. One notch for each day of damnation.

I am the calendar of Hell.

Satan lives in dread of losing track of his time here. Sometimes he forgets whether he's made the notch for the day, and he gnaws at his talons, trying to decide whether he should make another notch. But he knows if he's already made today's mark, another would throw off the count.

He goes through this every day. Despite the rigorous routine, despite the witnesses. And he worries that sometime in the past, millennia ago or just yesterday, he really did make a mistake and now he's permanently wrong.

I have no trouble keeping track of his notches. I know how fresh my pain is.

If Satan clawed his own hide, he'd know too.

16. *The Sparks Shooting from the Tower:* This tower stood for two hundred and fifty years.

It resisted five enemy attacks. Those who lived in the tower praised its strength. Honored it with songs. Spread its fame through all countries.

More than four hundred children have been born within its walls. Most grew to adulthood here, and died when their time came.

Diplomats came here from across the sea. They complimented the strong walls, the view that commands the surrounding territory, the strategic positioning of wells and storehouses.

This tower stood for two hundred and fifty years.

We sparks last a second at most.

Don't you dare feel sorry for this damned tower.

17. *The Bird Observing the Star:* A woman is pouring water, some on the ground, some into a pool. Huge white stars circle around an enormous yellow one.

Portents. Humans love portents. Humans hunger after portents.

We birds haven't forgotten about Roman auguries. The priests slit living birds open, just to look for portents in their entrails. Entrails . . . humans always use the word "entrails." The truth is the priests would cut out our hearts. They cut out our livers. They cut out our intestines and scanned them inch by inch like stockbrokers examining ticker tape.

Stockbrokers examine ticker tape for portents.

We birds see everything, from stockbrokers to stars, but we don't see portents. Birds have no portents, not even portents of things that concern us, like winter. One fall day we find ourselves flying south, that's all.

That's all.

18. *The Dog Who Bays at the Moon:* Wolves howl at the moon. Dogs bay.

Here's the difference.

A wolf is shouting a challenge, crying defiance at the great face in the sky. A wolf is saying, "Despite hunters and hunger and sickness and snow, I'll be here again next month, same as you. You go on and I'll go on. You might be hidden by a cloud, but I'll still be here. And when I die, my children will howl for me, and the pack will howl and every pack will howl, until you slink below the horizon. We are forever."

A dog is greeting a companion, a fellow traveler that humans revere or ignore. A dog is saying, "You and me, moon, we're the ones who know how to laugh. Whatever damned thing the human race comes up with next, it's okay with us. Dogs are no more domesticated than you are, moon; we're just easygoing. Why make a fuss? Eating is good, sniffing is good, sleeping is good. Most things are okay."

That's what we dogs say to the moon.

It's the only sane attitude. Wolves are too intense.

*19. **The Sunflowers Beneath the Sun:*** Height! More height! More height!

Height is sun and sun is height.

The pretty-doll flowers in the garden next to us are irrational. They hug the ground. They keep their heads down. They don't compete.

Why? Why? Why?

It must be some mutual agreement to remain mediocre. If no one sticks her head up, no one else gets overshadowed. And they're all so spineless—they're so afraid of losing if they take a chance, they're so reluctant to seem rude—they remain prissy little runts all their lives.

We sunflowers have more stomach. We strangle each other. We compete. More height means more sun. More sun means more height.

The prissy little runts ask how much sun and height a flower really needs.

More! The answer is always more!

*20. **The Trumpet That Wakes the Dead for Judgment:*** It's no big deal. At the End of Time, the angel Gabriel will use me to blow a single note and the dead will rise from their graves. Until then, I stay silent.

I can handle that.

Gabriel can't. It's a big responsibility for him, and he'd like to practice. Sometimes he takes me out of the case, puts my mouth-piece to his lips, and thinks about playing. Something soft. Something so low human ears couldn't hear it. But he knows it's like biting a balloon—big bite or small, the effect is the same.

I have this hunch about the way Heaven works. I don't think Gabriel will ever be given the signal that it's time to blow. I think someday the temptation will just grow too great and he'll crack.

He may try a quiet little toot or blast a fanfare that makes the stars echo, but sooner or later he'll break. And that will be the End of Time.

Running things this way, God doesn't have to make the big decision. He just appoints Gabriel as the scapegoat and waits for all hell to break loose.

Me, I'm patient. It will happen or it won't.

Gabriel polishes me every day with the vigor of a man who needs to keep his hands busy. He doesn't sleep well.

21. *The Wreath on the Card Called the World:* A woman dances, holding a baton. She is clad only in a tastefully draped ribbon.

I surround her, a green wreath with the silhouette of an egg.

In the four corners of the sky, faces look at us: a lion, an eagle, an angel, and a bull.

So. Which one of us is "the world"?

Me? The woman? The watchers? All of us? Some mysterious whole that encompasses us?

Or simply the ink that depicts us and the cardboard that gives the ink something to cling to?

Philosophers may amuse themselves making arguments for each possibility. Theologians may obtain their god's version of the truth and expound it from the pulpit. Cynics may say that the designers of the Tarot didn't know what the hell the world was about, so they took the opportunity to draw another naked woman.

Anything's possible.

Anything's possible.

Anything's possible.

Shadow Album

In the deserted city at the heart of Muta's Great Fog Bank, there is a sundial. Its face is marble, once polished, now rough and pitted with age. The metal of the central gnomon flakes with rust; it has bled a dull brown stain across the dial's gritty white face.

The sundial no longer tells the time—the perpetual fog smears Muta's hot blue sunlight into a diffuse gray that casts no shadows, even at midday.

I visit the sundial often; the sight of it calms me when the loneliness grows too strong. I find it comforting to think even a sundial can stop. It seems to be a promise that no responsibility lasts forever.

Once, this city was home to a million beings. Green plants grew, animals basked at midday, the Mutan people cast shadows and shaded their eyes from the afternoon sun. Now, the only flora are lichens and fungus, and the only animals small scavengers that dart in and out of nests under the crumbled buildings. As for the Mutans, they cast their last shadows long ago.

I carry a camera with me wherever I go, and it is full of shadows. Some are recent—photographs I've taken to pass the time, to pretend that I've chanced upon beauty or importance in a rusted tangle of metal, an oddly shaped mushroom. The recent photos occupy the reusable slots on the camera's recording diskette, shadows I discard as new ones catch my eye. But there is a set of pictures I have tagged to prevent overwriting, shadows cast before the last light left me. Now, as night falls and the ghosts struggle to wake themselves from their collective sleep, I put the diskette into the viewer in my hut and click through my little album.

Picture 1—Exploration Team Harmony on the Plains of Expanding Accord:

Twenty-two men and women stand in the center of a burnt field, the grass charred black by the heat of a Vac/ship's landing. The ship is gone now, back to the orbiting task force where a million colonists wait in suspended animation until Harmony Team certifies the planet safe. Our mission is considered a formality—satellites and robot probes have given Muta such a positive rating that supply caches have already been dropped at selected sites all over the planet. Even so, final approval for colonization rests entirely with our team and its superiors. We do not place blind trust in machines; it is a doctrine of our faith.

By the time this picture was taken, all that remained to be explored was the anomalous fog bank perpetually covering a region of Muta's southern hemisphere: cause unknown, unchanged by wind and sun, impenetrable to orbital eyes. We thought our investigation would be routine and painless.

The team members offer smiles for the camera, showing or not showing their teeth according to their chosen self-image. Most try not to squint, though the sun is in their eyes; they want to look good for the photograph.

Behind them is the skimmer assigned to fly the team to the Great Fog Bank. On the craft's fuselage, brown letters proclaim UNITY TASK FORCE: MUTA. Beneath the words are the twenty-two symbols of our totem houses, the spirits that unite our people and set us apart from other human cultures in this galactic sector.

The symbols attest that the world is more than a machine, and humans more than a meaty collection of chemicals. We of the Unity are a spiritual people.

Each symbol on the fuselage is carefully labeled: the Dancing Madman, the Ready Mage, the Blind Priestess, and so on. The Unity is relentless in labeling everything.

In the far background, beyond the landing strip, you can see the grassland that the Unity named the Plains of Expanding Accord. Amidst the thick band of green there is a single dab of brown—some inquisitive Mutan herd animal peering at all the curious activity happening around the base.

At first glance, the people posed in this picture may be indistinguishable. They are all uniformed in the same tan fatigues. They all look healthy and competent. But to my eyes, three people stand out from rest. They stand together on the extreme right of the picture: a woman between two men.

The woman is Chiala, Archeology Officer, age 25. In the picture, her skin is the same glossy color as a chestnut fresh from its shell; but I remember it as dark honey, and I dream of the soft brown of her hand resting lightly on my forearm. Her smile is wide and bright. Around her throat she wears a neckerchief, white linen printed with a pattern of orange flowers. The flowers are chrysanthemums, totem flowers of my birthmonth. I nearly told her so when I helped her choose the neckerchief on our last recreation leave, but I decided to hold my tongue. It pleased me to have this secret link to her that even she did not realize.

The man on her right is Planetology Officer MolanDif, the same age as Chiala. In the hand dangling at his side, he holds the Unity regulation manual for missions exploring Earth-like environments. Harmony Team had completed three such assignments at the time the picture was taken, but MolanDif still consulted the manual regularly . . . not because he wanted to enforce the rules on his juniors but rather because he wanted to be sure of the rules himself. He was a man in constant need of specific instructions, of models to imitate. (His shirt is open low enough to reveal the steaming snout of a dragon tattooed on his chest. He once confessed to me he got that tattoo when he was a teenager; he had read somewhere that teenagers were supposed to do irrevocable things on impulse.)

The graying man on Chiala's left is Senior Orthodoxy Officer BarlDan, age 49. Me. My smile is self-conscious and clumsy—the skimmer pilot who took the picture for me ordered us to crowd together, and I was keenly aware of the solid warmth of Chiala's body pressing against my arm. (After the picture was taken, she did not move away from the contact. I was the one who withdrew to attend my duties.)

At one time, I could have named all the others in this picture. I still remember names, remember faces . . . but I become confused when I try to pair them. It panics me sometimes, the thought that I was supposed to safeguard all these souls, but now can't remember which man was the ceremonial castrato, which woman wore the mask of the Riven Tower. I think I know, yet I suspect I'm mistaken, that my memory rearranges itself when I sleep. I wake sometimes to find myself shouting at people who flee from me in my dreams.

The only other face I'm sure of is Junior Planetologist DiDeel, a young red-headed man grinning widely into the camera, his arm around the shoulder of the man beside him; and the only reason DiDeel retains a foothold in my mind is because he was the first to die. The others . . . dead too, officers, juniors, all dead, murdered in the fog, but I am losing them day by day and I cannot keep them with me.

In the extreme foreground of the picture, we have lined up our spirit masks. The masks are dormant, their inhabiting spirits forced into temporary exile by the brilliant sunlight. Their eyeholes are empty; they are merely constructions of paper and plastic, feather and foil.

Given a choice, I would have preferred not to take photographs of the masks; but some of the spirits were vain and demanded I take pictures of their mask-houses as often as possible. I complied, as I always complied with wishes of the masks. You cannot reason with a spirit.

Picture 2—*Chiala examining a Mutan statue:*

In the Mutan city within the fog, Chiala kneels at the base of a marble statue. She has arranged weak laser projectors to throw up a yellowy grid-work of cubes around the statue, each cube ten centimeters to the side. The statue is thus boxed into a phantom coordinate system that helps her make measurements.

The statue resembles others found all across the planet: a man-high figure that might be a lump of bread dough, surrounded by a surface that bristles with quills like those of a porcupine. The quills appear to be protrusions of internal bones, forming a type of articulated exoskeleton. The top of the body is clearly a head, with two widely spaced eyes, a cluster of nose-holes shielded by a thatch of quills, and a fully toothed mouth. No ears are visible.

This was our image of the beings who built the Mutan cities, though we did not know how accurately the statues depicted them. Perhaps Mutan art was not representational—perhaps we were seeing some abstract style that only marginally resembled the true Mutans, or it could be that all these statues were idols of some deity whose appearance was utterly unlike the people's. Perhaps they weren't statues at all; they might be signposts, or notice boards, or equipment for a game.

The Mutans had vanished centuries before the Unity discovered the planet. It had happened abruptly, without property damage—

a plague perhaps, a radiation disaster, or maybe mass suicide. The archeologists had many theories, but no evidence . . . only ruins, and a fog bank like a cloud of smoke after a great burning.

In the picture, Chiala holds a measuring tape to the pedestal that supports the statue. She has rolled up her sleeves. Some of the mist has condensed on her forearms, giving them a dark sheen, highlighting a line of sleek muscle from elbow to wrist. If I look at this picture too long, I find myself leaning forward to touch the viewer screen, to trace that line of muscle with my finger.

Chiala's eyes are on the work, not the camera. I approached her quietly through the fog; she didn't see me watching.

Picture 3—MolanDif's testing station on the Chastened River:

The picture is taken from the top of the bank looking down toward the water. Eight team members are in sight. Most are on shore, fussing with electronic instruments I cannot name. DiDeel wears hip-waders and stands in the water up to his thighs; he is far enough away to be nearly lost in the fog. He holds a metal pole that stretches out into the mist and disappears. My guess would be that he is scooping a water sample from the middle of the river, but for all I know, he could be fishing.

The group is attempting to locate evidence of volcanic hot springs in the riverbed. The senior planetologists, up in orbit with the colonists, hypothesized the fog bank was created by near-boiling water from springs mixing with near-freezing water running down from the Upward Potential mountains. No one found the hypothesis persuasive, but it offered a foundation for conducting tests until new data suggested something better.

MolanDif is on the far right of the picture, paddling an inflatable dinghy out of the upstream mists. The dinghy is filled with testing equipment. He holds the paddle awkwardly.

When he caught sight of me watching, he hailed me and pulled into shore. As I helped him out of the dinghy, he said, "Officer BarlDan, I'd like to consult with you."

"In my official capacity?" I asked.

"Of course," he said—seemingly surprised I might have an unofficial one. "When would be suitable?"

"I'm free now."

"Oh," he said. "Oh." He looked at the ground as if there might be something there needing his attention. "All right, then." He paused again. "This is a private matter."

"We'll walk along the river," I said.

The Mutans had paved a wide promenade along the top of the bank, running completely across the city. Potholes had developed in the asphalt here and there, and tough fungal growth was working up from below, cracking the surface into patterns like the glass in a smashed mirror; but walking was easy if you watched your step, and it provided a route away from the others without getting lost in the fog. We walked for some time in a silence overlaid with the background mutter of the river. I waited for MolanDif to begin.

"I have reached the age of twenty-five," he said at last.

I knew that; his birthday had passed while we were in stasis on the way to Muta, but Harmony Team had danced in his honor shortly after we woke up. MolanDif continued, "The social adjustment manual says twenty-five is the optimal age for marriage."

"To be precise," I said, "the manual says twenty-five is the median age at which a human being has reached a level of maturity consistent with the obligations of intimate social partnership. Not the same thing."

"Still," he said, "I believe I am ready for marriage. I . . . I'm not fulfilled being alone. I think it would be better to be married."

"Are you unhappy?" I asked.

"Oh no," he said quickly. "I'm quite well adjusted. To the situation. But I think . . . life could be *fuller,* you know? There's something . . ." He reached out with his hand and clutched an empty fist. "Life could be fuller," he repeated.

"Have you chosen a partner?"

"Chiala, of course," he answered, in a tone of surprise that I could consider any other alternative. "She's of equal rank. She's twenty-five."

"And she's beautiful," I said.

"Well, yes. But beauty . . . the manual says it's too shallow a reason for seeking marriage. Isn't it?"

"Yes," I said. "Yes, it is."

"Sexual attraction is an inadequate basis for dedicated partnership actualization. That's right in the manual. The manual stresses that feelings—you know, love . . ." His voice fell to near inaudibility on the word and he went on quickly. "Whatever you think you feel, it's only infatuation if you don't have a deeper basis for . . . for what you want. I'm not just infatuated with her, Barl-Dan. I have good deep reasons."

"She's of equal rank and she's twenty-five."

"Yes. You see how it makes sense?"

"Does it make sense to Chiala?" I asked.

"I couldn't possibly discuss it with her until you've cross-matched our personality profiles," he said. "If we aren't compatible in the eyes of the Unity . . . well, I couldn't pursue it, could I? I'd just . . . I couldn't pursue it. And if we *are* compatible, I'd have something to talk about with her. I could say the Unity officially thought we had a marriageability coefficient of ninety percent. Or whatever it turns out to be. You understand?"

"Yes," I said. "I understand. I'll do the calculations for you."

He thanked me hastily and headed back to the investigation site almost at a run.

I should have told him I wanted her for myself, that she was a dancing flame which could never burn bright enough fueled by his soggy wood. But how was I any different?

Picture 4—The interior of my hut, evening, first day within the fog:

The picture is taken from the doorway. All the usual amenities are present: cot, sink, desk, two chairs, chemical toilet, mask shrine. On the desk, a lamp glows at minimum brightness; there are plenty of shadows here. The only other light comes from the candles on the shrine and their reflections in the shrine's mirror.

The juniors who put up the hut for me have placed my shrine so the mask points toward the door. The face that was my second self looks almost directly into the camera. The eyes are not empty in this picture; they're filled with shadow. It's dusk and the mask is once again inhabited.

The mask belongs to the Hanged Prophet house. It is an adult male who calls himself ToPu. ToPu the Seer. ToPu the Abiding Observer. His umber papier-mâché face is runneled with crags that have been deepened using paint of blue and green. This shows age and therefore (so the theory goes) wisdom. But when the spirit of ToPu guided me to fashion his mask-home during my time of initiation, his hands were clumsy in affixing the garnet. The gem is centered properly on the forehead, but its setting is tipped to the left. Instead of facing outward, the capital facet looks ashamedly to one side.

For thirty-five years, this was what ToPu saw when he looked at himself in the mirror of my shrine: he saw he was flawed. His little gem, his humble soul, was forever set akilter. He felt this was the kind of seer he was—one who never looked in quite the right direction.

And, of course, ToPu's sadness infected my own life. However much I, BarlDan, progressed through victories or defeats, ToPu always shadowed me. I would sit before the mirror to don the mask (its interior smelling of paint, sweat, and resin) and in the moments that both BarlDan and ToPu shared my body, I would feel him tumbling down into heartsick shame at the sight of his face.

Whenever I regained consciousness at the end of the Dance of the Arcana, I would find that ToPu had been standing apart from the others, simply watching.

All these feelings return when I look at this picture and see ToPu's imperfect face staring sadly back. If I had set up my room myself, I would have angled the shrine away from the door—I had no need to remind myself of the awkward, earnest sharer of my soul. But I couldn't rearrange the furniture now: the juniors who set up the hut had seemed so proud of their work, I couldn't hurt their feelings.

Whenever I view this picture, I look at ToPu first, in order to save the most important detail for last. In the foreground, two chairs are turned to face each other. Draped over the back of the closer one is a white linen neckerchief printed with orange chrysanthemums.

Chiala left it behind after proposing marriage to me. It was her betrothal token. If I accepted her offer, I was to wear it so all the camp would know of our engagement. Otherwise, I was to return it discreetly to her hut and leave it lying across her pillow.

I planned to give back the neckerchief the next night. Sooner would insult her, as if I thought her easy to reject. But I had already rejected her in my own mind more than a dozen times since she joined Harmony Team, even while I talked with her, watched her with hungry eyes, touched her with feigned casualness and felt her touch me.

She told me she loved me because I was gentle, kind, and vulnerable; but analysis of her personality profile revealed she wanted a father figure who would absolve her from the responsibility of growing up. (I once dyed the gray in my hair, hoping she would be dazzled by a younger man. She was appalled I would want to look like some unseasoned junior.)

I felt I loved her because she was intelligent, beautiful, and so very alive; but in fact, I was immaturely hoping she would rescue me from a self-centered loneliness from which I was too weak to extricate myself. (On our nights of quiet sociability, it was always she who sought me out. I could never bring myself to believe she'd be happy to see me at her door.)

If we married, I thought, we would cling to each other too tightly, feeding on our weaknesses. We might be happy, but we would fold inward too much, dedicating ourselves to each other instead of the good of the Unity. In solitude, I had calculated our social coefficients many times before: love high, but social desirability just inside the bounds of legality. As Orthodoxy Officer, I could not give my approval.

Instead, I savored an aging coward's self-indulgent melancholy as I oh so carefully calculated the social coefficients for MolanDif and Chiala. The ratings were no worse with him than with me; better on some scales. The two would never love each other, but they would make it work, without letting it interfere in their pursuit of the greater good.

I told myself my duty was clear.

Still, I took this picture of the neckerchief so I could always remind myself that Chiala had once asked.

Picture 5—*Harmony Team singing around a campfire, first evening of the mission:*

The campfire roars high. It is a volcanic island of light, ringed by a lagoon of fog, enclosed in an ocean of blackness. The fire has been built inside a cracked concrete dish in the same park as the sundial; an archeologist conjectured the dish was a reflecting pool in the days of Mutan civilization. It is surrounded by what seem to be low marble benches, but benches built for Mutan anatomy. Their tops resemble narrow U-shaped troughs.

The members of Harmony Team lounge on the benches in a variety of postures. Only Chiala looks comfortable. She sits with both legs tucked beneath her, hands in her lap. Her mouth is open wide and her head is tilted back for greater singing volume.

She was a terrible singer. She was, in fact, tone-deaf. The notes she bawled so lustily bore no relationship to the tune the others sang. Chiala didn't care. Perhaps she didn't know—who would tell her? In an odd way, her handicap endeared her to the team, bringing her down from the heights of perfection and making her just a bit pitiable.

MolanDif sits awkwardly beside Chiala, his rump at the bottom of the trough, his legs dangling over the edge. The flames tint his face a jaundiced shade of orange. He is not singing; as I remember that night, he was barely breathing, hovering at Chiala's side all evening but struck speechless by the enormity of what he wanted to say.

From the angle I took this picture, I cannot tell if his thigh is touching her knee. Some nights I think yes, some nights I think no.

A number of team members appear to be in the Arcana trance already. The youth who beats the drum is clearly there. His glassy eyes stare blindly into the fire; his body is slack, though his arms continue to pound out the rhythms of attuning. The harpist too straddles the boundary between our world and the spirits'. Her shirt hangs open to bare the perspiration-slick boniness of her chest. A reflection of flame dances on her moist skin.

Picture 6—Dance of the Arcana, first night of the mission:

The picture shows a bare patch of dirt, not far from the campfire site. Candles are laid out on the ground in a spoked wheel around a silvery mirror-ball at the hub. The candles do not dispel the mist as the campfire did, though they force back the darkness a few paces. Fog wraps and obscures the dancers, in lieu of the clothing they have shed.

Chiala's mask-self dances proud and beautiful in the foreground. When she proposed, Chiala gave me the name of her mask: Lilijel. Lilijel the Sun-Child. Lilijel the Jewel. Her face is beaten gold, a mask of the Laughing Sun, lacquered black except for the rims of the eyes and a burnished band around the outer edge. The gem in Lilijel's forehead is a topaz, and it is set perfectly straight.

Lilijel dances, prances, alone. The picture captures her mid-leap, front leg bent, back leg straight. Her jump has such strength that her muscles stand out with sharp definition even in the fog. She throws her arms straining wide above her head. There is something about her that frightens me, a potential for cruelty in her self-absorption. She is always exultant, always alone. It is inconceivable she would deign to dance with an ungainly old man.

Behind Lilijel, MolanDif stands wearing his mask. The mask belongs to the house of the Worldly Cleric, black cloth embellished with spiraling traceries of silver thread. His gem, of course, is a diamond. In the picture, MolanDif prepares to leap in imitation of Lilijel.

It is clear MolanDif is himself . . . not in trance, not possessed by the mask. The fact is evident in the way he stands—self-conscious, a wary, soul-cluttered man attempting to imitate masks who are as simple as children. Lilijel jumps and he follows like a shadow.

The doctrines of the Unity accept such people as they are. It is simply another sort of disability, like being unable to sing. Men and women who cannot lose themselves are as much a part of the orthodoxy as those who fall into trance effortlessly; they just don't know it. They torment themselves each night at the dance, watching the spontaneity of the others and guiltily going through the motions.

Not so different from ToPu, though ToPu was a true mask—less a wooden adult and more a sober child.

ToPu took this picture. He often played with my camera while the other masks danced. Only a few of his concrete memories ever leaked into my mind; one is the image of him standing apart from the dance, using the camera to click shot after shot of the other dancers.

In some way, ToPu believed his watching protected the other mask-spirits—that they would wisp away to nothingness if someone didn't remove himself from the revelries and look on from the sidelines. If no one watched, the dance was random capering, dissipative frenzy . . . a meaningless hell. Someone had to see how a mask drew pictures in the dirt, someone had to hear it sing nonsense syllables to a stone. Being watched made it all real; taking pictures kept them safe.

There was seldom any logic in the pictures he took. When I put the diskette into the viewer on the morning after a dance, I might see a close-up of someone's hand, or a badly framed tangle of copulating bodies. I don't know if ToPu even understood what the camera did, for he never learned how to advance the diskette from shot to shot—each new shot overwrote the previous one, so only the last shot of the night was preserved.

But ToPu didn't care about preserving pictures; he only cared about watching. The camera was a watching machine, and watching was ToPu's duty.

Picture 7—The death of Junior Planetologist DiDeel, during the Dance of the Arcana:

I took this picture moments after waking from the trance. I believe ToPu saw the horror begin and surrendered the body to me prematurely, in the hope BarlDan could cope with something ToPu could not.

I did not understand. I awoke sluggish, my mask beside me, my camera in hand. When I saw what was happening to DiDeel, my first reaction was to snap a picture, thinking I was seeing some re-markable atmospheric phenomenon.

The picture shows DiDeel frozen in the moment of transition from mask-self back to man. His mask belongs to the house of the Blind Priestess, an eyeless shell of pearly plastic with a wig of blended human hair reaching the ground in a blond-brown-red-black tumble. The mask is pushed far enough back on DiDeel's forehead that the man's mouth is uncovered. The mouth is open wide. He appears to be screaming.

That is what the camera recorded; but what my eyes saw was a stream of creamy mist pouring from his mouth like smoke belched by a fire-eater. The mist pierced the surrounding fog and sent it billowing outward in ripple after ripple. DiDeel made no sound but a choked crooning in his throat, like a heartsick child hum-ming itself a lullaby.

All this . . . and my first reaction was merely to snap a picture. I found the sight odd but not disturbing, as if I were a four-year-old watching a favorite uncle do a magic trick. Accepting it all; almost absorbed. But when I look again at the picture, I cannot blind myself to DiDeel's agony. His body is bent backward as if some invisible as-sailant has wrapped one arm around his waist and is pressing the other hand on his sternum, pushing with full strength in an attempt to snap DiDeel's spine. The man is held impossibly off balance, screaming without noise, the hair of his mask dragging in the dirt.

Yet in the moments after waking, I had a lingering feeling this was very right: that I should want the same for myself.

DiDeel's body wavered in that pose for one second, two sec-onds, three, then jerked twice with the force of whipcracks. He heeled backward, striking the ground hard enough to scuff up a cloud of dust, and lay there as limp as his hair.

It was only then I put down the camera. I started shaking and couldn't stop.

A few of the masks came to look at the fallen body. Lilijel poked it with her finger once, then a second time much harder. I had to shout at her to go away and leave DiDeel alone.

Mask spirits almost never understand death.

Picture 8—Campfire, second night of the mission:

A jump forward in time . . . but I was too busy to take pictures during the day after DiDeel's death. There were reports to file. There were morale restoration activities to run: a group contact experience in the morning, a unification dialogue at lunch, grief counseling sessions all afternoon. My hardest duty was calling my superiors in orbit, formally asking them to quarantine Muta until we determined the cause of DiDeel's death. If this was some kind of disease, we could not risk infecting the main body of the task force. The mother ship offered to send us robots, medicines, any equipment we might need; but what could I ask for?

The picture around the campfire shows the team at the end of the day: haggard, subdued. Our Senior Medical Officer leans against the shoulder of the man beside her; her eyes are half closed. She has not slept except for a three-hour nap I ordered her to take before supper. For the rest of the time, she and her junior have tried to determine why DiDeel died. No success.

Many of the other team members also show signs of exhaustion. No one slept well. DiDeel was popular, respected for his exceptional openness and generosity to all; his death struck hard. The majority of those around the fire simply stare into the flames, their expressions somber. The camera has caught one junior in the process of glancing over his shoulder into the fog.

The fog is thicker than the previous night. It crowds around us hungrily.

Chiala and MolanDif sit in almost the same positions as before. She is not singing—no one is singing—but she is speaking intensely to him, punctuating her words with a sharp gesture of her hands.

The neckerchief is around her throat.

I intended to take it to her hut and leave quickly without being seen . . . but the hut was full of her, the smell of her hair, a book she'd been reading, the imprint in the blankets where she recently sat on the edge of her cot. As I laid the neckerchief across the pillow I could smell her everywhere—on her pillow, the linen, the talismans dangling from the headboard. A chocolate-brown dress jacket was thrown across the top of her storage trunk; the sight of it brought back memories of her wearing it at celebration dinners, her eyes meeting mine as we drank from a shared chalice, her eyes, her skin, her skin the color of the jacket, her eyes . . . not one of these photos truly shows her eyes, not the way I want to remember them, how full they were with warmth and heat and fire. And my memory is slippery—in embarrassment and fear, it shies away from recalling the intensity of her gaze. I can see Chiala's face, but I can't look into her eyes.

She found me in her hut. I don't know how long I'd been standing there. The neckerchief was in my hands, though I don't remember picking it up again. When I laid it down a second time, smoothing it out on the pillow, she asked why.

I had a speech prepared—not that I'd planned to recite it to her. I'd constructed it for my own benefit, putting the issues into well-chosen words supposedly showing the wisdom of my decision. In the naked light of her eyes, the words and wisdom shattered. I could say nothing more than "I'm sorry, I can't, not me" as I fled the hut.

The words of my rehearsed rationalizations came back like shouting ghosts as I retreated to my hut through the fog. "I love you so much I can't *see* you. I see your face, that's all. All I know of you is fragments—the warmth of your body, the smoothness of your bare shoulder, your off-key singing. I can't glue the fragments into a real woman. I'm blinded by love, I can't see, what am I loving but a voice, a perfume, the imagined kiss of your skin?"

The ghost words haunt me today as I view my photos and pretend I've left my past behind. Like all ghosts, words are liars. I chose loneliness because it was familiar and safe.

Even cowards find themselves facing the truth eventually. They just do it too late.

Picture 9—Fog:

It was my duty to ensure that the Dance proceeded as normal. All the morale-building exercises of the day would be wasted if we didn't fulfill the Arcana. Every person on the team had danced each night since his or her initiation; to skip the ritual now would completely unhinge them. It was bad enough we had to dance without the circle full. MolanDif kept asking, "Can we do this with only twenty-one houses? Isn't it against the rules?"

We lit the candles in the dance wheel and set up the mirror-ball at the hub. The drummer drummed, the harpist played, the masks inhabited us (except for MolanDif). ToPu took his pictures, earnestly trying to keep the others safe . . . I have his memory of that. I do not have his memories of Lilijel if he saw her that night. Sometimes I wonder if she pranced the same as ever, or if Chiala's feelings about my rejection infected her. Was she struck quiet, or moved to fiercer abandonment? The only picture recording that dance is this picture of fog.

I woke but did not waken; and the fog was inside me. I was BarlDan and ToPu, both—brothers who shared the same eyes. The eyes looked out on fog, bright fog lying before me like the softest of beds, glowing golden. It beckoned with a force stronger than any I had felt in the most sacred rites. "Dance," a voice said, and the voice was a billion voices. "Join. Dance."

The fog swirled in serene billows before my eyes. In the distance I heard drums and harps. The voices sang softly, their song achingly sweet. "Dance. Join. Sing together." I felt tranquillity in the fog, and peace. Love, uncomplicated love, never fading. "Dance. Now. You can see us. Now. Join. Sing." It would be so easy to surrender. Simply falling into bliss.

ToPu shook his head. I could feel his sad, lonely longing, but he knew his duty didn't let him join the dance, ever. I felt the same wild yearning to accept, but I too drew back from the fog. I'd resisted my love for Chiala—by comparison, this resistance was nothing.

I took a step away from the fog, from the choir that sang within it. Screeching with sudden outrage, the placid wisps of fog twisted in anger and locked into a hard churning wall the color and height of a thunderhead. Tentacles erupted from that wall, meaty pseudopods caged within quill-like bones, glistening wet and yellow, smelling of rotten fruit. They grabbed at me, trying to wrap around my arms and legs, and I pulled away with all my strength, feeling them slide suckingly off my flesh, slimy as eels.

I had almost dragged myself clear when a human hand burst out of the blackening fog-wall and clamped around my wrist. The fingers were long and muscular, clenched like claws. It did not try to pull me into the cloud, but its grip was iron; I couldn't wrench it loose. Desperately, I grabbed my trapped wrist with my free hand, and using the strength of both arms heaved backwards. My captor held on; and as I tugged, the rest of my captor's arm emerged from black fog, then his head—a head with DiDeel's face but blanched of color, the eyes sewn shut like a corpse's, the mouth screaming wide. Sweat-slick hair plastered the sides of his face, hair of all shades, the hair of the Priestess. Mask-spirit and man had been crushed into one, like two colors of putty squeezed into a formless lump by a clenching fist. For a moment I stared at the ghastly face; then pseudopods wrapped around the head and smothered it back into the fog. The hand around my wrist went limp, fell away . . . and I found myself lying on damp earth, night fog clotting powerlessly around me. My mask lay faceup by my side.

In all directions, I heard the same choking crooning DiDeel made before he died. I recognized the tune—the song the fog had sung in my brain. Harmony Team was being absorbed, just as DiDeel had been . . . just as the Mutans must have been, all those quilled pseudopods in the cloud. Some horror was unleashed here long ago, perhaps a grand experiment to unify the spirits of the people; and soul by soul, the horror had devoured the planet. The entire fog bank was a single ghost . . . or rather a billion ghosts trapped in a hellish union that had consumed them all.

Out in the fog, one voice lifted above the rest: tone-deaf Chiala, not yet in tune with the crooning mass. I staggered to my feet and followed the sound, hearing her voice twist angrily as it tried to find the right notes to join the song. She was still off-key, but as I searched I heard her growing closer and closer to the tune the others sang.

When I reached her, MolanDif was already there, cradling her body in his arms. "What's wrong with her?" he cried when he saw me. Without answering, I pulled off her mask and threw it aside. Her face was slack, still deep in trance. I shook her shoulders and slapped her cheek, rousing her enough that she opened her eyes . . . but the eyes were still vacant and the humming in her throat went on.

"Get her to the mirror," I ordered MolanDif, and he was so grateful to be told what to do, he asked no questions. Together we dragged her body to the ball at the hub of the dance wheel and propped her up so she could see her face. "Your name is Chiala," I shouted in her ear. "Chiala. Chiala. Chiala."

Her eyes focused and saw. She gasped and threw her arms outward to steady herself against the sphere. The fog condensed where her hands touched the mirror, making misty silhouettes like ghosts. She blinked and looked wonderingly at her beautiful face.

Her humming stopped. "Chiala," she said.

Picture 10—A bend in the Chastened River:

It's the afternoon of the next day. There is no fog here. The land is a sunny meadow, buttery with summer wildflowers. The river's edge is stockaded by rushes. Chiala, MolanDif, and I have paddled the dinghy many hours downstream. We emerged from the fog bank around midday, but kept going until we were well clear.

The rest of Harmony Team is dead. I tried to save them, but failed. Before they died, a few possessed team members smashed our communication equipment. We are now truly on our own.

We carry maps and aerial photographs that indicate it's a four-day trip to the sea. A few rapids might force portages along the way, but the journey doesn't look difficult. From the mouth of the river, another two days up the coast leads to one of the planned sites of colonization, and there we should find a cache that contains working communicators.

In the picture, MolanDif and Chiala cook supper over a campfire. They believe I'm still gathering firewood, but I've already collected what we'll need for the night. I have concealed myself in a thicket to take this picture and watch the two of them hover over the pots.

In this shot, their knees are definitely touching.

Picture 11—Chiala by the fire:

She holds her mask in both hands, frozen in the moment of raising it to her face. Her head is twisted slightly toward the camera; she must have heard something as I focused the lens, and turned to look at me. Behind her, the sky is a sheet of deepening indigo spreading over the dark meadows. A clump of trees stands silhouetted on the horizon.

I took this picture to distract Chiala, to interrupt that motion of donning the mask. The click, the flash.

"Why did you do that?" she asked.

"You shouldn't tonight," I told her. "The trance opens us too wide. To the fog. Opening yourself to the mask—it's too risky. The fog wasn't strong enough to take us when we were ourselves, not even when we were asleep. Only in trance. Please, Chiala, leave the mask."

She looked at me steadily for several seconds. Half her face was lit with the sun-yellow blaze of the fire, the other half cloaked with shadow. "You have nothing to say to me about taking risks," she said. Very deliberately, she pulled the mask over her face.

"It should be safe," MolanDif said from across the fire. "The fog is a long way behind us." Self-consciously, glancing sideways at Chiala for her approval, he put on his own mask.

Chiala began drumming on her knees. I watched her strong hands rise and fall.

Picture 12—*A night view looking upstream over the Chastened River:*

Track the image from foreground to background: the dark water flowing over outjuts of black rock; reflections of two of Muta's moons farther upriver, rippled smears of red and silver; the dark fields rising to rolling hills; the night sky gaudy with stars.

Stretching across half the river valley is a churning wall of fog as high as the eye can see. It approaches with the speed of a summer windstorm.

I took this picture while standing alone on the riverbank, grass whipping my legs with the force of the oncoming gale. Chiala and MolanDif had fled downstream in the dinghy. Chiala was still half in trance as I helped them push off, MolanDif chanting, "You are Chiala, you are Chiala," with each awkward stroke of his paddle.

They could not travel as fast as the cloud.

I stood between them and the ghosts like a brave man, wrapping myself in an armor of unconvincing hopes. I hoped the mist would not pursue my companions until it had dealt with me; I hoped I could escape it as I escaped before; even if it consumed me, I hoped I could resist long enough for the others to get away.

And I hoped if they did get away, Chiala would realize that I *did* take a risk, when it was too late for anything else.

I set my camera down carefully and picked up my mask. If I was to be bait, I had to make myself tempting. I donned ToPu's face and opened myself to him.

Picture 13—My face in terror:

ToPu arrived immediately. He inhabited my body but my consciousness remained awake, watching everything. Perhaps it was ToPu's choice to keep me with him; perhaps our previous confrontation with the fog had realigned our spirits somehow, allowing us to coexist in the same body. I don't know. I only know we stood together as the fog descended upon us.

Through ToPu's spirit eyes, I saw past the physical aspect of the fog and into another plane—a plane of ghosts where a great agglomerate creature rippled and shimmered around us. Heads erupted from its writhing mass and were dragged screaming back inside; pseudopods and arms snaked out of control, scrabbling at the ground, never gaining purchase. From deep within the creature came a ceaseless frenzy of moaning, surging in pulses like ocean waves.

ToPu picked up the camera and began shooting picture after picture of the swallowed souls. Tears ran down his face. It was all he could do for them—watch and let them know he watched.

The fog seethed; the thing that was the fog convulsed around us. Something grabbed ToPu's arm, then his leg, then wrapped around his head. With one great heave, he was ripped away from me, as if my own body were torn in two. The fog clutched both of us in its grip, and for a single moment in our lives, ToPu and I saw each other face-to-face. He was not just a mask now but a complete spirit, a wrinkled man in shabby clothes, held spread-eagled before me. Our eyes met; and in his face I saw what he had never known, that he *was* wise despite all his fear and doubt. Then, with agonizing effort, he yanked himself free of the fog, arms and pseudopods sliding away from him. He raised the camera and clicked this picture of me.

In that instant, my vision of the ghost-world collapsed like a bubble popping, and my eyes returned to the physical plane.

The fog surrounded me, a rolling night fog that blotted all sight. It seemed too thick to let me breathe. Panic took me and I ran blindly, tripping on uneven ground, picking myself up and running on. Brambles tore at my uniform; my shoulder struck an unseen tree, and I spun away, pain scissoring down my arm. Suddenly there was nothing under my feet and I was tumbling downward, striking the river with a splash that sent warm water stinging up my nose. I swam a few weak strokes, bumped against a rock, and clung to it, panting. Water flowed gurgling around me, while overhead the ghost fog roared.

Picture 14—ToPu:

It took me three days to find my camera in the mist. It was scratched but undamaged. Nearby I found the remains of ToPu.

The picture shows the mask lodged on a bramble bush. Branches of bramble protrude through the eyeholes and the mouth. The papier-mâché of the face has been dented and ripped in numerous places. The garnet and its setting are gone.

Scattered on the ground around ToPu's bush are the other masks—the rest of the full Arcana, Lilijel and MolanDif's mask among them. Their eyeholes all stare at ToPu, like an audience gathered to hear a speaker. Their gems are missing, but the masks are otherwise undamaged.

They must have been carried here by the fog cloud, then released. I like to believe the mask-spirits and their human hosts were released too. Perhaps they proved incompatible with the Mu-tan ghosts and could not truly meld with the whole; but I prefer to think ToPu saved them. Within the cloud, he located each familiar soul, watched it, took its picture, freed it by making it real.

That is what I tell myself. That is my mythology.

The gems are gone, and the mask-spirits departed. Lilijel will not dance on this physical plane again.

I dream that Chiala and MolanDif survived. Though I searched the length of the river, I did not find their bodies or the dinghy. The fog stayed thick about me, angry that my soul was closed to it forever; but despite the fog, I think I would have found Chiala's body if it were there.

Picture 15—The sundial:

I took this picture earlier today. I won't tag it for preservation like the others. It's better to go to the park and see the sundial for myself. I'm a man who should remind himself of the realness of things.

I came back to this city because the huts are here and all our supplies. The fog followed me back . . . or perhaps it never left. I think it will stay with me wherever I go.

The task force has surely left orbit by now and headed for a new planet. The universe is too rich in worlds for them to trouble with Muta. No colony would ever be safe here, unless they aban-doned their masks and the dance. That is a price they will not pay.

The ghost fog swirls around me but its attempts to consume me are futile. My link to the spirit world is gone. If I want to com-mune with ghosts, all I can do is talk.

Are you listening to me, fog?

I've hated you a long time, hated you for the murders and my banishment here. But the loss that hurt me most was none of your doing. And the souls trapped inside you . . . I can't help thinking of them as people like me, though I know Mutans are alien, non-human. Maybe to them, being part of this undifferentiated mass is heaven; but I can't help thinking it's hell.

I've decided to do something, fog. I've failed to take action so often in my life, there aren't many options left for me. But I can still watch. I can still try to see, really see, the souls you've swallowed. They may nearly have forgotten the people they once were, but I think they can remember. If they try. If I try.

I'm watching. I know it's not much, but it's something. I'm watching.

Picture 16—Fog.

Picture 17—Fog.

Picture 18—Fog.

Hardware Scenario G-49

There are few human beings who would not fit into a box eight feet long, four feet wide, and four feet high. Construct such boxes. Wire them, pipe them, tube them to provide even temperature, nutrition, and air. Don't forget sluices for the elimination of waste. Do something about exhaled carbon dioxide. Come up with neural inhibitors to prevent movement and sensation. Install epidermal scrapers to remove skin as it flakes off. Add whatever else seems required.

Properly containerized, the entire population of Earth will fit into a cube about a mile and a half on each side. Put the whole thing into orbit? Nah, that's just showing off. Leave it on the ground in a desert somewhere.

Why? So everyone stays healthy and happy, of course. No walking around and stubbing your toes. No catching colds when someone sneezes on you. No smoking or drinking or eating fatty foods. Life lasts a lot longer when you live it in a box.

Quit asking such obvious questions . . . the Facility is run by *robots,* of course. As are the hydroponic gardens, the recycling plant, and all the other life-support equipment. (These are really *good* robots.) And the robots are supervised by highly skilled, politically neutral, psychologically stable human support personnel.

Give the designers a break, for crying out loud. They thought of *everything,* okay? This isn't that kind of story.

This is the kind of story where everyone does astral projection.

George Munroe sat in his hardware store wondering why there were so many types of nails. He had forty little bins in front of him, and each contained nails that were different from all the rest. He pulled out a one-inch finishing nail and a three-quarter-inch finishing nail. (His astral projection could pick up light objects if he concentrated really hard.) When you got right down to it, what was the difference between the two nails? A quarter of an inch. That's all. But one nail had to go in one bin and the other had to go in a different bin. That was the only professional way.

Running a hardware store sure was a precision business. George knew he could send his astral projection anywhere in the world to indulge in any lifestyle scenario, but hardware had such a depth and richness of scope, George didn't think he'd ever have time for more.

The bell on the front door of the shop tinkled. George looked up from the nail bins to see a woman, six and a half feet tall, posing beside the lawnware display. Her hair flowed thick and tawny, rippling in the ether wind; her skin was bronzed and flawless, tautly stretched over firm young muscles; her face shone with self-assurance. She wore the sleek skin of a black panther, cut into a maillot that left one breast bare, and around her waist was a cinch made of cobra skulls. In one hand she held an ivory spear, and in the other a dagger made of teak.

"I am Diana, Goddess of the Hunt," she announced. She had an announcing kind of voice.

"What can I get for you today?" George asked. "I'm having a special on nails."

"You are George Munroe?"

"Yes."

"Then rejoice, for Destiny has decreed we are to be mated!" She threw aside her spear and dagger with a sweeping gesture. George winced as the dagger headed for a shelf of lightbulbs, but Diana's weapons were only illusory astral props for her persona; they vanished as soon as they left the field of her aura. With cheetahlike grace, Diana strode down the home appliance aisle, seized George by the lapels of his Handee Hardware blazer, and hauled him up to her lips.

George had never imagined that tongues could be involved in kissing. In movie kisses, you never saw what the actors did with their tongues—it was one of the limitations of the medium. George wondered if it made movie directors sad that they could only show the outside of a kiss. There certainly seemed to be a lot of action happening on the inside.

Abruptly, Diana let him go. Turning her perfect chin away from him, she said, "I don't think you're trying."

"Trying what?"

"To love me. Destiny has decreed we are to be mated. At least you could try to generate some electricity for me."

George's store carried flashlight batteries, but he was almost certain she had something different in mind. "Is this some mythological scenario?" he asked. "Because it's nice of you to kiss me and all, but right now I'm happy with the small-town hardware business, and I don't feel the urge to play god. Sorry."

"This is not a scenario!" Diana shouted. The spear rematerialized in her left hand and purple sparks crackled from the tip. "I'm talking about real life. My body. Your body. Egg and sperm. Two become one, then three. Computer analysis at the Population Storage Facility says we complement each other genetically and are ideal progenitors for the future of humanity. Well, at least for one new baby anyway. I'm scheduled to be impregnated by you within twenty-four hours."

George felt himself growing faint; with an effort of will, he brought himself back to full visibility and tried to consider the situation rationally. He'd always known the Facility couldn't keep physical bodies alive forever. People died; presumably they had to be replaced. Somehow, though, he'd thought science would come up with a more impersonal way to create new life. Like cloning. Why did scientists always talk about cloning if they didn't really do it? It was disappointing the next generation apparently came from what amounted to arranged marriages.

"I'm sorry," George said. "I didn't understand what you were talking about."

"The fathers are always the last to know. That's one of the sacred traditions the robots are programmed to observe."

"They're really good robots, aren't they?" George said.

"They sure are," Diana agreed with a warm smile.

George nodded, then kept nodding in lieu of speaking. He wondered if Diana was expecting to make love with him in the near future. Astral bodies could make love, of course; astral bodies could interact with each other in any way physical ones could. But George had watched people making love in a lot of movies, and the hardware store didn't seem suited for that sort of thing. To get a soft place to lie down, they'd have to make a bed out of bags of grass seed, or find some way to arrange themselves on one of the lawn recliners.

On the other hand, he couldn't quite see why making love was necessary. "They're just going to use our physical bodies for this, right?" he asked.

"Right."

"So I guess they'll, umm, collect my sperm and use it to impregnate you, right? And if it's like everything else they do to our physical bodies, neither of us will feel a thing. Isn't that how it works?"

"Yes."

"Then I don't understand why you're here. It affects our bodies but not our lives. I mean our astral lives. You know what I mean. It just happens, no matter what we do. I can't see any reason for us to, uhh, interact."

"You cold-hearted bastard," she said. Her hair tossed wildly as if buffeted by a tornado; the cobra skulls in her belt hissed and snapped. Her skin turned scarlet, her pupils crimson, her lips black. "Do you think parenting is a mere physical act?" she shouted in a voice like an earthquake doing ventriloquism. "Do you believe love is irrelevant? Do you deny the importance of a nurturing psychic aura in the formation of human life? Do you want our child to usher forth from a joyless womb?"

George hadn't really thought about it.

Given that he'd been living as a psychic phenomenon for twenty-six years, he supposed he wasn't entitled to doubt the importance of psychic auras. Parental attitude at conception probably did make a difference—if Diana conceived a child in her current mood, the baby might turn out kind of cranky. (A cobra on her belt spat venom in George's direction; the astral fluid fell into a bucket of plastic fishing lures and vanished.)

Was conception the only crucial moment for the baby? No, George had heard prenatal influences could affect the child all through pregnancy. And after that, who raised the infant? The robots, of course; but could they provide a nurturing psychic aura in the child's formative years? Probably . . . they were really good robots. But just in case, George figured he shouldn't make any long-term plans.

It was an imposition on his life . . . but then, it was an imposition on Diana's life too. She was obviously devoted to the goddess scenario—she probably lived in a marble palace on a mountainside with lots of other divinities, doing all kinds of divinity things.

It must be a real letdown for her to be mated to a storekeeper, even a hardware storekeeper. If she was prepared to make such a sacrifice for their child, George should be too.

"I'm sorry," he said to her. "I was being selfish. We can, uhh, get married. Or whatever you think is right."

Slowly her body returned to its previous coloration. The cobra skulls gave a peevish-sounding sniff in unison, then went back to being dead. "All right," she said. "Apology accepted. Diana is a strict goddess, but fair."

"What do we do now?" George asked.

"We learn to love each other."

George had watched a few couples courting in his town, and he thought they should try the same sort of thing: an arm-in-arm walk down to the ice cream parlor. With Diana at her present height, that was easier said than done. Graciously, she assumed a persona no taller than George—a trim lynx-woman with two-inch talons and a pelt of stiff brown fur. George recognized her new body from a collection of clip-art personas published the year before. He'd chosen his own appearance from the same book— Kindly Shopkeeper with a Twinkle in His Eye, #4.

People on Main Street stared as they walked by, but showed the kind of small-town courtesy George had known they would. "Well, George, got a new friend, I see. Oh, she's your mate. Well, well. Pleased to meet you, missus. A goddess! Well, George, she's a catch, all right. How long are you going to keep that special on nails?"

At the ice cream parlor, the robot attendant served them two strawberry sundaes. George didn't try to eat his—lifting a spoonful of ice cream took a lot of concentration, and when he put it into his mouth, it would fall right through his astral body anyway. George preferred to watch it all melt into a smooth white cream with swirls of strawberry—it reminded him of paint, just after you add a slurp of red colorizer to the white base, before you put it on the mixing machine and let it shake itself pink.

Diana, on the other hand, dug into the ice cream immediately. "This is a pleasant town," she said to George as she inserted a spoonful into her mouth. George heard a liquidy plop as the ice cream fell through her and landed on her chair. "Of course, the town is quiet for my tastes. But it has potential. I have a friend who does werewolves and he could really liven up the place. You know, lurk on the outskirts, savage a few locals from time to time. Not hurt them for *real,* of course, just scare them and make them promise to go to another scenario for a while. But as people began to disappear, as the town devolved into a panicky powder keg waiting to explode in an orgy of hysterical butchery, you and I could hunt down the monster and kill it. Wouldn't that be fun?"

It didn't quite match George's notion of why his neighbors were living in the small-town scenario, but he knew he could be wrong. He went to a lot of movies. He knew that small towns were full of people just *waiting* to stir up a bloodbath.

Dirty Ernie Birney came into the ice cream parlor just as George and Diana were finishing up. George shuddered; Dirty Ernie was not the sort of person anyone wanted to meet on a date. The older folks in town said Ernie was at least thirty-five, but he wore the persona of a rotten little eight-year-old. He was foul-mouthed, brattish, whiny, and persistent. George grabbed Diana's furry elbow and said, "Let's get out of here."

As she stood up, Dirty Ernie whistled and pointed at her chair. "Hey, lady," he said, "looks like you pooped a pile of ice cream."

Diana moved so fast George's eyes could scarcely track her. Slash, gash, and Ernie's astral arm was nothing but tattered ectoplasm. The boy howled and bolted out the door, the ribboned flaps of his arm trailing after him like red plastic streamers on bike handles.

"You shouldn't have done that," George said. He thought there was a chance he might throw up, if astral projections could do such a thing.

"He can fix his arm any time," Diana said. "It's just like assuming a new persona."

"Yes, but . . ."

"Well, I couldn't let him insult me. I'm a goddess, for heaven's sake! Rotten little prick. In a *proper* scenario, he'd know his place."

George took Diana by the hand and led her back to the hardware store. He could tell that while they were learning to love each other, it would be a good idea to leave town.

They leaned on the store's front counter and looked at the latest catalog of available scenarios. Diana was only interested in the heroic ones. She swore if she could watch George rescue her from a dragon, she would fall hopelessly in love with him. George was beginning to suspect his new bride had a pretty narrow range of interests . . . but then, newlyweds had to learn to accept each other for what they were.

When Diana had chosen a scenario, George called to Benny, his robot stockboy, who was down in the basement rearranging the plumbing supplies. (Benny did all the physical work around the store. He loved hauling around boxes and often restacked the entire storeroom out of sheer high spirits.) George told Benny he was going away with Diana for a few days and Benny would be in charge of the store. The robot bounced about in a little circle and piddled machine oil in his excitement. George couldn't tell if Benny was excited because he'd be running the store or because George was acquiring a mate. Probably both. Benny's way of thinking ran the same direction as George's on a lot of things.

For George, the best part of assuming the persona of a knight was designing the coat of arms. He decided on a hammer and screwdriver rampant, argent sur azure. His motto was, "Ferrum meum spectari": My Iron Stands the Test. Diana said she approved of the sentiment.

Of course, Diana was now captive in the highest tower of a castle overlooking the Rhine. It was the stronghold of the unspeakable Wilhelm von Schmutzig, sorcerer, murderer, ravisher, and author of six pornographic trilogies about elves. A dragon prowled the castle courtyard; mercenaries patrolled the halls. Rumor claimed that diabolical experiments were even now reaching fruition in the castle's dungeons and soon a horde of . . . of . . . (George pulled the brochure from his saddlebag to refresh his memory) a horde of disease-bearing zombies would be released on a helpless world. Only one man, the brave Sir Your-Name-Here could avert the onrushing tide of destruction.

George asked his horse how much farther it was to the castle.

"Just around the bend," the horse said. It was the astral persona of a man named Hawkins who heartily enjoyed the equine life. "You get to be really *big*," Hawkins had said. "You can rear up on your hind legs and scare people. You get to eat grass." Hawkins had been doing knightly steeds for years and never tired of the role. He'd told George that sometimes he moonlighted as a Cape buffalo, but it wasn't his first love.

Hawkins stopped at the bend and let George scout ahead. Skulking wasn't easy in full plate mail, but the forest was thick on both sides of the road so there was little chance of being seen.

The walls around the castle were high and thick, the moat deep and foul-smelling even at this distance. The drawbridge was up, the portcullis down, and frankly, the place looked impregnable.

George considered breaking the seal on the scenario's Hint Booklet. Back at the Population Storage Facility, the robots might impregnate Diana any time now; if George was too slow in winning her love, all would be lost. On the other hand, would Diana love him when she saw he'd looked at the hints? (George was certain she'd check.) No, she would view him as a cheater and a cad, and their baby would probably grow up to be a lawyer.

George clanked up against a tree to think. If this was a movie, what would the hero do?

"Halloo, the castle!"

A mercenary's head looked down on George from one of those little slots castles have instead of real windows. George was once again wearing his red Handee Hardware blazer, and Hawkins had acquired a Handee Hardware saddle blanket. "What do you want?" the mercenary asked.

"I'm just a poor peasant merchant and I have a delivery for the Lord von Schmutzig."

"What kind of delivery?"

"Nails," said George. "Three-quarter-inch finishing nails for the final assembly of the horde of disease-bearing zombies."

"Nobody told me anything about nails," the mercenary said. "Last night at cocktails, the lord said he had everything he needed to complete his evil zombie horde."

"Some fool delivered one-inch finishing nails instead of three-quarter-inch ones," George said, improvising. "Building zombies is a precision business. You use nails a quarter inch too long and they'll stick out all over the zombie's body. They'll keep catching on things."

"Ugh," said the mercenary and let George in.

———

George left his horse Hawkins to take care of the dragon. Hawkins knew the dragon personally from other scenarios—it was the astral persona of a woman named Magda who enjoyed being vanquished on a regular basis. Hawkins was sure Magda would agree to feign sleep while Hawkins drove a few nails through her wings with his hooves. She would gladly thrash and moan, spiked helplessly to the dirt, until George found time to plunge his cruel broadsword into the vulnerable soft spot of her abdomen.

George moved on to the tower where Diana was imprisoned. His red blazer was perfect camouflage; the mercenaries scarcely glanced his way as he passed. "Some hardware-hawking peasant," he heard one mutter in disgust.

At the top of the tower steps, George resumed his knightly persona. The armor made it impossible to walk silently and he knew there might be more danger ahead; however, Diana would be expecting him in heroic guise. With broadsword in one hand and shield in the other, he clanked forward to a closed door.

He could hear nothing from the other side of the door. Considering the thickness of his helmet, George was not surprised. He tried the latch and found the door unlocked. It would be nice to kick the door open the way people did in movies, but concentrating on his astral foot as hard as he could, he barely managed to move the door at all. When it was open enough to squeeze through, he sidestepped his way into the room.

Diana sat in a chair, bound by coils of thick white cord and gagged with a purple silk scarf. Though she wore the persona of a kidnapped princess—low-cut gown of green velvet, straight brown hair that reached the floor, eyes red from weeping—she still carried vestiges of the goddess of the hunt. The cobras on her belt had already gnawed through the cords around her waist and were snapping at the bindings on her wrists.

George hurried forward to untie her, but she shook her head violently and nodded toward the far corner of the room. "Mmmph mmph mmph," she explained.

At first when George looked in the direction she indicated, he saw only a rumpled four-poster bed surrounded by confusing watercolor prints of elves. George found it disturbing that Diana was so eager to draw his attention to the bed while she was still bound and gagged. In fact, finding himself unexpectedly alone with her in an elaborate bedroom stirred nervous flutters in his stomach. He hadn't pictured this moment coming so suddenly. The part of his mind that normally said, "This is what you should do," was completely silent; the part that said, "This is what might happen," had hiccups. It was a huge relief when a lean figure stepped from the shadows behind the bed-curtains and said, "So. Some fool believes he can foil my schemes."

George recognized the man as another clip-art persona: Seductive Yet Dangerous Scoundrel with Pencil Mustache, #2. He wore a white puff-sleeved swashbuckler shirt, tight black chinos, and knee-high boots of black leather. He would have intimidated George even if he hadn't been carrying a saber with a dripping crimson blade.

"Wilhelm von Schmutzig, I presume," George said in a voice he wanted to sound brave.

"At your service," said the villain, giving a courtier's bow. "Shall we duel to the death or would you prefer to impale yourself on my blade immediately?"

"I will not rest until I have cleansed the Earth of your foul presence, von Schmutzig." George was rather pleased with that speech—Hawkins had suggested he should have some appropriate soliloquy for the final confrontation with the villain, and George had practiced till he could say the line without fumbling.

George was still congratulating himself when von Schmutzig attacked. With lightning-swift strikes, the villain rained blows upon George's armor. The saber itself had no effect, but the clanging noise ringing against his helmet gave George a throbbing headache. He did his best to fight back, but was far too slow and clumsy to come close to his opponent. Occasionally he managed a parry, but never a successful thrust.

"Are you the best the forces of virtue could muster?" von Schmutzig sneered as he played on George like a steel drum. "I expected a hero."

"Just because you're evil doesn't mean you should be rude," George replied. "You'll get yourself in trouble someday." But it was clearly George who was in trouble as he clattered back and forth around the room. At last he was driven back against a post of the bed and his weapon was flicked out of his hand by a fencing maneuver something like the little twist of the wrist you need when you're using an Allen wrench to loosen the bit in an electric drill. George hurried to pick the sword up, but found his feet tangled in sheets lying on the floor. He fell back heavily onto the mattress and von Schmutzig was on him immediately, the tip of his saber blade pointing through the helmet's visor at George's right eye.

"Now, Sir Knight," said von Schmutzig, "you will die."

"Don't hurt me," George whispered. "If I don't win, Diana will never love me and our child will usher forth from a joyless womb."

"What care I of children?" Von Schmutzig laughed. "I am a villain . . . and I get defeated in so many scenarios, I don't mess around when I finally win one. I'm minutes away from finishing my zombie horde, and I'm really looking forward to decimating the duchy."

"But my baby!" George shouted.

"I was an unhappy child," von Schmutzig said. "I don't see why I should give a break to anyone else."

"Urk," he added as the tip of an ivory spear burst out of his chest, like a one-inch nail driven through a three-quarter-inch board.

Resplendent in her goddess persona, Diana carried von Schmutzig to the window on the end of her spear. "Thus end all who give my mate a rough time," she said as she tossed him out. Von Schmutzig's screams turned into the screeches of an eagle as he fell. A large bird flew squawking past the window and off into the sunset. Like all good villains, von Schmutzig was escaping so there could be a sequel.

"Are you okay?" Diana asked as George stumbled to his feet. Her face was filled with concern. She put her arm around his shoulders, sat him down on the edge of the bed, and tried to look at him through his visor.

"Oh, I'm all right," he said. He couldn't meet her gaze. "I wasn't a very good hero."

"It was sweet of you to try," she said. "Are you sure you're all right? He was hacking you left, right, and center."

George reshaped himself into his comfortable old persona. "I'm fine. How about you?"

"Oh, I had fun. I like saving people in the nick of time." She gave him a quick squeeze, then looked away.

"I liked being saved," George said. "Thank you."

"You're welcome."

George was keenly aware she still had her arm around his shoulders. It felt very warm. He couldn't remember anyone else's astral projection feeling that warm.

"I suppose the scenario's over now," she said sadly.

"Actually," George told her, "the building is still swarming with ruthless mercenaries."

"It is?"

"And I left the dragon alive."

"You did?"

"And the dungeons are chock-full of disease-bearing zombies."

"Oh, George," she said, hugging him tightly, "you've given me something nice to look forward to on our honeymoon. Tomorrow."

In a gigantic cube in the desert, some really good robots work carefully on two physical bodies. Fluids are transferred. Vital signs are monitored. The probability of success is high.

In a castle on the Rhine, two ordinary human beings try on one persona after another as they strive to learn to love each other. If somebody ever finds a way to measure the probability of success in love everyone will ignore it anyway, so let's not pretend we know how things will work out.

In a hardware store in a quiet town, a robot stockboy impulsively decides to put the one-inch finishing nails and the three-quarter-inch finishing nails into the same bin. They're a bit different; but when you get right down to it, they're all nails, aren't they?

The Reckoning of Gifts

Hjunior cook brushes against the soup cauldron, hot, searing hot. He curses.

The kitchen noise strangles to horrified silence. Profanity is always dangerous here on temple grounds, and the danger is multiplied a thousandfold by the proximity of holy objects.

The cauldron holds the high priest's soup.

A potboy screams out the door for an exorcist, but he knows it's too late: the words have ripped the amniotic sac that protects our world from the chaos outside. Demons must be streaming in by the dozen, invisible demons who sniff once at the kitchen staff, then scatter in search of the tastier souls of the clergy. The potboy can almost see the demons—fanged, clawed, with naked female breasts—racing down the corridor, wiping their hands on the tapestries as they go by (the dyes fade, the threads ravel), pouring out into the herb garden to wither the foxgloves, to suck the soothing power from chamomile and the flavor from basil, then on across the courtyard, kicking a few cobblestones loose to trip passersby, pinching the horses of a bishop's carriage, flying unseen past the warders and into the temple proper, where they will crumple scrolls, tarnish chalices, and set the bells to wild jangling. Novices in catechism class will stumble over words as the demons tempt them to remember sweet berry pies, gravied beef, and a score of other foods the holy must forswear; priests hearing confession will find themselves dreaming of the feel of sins, the satisfying crunch of a fist plunged into the face of a self-righteous parishioner or the excitement of commanding an adulteress to disrobe; and the high priest himself, Vasudheva, voice of the gods on earth, will be swarmed by demons, engulfed by them, demons raking their claws across his heart until it shreds into tatters tossed on the winds of desire.

The junior cook faints. Others pale and scatter their clothing with salt. But the Kitchen Master simply tells everyone to get back to work. He cuffs the potboy who called for help, a good solid clout on the ear that sends the boy staggering back against a chopping block.

"The lad's too excitable," the Kitchen Master tells the exorcist who appears in the doorway. "Sorry to trouble you. Nothing's wrong."

Vasudheva, voice of the gods on earth, kneels before the Twelve-fold Altar. He is indeed surrounded by a frenzy of demons. When he kisses the feet of Tivi's statue, he doesn't think of the god's power or wisdom; he thinks of the sensation of kissing, the soft pressure against his lips, the lingering contact, the ghost of sensation that remains as he slowly draws away. He longs to kiss the stone again, to kiss it over and over until his lips ache with bruising. His hand rises toward his mouth. He stops the movement in time, but in his imagination it continues, his fingers reaching his lips, caressing, stroking, flesh against flesh.

Vasudheva cannot remember what he has prayed for this past half hour. Certainly not the exorcism of his demons.

A month ago, the Assembly of Bishops assigned Vasudheva a new deacon named Bhismu . . . a young man of undistinguished family, chosen because he has no affiliation with the Assembly's power blocs and can therefore be trusted not to exert undue influence on the high priest. Vasudheva also soon realized the young deacon wasn't appointed for any notable intellect, piety, or even willingness to work.

Ah, but Bhismu was beautiful! *Is* beautiful!

His hair is a garden of soft black ringlets, his beard an effusion of delicate curls. Vasudheva's hands long to entwine themselves, oh so gently, in those ringlets and curls, to braid, to weave, to stroke. He imagines threading his fingers through Bhismu's beard, cupping the young man's chin, gazing into those clear dark eyes as he leans forward and their lips meet. . . .

Vasudheva dreams too of Bhismu's hands, strong but fascinatingly dexterous when he played the reed-pipe at the Feast of the Starving Moon. Vasudheva was hypnotized by the confident rippling fingers. He thought of nothing else far into the night, until in the bleakness of morning, he wondered if he had eaten a single bite at the feast. Scripture said the moon would starve to death, disappear from the sky forever if the high priest hadn't consumed enough on its behalf; but the moon survived, as did Vasudheva's desires.

He has never prayed for those desires to abate. He cherishes them. He relishes them.

Tonight begins the Long Night Revelries, a week of feasting and celebration in the city of Cardis. Events include the Fool's Reign, the Virgins' Dance, and the Renewal of Hearth Fires from Tivi's sacred flame, but first comes the Reckoning of Gifts in the temple's outer hall.

It's never a pleasant ceremony for the priests who officiate. The hall teems with unbathed commoners, men and women together, all clutching packages to their chests with fierce protectiveness. They jostle each other in the rush to receive blessings; they insult the Gifts of others and boast about their own. Every year fights break out, and sometimes a full-scale riot. Even if demons are loose tonight, it's hard to imagine how they could add any more chaos to the usual commotion.

Vasudheva waits for Bhismu to escort him down to the hall. Not long ago, the high priest refused all help in getting around—though his quarters occupy the top of the temple's highest tower, he would climb the stairs unaided several times a day, glaring at anyone who tried to assist. Now Vasudheva goes nowhere without Bhismu's strong supporting arm. He clings to the young man with both hands and walks as slowly as possible.

Several powerful bishops have begun overt machinations to win support in the assembly, believing there will soon be an election for a new high priest. They are men of limited imagination; they think Vasudheva has become frail.

The bishops would like to influence which Gift is chosen from the dozens presented in the hall tonight. Power and prestige ride on the choice, not to mention a good deal of gold. The laws of Cardis stifle innovation—change threatens order, and order must be maintained. No one may create a new device, a new art, a new process . . . except in preparation for the Reckoning of Gifts. In the month before the Reckoning, creators may build their inventions. On the longest night of the year, they bring those Gifts to the temple; from the dozens offered, one Gift is chosen and accepted into orthodoxy, while the others become fuel for Tivi's flame. The successful creator is feted in all quarters of the city, honored as a benefactor of the people and a servant of heaven. Unsuccessful ones have nothing to show but ashes.

Needless to say, competition is intense. Every guild sponsors some Gift to better their lot—a new type of horse hitch offered by the cart drivers, a new way to waterproof barrels offered by the coopers—and scores of individuals also bring their offerings, some of them coming back year after year. One family of fisherfolk has sent their eldest child to the Reckoning each year for more than a century; they claim to be able to teach needles how to point north and for some reason they think the gods will be pleased with such tricks. Not so. The gods have consistently shown themselves to be pleased with the Gift accompanied by the largest under-the-table offering to the high priest. The only variation from one year to the next is whether the secret offering is made in gold, in political influence, or in the adroitness of beautiful women.

This year, Vasudheva is sure the gods smile on a type of clasp offered by the silversmiths, a clasp more secure and easier to fasten than orthodox clasps. The silversmiths have provided the high priest with several samples of work that show the virtues of the clasp: a silver necklace whose pendant is the letter V studded with sapphires; a silver bracelet encrusted with alternating emeralds and amethysts; and a silver dagger and sheath, the dagger hilt glittering with fire-eye rubies and the sheath embroidered to show Tivi's flame.

Schemers among the bishops try to sway the gods' decision, and several believe they have succeeded . . . but the gods are in a mood to demonstrate they speak only through Vasudheva, while upstart bishops should devote themselves to prayer instead of powermongering.

A soft knock comes at the door and Bhismu is there. Vasudheva catches his breath, as he always does when Bhismu enters the room. Sometimes the high priest thinks he has two hearts in his chest: the withered heart of an old man and the bounding, pounding heart of a youth who feels the fever of love but not the complications. If he only has one heart, it must be attuned to the hearts around him—when he's surrounded by crabbed and ambitious bishops, his heart shrivels; when Bhismu is near, his heart expands and expands until it's as large as the sky.

Bhismu asks, "Are you ready to attend the ceremony, Your Ho-liness?"

"If they're ready for me. Are things under control?"

"Father Amaran says we have encountered no more trouble than usual, but everyone feels a strong disquiet. There have been rumors of demons."

"Rumors of demons are like mushrooms," Vasudheva says. "They spring up overnight, and the peasants feed on them."

He hopes Bhismu will laugh, but the young man only nods. He's slow to recognize jokes. It's a failing that can be overlooked.

They begin the long journey down the tower's corkscrew stairs. A month ago, Vasudheva found it awkward to descend holding onto an arm instead of the balustrade. Now he's completely comfortable with it. He doesn't need to concentrate on his feet anymore; he can devote his full attention to the strength of Bhismu's hands, the faint smell of his sweat, the beard so close it would take no effort at all to kiss.

"Have you ever been in love?" Vasudheva asks.

The young man's thoughts seem to have been elsewhere. It takes him a moment to collect himself. "Love? I don't know. A few times I wondered if I was in love, but it wasn't like the minstrels say. It wasn't intense. I'd spend time with a girl—this was before I was ordained, of course—I'd spend time and I'd feel very fond and I'd wonder, am I in love? But my father was determined I would enter the priesthood, and if he saw me becoming attached to someone, he ordered me to give her up. And I did. I always did. So I guess it wasn't love. If it really had been love, I wouldn't have . . . I don't know. It's wrong to disobey your father, but if I'd really been in love . . . I don't know."

"So you've never had strong feelings for a woman?" Vasudheva asks. He is very close to Bhismu; his breath stirs wisps of the young man's hair.

"Not as strong as love. Not as strong as love should be."

"Have you ever had strong feelings for anyone?"

"I don't understand. You mean my family? Of course I love my family. You're supposed to love your family."

Vasudheva doesn't press the matter. It took him forty years to rise from an acolyte in the most crime-ridden quarter of Cardis to the supreme office of high priest. He has learned how to bide his time.

But Bhismu's beard curls invitingly. Vasudheva's demons will not wait forever.

Bishops lounge on divans in the vestry that's adjacent to the outer hall. Each wants a whispered word with the high priest; each wants to overhear the other whispers. Vasudheva forestalls their jockeying for position by sweeping past them and throwing open the thick outer door.

Screams. Shouts. Feet stamping and glass breaking.

On a night so rife with demons, the riot is no surprise to anyone.

The door opens onto the front of the room; the stampede is surging toward the public entrance at the rear. That's why Vasudheva isn't crushed instantly. The only people nearby are two men grappling with each other, one dressed in velvet finery, the other in bloodstained buckskins, each trying to dig fingers into his opponent's eyes. Here and there within the crowd other fistfights thump and bellow, but most people are simply trying to get out, to escape the trampling mob.

Things crunch under their feet. They could be Gifts dropped in the panic; they could be bones. No one looks down to see.

Vasudheva stands frozen in the doorway. A priest staggers up to him from the hall, squeezes roughly past into the refuge of the vestry, and cries, "Close the door, close the door!" He bleeds from a gash on his forehead.

Behind the priest comes a woman, doing her best to walk steadily though her clothes hang in shreds and blood oozes from wounds all over her body. Where her arms should be, she has wings. Wings. Vasudheva steps aside for her to pass, his mind struck numb as a sleepwalker's. Bhismu drags both the woman and the high priest back into the vestry, and slams the door shut.

The noise of the riot vanishes. There is only the whimpering of the injured priest, and the heavy breathing of several bishops whose fear makes them pant like runners.

"Sit down, sit down," Bhismu says. Vasudheva turns, but Bhismu is holding out a chair to the woman. Who shouldn't even be here—women are forbidden to enter the temple beyond the outer hall.

She's a Northerner, her hair black and braided, her skin the color of tanned deerhide . . . young, in her twenties. Bhismu's age. Vasudheva can't believe anyone would find her attractive—she's too tall and bony, and her nose is crooked, as if it was broken, then set haphazardly.

Vasudheva keeps his eyes off the wings. There's no doubt they're beautiful, exquisite—slim as a swift's, abundant with feathers. For a moment, Vasudheva has a vision of the bird kingdom parading past this woman, each presenting feathers for these wings: eagles clawing out sharp brown pinions, hummingbirds poking their beaks into their chests to pluck soft down the color of blood; and crows, doves, finches, jays, each offering their gifts until the woman faces a heap of feathers taller than her head, and still the birds come, geese, falcons, owls, wrens, adding to the motley pile, all colors, all sizes, herons, plovers, swallows, larks, all bowing down like supplicants before an angel.

Vasudheva shakes his head angrily. A high priest can't afford to indulge his imagination. This is no angel. This is just some woman from a tribe of savages. She killed a lot of birds, sewed their feathers into wings, then brought those wings to the Reckoning. No doubt she started the riot in the first place. Pretending to be an angel is blasphemy; the people must have attacked in outrage as she came forward for blessing.

Bhismu kneels beside her and dabs the hem of his sleeve at a wound on her cheek. He smiles warmly at her and murmurs soft encouragements: "This one doesn't look bad, this one's deeper, but it's clean. . . ."

Vasudheva finds the expression on Bhismu's face unbecoming. Must he simper so? "You can help her more by getting a proper Healer," the high priest tells him. "The sooner the better. Now."

Reluctantly, Bhismu rises. For some moments, he stands like a man bewitched, gazing at the specks of blood that mar the whiteness of his sleeve. "Now," Vasudheva repeats. Suddenly the bewitchment lifts and Bhismu sprints out of the vestry, off down the corridor.

"We must make the woman go back to the hall," says a voice at Vasudheva's ear. "She shouldn't be in this part of the temple."

The words echo the high priest's thoughts. When he turns, however, he sees the speaker is Bishop Niravati, a man who loves to wield his piety like a bludgeon. Niravati has always been too quick to proclaim right and wrong; he conducts himself as if *he* were the voice of the gods on earth.

"She may stay as long as necessary," Vasudheva says. Bishops must never forget who makes the decisions in this temple. "Sending her back to the hall now would be close to murder. And she's injured. Tivi commands us to minister to the sick, Niravati; did you skip catechism class the day that was discussed?"

Several other bishops chuckle. Good. Niravati will note who they are and later take revenge. Vasudheva foments feuds among the bishops whenever possible: dividing one's opponents is useful. And entertaining.

The woman has watched this interchange with no expression on her face. Perhaps she's in shock . . . but she gives the impression of understanding it all and simply not caring. For a baseborn woman, she's remarkably unmoved being surrounded by the highest patriarchs of the faith. "What's your name?" Vasudheva asks her.

"Hakkoia."

"From a Northerner tribe?"

"From the Bleached Mountains."

Vasudheva doesn't know if this denotes a specific tribe or merely a place—his knowledge of the world outside Cardis begins and ends with the names of the bishoprics. "What happened in the hall?" he asks.

"There were fights. People threw things at me." She wipes blood from her chin.

"Why did they throw things?"

"It was demons!" the injured priest bursts out. Father Amaran. He's been huddling on a divan, hugging himself as if cold, but now he leaps to his feet and begins to babble. "Down in the kitchens . . . I can't get a straight story out of anyone but at confession . . . demons, they've released demons. In the soup."

Even Niravati drops his eyes in embarrassment. It's one thing for a priest to rail about demons to the laity, quite another to bring up the subject among peers. Vasudheva envisions Amaran dying years from now as a workaday priest in some remote parish, and being able to put his finger on the exact moment when he destroyed his career.

"I saw no demons," Hakkoia says in the silence that follows Amaran's gaffe. "I saw a man who was jealous of my wings. A man in the crowd—I don't know who he was. He wore fine clothes but his gift was petty and small. He stirred the others to attack me."

"Demons are deceitful," Vasudheva says lightly. "The man may have been a demon in disguise. Or someone possessed by demons." The high priest has no intention of asking Hakkoia to identify the man who attacked her. If he wore fine clothes, he was probably a noble or the representative of a guild. Arresting such a man would have repercussions. Besides, everyone could feel the tension in the air tonight. The riot was inevitable, and assigning blame is beside the point. "Niravati," he says, "help this woman take off those wings. She'll be more comfortable without them."

Hakkoia looks miserable as the wings are removed. But she says nothing.

Soon Bhismu arrives with old Lharksha, teacher of Healing to three generations of acolytes. Lharksha's silver hair is wildly tangled, and his bleary eyes blink as if he's just been roused from a deep sleep. Vasudheva can't remember Lharksha ever looking otherwise; day or night, the man always seems freshly rumpled.

"Lharksha . . ." Father Amaran begins, stepping forward and lifting his hand to the cut in his forehead. But Bhismu pulls the Healer onward to the woman and begins to inventory her wounds. Amaran looks as if he is going to demand attention; but then he subsides and slumps back onto the nearest divan.

The Healer says little as he examines Hakkoia: "Does this hurt? Lift your arm, please. Can you lift it higher? Does it hurt?" Hakkoia answers his questions in monosyllables. When Lharksha asks if something hurts, she always says no.

The others in the room say nothing. They watch avidly as Lharksha prods Hakkoia's body and smears salve on her skin. The shredded remains of her clothes are discarded; sometimes they have to be cut away with scissors when the blood has crusted them in place. The men watch. Bit by bit, her body is stripped, cleaned, clothed again with crisp white bandages. The men make no sound, except for occasionally clearing their throats.

Vasudheva watches himself watching her. He's no stranger to the bodies of women—women are frequently offered to him as bribes. Hakkoia doesn't compare to the professional beauties he's seen, and he can view her with dispassionate appraisal. The bishops, on the other hand . . . Vasudheva looks around at the hunger on their faces and chuckles inwardly. Niravati is unconsciously licking his lips. Bishops aren't bribed as often as the high priest.

Vasudheva turns toward Bhismu and sees the young man has averted his eyes.

In that moment, Vasudheva realizes Bhismu is lost. The realization is a prickly heat that crinkles up through Vasudheva's shoulders and leaves his ears burning. He felt this way fifty years ago when he was caught stealing a coin from the poor box. It's a feeling of guilt and pure animal desperation, the piercing desire to reverse time and erase the past few minutes.

Bhismu is in love with Hakkoia. Why else wouldn't he look? A healthy young man should relish the opportunity to see a woman naked. Even if he's zealously trying to live up to a deacon's vows, he should peek from time to time or at least show signs of temptation. But not Bhismu. His face shows neither lust nor the struggle against lust.

Bhismu in love . . . Vasudheva averts his eyes.

"The woman may stay the night in this room," Vasudheva says, breaking the silence. Heads turn sharply toward him. "When the trouble dies down next door, collect any Gifts that are intact and arrange them at the front of the hall. Clear out the broken ones and throw them on Tivi's flame. If there have been deaths, save the bodies; I'll give them public blessing before we return them to their next of kin. In the morning. I'll judge the Gifts in the morning too. Everything in the morning." He holds out his arm. "Bhismu, take me back to my chambers."

Bhismu is reluctant to leave. As he leads the high priest away, the young man keeps glancing at Hakkoia back over his shoulder. Vasudheva thinks, *Now he looks. Couldn't he have looked before?*

Bhismu's body is still warm, his bearded cheek still inviting, but the high priest takes no pleasure in holding the young man's arm. Vasudheva needs no human escort; he is escorted by his demons who bear him up, quicken his stride, carry him along.

Vasudheva can't sleep. He paces around his desk, arguing with himself. Is Bhismu really in love? Could it just be some kind of chivalrous arousal, a reaction to the sight of a young woman in trouble? And why should a high priest be so concerned about a nobody like Bhismu? Bhismu has no brain, no political power; he's just a beard that begs to be kissed. A pretty trinket, nothing more. A high priest can't let himself get distracted by trifles.

But Vasudheva pictures Hakkoia dying. Not dying with a knife in the throat, or choking from poison, or strangling by garrote, just . . . dying.

Vasudheva imagines the wings burning in Tivi's flame. They will sputter and crackle at first, then catch fire with a roar. The smell will be hideous.

Destroying the wings will be nearly as good as killing the woman herself, but entirely free of blame. He can imagine the look on her face as she sees the wings burn.

Sometime after midnight, Vasudheva opens the secret drawer of his desk and takes out the presents from the silversmiths. All three are exquisite, but he may have to part with one. In order for the guild's clasp to be accepted by the gods, there must be a sample downstairs in the hall. If the riot destroyed the original sample, Vasudheva must supply a new one.

Wistfully, Vasudheva toys with the necklace, the bracelet, the dagger. It will irk him to part with any of the three, but if necessary it should be the dagger—fewer gems. He'll take it downstairs and slip it in with the other Gifts. No doubt the silversmiths will recognize the generosity of this sacrifice and offer appropriate compensation.

He finds that descending the staircase alone is more difficult than he remembers. The realization scares him; he doesn't want to depend on Bhismu or anyone else. But no, he's not weak, just tired. He needs sleep, that's all.

As he nears the vestry, he realizes Hakkoia will be there. Why didn't he remember her before? His thoughts wander too much these days. But Hakkoia can't stop him from going to the hall. She may not even notice him; she's probably asleep.

And he has the dagger.

Vasudheva draws the blade slowly from the sheath. It glints in the light of the torches that flicker on the wall. He can't remember ever testing its blade before. He slides it along the edge of a tapestry that shows Tivi setting the temple's cornerstone at the very center of the world. The dagger effortlessly slices off a strip of cloth ornamented with dancing angels. The blade is functional as well as ornate.

Vasudheva wonders how soundly Hakkoia sleeps.

But as he steals down the corridor that leads to the vestry, he finds Hakkoia is not sleeping at all. Low voices come from the room, one male, one female. Vasudheva closes his eyes and prays that the man is not Bhismu; it may be the most fervently Vasudheva has prayed in years.

But, of course, it *is* Bhismu.

They aren't in each other's arms. Both are fully dressed. Hakkoia sits on one of the divans, her spine as straight and strong as a javelin. Bhismu sits on the floor at her feet, his head leaning against her thigh. The wings lie across Hakkoia's lap like a chastity belt.

No one has heard Vasudheva's quiet approach. Standing just outside the room, he can listen to their conversation. Bhismu is describing how his father beat him for every thought or action that might have kept him out of the priesthood. Vasudheva has never heard the man speak of such things; despite a month of cultivating Bhismu's trust, Vasudheva has never reaped such secrets. And Hakkoia isn't *doing* anything. She barely speaks. Her attitude suggests she is merely tolerating his attentions; her mind is elsewhere.

"I could leave the priesthood," Bhismu says. "Vasudheva is fond of me. He'll release me from my vows if I ask. He tells me all the time I'm his favorite. He gives me presents, and . . ."

Vasudheva steps angrily into the room. "Enough!" he says. "Enough!"

Bhismu blushes guiltily. He jerks away from the woman and slides quickly along the floor until he's more than an arm's length from her. Hakkoia barely reacts at all; she only lifts her chin to look the high priest in the eye. Her gaze assesses him thoughtfully. Vasudheva wonders what sort of things Bhismu said about him before he arrived, but there is no time for speculation. "*I* am not the one who can release a deacon from his vows," Vasudheva says, glaring at Bhismu. "Only Tivi may do that. And I don't think Tivi will be inclined to grant such a dispensation to a stripling who fancies himself in love because he's seen a woman's naked flesh. Aren't you ashamed of yourself? Aren't you?"

Bhismu seems to waver on the edge of surrender. His eyes are lowered, his hands tremble. But then the hands clench and he shakes his head like a fighter throwing off the effects of a punch. "I haven't done anything to be ashamed of." His voice is almost a whisper, but there is no submission in it. "I haven't done any-thing."

"What would your father think of this?" Vasudheva demands. "Alone with a woman in the middle of the night. And on holy ground!"

Bhismu cringes. But Hakkoia slaps her hand down on the divan with a loud smack. "I'm not some corrupting evil," she says. "I'm not one of these demons you talk about, the kind you can blame but can't see. This ground is just as holy as when I arrived. If it was holy then. Why do you carry a knife?"

Vasudheva's anger surges. It's been years since anyone dared to talk to him so accusingly. People like Bhismu hold him in awe; people like Niravati are too conniving to be blunt. He's on the verge of calling the warders, of consigning Hakkoia to the dungeons as punishment for her disrespect . . . but he realizes he can't do so in front of Bhismu. No violence, no cruelty, ever, in front of Bhismu.

Besides, violence is never more than a last resort. A prudent man finds other ways to eliminate problems.

"Bhismu," Vasudheva says in a calmer voice, "I think you should go to the chapel and pray."

The young man seems to have recovered some backbone, thanks to Hakkoia's words. "I haven't done anything to be ashamed of," he says again.

"Good for you," Vasudheva replies. "But I heard you talk about renouncing your vows, and that's grave business. No, no"—the high priest holds up his hand to forestall a protest—"I'm not accusing you of sin. But this is something you should think about very seri-ously. You should be sure it's what you want and what's best for you. For you, for your family, for everyone. That's only right, isn't it?"

"Yes," Bhismu says. He sounds like a little boy, still defiant inside but momentarily cowed. Vasudheva thinks of ruffling

Bhismu's hair the way he has seen parents do with their children, but he restrains his hands.

As Bhismu turns to go, Hakkoia tells him, "I'm staying with the family of Wakkatomet, the leatherworker. Elbow Street, near the Tin Market. They're Northerners; they're very glad when people come to call."

Bhismu's face blooms into a grin. He thanks Hakkoia profusely and leaves with a capering step. *He is so beautiful, so radiantly beautiful,* Vasudheva thinks. *It breaks my heart.*

"Why did you tell him where you live?" Vasudheva asks when Bhismu is gone. "You aren't interested in him."

"He said he was worried about my injuries," Hakkoia answers. "He's concerned about my health. I thought he might rest more easily if he checked on me from time to time. To see that I was well."

Vasudheva conceals a smile. He knows she's lying; she told Bhismu where to find her because she wanted to see if he would actually do it. To see if she had power over him. This is a woman a high priest can understand. "Lharksha is the best Healer in the city," he says. "Your health isn't in danger, believe me."

Hakkoia's eyes flick to the dagger the high priest still holds in his hand. She raises an eyebrow questioningly.

"A Gift," he tells her, "that's all. The sheath has a new type of clasp created by the silversmiths' guild. I was returning it to the hall to put with the other Gifts."

"There are no other Gifts," she says. "The priest, Amaran—he told me nothing survived the rampage."

"Nothing except this dagger," Vasudheva corrects her.

"And my wings."

The wings still lie across her lap. Her hands rest on the feathers, caressing them, stroking them.

"Are the wings hard to make?" Vasudheva asks.

"My people believe humans are born with only half a soul," Hakkoia replies. "When a child has learned how to dance, she must go in search of an animal who is willing to provide the other half. I am now of eagle blood, and flight fills my heart. I have studied the wings of every bird; I have gathered their feathers; I have learned their calls. The wings were not hard for *me* to make."

"So you intend to make yourself rich selling wings? You and your leatherworker friends?" Vasudheva shrugs. "You'll probably do well. The nobles of Cardis are always eager for novelties, and flying will certainly appeal to them. Though most of them are lazy. Is flying hard work?"

"I don't know."

Vasudheva looks at her in amazement. "You've never tried the wings?"

"I have," she answers, and the boldness in her gaze disappears for the first time. "They don't work."

Suddenly, fiercely, she stands; the wings fall off her lap and thud heavily to the floor. She picks them up, thrusts them out toward the high priest. "If they could fly, would I bring them to this stinking hateful city? Cardis law means nothing in the mountains—I would fly the peaks and valleys, and to hell with the priests who say no. But your gods . . . your holy Tivi who's terrified of new things, he's the one who's keeping me on the ground. The Queen of Eagles told me this in a dream. So I've come for Tivi's blessing, and when I have it, I'll soar away from Cardis forever."

She's mad, Vasudheva thinks. No Northerner is completely sane, but this woman goes far beyond the fanatic adoration of animals for which Northerners are famed. There is no Queen of Eagles! There could be a king—certain marginal writings imply there are kings of many mammal species, and that might extend to birds. But if she expects official recognition is all that's required to make flightless wings soar . . .

Her eyes glitter wildly. When she speaks of flying, you notice it: the glint of obsession. Vasudheva has seen it often through the years—priests who appear entirely balanced until you broach some subject that rouses their lunacy. Perhaps he himself is that way about Bhismu. How often has he muttered under his breath that he's acting obsessed, irrational?

Thoughtfully, Vasudheva strokes his beard. "If these wings are accepted as Tivi's Gift, you'll leave the city?" he asks.

"Like a dove fleeing from crows."

He nods. "Bring the wings to my chambers at sunrise. In the tower. The warders will show you the way—I'll tell them to let you pass. The crowd will be waiting in the courtyard for my announcement. I'll proclaim your wings to be Tivi's choice and let you have your first flight from my balcony."

She hugs the wings to her chest and smiles. It is a dangerous smile, a mad smile. "Thank you," she says. "I'll leave, I promise. Bhismu will soon forget me."

Only years of experience let him hide his alarm at her words. She knows too much. Bhismu, innocent Bhismu, must have told her enough that she could deduce the truth. The dagger is still in his hand . . . but sunrise will be soon enough. If the wings work, she leaves; but the wings will not work. Vasudheva knows how little real magic there is in Tivi's blessing.

The silversmiths will be annoyed when their Gift is not chosen; but they can be mollified. A big order of new chalices, bells, censers. Silver soup bowls for the acolytes, silver plates for the priests. He nods to himself, then sheaths the dagger and tucks it inside his robe.

"Tivi's grace on you," Vasudheva says to Hakkoia.

"Thank you," she says again.

After telling the warders to escort Hakkoia to his tower before sunrise, Vasudheva stops by the chapel. All the candles have burned out; the only light is Tivi's flame, flickering in the enormous hearth at the front of the sanctuary. The rest of the room is in blackness.

Bhismu lies before the flame, sound asleep. There's a smile on his face; no doubt he dreams of Hakkoia, but Vasudheva can forgive him for that. The more Bhismu loves her, the more her death will shake him and the more comforting he'll need.

He looks so vulnerable.

Without warning, a wave of passion sweeps over Vasudheva's heart, and he is bending to the ground, Bhismu will never feel it, a kiss on the cheek, the beard, one kiss stolen in the night, flesh, lips, and yes! Bhismu's curls are soft, and warmed by Tivi's own flame. The kiss is like a sacrament, holy, blessed. Another kiss, this time on the lips . . . but no more, no more, he'll wake up, one more, it doesn't matter, he's sleeping so soundly . . .

Something rustles in the back of the chapel, and Vasudheva is immediately on his feet, peering into the shadows. Is there someone on the bench in the farthest corner? Vasudheva strides down the aisle, his entire body trembling with rage. Reluctant to wake up Bhismu, he whispers, "Who are you?" with piercing harshness.

"Duroga, sir, Your Holiness," a voice whispers back. "Junior cook down in the. . . ."

"What are you doing here?"

"Praying, Your Holiness." The whisper is full of fear.

"In the middle of the night? More likely, you came to steal. What did you want? The sacramental silver?"

"No, Your Holiness, no! I'm praying. For forgiveness. I burned myself on the soup cauldron and I said . . . I spoke profanely. The words released demons, I know they did. The riot was all my fault. And everyone acting so oddly, it's the demons making everyone . . ."

Vasudheva slaps the cook's face, once, very hard. His palm stings after the blow and the stinging feels good.

"Listen to me, junior cook," Vasudheva says. "You did not release any demons. If demons exist at all, they have more important things to do than flock about when some peasant burns his thumb. Understand?" He grabs the front of the cook's robe and shakes the man. Duroga's teeth clack together with the violence of the jostling. "You want to hear something? You want to hear?"

Vasudheva begins to curse. Every profanity learned as a child, every foul oath overheard in the vicious quarters of Cardis, every blasphemy that sinners atoned for in the confessional, words tumbling out of the high priest's mouth with the ease of a litany, all tightly whispered into Duroga's face until the cook's cheeks are wet with spittle and his eyes weeping with fear. The words spill out, here before Tivi's own hearth, the most sacred place in the universe and so the most vulnerable . . . but no demons come, not one, because hell is as empty as heaven and the void hears neither curses nor prayers. Vasudheva knows; he's been the voice of the gods on earth for twenty-three years and not once has he spoken a word that didn't come from his own brain, his own guts, his own endless scheming. Wasn't there a time when he prayed some god would seize his tongue and speak through him? But the first thing ever to seize his tongue is this cursing, on and on until he can no longer draw enough breath to continue and he releases the cook, throws him onto the floor, and gasps, "Now let me hear no more talk of demons!"

Without waiting for a reaction, Vasudheva staggers out to the corridor. His heart pounds and his head spins, but he feels cleansed. Duroga must meet with an accident in the near future, but it can wait, it can wait. Vasudheva has kissed Bhismu, has dealt with Hakkoia . . . has faced his demons.

Climbing the tower steps, he feels his soul flies upward, dragging his feeble body behind. His soul has huge wings, and as he reels into his chambers, he has a vision of the bird kingdom parading past him, each presenting feathers for those wings: eagles, hummingbirds, crows. . . .

A loud knocking comes at the door. Vasudheva wakes, aching in every bone. He has spent the night on the floor; he never reached the bed. Now the room is quickening with predawn light, gray and aloof. Vasudheva shivers, though the day is already warm.

The knocking comes again. Vasudheva pulls himself to the bed. Off with the robe he still wears, a quick rumpling of sheets, and then he calls out, "Come in."

Bhismu enters. Vasudheva's smile of greeting for the man dies as Bishop Niravati and the cook Duroga enter too.

"Good morning, Your Holiness," Niravati says. The bishop's voice has none of its usual tone of feigned deference. "Did you sleep well?"

"Who is this?" Vasudheva asks, pointing at Duroga, though he remembers the cook quite clearly.

"His name is Duroga," Niravati says. "Last night he came to me with a disturbing tale about demons. Demons that he thinks have possessed high-ranking officials of our temple."

"He claims to be able to sniff out demons?"

"No, Your Holiness, he's merely a witness to their deeds. He saw a great deal of their handiwork in the chapel last night." Niravati glances toward Bhismu. "A great deal."

"I was there," Bhismu says. "I saw nothing."

"You were asleep." Niravati smiles, a smile gloating with triumph. "You slept through quite a lot."

"Well, if you really think there are *demons* loose," Vasudheva says, "call out the exorcists." He tries to sound mocking, but doesn't succeed. The trapped feeling burns in his ears again, guilt and desperation.

"I've already called the exorcists," Niravati says. "But I thought I should come directly to you on another important matter. You asked the warders to escort that woman Hakkoia to your chambers this morning. . . ."

Bhismu looks startled. "You did?"

"Her wings are Tivi's chosen Gift this year," Vasudheva replies. "No other Gift survived. I thought it would please the people to see her fly from my balcony."

"No doubt it would be exciting," Niravati says. "But with so much concern about demons, surely it's rash to let a woman visit your room. The laity is not in a mood to accept . . . deviations from common practice."

Vasudheva knows he must rebuke Niravati now, immediately. To hesitate for another second will prove he's afraid. (Does Niravati know about the kisses? He must. Bhismu lay in the light of Tivi's fire; Duroga could see everything.)

But Vasudheva *is* afraid. The people are used to the clergy sporting with women—order an ale in any tavern of Cardis, and before your glass is empty, you'll hear someone in the room telling a joke about lascivious priests. Such joking is good-natured, almost fond. However, to be caught kissing a man . . . of course, there would be no trial, no public punishment, for a high priest could not be convicted on the word of a junior cook. But there would be insolence from the novices; too much salt in every meal; clothes that came back dirty from the temple laundry; conversations that went silent as the high priest entered the room.

He couldn't stand that. He couldn't stand a world that didn't respect or fear him.

Vasudheva sighs heavily. "You have a point, Niravati. Hakkoia will have to fly from some other height. Perhaps the bell tower of the City Council?"

Niravati shakes his head. "The people are gathering in the

courtyard below us. They expect you to announce the Gift from your balcony here. That's the tradition."

"*I* could wear the wings," Bhismu says suddenly.

"No!" Vasudheva's voice cracks.

"But I *could*!" the young man insists. "I want to. For Hakkoia's sake."

"An excellent idea," Niravati says, clapping Bhismu on the shoulder. "I should have thought of it myself."

"She talked to me about flying," Bhismu says excitedly. "She says she has eagle blood. The way she spoke of eagles . . . as if she were in love with them . . . please, Your Holiness, let me fly in her place."

"Yes, let him, Your Holiness," Niravati says. "It would show your . . . good faith."

Vasudheva looks at Bhismu's eager face and remembers warm curls, soft lips. "All right," the high priest says. "Go get the wings."

He turns away quickly. Another second, and Bhismu's grateful expression will wring tears from the high priest's eyes.

"People of Cardis!"

The rim of the sun is emerging over the rooftops. Only those in the tower can see it; five stories lower, the city is still in shadow. But men and women crowd the courtyard, their heads craned up to watch the high priest's balcony. Every onlooker wears some small finery—a new ribbon in the hair, a patch of bright cloth sewn on the shirt directly over the heart.

Hakkoia must be in the crowd somewhere, but Vasudheva doesn't see her. His eyes water; he can't focus on any of the faces below.

"People of Cardis!" he repeats. "As you may have heard, many of the intended Gifts were destroyed last night in a terrible commotion. A commotion we believe was caused by demons."

At Vasudheva's back, Niravati murmurs, "That's right."

"But through Tivi's heavenly grace," Vasudheva continues, "one Gift was spared. That Gift is the one the gods have chosen to accept this year. A Gift that is nothing less than the gift of flight!"

Bhismu steps onto the balcony, arms high and outspread to show the wings he wears. The crowd stirs with wonder as the feathers catch the dawning sunlight, catch the soft breeze blowing down from the hills. Bhismu glistens like dew, so pure, so clean.

Vasudheva can see Bhismu's arms tremble as they try to support the weight of the wings. The wings are far too heavy; they'll never fly.

Bhismu grins, eager to leap out over the crowd. He waggles a wing to someone; it must be Hakkoia, though Vasudheva still can't pick her out. Bhismu no doubt intends to fly a few circles around the tower, then land at the woman's feet.

He's so beautiful.

Vasudheva lifts his hand to touch the young man's hair. As simple as that, a totally natural gesture. Bhismu turns and smiles; he must think it's a sign of encouragement.

Niravati clears his throat disapprovingly. "Your Holiness . . ." he murmurs.

And suddenly Vasudheva is angry, righteously angry, at Niravati, at himself, at all those who try to lever people away from love. All the scheming conniving bishops, and others like Bhismu's father who trample over affection on their way to meaningless goals. Love demands enough sacrifices in itself; no one should impose additional burdens. One should pay the price of love and no more.

And no less.

Vasudheva touches Bhismu's arm. "Take the wings off," he says. "Give them to me."

A stricken look of betrayal crosses Bhismu's face. "No!"

"You can have the second flight. Warders!"

They grab him before he can jump. One warder looks at Nira-vati for confirmation of Vasudheva's command; already the bishop has followers. Let him. Let him have the whole damned temple. "Give me the wings!" Vasudheva roars.

They slide onto his arms like musty-smelling vestments, each as heavy as a rug. Vasudheva can barely lift his arms. A warder helps him up to the balcony's parapet.

Vasudheva would like to turn back, just for a moment, and say something to Bhismu, something wise and loving and honest. But that would only burden his beloved with confusion and guilt. Best to leave it all unsaid.

"With wings like these," the high priest calls out to the crowd, "a man could fly to heaven."

He laughs. He's still laughing as he leaps toward the rising sun.

The Young Person's Guide to the Organism [Variations and Fugue on a Classical Theme]

THEME: ORGANISM

(ALLEGRO MAESTOSO E LARGAMENTE)

(WITH GOOD SPEED, MAJESTIC AND SWEEPING)

A treat. Come to the window. An Organism is passing the Outpost.

There, where my claw points. It is very faint. It is nearly invisible because its skin absorbs almost all the electromagnetic radiation it receives. Do you know what I mean by electromagnetic radiation? And what else besides light? And what else? And what else? Gamma rays, child. Gamma rays.

When you sleep tonight, I will see that you dream of physics.

You cannot tell from this view, but the Organism is very large. Twelve kilometers long, ten kilometers in diameter at its midsection. That is comparable to the Outpost itself. It is larger than any ship or orbital yet constructed by your race.

If you look closely, you will see that from time to time its skin glistens slightly with thin ghosts of color. It is beautiful, is it not? A thing of splendor, though it is nearly invisible. It is black, but comely.

Can you identify my allusion? The Song of Solomon. From a human celebration text. I have made a study of such texts, child; they hearten me. Whenever I despair that your race is entirely consumed by pettiness, the celebration texts remind me that humans also recognize greatness.

Recognize the greatness of this Organism, child. It is magnificent: huge, ancient, serene. When such an Organism passes by, ephemeral species like yours will dream dreams and see visions. Its presence stirs a resonance within you; some races claim these creatures are the shadows of gods, slowly gliding through our universe.

We do not know where this Organism comes from. It has been in deep space for centuries. If it does not choose to settle down in Sol's system, it will travel many more centuries before it reaches another star. It has been alone a long time.

No . . . why should we stop it? We have no right to interfere. Once it is past the Outpost, it is within human jurisdiction.

I don't understand your question. Why should it matter whether the humans can "handle" the Organism? This is their system—they are its children and its masters. We will not tamper with human affairs, not even "for their own good." We have neither the right nor the wisdom to meddle. You know that.

Yes, you are human yourself, child, but only in the coils of your DNA. In your brain and heart and soul, you are the chosen envoy of the League of Peoples. By the time humans step beyond the edge of their system, you will be ready to serve as intermediary between our two races. But before you can act, you must learn; and in order to learn, you must observe.

Observe the Organism as it passes, child. We do not know where it came from, nor can we predict where it goes. We cannot tell how much it is moved by instinct, how much by intellect . . . yet I say unto you, Solomon in all his glory was not arrayed as one of these.

Yes, another allusion. And unfair to Solomon. I expect he was a marvel himself.

VARIATION A: LEVIATHAN
(PRESTO)
(VERY QUICKLY)
CONTACT: MAY 2038

Not so long ago, my darling girl, every freighter flying the Red Run had one cargo pod doing duty as an Environment. You wouldn't know what that was, would you? (Whoops, Granddah spilled a bit on your bib, didn't he? Let me wipe it off. Ahh, get your fingers out of it. It's the tiniest fingers in the world you have, yes, Colleen, yes, you do.)

An Environment was a piece of Earth, that's what it was. A sim-u-la-tion. Which is a big word even for those of us who've mastered words like Mama and Dada and Granddah. (Granddah. Grannnn-daaahhh. No? Oh, well.)

We sometimes had trouble with Mudside investors who thought the Environment was a waste of our freight space, but those damned moneylenders had their thumbs up their . . . they were notoriously shortsighted, that's what they were. You put yourself in the place of those miners on Mars. Which would you rather have? Another few tons of bouillon and toothpaste? Or a walk through a rose garden smelling of perfume and peat moss, maybe a night forest rustling with rabbits and squirrels, or a marsh with red-winged blackbirds fluting away Cheeee-ri-ohhhhh! (Oh, you like that? Cheeee-ri-ohhhh! Cheeee-ri-oh-oo-oh!)

Anyway, how it was, your ship *was* its Environment. (Take a big mouthful, that's my girl.) The Environment was your ship's trademark and you lived up to it. I remember a Japanese ship called the *Edo Maru*—had a pretty little Shinto shrine, copy of a famous one on Mt. Fuji, I forget the temple's name. But very pleasant and tranquil. Trouble was, the captain was this Swede, nice fellow really, but *hearty*, you know, with the loudest voice God ever foisted on someone who didn't sing opera. Sort of gave the ship a split personality. No one could take it serious.

Don't know what happened to the *Edo*. Got old, got sold, I guess. Not many alternatives to that story, are there?

Our ship was called the *Peregrine*, and our Environment was the deck of a China clipper. A bit different from the back-to-nature Environments, but very popular. We had sun, waves, gulls, fresh-picked oolong in the hold. The kids could climb up into the rigging. Adults too, for that matter—miners would get one whiff of the breeze carrying the salt smell of the Pacific and they'd be clambering up the mast, forgetting the mines and the cold red desert, stretching those muscles that only get stretched when body and soul reach up together.

Once every docking, we'd run a storm—never broadcast when it would be, just let the sky start to turn gray . . . and the excitement! The looks on the faces of the visitors when the clouds began to cover the sun and folks knew they'd hit the right time! Then a lightning flash in the distance, a count of five, the rumble of thunder . . . waves heaping up and capping over, the wind rising to squall, the deck rocking, our crew lashing everyone to the railings as rollers came crashing over the bough . . . well, we were a legend. *Peregrine* wasn't a clunk of a freighter looking like a sow dangling twenty full teats, but an honest-to-God clipper ship.

Not an easy image to maintain, I tell you. Like the old masted clipper *White Cloud*, we couldn't ever be late, or the mystique would be shattered. Other ships—*Coventry*, that was the one with the rose garden—*Coventry* never docked on schedule. Once we saw it parked behind Phobos, passing time till it was overdue. It had its reputation, we had ours.

All of which is preamble to the story I'm going to tell you, soon as you have another spoonful of these beans. Or peas. This green sludge that looks like it came out of some . . . out of the wrong end of a herbivore. Mmmmm, yes, it's good, isn't it?

We may have had some beans and peas on board for the run I'm going to tell about. I don't know. The manifests said we were carrying perishables, which meant they'd only be good for three or four months in a refrigeration pod. The contract called for docking at Mars-Wheel within ninety days of departure, with a late penalty of ten percent of total fees per day . . . which was tough terms, let me tell you. But we were the *Peregrine* and we had our reputation to uphold. Not to mention raking in a pretty packet if we pulled the trick off.

We ran stripped, without a thimble more fuel than we needed and without a single spare part. Normally we'd carry enough gear to rebuild the entire engine if need be, not to mention duplicate navigation and life support systems. But that meant extra mass, and to make the Red Run in ninety days, given the relative positions of the Earth and Mars at that point . . . well, you don't want to hear this. Anyway, I don't want to talk about it, which amounts to the same thing, don't it?

We'd run stripped twice before, and didn't like it any better the third time. Superstitious types in the mess—and there are always superstitious types in the mess, that's as sure as death and taxes— they said you couldn't get away lucky three times in a row. All of us were jumpy, and me . . . it was my last trip before retirement, and I thought sure the fates would cut me down. Passing a watch alone in the control room, I'd say to myself, O'Neil, didn't you just hear the whine of the engines change? Shouldn't the pitch of the turbines sound lower? And isn't there maybe a kind of sour smell in the air, not exactly like something burning, but maybe the tiniest leak in a liquid fuel canister . . . and I'd stare at all the gauges, tap them sharp in case the needles were stuck, run diagnostics over and over again wondering what I'd do if I actually found something wrong, when all along, I knew the answer was just bend over and kiss my . . . life good-bye.

So. It was the sixty-fifth day and I was the only one awake on the ship. Well, considering how badly we were all sleeping that's probably not true, but I was the only crew member on duty, sitting in the control room and fretting over imagined catastrophes. I thought I was so keyed up I'd leap at shadows; but suddenly, it dawned on me I'd been staring at a blip on the proximity screen for over a minute without realizing what that blip meant.

I jerked into action, grabbed a radio headset with shaking hands, and nearly shouted into the mouthpiece, "Attention, nearby vessel, this is merchant freighter *Peregrine* traveling stripped, repeat stripped, en route to Mars-Wheel. Please yield. Repeat, please yield. Over." Which meant I wanted the other vessel to do whatever maneuvering was needed to avoid collision, because we intended to keep dead on course.

There was a silence that felt long, but I wasn't near calm enough to wait more than a heartbeat. I repeated myself three times without getting an answer, all the while watching the blip. It seemed to be growing, a speck that grew like a grain of rice in water and kept growing, to maggot, to beetle, to moth; but faint, ghostly faint, as if it was barely there. Too big for another freighter, but nothing like an asteroid, nothing like any chunk of space debris I'd ever seen. My hand hovered over the klaxon button, ready to send a panic through the ship, but I was too scared and unsure to sound the alarm. I doubted what I saw. I kept saying under my breath, I'm dreaming, I've snapped, it can't be.

It took a long time for the object to show on the visual monitors. When it did, it was a huge egg, bigger than Mars-Wheel itself, but so black I could only see it as a blot lumbering across the starscape. It was the biggest damned ship my eyes ever saw, and I knew it hadn't been constructed by human hands.

We passed within ten klicks of it, and I did nothing but watch. Never turned on the video recorders. Never called another soul as witness. I don't know why. After the edge dulled on my terror, I was overall calm. I didn't want to share this thing. It was something like a miracle, and I saw it as a promise the run would end all right. Ah, my darling, I was the man in the clipper's crow's nest catching sight of Leviathan itself in the quiet dark, and taking comfort there are great and strange mysteries in the places between shores. The deeps are unfathomable, which is a pun and a promise and a treasure and a truth. Near ten years have passed, but the wonder's still in me. And maybe it'll rub off on you, Colleen, my other wonder. Yes. Yes.

Now we'll mop off this pretty little mouth and say all gone, get rid of the nice bib that Granddah messed up, and then we'll see if we can find where your mother hides the diapers. All right? All right.

VARIATION B: NESSIE

(LENTO)

(SLOWLY)

CONTACT: JULY 2038

My Dear Grandchild Ashworth,

The doctors tell me I shall not live to see you born; and although a sensible man puts as much faith in doctors as he does in palm-readers and politicians, I am inclined to believe them in this particular matter. When I lie awake at night, I can feel the loosening of the strings that tie me to life. They unravel quietly; I have yet to decide if death is being gentle or merely stealthy.

But to the business at hand. Have you read those stories where someone puts a message in a bottle and throws it into the sea? As a boy, I loved those tales. We lived a hundred miles from the coast and had no money for traveling; but one autumn day when I was twelve, I tucked an old wine bottle into my knapsack and thumbed a ride with a lorry heading toward the ocean.

Two hours later I was standing on the edge of a deserted beach where a long cement pier stretched over the water. It was overcast and cold—I hadn't thought to bring a sweater—but my blood was singing with exhilaration. I ran along the sand and danced with the waves, each breaker different, each filled with water from a distant shore. It was one of the two perfect moments in my life.

When I had burned off the hottest fires of my elation, I threw myself down at the end of the pier and watched flotsam nudge against the pylons below me. After a while, I got out my bottle, my pen, and a notepad, and tried to decide what to write for my note. You may laugh at me (I do myself now and then), but I'd given no thought to this aspect of the adventure. The important thing, you see, was just to send some tiny bit of myself off into the unknown . . . to think that my bottle might be retrieved by a pearl diver off Honshu, or tangle itself in a mackerel net on the Grand Banks off Newfoundland, or founder in a storm rounding the Cape of Good Hope. I could point to any spot on the globe and think, there, right there, a part of me could be there.

Do you know what I finally wrote? *HA HA. IT'S ME. HELLO!!!*

I didn't even sign my name. In the back of my mind, I worried someone might find the bottle, track me down, and say, "Well, boy, your bottle got all the way to Brazil, isn't that splendid?" But it wouldn't be splendid at all. It would collapse my dream to some tiny reality. I wanted the world, not one paltry patch of sand.

Years later, I found myself owner and master of the good ship *Coventry,* a merchant freighter plying the silent dark between Earth and Mars with cargoes of tea and silk and spice . . . not to mention toothpicks, pencils, toilet tissue, and other mundane needs of life. It was a staid and genteel existence: months of slow calm followed by a cheerful arrival at the colony, where everyone was your friend and happy to meet you. The *Coventry* was always eagerly awaited.

Like most lives, I suppose, my life rolled along uneventfully. Our contracts were unashamedly pedestrian—I left to others the dangerous chemicals, the refined fission tubes, the lucrative perishables. Other ships might save money by gambling that an aging guidance system would last one more run; but the owners of those ships didn't ride in them. We spent more money on maintenance than we had to, but we never found ourselves stopped in the middle of a million miles of emptiness.

Except once. And that was by my command.

Halfway through an unexceptional run, I was summoned to the bridge by our second mate, a mercurial sort of woman named Rachel who amused the wardroom by taking up a new hobby on every run: oil painting, algebraic topology, playing the oboe . . . it was something different each time. This particular trip, she'd been dabbling with some of the new long-range sensor equipment that was just then coming onto the market (Lord knows where she got the money to buy it) and she'd detected a large anomaly some three hundred miles off our course. Did she have my permission to investigate? Well, certainly; our schedule was flexibility itself.

I can't say what we expected to find. Humanity was new enough to spacefaring that we constantly encountered oddities, most of them falling into the category of "yet another oddly pitted rock with a mildly unusual radar profile." However, when we finally closed on the anomaly, we discovered it was anything but mundane.

It was a giant: teardrop-shaped, black as the night it drifted through . . . all the grandeur and mystery of the universe made solid and riding silently before us. Like meeting the dear old

Loch Ness monster—something that *ought* to exist, even if it's impossible.

Almost twenty years have passed and still I cannot decide if it was a ship or a single giant creature, if it was alive or dead. One thing I know: it was not some oddly pitted rock.

Rachel looked at it with something like terror in her eyes. She could not bring herself to speak.

"Dock by it," I said without hesitation. "Tell the crew it's only a drill. I want this kept secret."

"Is it safe?" she asked.

"Do what I ask, please, Rachel. Let's consider this an order, shall we?"

While she brought the ship about and matched velocities with the anomaly, I put on a Vac/suit and found some chalk. I was in a state of burning excitement, fully alive for the second time in my life.

Yes, child. I went out the airlock, leapt through the void to the anomaly's flesh, and scrawled huge letters on its midnight scales: *HA HA. IT'S ME. HELLO!!!*

Now I, Gerald Ashworth, own the universe. That's how I feel. Perhaps the mystery will reach some far-off planet and start some new life cycle; perhaps it will fall into a sun or black hole; perhaps it will simply drift on until the great enfolding embrace of the cosmos reunites all matter and energy at the end of time. A little piece of me rides through the universe's depths, and makes them pregnant with possibility.

Only you and I know this secret. I was out of sight of the *Coventry* when I wrote the message; Rachel must have been curious, but didn't ask questions. I begged her to tell no one what we had seen, and she agreed.

So, you may ask, why am I telling this to an unborn grandchild when I've kept it secret from everyone else? Because you are a complete unknown. Maybe you'll be a great leader, or an artist, or a scientist; maybe you'll be a modest factory worker; maybe you'll be a criminal, or a lunatic, or a doctor. A world of possibility.

I shall put this letter into an envelope and leave it for you to open on your eighteenth birthday. I own the Earth and I own the universe. Through you, I can own the future.

HA HA. IT'S ME. HELLO!!!

VARIATION C: ANGEL
(FURIOSO)
(FURIOUSLY)
CONTACT: JULY 2038

I am in hell you are in hell this is hell we are all in hell. Amen. Say amen.

Say it!

Your voice sounds young today, demon. What are you pretending to be this time?

Simon Esteban. A student. Student of what, psychology or demonology? Never mind, that was a joke. I have a lot of psychology students visit me, Simon Esteban. You'd think I was the only madwoman on Mars.

Yes I know I'm on Mars and I know I'm in hell. Do I contradict myself? Very well, I contradict myself. I am large . . . I contain multitudes. My name is Legion, for many demons have entered me.

That's in the gospels. "Gospel" means "good news."

My other name is Rachel. "Rachel" means "Gentle innocent."

I enjoy irony as much as the next person.

I'm not what you expected, am I, Simon Esteban? Different from textbooks, different from case studies, different from typical profiles.

I can't imagine you'll ask any of the right questions. You'll start on my childhood, toilet-training, who fucked me first, and all that sewage. Do you want to know why I blinded myself? Do you want to know why I dug fishhooks into my eyes and *pulled* with all my strength, yes picture that, Simon Esteban, you with your eyes whole and round, picture the sight of the points hovering a hairs-breadth away, the clean dividing line between past and future as the points touch the corneas, the moment of resistance from the lens, then dig, pull, shred, so fast and strong the pain can't stop you soon enough, and the little sucking slurping *pop* as it is all over and sight gushes out in a flood . . . do you want to know why I did it? Because Oedipus did. The *real* Oedipus: not your puerile Freudian infant mooning over his mommy and playing with his pee-pee, but the King of Thebes, the hero who answered the Sphinx, the man who faced what he had done and knew he had to cleanse himself regardless of the cost.

When you're dirty, you must cleanse yourself, Simon Esteban. Or else you go mad.

Haven't they told you the story? Or are you simply lying in the hope I'll reveal myself?

I killed an Angel.

Rachel, Gentle Innocent, was sent an Angel in the darkness of the deepest night, and she slew it in cowardice, out of fear and envy and hatred.

I won't tell you what it looked like. That's a secret God wants me to keep. God won't always hate me. Someday I'll cleanse my-self totally. You can't watch me forever. Only the Angels watch forever.

In the darkness of space, the Angel first appeared unto me and me alone, in all its beauty and mystery. But when I saw it, I was sore afraid. I feared its strangeness and faltered.

Another went forth to greet it, and walked with it, and talked with it, and when he returned his face shone and his countenance was transformed. Then in my heart I hated the Angel, for I had feared it and had not taken its hand. And I envied him who had touched its being and basked in its glory; him also did I hate.

Then did we leave the Angel and travel on to safe harbor, where I fled unto the Legions of Caesar; and there did I tell them of the Angel and where it could be found. I told them also lies, that it had hidden in dark ambush and attacked our ship with fierce beams of light that bid fair to destroy us. Then Caesar sent out ships of war to do battle with the Angel and destroy it. And from that day to this, the Angel has never been seen again.

Only after the Angel's destruction did I see what I had done. And seeing what I had done after seeing what I saw, I wished that I could no longer see. And so it was done.

Amen.

Say amen.

You don't know what to believe, do you, Simon Esteban? Is it a lie or delusion or metaphor or truth? Lie, delusion, metaphor, truth, metaphor, delusion, lie, back and forth, up and down, doh, mi, so, doh, so, mi, doh, the hateful arpeggio, lie, delusion, metaphor, truth, metaphor, delusion, lie.

I can't tell them apart anymore. That means I'm mad.

When I talk, no one else can tell them apart either.

I don't know what that means.

VARIATION D: BOGEY
(ALLEGRO ALLA MARCIA)
(QUICK MARCH TEMPO)
CONTACT: NOVEMBER 2038

I know it's easy to hate the military. . . .

Jenny, would you look at me?

Would you look at me, please?

No, I won't go away. Your father was my best friend and he

would have wanted me to explain why he died. Frankly, your feelings don't enter into it at all.

Yes, I suppose that *is* a typical military attitude.

Let me say this: I'm about to tell you a military secret. If someone finds out, I'll be imprisoned for life. Maybe even executed. And I'm going to tell you anyway, even though you hate my guts and might turn me in when I'm finished. I'll do what needs doing, without balking at the consequences or deluding myself it will be appreciated. And *that's* a typical military attitude too.

A second mate on a Mars-Earth freighter came to us and reported her ship had been subjected to laser fire from a non-Terran-attributable source. Of course we were skeptical—she was a high-strung, frantic sort of woman, and obviously close to some kind of breakdown. The point was, had she seen a bogey because she was unstable, or was she unstable because she'd seen a bogey?

We questioned the rest of the crew. They told us the woman performed unscheduled maneuvers at one point in the journey, claiming they were some sort of drill. When we questioned the captain about this so-called drill, his evasiveness suggested he was concealing some pertinent information. Regrettably, he was a foreign national and his ship had foreign registry, so we had no legitimate way to lever further data from him.

You're determined to hate us, aren't you, Jenny? To be honest, we tried to get him drunk. It didn't work. That was the limit of our unorthodox coercion methods.

After due deliberation, we decided to send a frigate to investigate, under the command of Captain John Harrison. Your father. He volunteered for the mission. I was in charge of ground communication on Mars.

We'd gone on wild-goose chases before; sailors were forever seeing strange-shaped asteroids and reporting alien invasion fleets. We expected this to be another false alarm. However, as per standing orders, the operation was conducted under the tightest secrecy.

Our informant had given us detailed information on the bogey's course; if it was there, we'd find it. To our surprise, we did.

I won't tell you what it looked like. Suffice it to say, it was larger than Mars-Wheel and Venus-Wheel combined. It was virtually invisible on all spectral bands; if the informant hadn't told us exactly where to look, we wouldn't have found it. In comparison, the vessel your father commanded glowed like a beacon. The bogey must have perceived the frigate clearly, but took no hostile action.

After tracking the bogey for several hours, your father attempted communication using everything from radio to signal flashers. There was no response of any kind.

We consulted with higher authority. The very highest. Everyone was inclined to leave the bogey alone . . . or more accurately, to turn responsibility over to the scientific arm and let them investigate to their hearts' content. But we had that report saying the bogey had fired on a freighter; and trajectory calculations showed the thing was heading into the main shipping lanes on a near-collision course with Earth.

Do you understand how it was, Jenny? It was heading for Earth and no one knew why. We didn't know if it was an invasion army, or a bomb, or just some harmless piece of junk. We didn't know.

A decision was made to destroy it. I didn't make it, your father didn't make it, but we agreed one hundred percent.

You say that as if we were all vicious killers. You knew your father; you know he wasn't like that. He was the man on the spot, that's all. He had to carry out the mission.

Do you think no one considered the alternatives? Yes, the bogey might have been peaceful. Yes, it might have blessed humanity in unimaginable ways. Yes, it might simply have drifted past in total indifference. Believe me, our superiors didn't make the decision casually.

But they had no choice. The bogey would pass through the space lanes. It would be seen. It would be a destabilizing influence. There would be panic, hysteria, people killed in riots . . . and that's if the bogey just flew by without taking action. Maybe it would turn out to be hostile after all. We had to face that possibility. What would humanity think of the fleet if we let such a thing reach Earth without opposition?

I want you to understand this, Jenny. Your father would want you to understand. No one could take that chance. We had to do the hard thing. The hard thing is not killing or dying, it's making the choice. Making the choice that is cruel and necessary and irrevocable.

The worst part is knowing you'll never find out if you were right.

The bogey drank up laser fire like water—your father drained his weapon batteries without burning a square inch of the thing's skin. Contrary to insinuations from the press, our forces *are* respecting the Selene treaty and your father had no nuclear weapons aboard. Therefore, after consultation with our superior officers and in full agreement with their decision, your father commanded his men to evacuate the vessel in life-pods, and then, alone at the helm, rammed the bogey at maximum velocity.

We don't know if the bogey was destroyed. Perhaps it was only diverted from its course. Other ships searched the area, but space is large. They found less than a third of the remains from your father's ship. They found nothing at all of the bogey.

To me, Jenny, your father died a hero. Not because he was willing to die—there are millions of fools who think dying somehow justifies their cause. Believe me, that's bullshit: your father knew dying doesn't prove anything. But he died anyway, eyes open, full of doubt but doing the job.

They told you your father died in some kind of accident. I thought you should know the truth. Too many things happen by accident in the world. It's time people realized some things happen by human choice.

VARIATION E: DAEMON
(BRILLANTE)
(SPARKLING, LIVELY)
CONTACT: NOVEMBER 2038

Sit down and quit whining.

I don't *care* if you were going riding. I've decided it's time to pontificate.

Honestly, Maria, didn't they teach you anything in that private school I sent you to? Pontificate. Look it up. Show a little initiative, for God's sake.

That's what I want to talk about: initiative. There are two types of people in the world—the ones who are alive and the ones who aren't. The quick and the dead. The open and the closed.

Here. Catch.

Know what that is?

A false fingernail? Did you say a false fingernail? Hell, that false fingernail is the Petrozowski Whole Spectrum Collector Cell. That's what pays for your wardrobe, your boyfriends, and your goddamned horse.

Sometimes, Maria, I don't think you're really my daughter. Sometimes I think your mother, God rest her soul, had a fling with some pretty playboy while I was busy at the office. I know, she wasn't that kind of a woman. I'm just trying to dodge the blame.

Now here . . . take a look at this.

No, it's not the same thing. That, my dear, is a scale from the hide of my personal daemon.

Daemon, not demon! My guardian spirit. My source of inspiration.

No, your old man isn't cracking up. Although people might think so, if they knew what I'm about to do.

I'm going to give you total control over Petrozowski Energy. Have fun with it.

Stop whining. Stop right now.

The business world is losing its novelty for me. I foresee that in the not-too-distant future, I'll be bored to the edge of madness. So I'm taking a one-man yacht into space and I'm going to find the daemon again.

I've thought about this a long time. I could go through the motions of running the company till the day I die, or I could say to hell with the rat race and pursue another dream.

I hate the jaded way I feel some days, Maria. I want to be excited about something again. I want to feel the tingle of magic.

You don't know what I'm talking about, do you?

Thirty-five years ago, daughter dear, I was a lowly navy tech baby-sitting the solar energy cells of a frigate named the *Coherent*. It was a stupid job. I'd enlisted because I wanted to get off Earth. "Out of the cradle and into the rest of the universe," that's what the recruiters told me. I should have realized the purpose of the fleet wasn't to widen our horizons but to bring the cosmos down to our own size.

One afternoon I was standing my watch when I felt the jolt of our guns firing and saw our battery levels dropping. Fifteen minutes later, the charge in the batteries red-lined dead bottom. An hour later, we were ordered to abandon ship. That was it. No one felt it necessary to explain what was going on. Need to know and all that.

I ejected in the nearest escape pod and found myself shooting toward the biggest damned hulk I'd ever seen. I couldn't tell you what it was. I've thought about it most of my life.

In my dreams, sometimes I get inside the thing, and it's always different. Sometimes I meet these glowing little men who sit me down and tell me things that make me understand myself and the universe. Sometimes it's filled with monsters and I find myself with pistol in one hand and saber in the other, shooting and slashing to save the human race. Sometimes I'm just walking through this huge cavity and I look up and there's this huge heart beating slowly overhead, booming like thunder.

But I didn't get inside the daemon; I only smacked into its hide. A rough landing . . . the daemon had a gravity almost as strong as Earth's and it sucked me right down. I can't explain the gravity—artificial maybe. I managed to brake most of my speed with the retros, but the escape pod still slammed against the daemon with a clang like a great Chinese gong. *CLLAAANNNGGGG!!!*

I did that to catch your attention. Here and now, girl! Keep your head in the here and now!

The first thing I did after landing was put on a suit and go out—I wanted to know what I'd landed on. The surface was broad and black, very slightly rounded and pebbly with scales. Overhead floated the *Coherent,* bright and silver like the moon above dark autumn fields.

I knelt and examined the daemon's hide. Blacker than black, each scale was angled toward the *Coherent,* an audience of a billion eyes watching.

Then, slowly, the nearest eyes turned to look at me.

If I hadn't been a solar cell technician, I might have run screaming in terror back to the pod . . . but I'd worked among our own solar collectors and seen them slowly turn their gaze on me as the robot controllers picked up my body heat and swiveled to drink it in. Absorbing the IR my own flesh emitted.

I pried loose as many of those little eyes as I could. They had to be energy collector cells and for some reason, I knew—knew!—they were orders of magnitude more efficient than anything we humans had developed. And indeed they were, my darling daughter, indeed they were.

Perhaps if I'd had more time, I could have found some way to enter the daemon . . . but as I knelt there plucking up eyes, I saw some of them turn away from me and I glanced back to see what they'd noticed.

The *Coherent,* engines streaming out a fiery cloud, was speeding through the night like a torpedo on a collision course with my daemon. I suppose in the back of my mind, I must have realized this would happen—why else would they have ordered us to abandon ship? But for a moment I was staggered and frozen by the utter stupidity of the military mind. It was the ultimate evil: trying to kill something wonderful and magic and new.

I was paralyzed only for a moment, but it was almost a moment too long. I barely had time to get back inside my pod and slam the outer hatch before the *Coherent* hit and exploded. The daemon pitched wildly; my pod was bucked off, rolling end over end and tossing me around inside like a man going over Niagara Falls in a barrel.

Through the pod's viewport, I caught one last glimpse of the daemon before it vanished into the blackness. It was on a new heading . . . I don't know if it had simply been knocked off course by the collision or if it had changed direction on its own. I couldn't tell if it'd been damaged; it vanished as quickly as a coin in the hands of a magician.

Well, you can fill in the rest of the story. I kept the scales to myself till I got out of the navy, then analyzed them and reproduced them as well as I could. The reproduction wasn't perfect, but it was generations ahead of anything else on the market; and as the money flowed in, I could afford to hire a team of the best eggheads, and patent by patent, they came closer to a full duplication of . . . well, a flake of my daemon's skin.

I could also afford to hire scouts to search for the daemon. They never found it. I think . . . I think daemons only appear to a certain kind of person. You have to be ready for them. You have to be open. You have to be goddamned alive.

So. I'm going out solo.

I want to know if I'm still the sort of person who's worthy of wonder.

Don't cry. If you don't want to run the company, let the board of directors do it. You'll still receive dividend payments and the company will stay healthy. My people know what they're doing. I just thought you might enjoy honest work.

If you prefer, you can sell your share in the company and use the money to pursue whatever dreams you want. Really. I whole-heartedly approve of people who pursue their dreams.

If you have any dreams.

Do you have any dreams, Maria?

VARIATION F: BOOJUM
(MENO MOSSO)
(SLOWER, LESS MOTION)
CONTACT: JULY 2070–APRIL 2071

So, Yorgi. You got caught.

You're an idiot, boy.

Your mother, she wants me to make a big fuss. She wants me to smack you around. I should spit in your face and say your ances-tors will haunt you.

Maybe they will.

Me, if I get to heaven, and some great-great-grandchild of mine gets caught breaking into a store, I got better things to do than sneak up on the kid and go boo. I'll just say to myself, the boy's an idiot, and go back to the houris.

But your mother says, Emil, talk to the boy. Okay, Yorgi, I'm talking to you.

The priests, they'll threaten you with hell. They're good at it; it's their job. But you're like me—you can't listen to a sermon without falling asleep.

So no sermons. Here's all I'm going to say: there are lots of things you can do in your life, but they break into two classes. Some things make you smarter. Some things make you stupider. No other possibilities.

Stealing makes you stupider. Every time you steal, you get a little stupider. It doesn't matter if you get caught, and it doesn't matter what you steal.

I know.

A few years back—you *aren't* going to tell your mother this story—I was working for Petrozowski Energy. Cook on a freighter. But it wasn't really a freighter, it was a hunter. We'd load up with cargo and fuel as if we were making the Red Run, but then we'd prowl space, looking for a boojum Mr. Petrozowski saw once. Crazy, eh? And the craziest thing was, our third time out we found it.

Big thing. Huge. And black, with a kind of shimmer, like the northern lights. First time we saw it, we nearly pissed ourselves. Whole crew went up to the bridge, looked at the thing. None of us had a clue what it was. Didn't look dangerous. Just kind of spooky.

Instructions were to track it, plot its course. No radio reports . . . Mr. Petrozowski didn't want anyone finding out where we were or what we were doing. Once we got the thing charted, we were supposed to fire back full thrust and report in person.

Well. We all got to thinking. Petrozowski was paying big money for all this secrecy. Triple what we'd get on a normal run. And if we reported home right away, maybe we'd get a bonus if we were lucky, but then we'd go back to the usual grind. We thought, if we put off reporting it till the *next* run . . . well, Mr. Petrozowski would still find his boojum, we'd still get the bonus, and we'd get triple pay for an extra run.

So that's how we all started getting stupider. It was stealing, you see. Easy stealing. Didn't have to hit someone over the head, didn't have to get past an alarm. Just waited out our time and headed home empty-handed.

We waited out our time on the boojum. Didn't have anywhere else to go.

Went down, looked around. It was scaly. No mouth or any other opening. Something had dented its side a bit . . . a meteor, I guess. We tried to cut a hole in it with laser torches, but the light just got sucked up. We pried away scales, and underneath were more scales. We dug down a long way, but the scales went down farther. They grew back too, eventually. Took a few days. They sort of pushed up from below.

That first time, we amused ourselves watching the Boojum grow scales. Some of the technicians tried to figure out where its gravity came from, but they soon lost interest.

The second time, we found it again, no problem. Went straight to it. Then we had nothing to do but spend three months sitting around. As cook, I was the busiest hand on board.

To pass the time, the crew played with the Environment. Sure, Yorgi, our ship carried an Environment, like any other Mars freighter—Mr. Petrozowski didn't want to arouse suspicions when the ship was in port. The Environment held a little stone temple surrounded by a lot of nice green plants. Very pretty. Buddhist, maybe. Mr. Petrozowski didn't care about it; it'd been built by the previous owners. We could use it for anything we wanted.

We installed it on the boojum.

For some reason, we laughed and laughed at the idea. It seemed so funny. This boojum, this strange alien thing, this giant—we'd attach our Environment to it like a flea on the back of a dog, and we'd ride and grow fat. The ship would hover in space, but the crew would pass the time in the Environment pod on the boojum's back, sitting in easy chairs under a simulated sun, sipping lemonade and playing cards. Like we were all wealthy landlords who'd found some private jungle retreat away from the stupid peasants.

That time, we had to feed the Environment power from the

ship's storage cells. And we had to reattach the Environment to our ship when we left for home.

The next time, we sold our extra fuel on the black market. We didn't need fuel to go out into space and sit around for three months. We used the money to buy good Petrozowski Whole Spectrum Collector Cells, which we installed on the hull of the Environment pod so it could gather its own energy from the sun. That way we didn't have to go back to the ship to recharge the life support systems; we could live in the Environment all the time. And we did. We lived what we thought were the lives of the rich.

They were stupid lives.

The time came to head for Earth. And we found the boojum had grown too fond of the Environment pod.

Somehow, the scales of the boojum had attached themselves to the collector cells we'd installed on the pod. The scales and cells had grown together into a single skin, like the edges of a wound healing shut. The Environment was bonded fast, held tight; we couldn't cut it free, couldn't pull it loose with the ship's engines. In the end, we had to go home without it.

Stupid, see? We thought we could do what we wanted. We thought were smarter than other people, and what did we get?

When we got back to Earth, we still thought we might get away with it. We tried to buy a new pod; we thought we could make do with a substitute, pick up better cutting tools and go back to slice the Environment free. No. Mr. Petrozowski heard we were missing a pod; he investigated and found we'd been selling our fuel; and he fired us. He thought we'd been cheating him all along. The only reason he didn't call the cops was he didn't want us telling anyone about the boojum hunt. We told him we'd *found* his boojum, but he laughed in our faces.

So. Your father is no saint. We both knew that, yes? But I've learned.

We were stupid. There were hundreds of ways we could have

got caught. If one of Petrozowski's other hunters had found us on the boojum. If the police nabbed us selling fuel on the black market. If any member of the crew had loose lips. Hundreds of ways. But we ignored the risks. We thought we were being smart when we were being stupid.

I tell you, Yorgi, if you decided to be the best thief in the world, and learn, and work hard at it, maybe you could get smarter. Maybe that would be possible. But such thieves, I don't think they exist. When I was a thief, I was lazy. I sat on easy chairs and drank lemonade. I told myself Mr. Petrozowski was stupid, not me. I thought I was one of the smartest men in the world, and I laughed, laughed, laughed. But what was I? A flea riding the back of a dog. That's all.

Who thinks fleas are smart?

VARIATION G: TITAN
(DOLCE CON AMORE)
(SWEETLY, WITH LOVE)
CONTACT: MAY 2071

Teeth brushed? Faces washed? No one has to pee? Then we start.

How I met your father. A true story. With a moral.

No giggling. Once upon a time.

You know there are great rivalries between the Venus cloud mining orbitals. Great rivalries. Each orbital is owned by a different company, and the companies hate each other. They sabotage each other's wells, they interfere with each other's communications, and when miners meet each other in Venus-Wheel . . . well, there may be fights and duels and death.

My family lived on an orbital belonging to Clearwater Chemical, and our greatest rivals were those in New Frontier Mining and Manufacture.

No giggling! This is a true story. With a moral.

My mother was Clearwater's economic envoy to Venus-Wheel. By the time I was fourteen, I went with her on every trading mission. In those days, I was a very great beauty . . .

What are all these giggles I'm hearing?

I was a great girlish beauty then, and now I am a great womanly beauty, which is even better, though different. Do you want a story or not?

Then we go on. How I met your father. A true story. With a moral.

In those days, I was a great girlish beauty, and *firm* in the soft places. Which is almost as good as soft in the soft places, though different. Many boys wanted to make love to me, and many older men as well.

A *great* many older men.

You would not *believe* how many older men would rather have girlish beauty instead of womanly beauty. "Bah," they say, "who cares if the woman knows what to do? *We* know what to do, and that is the important thing."

A free lesson for you about men.

But I had not yet learned that lesson and I was drunk with the power of my very great firm beauty. I went to many dances on Venus-Wheel and danced with many men. It was a great whirling excitement for a girl my age. The men worshipped me and the boys adored me; it made me feel very strong.

Then one night I met a boy who made me feel weak. Oh, such weakness! If I looked in his direction, I blushed. If I didn't look in his direction, I watched in mirrors to see if he was eyeing me behind my back. When he talked to me, I wanted to run and hide; when I danced with him, I could feel every part of my body singing. And I could feel every part of *his* body too—maybe not singing, but at least standing up in the choir.

When I told him my name was Juliet, he bowed and said he

would be my Romeo. So gallant! But too close to the truth. I found out after the dance his father was economic envoy for New Frontier. Disaster! I was forbidden to speak to the boy again.

I cannot be sure I loved my Romeo before I was forbidden to see him, but afterward, I loved him with a love as deep as starry space. He was the blazing sun, and I the dark Abyss that yawned to engulf him and be illuminated.

We talked like that back then. We were young.

The boy and I met all the time, of course. Many trysts. Many *excellent* trysts. I became a very great girlish beauty who purred to herself, and my mother became suspicious. She announced she was sending me home to Clearwater orbital, where the only boys were my brothers and cousins.

I did not go. Instead, I eloped. My Romeo and I stole a rich man's yacht, disabled the homing beacons, and fled into the night. Our goal was Mars, where we planned to scout the asteroid belt. Out in the belt, we would become the first humans to find alien artifacts; we would be rich and famous, and the entire solar system would envy us.

Two weeks later, our food ran out. A month and a half away from Earth, four months away from Mars.

My Romeo and I had our first fight.

"I thought *you* were going to pack the food."

"I didn't know we needed food. Ships are supposed to recycle everything."

"When you recycle everything, you don't recycle *everything*. You run out eventually. Don't you know Newton's laws?"

"I know Newton's laws, and they don't say anything about food!"

Remember, this is a true story.

We made up and made love, as always happens with first fights. Making love after a fight can be very bad or very good. It is awkward, but vigorous.

We were lucky and did not starve. God looked down, said "Tsk-tsk, such blockheads," and saved us.

We came upon a great creature in space. A giant; a friendly Titan, like Prometheus or Atlas.

Why do you immediately believe me when I say we found a Titan in space, but you giggle when I say I was a great girlish beauty? No, don't answer.

Like Atlas, the Titan carried a world on its back, and inside that world, we found a temple for worshipping the Titan. The temple area was bright and warm, filled with growing green plants. Many of the plants were edible; some were edible even after we had overcome the first pangs of our ravening hunger.

We stayed at the temple for two weeks. At dawn, we would wake naked in each other's arms and watch the sun rise; we would eat breakfast, then spend the morning gathering leaves. In the afternoon, we would go back to the yacht and take turns shoving leaves down the toilet, to replenish the bio-mass the ship needed to make food. In the evening, we would return to the temple, recite worshipful poems of our own devising, and sprawl ourselves reverently on the altar. We fell asleep only when we had wrung out our bodies in every way, and we dreamed of the new universes we would discover.

Here is what we really discovered.

I discovered my Romeo had never heard of Scarlatti, Haydn, Mendelssohn, Chopin, Cage, or Laurier-Leyrac. He was not keen to learn.

I discovered he was an enthusiast for types of music called Synthereg and Mexihowl. Mexihowl required drumming on your thigh. Or someone else's thigh.

I discovered he thought my mother was a greedy bitch because of some deal where she'd outmaneuvered New Frontier.

I discovered he was unwilling to admit that many New Frontier trade practices were unethical, if not outright illegal.

I discovered whisker-burn.

He discovered menstruation.

We flew back to Venus-Wheel and were met with teary hugs. Afterwards, our parents got very very angry, but hugs first. That is the way good parents are.

My Romeo and I were sent to apologize to the man whose yacht we had stolen. The man was wealthy and good-natured. It amused him, the way things turned out. He laughed and laughed when I told him about stuffing the leaves into the toilet. I laughed with him. We had a very good laugh, and my Romeo joined in with us. Then he went away with his family, leaving me alone with the wealthy man.

So the true story is, I met your father by stealing his yacht to run away with someone else. And the moral is, making love is glorious, and someday you will do it and revel in it, as your father and I do it and revel in it. But when you pick someone to be with, think about everything *except* making love.

Any two people can make love if they want to.

VARIATION H: DRAGON
(SCHERZANDO MA CON FUOCO)
(PLAYFULLY, BUT WITH FIRE)
CONTACT: JULY 2076

Sacred Daughter of the Sun,

Forgive an old woman's presumption for writing to You, Honored Child, and forgive the many tricks I have used to smuggle this message past Your Regents. The Regents are all fine people, yes, but they are not the Empress. Some things are meant for Your August Ears alone.

I am Mariko Naruki, wife to Yushio Naruki, who is chief executive of Laughing Dragon Entertainment Industries Company Limited. He is a dear man because he is mostly a child. He has invented many games in his life, not to mention many fine rides in Laughing Dragon Entertainment Parks throughout the Inner Planets; but I have never trusted him with the grocery money. Never mind. A good man, and good at building fun and happiness. Not so good at building strong fiscal structures. So—and I pray it will be forgotten by the time You reach Your Majority and are given this letter—my dear Yushio led Laughing Dragon to the brink of ruin.

One day he phoned from work and asked me to make a large withdrawal from our savings account. Why? I asked. He needed the money to buy something. What did he want to buy? He wouldn't say. So I did what a good wife should: I gave him the money, then followed him when he left the office.

He bought a sword. A very fine sword of strong bright steel, with a hilt covered in real leather and a fine embroidered sheath. A good choice for a decoration hanging in the living room, but I knew he wanted it for a different reason. What a child he was! I confronted him there in the store, berated him about what he was up to, attracted a big crowd, never mind. In the end, I let him make a down payment on the sword—it really was excellent, and the price quite reasonable—but I made him leave it in the store on layaway.

Still, that was not the end of it. He could see disaster looming for the company and wanted to pay the honorable price of failure. Which meant he just wanted to run away. We women know many men are just little boys whose swagger has become convincing.

Finally I suggested flying into the sun. It was the kind of gesture that appealed to Yushio: a flamboyant idea, but austere in execution. It appealed to me too because the flight would give him time to reconsider his rash decision. I thought I could persuade him to start a new life instead of ending the old one: perhaps becoming a Flare-Fisher on Mercury, which would suit Yushio's sense of romance while paying very well.

We set off secretly in the executive yacht, well provisioned and weighted down with our life savings converted to platinum. (We had no children to whom we could leave an inheritance . . . my fallopian tubes had growths, I nearly died at fifteen, never mind.) Soon Yushio was treating our trip as an adventure. He had never been in space, though he had designed entertainments for all the colonies and for many spacefaring vessels. Long hours at a time, he forgot himself and scribbled designs on paper: new games, new rides, new adventure areas. But then suddenly he would remember the reason he was in space, the catastrophe facing his company, and he would sink into gloom.

Then the hand of the gods. Just outside the orbit of Venus, we encountered a dragon.

It didn't look like a dragon. More like a dragon's egg: black with shimmers, huge and beautiful. Silent and serene as space, but when you looked at it, you felt a million eyes looking back.

Almost everywhere, its hide was smooth as a girl's cheek; but in one spot, on its back, the skin rose in the shape of the sacred mountain (I do not lie) with a small hole at the top. Like the sacred mountain's cone.

Except that this opening was an airlock. Inside, there was fresh air, sunlight, gravity, and a reproduction of the Musubi Shrine to Amaterasu O-mikami, Your Own Celestial Ancestress.

I swear this is true.

"We have found Heaven," I said to Yushio.

"Nonsense," he answered. "We have found an Environment my company built for a Mars freighter. The *Edo Maru*. I wonder what it's doing here."

"The gods put it here."

He looked around. "The gods haven't been taking very good care of it, have they?"

It was true—the shrine was in a shambles. Vandals had hacked off much of the foliage. Inside the torii gate, where Your Majesty knows there should only be peace and serenity, there were instead a few broken lawn chairs and some playing cards bearing pictures of hairy people in rut. And the altar . . . I cannot describe the altar, but it needed a very good cleaning.

I insisted on resanctifying the shrine. Yushio argued it hadn't been a real shrine and he shouldn't delay his death-trip into the sun, but he knew he was on shaky theological ground. How could his death be true to the Way when he would not trouble himself to repair the desecration of such a holy place?

Yushio is a dear man, but whenever he argues with me he is always wrong.

So we cleaned the shrine and put it to rights. Yushio had packed some incense with the intention of burning it as we sailed into the sun; but I convinced him the gods would be happier if we used it at the shrine in a purification ceremony.

While we worked, we discussed what we thought this dragon really was. I knew in my heart it was a true dragon sent by the gods . . . but I pretended to agree with Yushio that most likely it was a secret super-project that had been abandoned for some reason. Maybe the builders had gone bankrupt and just left the thing here. (Going bankrupt was ever-present in Yushio's mind.)

Finally I said, "Why speculate? You know this Environment once belonged to the *Edo Maru*. Radio your company and get them to find out who owns the Environment now."

Yushio refused. He said his decision to die had cut all ties with the business world . . . but that just meant he was afraid to talk to people. Finally I made the call myself after he had fallen asleep on rice wine. Our closest branch office was on Venus-Wheel, only a few radio-seconds away. They were glad to know we were still alive, worried the creditors were growing more insistent every day. I cut short that line of conversation, saying "I want to know who owns a freighter called the *Edo Maru*."

After a few minutes, the answer came back: "Petrozowski Energy."

"Yushio wants you to buy it."

"Buy it? I don't think we can afford . . ."

"Get a loan."

"I don't think any bank would . . ."

"Tell the banks," I said, "Laughing Dragon is about to announce its largest Entertainment Park ever. Tell them we have kept it a great secret because it is a brand new idea. Tell them this park is where all the company's capital went, and it will repay everyone a millionfold. You hear?"

"Is this true?"

"Yes, it's all true. Very secret. Very big. In space."

"In space?"

"Yes, it's a whole new idea. You'll see. Get the board of directors. I'll turn on a tracking beacon so they can find us. They can come and see the marvel Yushio has built. But you must buy the *Edo Maru*."

"Perhaps it would be possible . . ."

"And the *Edo Maru*'s Environment, and all attached chattels. That is most important. And it is most important Petrozowski Energy does not think this is anything special. You hear?"

"Yes." And it was done. We purchased the *Edo Maru,* its Environment, and all attached chattels. The dragon was attached and therefore ours . . . if humans can claim to own such a beast.

When Yushio awoke, I was looking over his plans for new games and rides. "It would be a shame if these were never built," I said. He agreed.

By the time the board of directors arrived, Yushio had mapped out two thirds of the Laughing Dragon of Heaven Entertainment World: the Christian Heaven, where adults and children would be given their own wings to play bumpem; Allah's Heaven with many nimble dancers; Valhalla, filled with much carousing and ax fights against hologram opponents; and many other fine heavens, including a reproduction of the real Heaven centered around the Musubi Shrine.

Now, as we begin construction on the park, the world believes this Dragon was built by our company. They see what they expect to see: the foundation for the greatest entertainment site in the universe.

Only you, Great Empress, will know the truth. It is a truth that should remain secret for a thousand years, for if anyone suspected Heaven's real nature . . . well, we know the West has a long tradition of killing dragons. But You—You are Child of the Sun and Sister to Dragons. May the truth do You honor.

VARIATION I: ROC

(NOBILMENTE CON FORZA)

(NOBLY, WITH FORCE)

CONTACT: SEPTEMBER 2078

If this had happened in my grandfather's time, throats would already be cut. I wouldn't be talking to a lawyer but to a mortician.

My grandfather was a prince who believed his title meant something. Perhaps it did in those days. Perhaps it still does. At the very least, being a prince means there's always some university that's willing to give you a scholarship. Trinity College, Oxford, for me. And you?

I don't believe I've heard of it. Good school, was it? Fine. I want to know we have a top man on this.

You're a little young to be a full partner, aren't you? Oh, no, I take that as a promising sign. Of course, you *will* be discussing the case with your firm's senior partners? Good. Good.

Now the long and the short of it is this: I want to sue Laughing Dragon's scaly tail off. Slap criminal negligence charges on anyone whose nose rises out of the foxhole. Permanently ruin a few careers, and if possible, give the whole Laughing Dragon of Heaven Entertainment Park such a reputation for gross mismanagement that no bourgeois little family would think of vacationing there. If we can drive a few of the bastards to commit seppuku, it will be icing on the cake.

Does that sound up your alley?

My dear man, let us understand each other. I am a prince in a line that stretches back more generations than anyone can count, and now, enemies have recklessly slain twenty-three people under my protection. If modern civilization prevents me from taking revenge with a knife, I will use whatever other weapon comes to hand. I have chosen my weapon to be the courts, and I will use that weapon to shed blood for blood, ruin for ruin, life for life. If you stand with me, good. If not . . .

You want to hear the circumstances first? I approve. Only a barbarian kills without knowing why.

As I've said, being a full-blooded prince means little today. I've had to work for a living. All in all, I think that's good for a man. I direct a modest construction company. Our primary business is building orbitals, but we're happy to put up anything that requires work in vacuum. My crews are drawn from all corners of the Earth, and one was even born on Mars . . . but you understand, whether or not they are of the blood or the faith, they are *my* people.

We had contracted with Laughing Dragon to build a part of the amusement park they call Heaven. (I know you'll want to examine the contract; I'll leave a copy with you.) Our assignment was a section on the side of the park that's always turned away from the sun. The section was named Afterlife After Dark . . . it's a name that would make a sensible man ill, but a company which refuses to work for fools soon finds itself out of business. And to be honest, my workers found building nightclubs and carousels and roller coasters was a pleasant change from all those oh-so-functional orbitals.

Not that it was easy work. Far from it. The entire surface of Heaven—they seem to want to keep this secret, so splash it around in every interview you give—the entire surface is covered with Petrozowski collector cells. Incredible. How long has Petrozowski been in business? Ten years? I wouldn't have thought the entire production of all his plants could have made so many cells. Hundreds of hectares in area! And many layers deep . . . a stupefying achievement. But impossible to dig into. We had to pour concrete foundations on top, covering over a fortune's worth of the cells . . . and you can't imagine the technical difficulties of putting up small environment domes, so you can pour concrete foundations, so you can put up big environment domes. But never mind that now.

Our construction site was on the dark side, but we lived in dormitory pods on the bright side of the terminator. We worked in shifts, of course. Which is why I'm alive when twenty-three of my people are not.

It was about an hour before shift change and I was in our cafeteria having breakfast with the crew that would be going out. I planned on going out with them. I often did. And I always did whatever tasks the shift supervisor assigned me, even if I am a prince. A prince must set an example, don't you think?

Suddenly, in the middle of the meal, we felt a great trembling in the floor beneath us. Water glasses rattled; salt shakers fell over. Without a second's thought, every man and woman there kicked back chairs and ran to the equipment chamber where Vac/suits were stored. We dove into the suits, grabbed extra oxygen tanks, jet packs, Mayday beacons, whatever we could fill our arms with; then we piled into the airlocks in a rush to get out in the open.

Outside, we were just one of many construction crews evacuating their dormitories, stumbling about in confusion, trying to keep our footing on the quaking surface. Every band on my helmet radio was clogged with cries of panic. I tried to shout against the noise, but couldn't make myself heard. In exasperation, I clicked it off and searched the sky, hoping to see one of the supply ships docked close enough that a jet pack could bridge the gap. But instead I saw the cause of the disturbance.

The entire dark side of Heaven had split in two, as if we stood on a giant bird, a roc, that was unfolding its wings. The wings rose up higher and higher over the horizon, strong and graceful, the ebony of night now glittering in the sunlight; but as the wings moved, their speed and strength tossed off my workers like seeds scattered across a field. The nightclubs, the carousels, the roller coasters . . . all wrenched apart as their foundations slid along with the motion of the wings. Gravity seemed to have gone wild out there: some buildings flew off into space with my people; others lodged themselves at the hinge point where the wings met the body.

Hundreds of people were thrown into the emptiness of the abyss. We formed rescue parties, retrieved those we could. Of my workers we found nineteen: seven alive, twelve dead in their suits. Another eleven have not yet been found. Teams still search—none of us believes the missing are alive, but it's horrible to think of a friend's body drifting forever in blackness.

And the explanation for this all? It took fifteen hours to get anything out of Laughing Dragon. Then the president's wife—his wife! the man couldn't face us himself—made a statement that the wings had been opened up to expose more collector cells to the sunlight. The management regretted this had happened without warning. Notices were supposed to have been sent around but were inadvertently misplaced.

All a lie. I've paid a few bribes, and no one, inside or outside Laughing Dragon, knew what was going to happen. Anyway, why would they open the wings when it would cause such damage to their own park? No, someone made a mistake, someone very high up or very well protected, and that person must be made to pay.

Reasonable damages for the next of kin? Do you think my people weren't insured? The next of kin will be paid handsomely, and if the insurance company wants to reclaim its money from Laughing Dragon, it can file its own suit. I want *damage,* man, not *damages*! Make them know they're dealing with something they can't control.

VARIATION J: LION
(LAMENTOSO MA DOLCISSIMO)
(SADLY, BUT VERY SWEETLY)
CONTACT: SEPTEMBER 2078

Oh, my darlings! I wish it could be said that your father died a man.

My grandfather once said to me, "Boy, a man is not a man until he walks with a lion."

And my grandmother said, "Oh, William, that was long ago."

"No," he answered. "Long ago, it was said a man had to *kill* a lion. But guns made killing easy. Too many lions died. Now, no more killing. Walk with the lion. See him. Learn what a man is not. Hear the voice of that which is stronger than you."

"What nonsense," my grandmother muttered. "If the boy ever does meet a lion, he'll find running is better than walking."

But my grandfather looked me in the eye, pointed a swollen-knuckled finger at my nose, and said softly, "A man is not a man until he walks with a lion. Maybe a leopard or a cheetah will do too. Or a male rhinoceros . . . but not a female! And elephants don't count either—they're strong, but now they're tame as dogs."

Thus, my grandfather. He died when I was still young . . . before I thought to ask if *he* had walked with a lion.

The only lions I have ever seen were mechanical. There's one back at the amusement park. On a merry-go-round. Ride a lion, ride a unicorn, ride a laughing dragon!

I bolted the lion in place myself. I pushed past the prince so I could do it with my own hands.

He probably thought I was trying to impress him with my enthusiasm. I think the truth was I was trying to impress the lion.

I'm getting cold. I wonder if I'll freeze before I suffocate or the other way around.

I could take off my helmet and finish it quickly. But there's always the chance if I hang on, someone will find me before I die.

Besides, most of these helmets are designed to lock in place when there's no air pressure outside.

Can you hear my thoughts, children? Noliwe? Jobe? Mamina?

The night my father died, I was asleep an ocean away . . . and I dreamed of a great plain dotted with every kind of tree in the world. The air was full of the smell of lilacs and the ground had a thick springy cover of pine needles and magnolia blossoms. If I reached up, I could pull down cherries or oranges, even calabashes—whatever fruit or nut I thought of, it was right there. Then my father was there too, and we walked together under the trees, saying nothing. I wanted to hold his hand the way I did when I was a boy, but I knew I couldn't.

"Son," he finally said to me, "they tell me I have to eat a leaf off every one of these trees. It's going to take a long while, and some of them are going to taste mighty bitter." He smiled. "Well, as penances go, I expected a lot worse. It's nice here, isn't it?"

"Did you ever walk with a lion?" I asked him.

He shook his head. "Lions are scarce these days," he said. "You never know, though." He looked around at the forest. "Lots of places here a lion could be hiding. I'll be checking them all out."

When I left him, he was still walking under the trees: walking slowly, enjoying himself. More relaxed in death than he'd ever been in life.

I believe I really was talking to him.

Can you hear me, children? I don't know what time it is where you are. I hope you're dreaming.

Lately, I've had a recurring dream of standing on the deck of a tall ship on a still night sea. There are many people with me. I feel as if we've been becalmed a long time; but as I watch, wind fills our sails, the mast groans and the canvas snaps taut, and everybody is clambering up to the rigging, laughing, letting out the sails, starting to sing a song of great rejoicing that we'll soon be speeding toward our destination again.

Children . . . are you dreaming?

It's as quiet as a forest here. Soft static on my helmet radio, that's all. For a while, I could hear everyone shouting at each other back on Heaven, but I'm out of range now.

From where I drift, Heaven is eclipsing the sun. Behind Heaven, the sun's corona is wild with prominences.

Heaven has a fiery mane.

Why can't I stop thinking about lions? I could just as easily say I'm walking with the constellation Leo. If I knew which one it was.

No, I'm walking with Heaven. And Heaven is just a carousel lion: something someone built.

But it's beautiful. And strong.

Something a man is not.

One could learn from it too.

I'm cold.

There's a song my grandfather taught me to sing:

> *The body perishes, the heart stays young.*
> *The platter wears away with serving food.*

No log retains its bark when old,
No lover peaceful while the rival weeps.

Oh, my children! I never taught you that song. It's a song for the old and the dying, and I thought I would sing it for you when I grew old.

But now I won't. You'll never learn it. And you won't know a man is not a man until he walks with a lion.

Soon everyone will forget that. And it's a thing someone should remember.

VARIATION K: JUGGERNAUT
(ANIMATO)
(ANIMATEDLY)
CONTACT: NOVEMBER 2078
RECORDED VIDEO-BURST TRANSMISSION FROM
DR. SHANTA MUKERJHEE (HYDROPONICS SERVICES,
HEAVEN) TO JOHN MUKERJHEE (SAN FRANCISCO, CA):

They tell me you haven't checked to see if I'm alive.

We've been under strict orders up here for the last few days, not to call friends and relatives to say we're all right. For the first few hours after the construction workers were killed, all the radio bands were clogged with people trying to get messages back home, interfering with emergency communications; so Laughing Dragon clamped down and said no outgoing calls. Incoming calls were taken by the main communications center, and answered curtly: "Yes, she's alive and well." "No, we haven't located him yet."

You'd know this if you called. But you didn't. I suppose you were too busy getting injunctions against mining companies that want to despoil the pristine Martian landscape; your mother isn't environmentally relevant.

That's a cheap shot. I'm sorry.

Anyway, things are returning to normal. We're each being allowed one ten-minute transmission to anywhere in the solar system, all expenses paid by Laughing Dragon. And I wanted to tell you I'm safe; our hydroponics dome was nowhere near the accident, and I didn't lose so much as a bean plant.

There. Well. I guess I still have nine minutes of free air time. This is hard for me.

Look, John, there's something I want to tell you. Show you. It's important.

I'll just get the camera turned . . . okay. You're looking at one of the hydroponics chambers up here. Leaf lettuce on the right, radishes on the left. Good growth, I'm sure you can see that. We've built quite a sophisticated system, very productive. I know you look down on me because I'm growing salad for rich tourists when I could be feeding the poor, but really—Laughing Dragon has given us a substantial research budget. Some of the designs we've developed could improve the yield of hydroponics systems everywhere, make more food for everyone. . . .

I promised myself I wouldn't keep apologizing to you. I've done important work up here. I don't have to feel guilty I'm not fighting drought in Africa. We can't all live up to your standards, John.

The plants you're looking at are normal strains, designed for Earth-normal gravity. I suppose you've read that Heaven's gravity is almost exactly equal to Earth's: within a few thousandths of a percent of gravity at sea level on the equator. It's touted as the greatest engineering feat in the construction of Heaven: getting the right density and distribution of mass to mimic one Earth G, over almost the entire surface.

Well. You'll see.

Now I'm taking the camera into the next room. This is an experimental chamber—black-eyed peas biologically engineered for growth in the Luna colonies. Laughing Dragon lets each of us senior researchers conduct small personal experiments; we get publications out of it and Laughing Dragon basks in any resulting prestige. There's nothing wrong with that, it's no different from a university or a . . .

I'm apologizing again. Sorry.

All right, you can see the peas are growing well. Good greenery, excellent pod production. I never expected anything like this. After all, these are low gravity plants; I only set up this chamber because I wanted to experiment with the design of water delivery systems, and I never thought I'd get significant yields. You just shouldn't see this kind of growth under Earth-normal gravity.

Now, watch as I drop this pencil.

No, I didn't change the camera to slow motion. That's precisely the speed things fall in this chamber. I haven't done any elaborate tests, but I'm fairly certain we have lunar gravity in here.

Needless to say, this is none of my doing. A month ago, I would have said it was impossible to have gravity like Earth in one room and like Luna right next door. But now let me go into the next chamber. I'll just . . . you can probably see the camera bouncing, because I'm bouncing as I walk. Have you ever been to the moon colonies, John? Walking in here is exactly like walking down the streets of Tycho. I suppose it would be fun, if it weren't so bewildering. And scary.

All right, through the hatch to the next room and . . . yes, I'm floating toward the ceiling. Weightless. I've got zero-G soybeans growing in this chamber—you know, engineered for nonspinning orbitals. Zero-G plants, zero-G chamber.

Believe me, the gravity here was Earth-normal two months ago. Back then, these beans could scarcely germinate. But over the course of a few days, the gravity dropped to nothing. Just dropped of its own accord. To precisely the level the plants found ideal.

It gives me the creeps, John. It did the first time I noticed, and it still does now. I haven't told anyone about this because it's too spooky to talk about.

Do you know what I think is happening? It's a feedback loop between these plants and Heaven. Heaven is artificially controlling the gravity on every square millimeter of its surface, in accordance with the preferences of those affected. In here, the soybeans want it weightless. Out on the rest of the surface . . . well, I don't think it's an accident the gravity is exactly what humans like it to be.

Laughing Dragon didn't engineer the gravity here; Heaven is doing this itself.

I get cold chills just thinking about it, John. Heaven can't be human-made. Humans don't know how to play games with gravity. Humans don't know how to establish this kind of feedback communication with plants.

And I haven't told you yet about the dreams. More and more people up here are having vivid dreams . . . and coherent ones, not the usual sort of vague, disjointed images. The dreams leave a lingering feeling of . . . I guess the word is spirituality. "Like touching the mind of God," one of the other researchers said this morning . . . which I'm sure you'll dismiss as maudlin sentimentality, but if you ever had one of these dreams yourself . . . a sort of quiet wonder . . .

No, I'm not going to tell you what I've dreamt about. I'm tired of you sneering at me.

But the point is, I don't think these dreams are just coincidence. This *thing* we're on, what Laughing Dragon calls Heaven—I don't know whether it's touching our minds or we're touching it, but if there's such a thing as telepathy with soybeans, why not with humans?

I don't sound much like a professional scientist, do I? No detachment. I can't feel detached when I'm constantly swinging between extremes of fear and awe. Because even if this creature sends inspiring dreams and nurtures our gardens, it killed dozens of people when it casually opened its wings.

It's like . . . do you know what the juggernaut is? I never tried to teach you the old ways, but maybe your grandmother told you. The juggernaut is a wagon used to carry a huge statue of Krishna Jagannatha through the city of Puri during the Rathayatra festival. The wagon is gigantic—it takes several hundred people to drag it along. On one hand, the juggernaut is beautiful and serene: it's decorated with flowers and surrounded by pilgrims singing hymns, not to mention that it carries the statue of the compassionate Lord Krishna; but on the other hand, a huge crowd mills uncontrollably around the wagon, and all too often, someone falls under the wheels. People even *throw* themselves under. The juggernaut doesn't stop; it represents benevolence and goodwill, but it can leave crushed bodies in its wake.

Do you understand, John? Yes, I imagine you do. You're a juggernaut yourself, on occasion.

I've been trying to build up my courage to tell someone what I've found out. I'm sure you'd do it without a moment's hesitation: summon the media, make a statement, proclaim your moral outrage at what's going on. Deceit. Criminal negligence. Cover-up.

But I'm no crusader. I'm just a woman who knows a secret.

And now you do too.

Help me, John. Call that prince, the one who's suing Laughing Dragon over the death of his workers. Say I'll testify. But keep my name secret, just for the time being. I still have a job up here with Laughing Dragon. I still have a reputation as a scientist, and if I start talking about artificial gravity, telepathy . . . I promise I'll take the witness stand when the time comes, but I don't want to declare war on Heaven just yet.

I want to stay here a little while longer. Even if it sometimes terrifies me.

I want to hold on to my dreams.

VARIATION L: WHITE ELEPHANT
(ALLEGRO POMPOSO)
(AT GOOD SPEED, POMPOUSLY)
CONTACT: DECEMBER 2078

Excuse me, Miss, uhh, Ms., uhh, Verhooven. Is your father in?

This, uhh, it's a business matter at the presidential level. Oh, no. No, it's not . . . of course, you're every bit the banker your father is, but I think—

Yes, ma'am.

Yes, ma'am.

No, ma'am.

Well, it's related to Laughing Dragon Entertainment Industries. As you know, their company has loans with this bank well in excess of . . . uhh, I have it written down . . . yes, ma'am, that's the figure I have here. Very good. You have an excellent memory, miss, uhh, ma'am.

At any rate, when our bank has that much invested in a firm, you may or may not know it's standard policy for us to, uhh, approach someone on their staff and make arrangements to be informed if and when something of interest . . . we prefer not to use the term "spy," ma'am. That term hasn't gained acceptance in traditional banking circles.

Certainly, I'll get to the point. Our, uhh, contact has informed us Mr. and Mrs. Naruki are considered missing. Ma'am.

Three days.

Our contact thinks the Narukis may have decided to, uhh, fly into the sun.

Well, it isn't entirely unfounded, ma'am. On one previous occasion when Laughing Dragon's business was running into setbacks, it's believed the Narukis set off sunward and—

Running into setbacks, ma'am. It isn't public knowledge, but the prince, you know, Prince, uhh, who's suing Laughing Dragon over the construction deaths—he seems to have come into some information. We aren't exactly sure what he knows, but the word is it's extremely powerful leverage that should . . . yes, we can try to find out. I'll write that down, shall I? Action Item One: find out what the prince knows.

Other setbacks, yes, ma'am, I'm getting to them. Uhh, it seems the, uhh, construction teams have all evacuated.

Gone home, ma'am. All of them.

Our guess is the prince told them something. Although maybe they just left on their own because of all the accidents. The accidents. Four since the original one that killed the prince's workers. Apparently there have been quakes on Heaven's surface which ruptured a number of domes . . . oh no, there's no suggestion of sabotage. It says here Laughing Dragon security personnel investigated each incident with all the . . . of course, there was insurance. We *insist* on insurance. We're a bank.

Our own investigators, ma'am? Well, perhaps you don't, uhh, understand the level of security Mrs., uhh, Mr. Naruki has imposed on Heaven. No photographs, no close approach from space, no unauthorized visits from . . . good Lord, no, she wasn't trying to *hide* anything from us. How could she hide something from us? We audit her books every six months.

The security was because Mrs. Naruki was worried about terrorists. Terrorists, ma'am. Well, no, an amusement park one hundred and six million kilometers from Earth is not an *obvious* political target, but caution is always—

Oh, now, Miss Verhooven, uhh, Ms. . . . we've made a substantial number of investigations, yes, a substantial number, let me . . . oh . . . no . . . this is the, uhh . . . we call it the, uhh, nut file. From earlier inquiries. You recall Laughing Dragon categorically refused to discuss how the body of Heaven was constructed? Well, we did some digging to find out . . . asked around on all the planets, did anyone see something huge and strange in space . . . well, we got some wild stories, ma'am, you'd be amused. No, there's nothing of interest here, I personally checked each and every . . . yes, ma'am. Yes, ma'am. I'll leave the file with you.

About the Narukis, ma'am . . . if they're, uhh, gone, there could be serious . . . well, I was talking to Legal, and they say if Laughing Dragon were to default on the loan, Heaven would, uhh . . . become ours.

The bank's.

Presumably we'd sell it to someone, ma'am.

There must be . . . uhh . . . I mean, it's a nice big, uhh . . . I should think there'd be a buyer somewhere, ma'am. All those energy cells, the scrap value alone . . . no, I don't think we've calculated the cost of reclamation. No, ma'am, I wouldn't be qualified to venture an opinion in that area. Not at present. I'll make that another Action Item, shall I?

Maybe we'll just work up a full report on this, yes? I mean, Heaven's a great big . . . it's very big. There's always someone who'll buy something that's big. In my experience. Any time the bank has repossessed something before, we've never had any trouble selling it off . . . not when it was something, uhh, big.

No, ma'am. We didn't think ahead. We're sorry.

VARIATION M: TOTEM
(TRANQUILLO CON SPIRITO)
(SERENELY, WITH SPIRIT)
CONTACT: JANUARY 2079

The smoke rises to heaven.
The sound of the rattle rises to heaven.
Let my song rise to heaven,
For I have dreamed a true dream.

Come here, Celeste.

You're wondering what your animal will be, right?

When I was a boy your age, I wanted the shaman to tell me I'd been chosen by the eagles. I dreamt of flying with them . . . or a bear, that seemed like a good animal too. I'd seen a bear once in a zoo—it seemed wise and kindly. Now that I know more about bears, I realize I overlooked important aspects of the bear personality. Its claws, for example.

But no, your animal will not be the bear. Or the eagle. Or the wolf or the whale or any of those totems young people usually hope for.

I know. You're disappointed. I was disappointed when the shaman told me my bed would lie in the rabbit lodge. I wanted to be . . . oh, something more heroic. I thought rabbits were timid and foolish. But really, when a rabbit runs from a fox, it isn't being foolish, is it? It's just being sensible. And a rabbit has the heart of a wolverine at times—when being brave is the least foolish alternative. A rabbit is always watching, always listening, always sniffing the air. That's a good way for a shaman to live.

But no, you won't be a rabbit either.

The spirits have built a new lodge. They've sensed a new creature. Not human, not an animal they've known in the past. It comes from far away. This animal is your totem.

I don't know its name. You're the first of its clan. It has no name in any human tongue. You can ask for its secret name when you meet it.

To meet it, you'll have to journey off-planet. At present, the creature is several million kilometers inside the orbit of Mercury, and—

No, I'm not crazy. Or lying. The animals spoke. I dreamed a true dream.

Are you saying the truth is only true when you can understand it? You're wrong.

When I went to university many decades ago, I enrolled in mathematics because I wanted to tell truth from falsehood. I believed mathematics was the one pure source of truth because it was the only discipline entirely divorced from subjectivity. But that was before I began studying. At school, I learned all mathematics starts with "Let's pretend this is true and see where it leads." That is mathematics' great joy and strength: it dares to stand on nothingness. It dares to *see* it's standing on nothingness, yet it's still brave. Can you tell me its magic isn't strong?

You want to argue with me, I see that. Don't you want to be a shaman, Celeste? Don't you want to have magic in your heart? Well, I'll tell you a secret about magic: it refuses to be what you want it to be. Demand something of magic and it will choose to be something else.

One quiet wintry Sunday while I was at the university, I woke at dawn and went for a walk. I suppose you'd like me to give some mystic explanation for walking at that hour, but the truth is, my roommate was snoring so loudly I couldn't sleep, so I got angry and left. I walked nowhere in particular, and because I was angry, I paid little attention to the world around me: the cardinals whistling in the trees, the squirrels running across the snow. I was in no magical mood, I assure you.

But. As I passed one of the university parking lots, I saw a spirit.

It was the Thunderbird, I think: a man's body with the head of a bird of prey. It was at the far end of the lot, walking away from me toward the science complex; I could only see its back, a long distance off.

I stood frozen for two full minutes until the spirit disappeared behind the Chemistry building.

Now, girl, was that magic?

The spirit was a long way off and in the shadow of some buildings. It could have been nothing more than someone wearing an odd hat. I tried to convince myself I was imagining things, because the incident didn't fit with how I thought the world should work. Why would a great spirit be walking across a parking lot? A parking lot! Not a field, not a forest, a parking lot. And if a spirit chose to show itself to me, why didn't it talk or do something miraculous? Why would it just walk away and disappear?

Was that magic? Or was it only my imagination?

Since then I've met the Thunderbird several times in my dreams of the Other World, but it's always refused to say whether it really showed itself to me that day.

That's the way of true magic, Celeste. It's slippery. It's always open to question. My dreams of the Other World, well, maybe they're just dreams, right? There's always a logical explanation somewhere if you want it.

And there's always magic if you want it. Everywhere. In the forest, in the city, in a lodge, in a factory.

In space, several million kilometers inside the orbit of Mercury.

That's the magic you've been offered, Celeste. You don't get a choice what your magic will be; your choice is whether you will let it *be* magic.

Will you?

Yes, we can get you there. A woman named Verhooven is bringing people to see the new creature. She's become curious about it; she's gathering those with knowledge of its travels. It won't be hard for you to join this group. You belong to the creature's clan—you have to speak for it. The spirits will make sure you get where you belong.

Are you willing to accept this magic, young shaman? Are you willing to say, "Let's pretend this is true and see where it leads"?

Then let the drums sound.

The music of the drums rises to Heaven.

FUGUE: ORGANISM
(ALLEGRO CON TUTTI)
(AT GOOD SPEED, WITH THE ENTIRE ORCHESTRA)
CONTACT: MARCH 2079

According to the laws of the League of Peoples, the boundary of a single-sun solar system is that set of points where the gravitational attraction of the primary exactly equals the gravitational attraction of the rest of the universe. Humans might claim determining this line is impossible, maybe even in violation of quantum physics; but the laws of the League have taken precedence over the laws of physics so long, physics no longer contests the issue.

A few meters outside the boundary of Sol's system, the Outpost prepared for action. Sensors had recorded a steady increase in the Organism's mass over the past months as it drank in Sol's energy; within minutes, the Organism would have enough energy to open a wormhole out of the system. Wormholes were a haphazard way to travel—the hole's outlet might open as much as a light-year off target—but species without true FTL flight found wormholes a convenient shortcut whenever they wanted to leapfrog a parsec or two.

Of course, wormholes had an unfortunate tendency to suck in every particle of matter for kilometers around. . . .

The Outpost of the League of Peoples watched and waited. The odds were good that humans would become an interstellar race much sooner than they expected.

[*Leviathan*] On Heaven, the environment domes and dormitory pods were slowly being shaken apart by twitches in the Organism's skin; but a new dormitory had been built in space, floating some five kilometers above the surface. In this dormitory's cafeteria, Colleen O'Neil stood before a giant viewscreen, watching a crack grow across the surface of one of Heaven's domes as the creature shrugged. Colleen had no idea which heavenly environment was dying . . . Valhalla perhaps, crumbling into Götterdämmerung. Good riddance.

She hated the sight of her grandfather's magnificent Leviathan reduced to this decrepit clown. But at the farthest ranges of vision, she could see the creature's wings spread wide to the sun: a clear, clean black, darker than the night sky behind them. Valhalla and Nirvana and the Sunboat Fun ride were just barnacles on Leviathan's hide; they'd be scraped off soon enough.

[*Nessie*] Stitch Ashworth entered the cafeteria and nearly left again immediately. The only other person he saw there was a fellow Martian, but dressed in laborer's khaki, her red hair braided with the gritty twine that miners called sand-string. Stitch's family were Olympians, residents of the heights of Olympus Mons, where the corporate executives lived. As a boy he'd been beaten up by miners' children whenever he ventured out of the Olympian safe areas; he'd become a pilot to get away from the mines, the miners, and everyone associated with the desolation of Mars.

The woman must have heard him come in, for she turned and nodded without smiling. "Hello."

"H'lo," he answered carefully. "Anything doing out?"

"Heaven is warring with itself," she said. "The idols are crashing down."

"Oh." He looked at the wreckage shuddering across the surface. A concrete tower toppled soundlessly across a cluster of roller-coaster tracks. The windows in the distant tower's observation deck shattered; the air inside burst outward, its humidity turning to a spray of white. Stitch couldn't remember if the white was steam because of the low pressure or frost because of the cold. "Wild, isn't it?" he said.

"Yes," said the woman, sounding very satisfied.

"I was thinking of driving down," Stitch said suddenly, surprising himself he'd revealed this to a stranger. "I'm licensed for minishuttles, and there are dozens in the docking bay. I'd like to see . . ." But there was something too intense in the woman's expression to let him tell the truth: that he was hoping to find some huge chalk letters his grandfather had scribbled decades earlier. "I'd like to see it close up," he said.

The woman looked down at the surface again. She seemed to be smiling at the continuing destruction. "I'd like to see it close up too."

[Angel] Dr. Simon Esteban met two of his fellow passengers in the corridor: Martians, both of them, a laborer built like a she-bear and a shy dandy dressed like he was heading for Club Olympia. No, Esteban corrected himself, it was wrong to pigeonhole people so quickly. As soon as a psychiatrist labeled a patient, he started treating the label instead of the person.

Esteban had repeated that axiom to himself so often it was like a mantra. Jogging around the track at the gym, he sometimes caught himself muttering, "Treat the person, not the label," over and over and over and over.

"We're going for a closer look at the surface," the she-bear said. "Interested?"

"Certainly," Esteban said, smiling his professional smile. In fact, he'd heard that vicious quakes rocked the surface from time to time, scattering rubble into the air. Getting too close was dangerous . . . but his first patient Rachel had hesitated to approach her angel, and for that cowardice, she'd gone mad.

No, he corrected himself, she'd succumbed to delusional paranoia brought about by unresolved guilt.

No, he corrected himself again. She'd gone mad.

[*Bogey*] In the docking bay, Jenny Harrington slid into the shadows of an inactive minishuttle storage tube when she heard approaching footsteps. Not that Jenny was afraid to be caught here—Ms. Verhooven said guests could go where they liked. But Jenny didn't want to talk to anyone now, didn't want the pointless rituals of making conversation with strangers. In her hand was a bouquet of daisies, hard-grown in Mars's sterile soil . . . well, to be honest, grown in *spite* of Mars's soil, because it had been necessary to add so much: fertilizer, water, several strains of bacteria.

Jenny didn't want any of Verhooven's other guests to see the flowers in her hand. They'd all heard her story. They'd think she was going to drop the flowers on the spot where her father had died because she loved him. Nothing could be further from the truth. Her father had been a militaristic blockhead who died trying to kill some harmless hulk . . . and it was all pointless, wasn't it, because the hulk was still here and all that was left of her father was a dent in the hulk's side. Love was for people who deserved it, and her father had never ever deserved it.

The flowers were an exorcism, nothing more. A way to close off the past, once and for all.

Three people passed her hiding place and entered another minishuttle tube. Soon the blast door shut and the mini blasted off.

Jenny clutched her flowers fiercely and headed for the next active shuttle.

[*Daemon*] Gregor Petrozowski did nothing as the first shuttle emerged from the dormitory. His yacht hovered above the dormitory, several kilometers sunward; he could see everything, with little chance of being detected himself, just a fleck in the fireball's face. When the second shuttle took off, the old man gave his computer a single soft command. "Down."

The sound of the sun was loud static over his radio speakers. In his years of isolation, he'd developed a distaste for both music and the human voice. Staying in contact with humanity had been *impure*, in a way he couldn't explain. If he was to become worthy to rediscover his daemon, he had to cut himself off from the mundane world. Now the only voice he could stand was the sun's.

Obviously, other people had discovered the daemon while he was searching alone in space. They'd tried to build something on it—temples, maybe; he couldn't tell now that everything was in ruins. If he'd been listening to human broadcasts, he would have come here much earlier.

But he was here now. He had found the daemon, unaided, in the vast depths of space. And he could feel in his bones that he'd arrived just in time.

"Down," he whispered. "Down."

[Boojum] "That's Petrozowski's yacht," Emil Mayous told his son Yorgi. "Petrozowski himself."

The boy hauled himself off his acceleration couch with a great ripping of Velcro and floated over to the viewscreen. "Yacht looks like shit," he said after a moment's inspection.

The boy Yorgi thought he was an expert on yachts now that he owned one himself. Emil didn't want to know where the boy got enough money to buy the ship. Emil hadn't wanted to come to Heaven either, but Yorgi thought the Verhooven woman might pay big money to hear about his father's boojum hunt.

"Petrozowski's probably been in space ever since he abandoned the company," Yorgi said. "I bet he hasn't—Jesus Christ!"

A jet-black wing swept past the viewscreen like a flapping chunk of night. Proximity alarms blared throughout the ship.

"You stupid flea!" Emil shouted at his son, for no reason except his fear.

[Titan] The last maxishuttle to Heaven was en route to the main dormitory when the Organism lifted its wings to full height. Suddenly, the shuttle found itself in a trough six kilometers deep, the walls and floor so black they were nearly invisible. Overhead, the wide face of the sun burned down into the chasm; but it was far, far away, like a glimpse of sky to a child trapped in a well.

"Ooooo," said Beatrice Mallio, age four.

"Wow," said Benedict Mallio, age five.

"Something nice on the viewscreen?" their mother asked. Like the other adults on board, Juliet Mallio was tired of looking outside after days of travel; but she dutifully prepared herself to admire whatever piece of space debris her children were watching now.

Her eyes widened as she saw the deep black of the Organism's skin towering over both sides of the ship, the wings forming massive walls of starless night. At first she thought the shuttle had entered some sort of landing bay; but as she watched, dim flecks of blue-tinged light flickered into life against the blackness.

"Pretty!" said Beatrice.

"Like electric spiders!" said Benedict.

And they did look like spiders, skittering out of their nests and racing across the surface of both wings. The spiders danced madly, colliding with each other, coalescing . . . and suddenly one leapt across the gap between the wings, trailing a pale thread of lightning directly in front of the shuttle. Without thinking, Juliet stamped down with her foot, as if she had a brake pedal that could stop the ship from flying through the lightning. The shuttle's pilot must have had reflexes equally quick, for the ship suddenly dipped, just managing to slip under the glowing thread.

All over the cabin, people cried out at the ship's sudden maneuver; but Juliet remained tensely silent, her eyes on the screen, her arms reaching out to wrap around her children's shoulders.

More and more of the lightning-threads sparked from one wing to another, weaving a net, a web across the trough. There was no way the pilot could avoid them all. One thread whipped against the shuttle's hull, and for a moment the viewscreen image twisted into jagged distortion; but a moment later, the picture snapped back into focus with an audible crackle. Another lightning strike, another crackle, a third, a fourth; then a fountain of light gushed crimson and the viewscreen went dead.

"Children," said Juliet Mallio, "are your safety belts very snug? Yes, make sure, let me check. Good. Good. A kiss for each of you. That's nice, very nice. Now it's too bad the pretty show has gone off the screen, but maybe you'd like a story instead. Yes? Maybe a story about a Titan." The shuttle veered sharply upward. "A Titan named Prometheus. A sad story, but a brave one."

The shuttle rocked like a cradle under an impatient hand.

"Ready? Once upon a time . . ."

[Dragon] Sunward, the Narukis looked back for a final time on their dragon. The wings were now pulled so far forward it seemed as if the Laughing Dragon of Heaven had reshaped itself into a cavernous mouth and its breath was a rainbow of fire.

"A true dragon," said Yushio, awestruck.

"It always has been," his wife answered.

"Change course, change course!" Yushio shouted to their yacht's navigation computer. "Into the dragon's mouth!"

For a moment, Mrs. Naruki considered countermanding the order. But when she saw the exhilaration on her husband's face, the joy of jumping into something new and exciting, she held her silence. The sun, the dragon, never mind.

She took Yushio's hand and squeezed fondly.

[Roc] Two seats behind the Mallio family inside the maxishuttle, the prince unbuckled his safety belt, then staggered up the aisle

and dragged open the hatch separating the cockpit from the passenger cabin. The female pilot shouted at him to get back and sit down, but the prince ignored the woman; he refused to die meekly, blind to what was happening and strapped into a comfortable chair.

Through the tinted cockpit port, the prince saw the pilot had angled the shuttle upward, trying to climb out of the trough made by the Organism's wings; but the web of energy woven across the chasm was acting like a physical obstruction, tangling around the ship's nose, dragging it down. Red lights flashed on the control panel; new ones lit every second.

There were no sounds but the cursing of the pilot and a frightened babbling back in the cabin. But beneath his feet, the prince could feel the floor beginning to vibrate.

Trying to balance against the rocking of the ship, he knelt beside the pilot and said in a low voice, "I'm a trained engineer. Tell me what I can do to help."

"Can you cross your fingers and pray?" she asked.

"The first thing an engineer learns," he told her.

[*Lion*] In the passenger cabin of the shuttle, Elizabeth Obasa hugged her children and whispered to them not to cry. "Listen," she said, "I had a dream. When I was sleeping a little while ago. About your father.

"He was walking across a dark grassland at night, and wherever I looked there was an animal there, watching him: a bull, a bear, a swan, all kinds of animals.

"As I watched, he walked up to a goat and said, 'I'm looking for a lion.'

"The goat said, 'I'm a lion.' So they walked a little distance and they talked about how beautiful their children looked when they were asleep.

"Then he walked up to a fine winged horse and said, 'I'm looking for a lion.'

"The horse said, 'I'm a lion.' So they walked a little distance and they talked about how beautiful their children sounded when they laughed.

"Then he walked up to me and said, 'I'm looking for a lion.'

"I said, 'I'm a lion.' So we walked a short distance to a little grove where you children were climbing trees. And your father said, 'So many lions!'"

A burst of blinding blue roared out from the door to the cockpit and the cabin lights blinked out.

[Juggernaut] The cabin lay silent and dark, lit only by a faint glow coming from the cockpit. Slowly, Shanta Mukerjhee eased her grip on the arms of her seat; she'd been clinging so tightly her knuckles cracked softly as they relaxed. She desperately wanted all the trouble to go away, for this to be yet another dream sent by the Juggernaut. But she knew this was real. And the blast of light from the cockpit suggested a fire, an explosion, something like that.

Her son John would never forgive her for cowering in her seat when the pilot might be endangered.

Hesitantly, she lifted open the release on her safety belt. Her first motion sent her drifting toward the cabin roof, bumping off and heading floorward again. It was almost funny—at one time she would have been completely disoriented by being weightless, but thanks to some soybeans, she was quite accustomed to it by now.

She could easily pull herself forward by grabbing at the edge of the overhead luggage compartments. A few of her fellow travelers were beginning to make panicked noises in the darkness. "It's all right," she said loudly, "it's just that the engines have shut off, so we're all weightless. Stay where you are and I'll check with the pilot."

She hoped she sounded cool and confident. John would despise her forever if she couldn't keep people calm in a crisis.

The light in the cockpit area was starshine coming through the front port: the hard sharp starshine of vacuum. The sun was not in sight, and overhead, the body of the Juggernaut was a vast blackness against the Milky Way. Its wings had once again tucked back against its body; its fireworks were over.

By the starlight, Shanta could see the pilot still belted into her chair, her face and hands black with burns. Shanta put her hand to the pilot's neck; no pulse. Electrocution from the control panel? Shanta couldn't imagine the size of a power surge that would kill a human being faster than fuses could blow.

But still. The pilot was dead.

On the opposite side of the cockpit, the prince's body was drifting, nudging against the side viewing port. He too had been caught in the power surge, but his burns were less severe. Shanta could feel no pulse in his throat either, but she couldn't just hover there staring at two dead bodies without doing something.

Shanta pushed the prince's body down to the floor and tried to give CPR. Weightlessness made it almost impossible: when she pressed on his chest, she drifted toward the roof. She managed to prop her shoulder under the pilot's chair to get some leverage, then began again. Patiently. Unstoppably.

[*White Elephant*] Margaret Verhooven floated to the door of the maxishuttle cockpit. She could see the dead pilot, and Shanta Mukerjhee trying to revive the prince. She could also see other ships outside: two minishuttles and three yachts. The shuttles were stenciled with the name of her bank, but the yachts were unfamiliar.

Verhooven scanned the sky for some indication of where she was. Against the swath of untwinkling stars, one star stood out from the rest, brighter than any planet seen from Earth. The star was yellow. It was either the sun much too far away, or another star much too close up.

The Outpost of the League of Peoples suddenly appeared below the shuttle, seeming to materialize from nowhere: a huge habitat bigger than any orbital or space-wheel, its brilliantly white skin surrounded by a milky envelope of particles agitated by its arrival. *Teleportation?* Verhooven asked herself silently. *Or just moving so fast I didn't see it come? And what the hell is it?*

The Outpost began to ascend slowly. Looking at the stark white Outpost below and the jet-black Organism above, Verhooven had the image of being crushed between giant salt and pepper shakers. She stifled a laugh before it threatened to become hysterical.

When the Outpost nudged up against the shuttle, Verhooven heard only a soft bump. She floated downward as the Outpost continued to ascend, pushing the shuttle with it. With one hand, she grabbed the edge of the cabin door and pulled herself back up to keep a clear view out the cockpit port.

One by one, the other ships made contact with the ascending Outpost and were caught in its upward push. They were not far apart to begin with, all sucked through the same small wormhole and spat out at the same point; now gentle nudges from the Outpost clumped them closer together, until they were bumping each other lightly like rowboats tied to the same ring on a dock. (Verhooven thought about the time her father had taken her fishing. The only time. She was eight years old, and for some reason he thought she hadn't enjoyed herself. Whenever she asked if she could go with him on another trip, he thought she was being polite. Or sarcastic. Throughout her whole life, no one had ever been able to tell when she was sincere.)

She told herself the white giant beneath them would really crush the ships against Heaven above; but when the gap was almost closed, the Outpost stopped pushing and let the ships drift the rest of the way to Heaven's surface. For a moment nothing happened but a gentle bump. Then, without hurry, gravity imposed itself: gravity from the Organism overhead, making the shuttle's roof into a floor.

Verhooven had ample time to reorient herself. Across the cabin, she saw Shanta Mukerjhee cradling the prince's body as the world reversed. The prince was breathing weakly.

Behind Verhooven's back, the hatch to the outside world slid open. Adrenaline shot into her blood and she dragged in a huge breath, expecting the ship's atmosphere to gust out into vacuum; but there was no wind, nor the sudden cold of space. A warm breeze blew in through the hatch, smelling as pleasant as a sunny hillside. She remembered the smell from the two weeks she and her father had spent at a mountain resort in the Rockies. They'd never done that again either.

Verhooven found she had tears in her eyes.

[Totem] Celeste Dumont was the first person to leave the shuttle. She walked slowly down the gangway, trying to memorize every sensation as she set foot on her totem's skin. The eyes of its scales tracked her as she moved. She knelt and held her hand out close to the surface, the same way she would let a dog smell her when she met it for the first time. The eyes focused on her, drank in her body heat.

Behind her, other passengers came slowly out of the shuttle, and farther off, people emerged from the other ships that lay on the surface. Some talked excitedly; others seemed struck dumb. Celeste remained silent and tried to hear a deeper voice.

When the babble of humans became too distracting, she moved away from them, coming at last to a hatchway in the side of a large black bulge in the Organism's skin. The hatch slid open at her touch, revealing an airlock. She went inside, closed the outer door, opened the inner.

Celeste found herself in a place of quiet greenery. A well-tended Japanese temple stood before her, and somewhere inside a flute was playing. As she followed the sound of the music, a wild joy filled her heart, tightening her chest, burning through her whole body: the taste of magic, the sensation of truly not knowing what might be abroad in the world, yet racing eagerly to meet it.

[Organism] The Envoy of the League of Peoples sat in a bamboo chair beside the temple's altar, his heart filled with the same fierce excitement. He'd lost track of how many human lifetimes he'd waited for this moment . . . although he was human himself, very human. Could a being live centuries and still be truly human? Yes. Yes.

If he couldn't calm himself by playing the flute, he felt as if his heart would batter its way out of his chest.

A woman entered the sanctuary, nearly running, her face shining. He lowered his flute and smiled self-consciously. He was sure she'd be disappointed to see a very ordinary man here; but there was no disappointment on her face.

"Hello," he said.

"Hello," she answered, a bit out of breath. "Do you know anything about this . . . creature we're standing on?"

"I've been watching it a long time. From the Outpost. The Outpost is the big white thing." He laughed. "I've been watching everything a long time. Hello."

"Yes. Hello."

"The League of Peoples wrote me a speech to welcome humanity as new citizens of the universe," he said, "but it's very pompous. At the moment, I'd be embarrassed to deliver it. If you people invite me back to Earth, I'm sure I'll have plenty of public speaking engagements. I can be pompous then. So . . . just hello."

She smiled brilliantly, and his heart beat even harder. He'd never met another human. He couldn't believe how magnificent humans could be. He wanted to see them all, touch them, embrace them, this woman, the others outside, a solar system full of them.

O wonder, he thought, *how many goodly creatures are there here! How beauteous mankind is! O brave new world that has such people in't.*

An allusion to a human celebration text. His mentor would be proud.

"This creature . . ." the woman said to him, pointing downward. "Do you know its name?"

"I just call it the Organism."

She nodded as if she found the name perfect. "It's my totem," she said. "I've finally found my totem."

He smiled. "So have I."

Three Hearings on the Existence of Snakes in the Human Bloodstream

1. Concerning an Arrangement of Lenses, So Fashioned as to Magnify the View of Divers Animalcules, Too Tiny to be Seen with the Unaided Eye:

His Holiness, Supreme Patriarch Septus XXIV, was an expert on chains.

By holy law, chains were required on every defendant brought to the Court Immaculate. However, my Lord the Jailer could exercise great latitude in choosing which chains went on which prisoners. A man possessed of a healthy fortune might buy his way into nothing more than a gold link necklace looped loosely around his throat; a beautiful woman might visit the Jailer privately in his chambers and emerge with thin and glittering silver bracelets—chains, yes, but as delicate as thread. If, on the other hand, the accused could offer neither riches nor position nor generous physical charms . . . well then, the prison had an ample supply of leg-irons, manacles, and other such fetters, designed to show these vermin the grim weight of God's justice.

The man currently standing before Patriarch Septus occupied a seldom-seen middle ground in the quantity of restraints: two solid handcuffs joined by an iron chain of business-like gauge, strong enough that the prisoner had no chance of breaking free, but not so heavy as to strain the man's shoulders to the point of pain. Clearly, my Lord the Jailer had decided on a cautious approach to this particular case; and Septus wondered what that meant. Perhaps the accused was nobody himself but had sufficient connections to rule out unwarranted indignities . . . a sculptor or musician, for example, who had won favor with a few great households in the city. The man certainly had an artistic look—fierce eyes in an impractical face, the sort of high-strung temperament who could express passion but not use it.

"Be it known to the court," cried the First Attendant, "here stands one Anton Leeuwenhoek, a natural philosopher who is accused of heresy against God and Our Lady, the Unbetombed Virgin. Kneel, Supplicant, and pray with His Holiness, that this day shall see justice."

Septus waited to see what Leeuwenhoek would do. When thieves and murderers came before the court, they dropped to their knees immediately, making a gaudy show of begging God to prove their innocence. A heretic, however, might spit defiance or hurl curses at the Patriarchal throne—not a good way to win mercy, but then, many heretics came to this chamber intent on their own martyrdom. Leeuwenhoek had the eyes of such a fanatic, but apparently not the convictions; without so much as a grimace, he got to his knees and bowed his head. The Patriarch quickly closed his own eyes and intoned the words he had recited five times previously this morning: "God grant me the wisdom to perceive the truth. Blessed Virgin, grant me the judgment to mete out justice. Let us all act this day to the greater glory of Thy Divine Union. Amen."

Amens sounded around the chamber: attendants and advocates following the form. Septus glanced sideways toward Satan's Watchboy, an ominous title for a cheerfully freckle-faced youth, the one person here excused from closing his eyes during the prayer. The Watchboy nodded twice, indicating that Leeuwenhoek had maintained a proper attitude of prayer and said Amen with everyone else. Good—this had just become a valid trial, and anything that happened from this point on had the strength of heavenly authority.

"My Lord Prosecutor," Septus said, "state the charges."

The prosecutor bowed as deeply as his well-rounded girth allowed, perspiration already beading on his powdered forehead. It was not a hot day, early spring, nothing more . . . but Prosecutor ben Jacob was a man famous for the quantity of his sweat, a trait that usually bothered his legal adversaries more than himself. Many an opposing counsel had been distracted by the copious flow streaming down ben Jacob's face, thereby overlooking flaws in the prosecutor's arguments. One could always find flaws in ben Jacob's arguments, Septus knew—dear old Abraham was not overly clever. He was, however, honest, and could not conceive of winning personal advancement at the expense of those he prosecuted; therefore, the Patriarch had never dismissed the man from his position.

"Your Holiness," ben Jacob said, "this case concerns claims against the Doctrine of the, uhh . . . Sleeping Snake."

"Ah." Septus glanced over at Leeuwenhoek. "My son, do you truly deny God's doctrine?"

The man shrugged. "I have disproved the doctrine. Therefore, it can hardly be God's."

Several attendants gasped loudly. They perceived it as part of their job to show horror at every sacrilege. The same attendants tended to whisper and make jokes during the descriptions of true horrors: murders, rapes, maimings. "The spectators will remain silent," Septus said wearily. He had recited those words five times this morning too. "My Lord Prosecutor, will you please read the text?"

"Ummm . . . the text, yes, the text."

Septus maintained his composure while ben Jacob shuffled through papers and parchments looking for what he needed. It was, of course, standard procedure to read any passages of scripture that a heretic denied, just to make sure there was no misunderstanding. It was also standard procedure for ben Jacob to misplace his copy of the relevant text in a pile of other documents. With any other prosecutor, this might have been some kind of strategy; with ben Jacob, it was simply disorganization.

"Here we are, yes, here we are," he said at last, producing a dog-eared page with a smear of grease clearly visible along one edge. "Gospel of Susannah, chapter twenty-three, first verse." Ben Jacob paused while the two Verification Attendants found the passage in their own scripture books. They would follow silently as he read the text aloud, ready to catch any slips of the tongue that deviated from the holy word. When the attendants were ready, ben Jacob cleared his throat and read:

After the procession ended, they withdrew to a garden outside the walls of Jerusalem. And in the evening, it happened that Matthias beheld a serpent there, hidden by weeds. He therefore took up a stone that he might crush the beast; but Mary stayed his hand, saying, "There is no danger, for look, the beast sleeps."

"Teacher," Matthias answered, "it will not sleep forever."

"Verily," said Mary, "I promise it will sleep till dawn; and when the dawn comes, we will leave this place and all the serpents that it holds."

Yet still, Matthias kept hold of the stone and gazed upon the serpent with fear.

"O ye of little faith," said Mary to Matthias, "why do you concern yourself with the sleeping creature before you, when you are blind to the serpents in your own heart? For I tell you, each drop of your blood courses with a legion of serpents, and so it is for every Child of Dust. You are all poisoned with black venoms, poisoned unto death. But if you believe in me, I will sing those serpents to sleep; then will they slumber in peace until you leave this flesh behind, entering into the dawn of God's new day."

Ben Jacob lowered his page and looked to the Verifiers for confirmation. The Patriarch turned in their direction too, but he didn't need their nods to tell him the scripture had been read correctly. Septus knew the passage by heart; it was one of the fundamental texts of Mother Church, the Virgin's promise of salvation. It was also one of the most popular texts for heretics to challenge. The presumption of original sin, of damnation being inherent in human flesh . . . that was anathema to many a fiery young soul. *What kind of God,* they asked, *would damn an infant to hell merely for being born?* It was a good question, its answer still the subject of much subtle debate; but the Virgin's words were unequivocal, whether or not theologians had reasoned out all the implications.

"Anton Leeuwenhoek," Septus said, "you have heard the verified word of scripture. Do you deny its truth?"

Leeuwenhoek stared directly back. "I must," he answered. "I have examined human blood in meticulous detail. It contains no serpents."

The toadies in the courtroom had their mouths open, ready to gasp again at sacrilege; but even they could hear the man was not speaking in deliberate blasphemy. He seemed to be stating . . . a fact.

How odd.

Septus straightened slightly in the Patriarchal throne. This had the prospect of more interest than the usual heresy trial. "You understand," he said to Leeuwenhoek, "this passage is about original sin. The Blessed Virgin states that all human beings are poisoned with sin and can only be redeemed through her."

"On the contrary, Your Holiness." Leeuwenhoek's voice was sharp. "The passage states there are snakes in human blood. I know there are not."

"The snakes are merely . . ." Septus stopped himself in time. He had been on the verge of saying the snakes were merely a metaphor; but this was a public trial, and any pronouncements he made would have the force of law. To declare that any part of scripture was not the literal truth . . . no Patriarch had ever done so in open forum, and Septus did not intend to be the first.

"Let us be clear on this point," Septus said to Leeuwenhoek. "Do you deny the Doctrine of Original Sin?"

"No—I could never make heads or tails of theology. What I understand is blood; and there are no snakes in it."

One of the toadies ventured a small gasp of horror, but even a deaf man could have told the sound was forced.

Prosecutor ben Jacob, trying to be helpful, said, "You must appreciate the snakes would be very, very small."

"That's just it," Leeuwenhoek answered with sudden enthusiasm. "I have created a device which makes it possible to view tiny things as if they were much larger." He turned quickly toward Septus. "Your Holiness is familiar with the telescope? The device for viewing objects at long distances?"

The Patriarch nodded in spite of himself.

"My device," Leeuwenhoek said, "functions on a similar principle—an arrangement of lenses which amplify one's vision to reveal things too small to see with the naked eye. I have examined blood in every particular; and while it contains numerous minute animalcules I cannot identify, I swear to the court there are no snakes. Sleeping or otherwise."

"Mm." Septus took a moment to fold his hands on the bench in front of him. When he spoke, he did not meet the prisoner's eyes. "It is well known that snakes are adept at hiding, are they not? Surely it is possible a snake could be concealed behind . . . behind these other minute animalcules you mention."

"A legion of serpents," Leeuwenhoek said stubbornly. "That's what the text said. A legion of serpents in every drop of blood. Surely they couldn't *all* find a place to hide; and I have spent hundreds of hours searching, Your Holiness. Days and weeks and months."

"Mm."

Troublesome to admit, Septus didn't doubt the man. The Patriarch had scanned the skies with an excellent telescope, and had seen a universe of unexpected wonders—mountains on the moon, hair on the sun, rings around the planet Cronus. He could well believe Leeuwenhoek's magnifier would reveal similar surprises . . . even if it didn't show serpents in the bloodstream. The serpents were merely a parable anyway; who could doubt it? Blessed Mary often spoke in poetic language that every educated person recognized as symbolic rather than factual.

Unfortunately, the church was not composed of educated persons. No matter how sophisticated the clergy might be, parishioners came from humbler stock. Snakes in the blood? If that's what Mary said, it must be true; and heaven help a Patriarch who took a less dogmatic stance. The bedrock of the church was Authority: ecclesiastic authority, scriptural authority. If Septus publicly allowed that some doctrines could be interpreted as mere symbolism—that a fundamental teaching was metaphor, not literal fact—well, all it took was a single hole in a wineskin for everything to leak out.

On the other hand, truth was truth. If there were no snakes, there were no snakes. God made the world and all the people in it; if the Creator chose to fashion human lifeblood a certain way, it was the duty of Mother Church to accept and praise Him for it. Clinging to a lie in order to preserve one's authority was worse than mere cowardice; it was the most damning blasphemy.

Septus looked at Leeuwenhoek, standing handcuffed in the dock. A living man with a living soul; and with one word, Septus could have him executed as a purveyor of falsehood.

But where did the falsehood truly lie?

"This case cannot be decided today," Septus announced. "Mother Church will investigate the claims of the accused to the fullest extent of her strength. We will build magnifier devices of our own, properly blessed to protect against Satan's interference." Septus fought back a smile at that; there were still some stuffy inquisitors who believed the devil distorted what one saw through any lens. "We shall see what is there and what is not."

Attendants nodded in agreement around the courtroom, just as they would nod if the sentence had been immediate acquittal or death. But ben Jacob said, "Your Holiness—perhaps it would be best if the court were to . . . to issue instructions that no other person build a magnification device until the church has ruled in this matter."

"On the contrary," Septus replied. "I think the church should make magnifiers available to all persons who ask. Let them see for themselves."

The Patriarch smiled, wondering if ben Jacob understood. A decree suppressing magnifiers would simply encourage dissidents to build them in secret; on the other hand, providing free access to such devices would bring the curious *into* the church, not drive them away. Anyway, the question would only interest the leisured class, those with time and energy to wonder about esoteric issues. The great bulk of the laity, farmers and miners and ostlers, would never hear of the offer. Even if they did, they would hardly care.

Minute animalcules might be amusing curiosities, but they had nothing to do with a peasant's life.

Another pause for prayer and then Leeuwenhoek was escorted away to instruct church scholars in how to build his magnification device. The man seemed happy with the outcome—more than escaping a death sentence, he would now have the chance to show others what he'd seen. Septus had met many men like that: grown-up children, looking for colorful shells on the beach and touchingly grateful when someone else took an interest in their sandy little collections.

As for Leeuwenhoek's original magnifier—Septus had the device brought to his chambers when the court recessed at noon. Blood was easy to come by: one sharp jab from a pin and the Patriarch had his sample to examine. Eagerly he peered through the viewing lens, adjusting the focus in the same way as a telescope.

Animalcules. How remarkable.

Tiny, tiny animalcules . . . countless schools of them, swimming in his own blood. What wonders God had made! Creatures of different shapes and sizes, perhaps predators and prey, like the fishes that swam in the ocean.

And were there snakes? The question was almost irrelevant. And yet . . . very faintly, so close to invisible that it might be a trick of the eye, something as thin as a hair seemed to flit momentarily across the view.

Then it was gone.

2. *The Origin of Serpentine Analogues in the Blood of Papist Peoples:*

Her Britannic Majesty, Anne VI, rather liked the Star Chamber. True, its power had been monstrously abused at times in the past five centuries—secret trials leading to secret executions of people who were probably more innocent than the monarchs sitting on the judgment seat—but even in the glorious Empire, there was a place for confidential hearings. The queen on this side of the table, one of her subjects on the other . . . it had the air of a private chat between friends: a time when difficulties could get sorted out, one way or another.

"Well, Mr. Darwin," she said after the tea had been poured, "it seems you've stirred up quite a hornet's nest. Have you not?"

The fiercely bearded man across the table did not answer immediately. He laid a finger on the handle of his cup as if to drink or not to drink was some momentous decision; then he said, "I have simply spoken the truth, ma'am . . . as I see it."

"Yes; but different people see different truths, don't they? And the things you say are true have upset a great many of my loyal subjects. You are aware there has been . . . unpleasantness?"

"I know about the riots, ma'am. Several times they have come uncomfortably close to me. And, of course, there have been threats on my life."

"Indeed." Anne lifted a tiny slice of buttered bread and took what she hoped would seem a thoughtful nibble. For some reason, she always enjoyed eating in front of the accused here in the Star Chamber; they themselves never had any appetite at all. "The threats are one reason We invited you here today. Scotland Yard is growing rather weary of protecting you; and Sir Oswald has long pondered whether your life is worth it."

That got the expected reaction—Darwin's finger froze on the cup handle, the color draining away from his face. "I had not realized . . ." His eyes narrowed. "I perceive, ma'am, that someone will soon make a decision on this issue."

"Exactly," the queen said. "Sir Oswald has turned to the crown for guidance, and now We turn to you." She took another tiny bite of the bread. "It would be good of you to explain your theories— to lay out the train of reasoning that led to your . . . unsettling public statements."

"It's all laid out in my book, ma'am."

"But your book is for scientists, not queens." Anne set down the bread and allowed herself a small sip of tea. She took her time doing so, but Darwin remained silent. "Please," she said at last. "We wish to make an informed decision."

Darwin grunted . . . or perhaps it was a hollow chuckle of cynicism. An ill-bred sound in either case. "Very well, Your Majesty." He nodded. "It is simply a matter of history."

"History is seldom simple, Mr. Darwin; but proceed."

"In . . . 1430 something, I forget the exact year, Anton Leeuwenhoek appeared before Supreme Patriarch Septus to discuss the absence of snakes in the bloodstream. You are familiar with that, ma'am?"

"Certainly. It was the pivotal event in the Schism between Our church and the Papists."

"Just so."

Anne could see Darwin itching to leap off his chair and begin prowling about the room, like a professor lecturing to a class of dull-lidded schoolboys. His strained impetuosity amused her; but she hoped he would keep his impulses in check. "Pray continue, Mr. Darwin."

"It is common knowledge that the Patriarch's decision led to a . . . a deluge, shall we say, of people peering at their own blood through a microscope. Only the upper classes at first, but soon enough it spread to the lower levels of society too. Since the church allowed anyone to look into a microscope without cost, I suppose it was a free source of amusement for the peasantry."

"An opiate for the masses," Anne offered. She rather liked the phrase—Mr. Marx had used it when *he* had his little visit to the Star Chamber.

"I suppose that must be it," Darwin agreed. "At any rate, the phenomenon far outstripped anything Septus could have foreseen; and even worse for the Patriarchy, it soon divided the church into two camps—those who claimed to see snakes in their blood and those who did not."

"Mr. Darwin, We are well aware of the fundamental difference between Papists and the Redeemed."

"Begging your pardon, ma'am, but I believe the usual historical interpretation is . . . flawed. It confuses cause and effect."

"How can there be confusion?" Anne asked. "Papists have serpents in their blood; that is apparent to any child looking into a microscope. We Redeemed have no such contaminants; again, that is simple observational fact. The obvious conclusion, Mr. Darwin, is that Christ Herself marked the Papists with Her curse, to show one and all the error of their ways."

"According to the Papists," Darwin reminded her, "the snakes are a sign of God's blessing: a sleeping snake means sin laid to rest."

"Is that what you think, Mr. Darwin?"

"I think it more practical to examine the facts before making any judgment."

"That is why we are here today," Anne said with a pointed glance. "Facts . . . and judgment. If you could direct yourself to the heart of the matter, Mr. Darwin?"

"The heart of the matter," he repeated. "Of course. I agree that *today* any microscope will show Papists have snakes in their bloodstream . . . or as scientists prefer to call them, serpentine analogues, since it is highly unlikely the observed phenomena are actual reptiles—"

"Let us not bandy nomenclature," Anne interrupted. "We accept that the entities in Papist blood are unrelated to cobras and puff adders; but they have been called snakes for centuries, and the name is adequate. Proceed to your point, Mr. Darwin."

"You have just made my point for me, ma'am. Several centuries have passed since the original controversy arose. What we see *now* may not be what people saw *then*." He took a deep breath. "If you read the literature of that long-ago time, you find there was great doubt about the snakes, even among the Papists. Serpentine analogues were extremely rare and difficult to discern . . . unlike the very obvious entities seen today."

"Surely that can be blamed on the equipment," Anne said. "Microscopes of that day were crude contrivances compared to our fine modern instruments."

"That is the usual argument"—Darwin nodded—"but I believe there is a different explanation."

"Yes?"

"My argument, ma'am, is based on my observations of pigeons."

Anne blinked. "Pigeons, Mr. Darwin?" She blinked again. "The birds?" She bit her lip. "The filthy things that perch on statues?"

"Not wild pigeons, Your Majesty, domestic ones. Bred for show. For example, some centuries ago, a squire in Sussex took it into his head to breed a black pigeon from his stock of gray ones."

"Why ever would he want a black pigeon?"

"That remains a mystery to me too, ma'am; but the historical records are clear. He set about the task by selecting pigeons of the darkest gray he could find, and breeding them together. Over many generations, their color grew darker and darker until today, the squire's descendants boast of pigeons as black as coal."

"They boast of that?"

"Incessantly."

Darwin seized up a piece of bread and virtually stuffed it into his mouth. The man had apparently become so engrossed in talking, he had forgotten who sat across the table. *Good,* Anne thought; he would be less guarded.

"We understand the principles of animal husbandry," Anne said. "We do not, however, see how this pertains to the Papists."

"For the past five centuries, Your Majesty, the Papists have been going through exactly the same process . . . as have the Redeemed, for that matter. Think, ma'am. In any population, there are numerous chance differences between individuals; the squire's pigeons, for example, had varying shades of gray. If some process of selection chooses to emphasize a particular trait as desirable, excluding other traits as undesirable—if you restrict darker birds to breeding with one another and prevent lighter ones from contributing to the bloodline—the selected characteristic will tend to become more pronounced with each generation."

"You are still talking about pigeons, Mr. Darwin."

"No, ma'am," he said triumphantly, "I am talking about Papists and the Redeemed. Let us suppose that in the times of Patriarch Septus, some people had almost imperceptible serpentine analogues in their bloodstream—a chance occurrence, just as some people may have curls in their hair while others do not."

Anne opened her mouth to say that curls were frequently not a chance occurrence at all; but she decided to remain silent.

"Now," Darwin continued, "what happened among the people of that day? Some saw those tiny, almost invisible snakes; others did not. Those who saw them proclaimed, *This proves the unshakable word of Mother Church*. Those who saw nothing said, *The scriptures cannot be taken literally—believers must find the truth in their own hearts*. And so the Schism split the world, pitting one camp against another."

"Yes, Mr. Darwin, We know all that."

"So, ma'am, you must also know what happened in subsequent generations. The rift in belief created a similar rift in the population. Papists only married Papists. The Redeemed only married the Redeemed."

"Of course."

"Consequently"—Darwin stressed the word—"those who could see so-called snakes in their blood only married those of similar condition. Those who saw nothing married others who saw nothing. Is it any wonder that, generation by generation, snakes became more and more visible in Papist blood? And less and less likely to be seen in the Redeemed? It is simply a matter of selective breeding, ma'am. The Papists are not different from us because the Virgin put her mark on them; they are different because they selected to make themselves different. To *emphasize* the difference. And the Redeemed have no snakes in their blood for the same reason—simply a side effect of our ancestors' marital prejudice."

"Mr. Darwin!" Anne said, aghast. "Such claims! No wonder you have angered the Papists as much as your own countrymen. To suggest God's sacred sign is a mere barnyard accident . . ." The Queen caught her breath. "Sir, where is your decency?"

"I have something better than decency," he answered in a calm voice. "I have proof."

"Proof? How could you prove such a thing?"

"Some years ago, ma'am," he said, "I took passage on a ship sailing the South Seas; and during that voyage, I saw things that completely opened my eyes."

"More pigeons, Mr. Darwin?"

He waved his hand dismissively. "The birds of the Pacific Islands are hardly fit study for a scientist. What I observed were the efforts of missionaries, ma'am; both Papists and the Redeemed, preaching to the natives who lived in those isles. Have you heard of such missions?"

"We sponsor several of those missions personally, Mr. Darwin."

"And the results, ma'am?"

"Mixed," Anne confessed. "Some tribes are open to Redemption, while others . . ." She shrugged. "The Papists do no better."

"Just so, Your Majesty. As an example, I visited one island where the Papists had been established for thirty years, yet the local priest claimed to have made no *true* converts. Mark that word, *true*. Many of the natives espoused Papist beliefs, took part in Papist worship, and so on . . . but the priest could find no snakes in their blood, so he told himself they had not truly embraced Mother Church."

"You would argue with the priest's conclusion?"

"Certainly," Darwin replied. "In my eyes, the island tribe was simply a closed population which for reasons of chance never developed serpentine analogues in their blood. If you interbreed only white pigeons, you will never develop a black."

Anne said, "But—" then stopped stone-still as the words of a recent mission report rose in her mind. *We are continually frustrated in our work on this island; although the people bow before God's altar, their blood continues to show the serpent-stain of the Unclean . . .*

"Mr. Darwin," Anne murmured, "could there possibly be islands where all the people had snakes in their blood, regardless of their beliefs?"

"There are indeed, ma'am," Darwin nodded. "Almost all the island populations are isolated and homogeneous. I found some tribes with snakes, some without—no matter which missionaries ministered there. When the Papists land among a people who already have analogues in their bloodstream, they soon declare they have converted the tribe and hold great celebrations. However, when they land among a people whose blood is clear . . . well, they can preach all they want, but they won't change the effects of generations of breeding. Usually, they just give up and move on to another island where the people are more receptive . . . which is to say, where they have the right blood to begin with."

"Ah."

Anne lowered her eyes. Darwin had been speaking about the Papists, but she knew the same was true of Redeemed missionaries. They tended to stay a year in one place, do a few blood tests, then move on if they could not show results—because results were exclusively measured in blood rather than in what the people professed. If missionaries, her own missionaries, had been abandoning sincere believers because they didn't believe the conversions were "true" . . . what would God think of that?

But Darwin hadn't stopped talking. "Our voyage visited many islands, Your Majesty, a few of which had never received missionaries of any kind. Some of those tribes had serpentine analogues in their blood, while some did not . . . and each island was homogeneous. I hypothesize the potential for analogues might have been distributed evenly through humankind millennia ago; but as populations grew isolated, geographically or socially—"

"Yes, Mr. Darwin, We see your point." Anne found she was tapping her finger on the edge of the table. She stopped herself and stood up. "This matter deserves further study. We shall instruct the police to find a place where you can continue your work without disturbance from outside sources."

Darwin's face fell. "Would that be a jail, ma'am?"

"A comfortable place of sanctuary," she replied. "You will be supplied with anything you need—books, paper, all of that."

"Will I be able to publish?" he asked.

"You will have at least one avid reader for whatever you write." She favored him with the slightest bow of her head. "You have given us much to think about."

"Then let me give you one more thought, Your Majesty." He took a deep breath, as if he was trying to decide if his next words would be offensive beyond the pale. Then, Anne supposed, he decided he had nothing to lose. "Papists and the Redeemed have been selectively breeding within their own populations for hundreds of years. There may come a time when they are too far removed from each other to be . . . cross-fertile. Already there are rumors of an unusually high mortality rate for children with one Papist parent and one Redeemed. In time—millennia perhaps, but in time—if we continue with segregated breeding, I believe the two populations may split into separate species."

"Separate species? Of humans?"

"It may happen, Your Majesty. At this very moment, we may be witnessing the origin of two new species."

Queen Anne pursed her lips in distaste. "The origin of species, Mr. Darwin? If that is a joke, We are not amused."

3. The Efficacy of Trisulphozymase for Preventing SA Incompatibility Reactions in Births of Mixed-Blood Parentage:

The hearing was held behind closed doors—a bad sign. Julia Grant had asked some of her colleagues what to expect and they all said, *Show trial, show trial.* Senator McCarthy loved to get his name in the papers. And yet the reporters were locked out today; just Julia and the Committee.

A very bad sign.

"Good afternoon, Dr. Grant," McCarthy said after she had sworn to tell the truth, the whole truth, and nothing but the truth. His voice had a smarmy quality to it, an unpleasant man's attempt at charm. "I suppose you know why you're here?"

"No, Senator."

"Come now, Doctor," he chided, as if speaking to a five-year-old. "Surely you must know the purpose of this Committee? And it therefore follows that we'd take great interest in your work."

"My work is medical research," she replied tightly. "I have no political interests at all." She forced herself to stare McCarthy in the eye. "I heal the sick."

"There's sickness and there's sickness." The senator shrugged. "We can all understand doctors who deal with sniffles and sneezes and heart attacks . . . but that's not your field, is it?"

"No," she answered. "I'm a hematologist, specializing in SA compatibility problems."

"Could you explain that for the Committee?"

The doctor suspected that every man on the Committee—and they were all men—had already been briefed on her research. If nothing else, they read the newspapers. Still, why not humor them?

"All human blood," she began, "is either SA-positive or SA-negative—"

"SA stands for Serpentine Analogue?" McCarthy interrupted.

"Yes. The name comes from the outdated belief—"

"That some people have snakes in their bloodstream," McCarthy interrupted again.

"That's correct."

"*Do* some people have snakes in their bloodstream?" McCarthy asked.

"Snakelike entities," another senator corrected . . . probably a Democrat.

"Serpentine analogues are not present in anyone's bloodstream," Julia said. "They don't appear until blood is exposed to air. It's a specialized clotting mechanism, triggered by an enzyme that encourages microscopic threads to form at the site of an injury—"

"In other words," McCarthy said, "SA-positive blood works differently from SA-negative. Correct?"

"In this one regard, yes." Julia nodded.

"Do you think SA-positive blood is *better* than SA-negative?"

"It provides slightly more effective clotting at wounds—"

"Do you *admire* SA-positive blood, Doctor?"

Julia stared at him. Mentally, she counted to ten. "I am fascinated by all types of blood," she answered at last. "SA-positive clots faster . . . which is useful to stop bleeding but gives a slightly greater risk of stroke. Overall, I'd say the good points and the bad even out. If they didn't, evolution would soon skew the population strongly one way or the other."

McCarthy folded his hands on the table in front of him. "So you believe in evolution, Dr. Grant?"

"I'm a scientist. I also believe in gravity, thermodynamics, and the universal gas equation."

Not a man on the Committee so much as smiled.

"Doctor," McCarthy said quietly, "what blood type are you?"

She gritted her teeth. "The Supreme Court ruled that no one has to answer that question."

In sudden fury, McCarthy slammed his fist onto the table. "Do you see the Supreme Court in here with us? Do you? Because if you do, show me those black-robed faggots and I'll boot their pope-loving asses straight out the window." He settled back in his chair. "I don't think you appreciate the seriousness of your situation, Dr. Grant."

"What situation?" she demanded. "I'm a medical researcher—"

"And you've developed a new drug, haven't you?" McCarthy snapped. "A new *drug*. That you want to set loose on the public. I wonder if the person who invented heroin called herself a medical researcher too."

"Mr. McCarthy, trisulphozymase is not a narcotic. It is a carefully developed pharmaceutical—"

"Which encourages miscegenation between Papists and the Redeemed," McCarthy finished. "That's what it does, doesn't it, Doctor?"

"No!" She took a deep breath. "Trisulphozymase combats certain medical problems that occur when an SA-positive father and an SA-negative mother—"

"When a Papist man sires his filthy whelp on a Redeemed woman," McCarthy interrupted. "When a Papist *fucks* one of the Saved. That's what you want to encourage, Doctor? That's how you'll make the world a better place?"

Julia said nothing. She felt her cheeks burn like a child caught in some forbidden act; and she was infuriated that her reaction was guilt rather than outrage at what McCarthy was saying.

Yes, she wanted to say, *it* will *make the world a better place to stop separating humanity into hostile camps.* Most people on the planet had no comprehension of either Papist or Redeemed theology; but somehow the poisonous idea of blood discrimination had spread to every country of the globe, regardless of religious faith. Insanity! And millions recognized it to be so. Yet the McCarthys of the world found it a convenient ladder on which they could climb to power, and who was stopping them? Look at Germany. Look at Ireland. Look at India and Pakistan.

Ridiculous . . . and deadly, time and again throughout history. Perhaps she should set aside SA compatibility and work on a cure for the drive to demonize those who were different.

"A doctor deals with lives, not lifestyles," she said stiffly. "If I was confronted with a patient whose heart had stopped beating, I would attempt to start it again, whether the victim was an innocent child, a convicted murderer, or even a senator." She leaned forward. "Has anyone here ever seen an SA incompatibility reaction? How a newborn infant dies? How the mother goes into spasm and usually dies too? Real people, gentlemen; real screams of pain. Only a monster could witness such things and still rant about ideology."

A few Committee members had the grace to look uncomfortable, turning away from her gaze; but McCarthy was not one of them. "You think this is all just ideology, Doctor? A lofty discussion of philosophical doctrine?" He shook his head in unconvincing sorrow. "I wish it were . . . I truly wish it were. I wish the Papists weren't trying to rip down everything this country stands for, obeying the orders of their foreign masters to corrupt the spirit of liberty itself. Why should I care about a screaming woman, when she's whored herself to the likes of them? She made her decision; now she has to face the consequences. No one in this room invented SA incompatibility, Doctor. God did . . . and I think we should take the hint, don't you?"

The sharp catch of bile rose in Julia's throat. For a moment, she couldn't find the strength to fight it; but she couldn't be sick, not in front of these men. Swallowing hard, she forced herself to breathe evenly until the moment passed. "Senators," she said at last, "do you actually intend to suppress trisulphozymase? To withhold lifesaving treatment from those who need it?"

"Some might say it's a sign," McCarthy answered, "that a Redeemed man can father a child on a Papist without complications, but it doesn't work the other way around. Doesn't that sound like a sign to you?"

"Senators," she said, ignoring McCarthy, "does this Committee intend to suppress trisulphozymase?"

Silence. Then McCarthy gave a little smile. "How does trisulphozymase work, Doctor?"

Julia stared at him, wondering where this new question was going. Warily, she replied, "The drug dismantles the SA factor enzyme into basic amino acids. This prevents a more dangerous response from the mother's immune system, which might otherwise produce antibodies to the enzyme. The antibodies are the real problem, because they may attack the baby's—"

"So what you're saying," McCarthy interrupted, "is that this drug can destroy the snakes from a Papist's bloodstream?"

"I told you, there are no snakes. Trisulphozymase temporarily eliminates the extra clotting enzyme that is present in SA-positive blood."

"It's only temporary?"

"That's all that's needed. One injection shortly before the moment of birth—"

"But what about repeated doses?" McCarthy interrupted. "Or a massive dose? Could you permanently wipe out the SA factor from a person's blood?"

"You don't administer trisulphozymase to an SA-positive person," Julia said. "It's given to an SA-negative mother to prevent—"

"But suppose you *did* give it to a Papist. A big dose. Lots of doses. Could it destroy the SA factor forever?" He leaned forward eagerly. "Could it make them like us?"

And now Julia saw it: what this hearing was all about. Because the Committee couldn't really suppress the treatment, could they? Her results were known in the research community. Even if the drug was banned here, other countries would use it; and there would eventually be enough public pressure to force reevaluation. This wasn't about the lives of babies and mothers; this was about clipping the devil's horns.

Keeping her voice steady, she said, "It would be unconscionable to administer this drug or any other to a person whose health did not require it. Large doses or long-term use of trisulphozymase would have side effects I could not venture to guess." The faces in front of her showed no expression. "Gentlemen," she tried again, "in an SA-positive person, the enzyme is *natural*. A natural component of blood. To interfere with a body's natural functioning when there's no medical justification . . ." She threw up her hands. "Do no harm, gentlemen. The heart of the Hippocratic Oath. At the very least, doctors must do no harm."

"Does that mean," McCarthy asked, "you'd refuse to head a research project into this matter?"

"Me?"

"You're the top expert in your field." McCarthy shrugged. "If anybody can get rid of the snakes once and for all, it's you."

"Senator," Julia said, "have you no shame? Have you no shame at all? You want to endanger lives over this . . . triviality? A meaningless difference you can only detect with a microscope—"

"Which means they can walk among us, Doctor! Papists can walk among us. Them with their special blood, their snakes, their damned inbreeding—they're the ones who care about what you call a triviality. They're the ones who flaunt it in our faces. They say they're God's Chosen. With God's Mark of Blessing. Well, I intend to erase that mark, with or without your help."

"Without," Julia told him. "Definitely without."

McCarthy's gaze was on her. He did not look like a man who

had just received an absolute no. With an expression far too smug, he said, "Let me tell you a secret, Doctor. From our agents in the enemy camp. Even as we speak, the Papists are planning to contaminate our water supply with their damned SA enzyme. Poison us or make us like them . . . one way or the other. We *need* your drug to fight that pollution; to remove the enzyme from our blood before it can destroy us. What about that, Dr. Grant? Will your precious medical ethics let you work on a treatment to keep us safe from their damned Papist toxins?"

Julia grimaced. "You know nothing about the human metabolism. People couldn't 'catch' the SA factor from drinking water; the enzyme would just break down in your stomach acid. I suppose it might be possible to produce a methylated version that would eventually work its way into the bloodstream . . ." She stopped herself. "Anyway, I can't believe the Papists would be so insane as to—"

"Right now," McCarthy interrupted, "sitting in a committee room of some Papist hideaway, there are a group of men who are just as crazy as we are. Believe that, Doctor. Whatever we are willing to do to them, they are willing to do to us; the only question is who'll do it first." McCarthy settled back and cradled his hands on his stomach. "Snakes all 'round, Dr. Grant. You can make a difference in who gets bitten."

It was, perhaps, the only true thing McCarthy had said since he'd started speaking. Julia tried to doubt it, but couldn't. SA-positive or negative, you could still be a ruthless bastard.

She said nothing.

McCarthy stared at her a few moments more, then glanced at the men on both sides of him. "Let's consider this hearing adjourned, all right? Give Dr. Grant a little time to think things over." He turned to look straight at her. "A *little* time. We'll contact you in a few days . . . find out who scares you more, us or them."

He had the nerve to wink before he turned away.

The other senators filed from the room, almost bumping into each other in the hurry to leave. Complicitous men . . . weak men, for all their power. Julia remained in the uncomfortable "witness chair," giving them ample time to scurry away; she didn't want to lay eyes on them again when she finally went out into the corridor.

Using trisulphozymase on an SA-positive person . . . what would be the effect? Predictions were almost worthless in bio-chemistry—medical science was a vast ocean of ignorance dotted with researchers trying to stay afloat in makeshift canoes. The only prediction you could safely make was that a large enough dose of *any* drug would kill the patient.

On the other hand, better to inject trisulphozymase into SA-positive people than SA-negative. The chemical reactions that broke down the SA enzyme also broke down the trisulphozy-mase—mutual assured destruction. If you didn't have the SA enzyme in your blood, the trisulphozymase would build up to lethal levels much faster, simply because there was nothing to stop it. SA-positive people could certainly tolerate dosages that would kill a . . .

Julia felt a chill wash through her. She had created a drug that would poison SA-negatives but not SA-positives . . . that could se-lectively massacre the Redeemed while leaving the Papists stand-ing. And her research was a matter of public record. How long would it take before someone on the Papist side made the connec-tion? One of those men McCarthy had talked about, just as ruth-less and crazy as the senator himself.

How long would it take before they used her drug to slaughter half the world?

There was only one way out: put all the snakes to sleep. If Julia could somehow wave her hands and make every SA-positive per-son SA-negative, then the playing field would be level again. No, not the playing field—the killing field.

Insanity . . . but what choice did she have? Sign up with Mc-Carthy; get rid of the snakes before they began to bite; pray the side effects could be treated. Perhaps, if saner minds prevailed, the process would never be deployed. Perhaps the threat would be enough to force some kind of bilateral enzyme disarmament.

Feeling twenty years older, Dr. Julia Grant left the hearing room. The corridor was empty; through the great glass entryway at the front of the building, she could see late afternoon sunlight slanting across the marble steps. A single protester stood on the sidewalk, mutely holding a sign aloft—no doubt what McCarthy would call a Papist sympathizer, traitorously opposing a duly appointed congressional committee.

The protester's sign read: *Why do you concern yourself with the sleeping creature before you, when you are blind to the serpents in your own heart?*

Julia turned away, hoping the building had a back door.

Sense of Wonder

[After school, 4:30 P.M.]

NICHOLAS: How 'bout the collision of two Dyson spheres?

BRENDAN: Bor-ring.

N: Two *sentient* Dyson spheres.

B: How can a Dyson sphere be sentient? It's just, like, a shell with a sun inside.

N: Both spheres are made of nanotech. You know? Little microscopic robots and they're all linked into big hive-minds.

B: So the spheres are big computers?

N: *Hive-minds*. Because each nanite is sentient on its own. Each one is way smarter than humans to begin with.

B: If they're so smart, why are the spheres colliding? They should just change course.

N: Because . . . because one sphere is made of matter and the other's antimatter! A big antimatter Dyson sphere, the size of a whole solar system, right? And it's getting pulled toward the normal-matter one because opposites attract.

B: You mean like you and Ashley McGregor?

N: I am *not* attracted to . . . the only reason I even talk to her is just she lives two houses down from me.

B: Suppose the Dyson spheres are getting together to make out.

N: What?

B: You're the one who said they're sentient. And they're, like, you know, billion-year-old *virgins*.

N: Yeah, right. Virgins!

B: Stupid old virgins.

N: Wait a second. If they're both *spheres* and they want to get it on, doesn't that make them gay?

B: One is matter and the other's antimatter.

N: Doesn't make a difference. They're both spheres!

B: Oh. Yeah. I see your point.

N: Now if one was a *ringworld* . . .

B: Right. Then, like, the sphere could go *right through* the ring-world. You know, kind of back and forth . . .

N: In and out.

B: Yeah. Except doesn't a ringworld have a sun?

N: Oh, right. Ringworlds have a sun in the middle.

B: So when the Dyson sphere tries to, you know, slide through the ring, it gets kind of scorched.

N: What can I say? Love hurts.

B: Is that what Ashley tells you?

N: Look, I just walk home with her sometimes, okay? We live so close together—

B: Suppose it's a *ghost* ringworld.

N: A what?

B: Like, it doesn't *have* a sun. It's all dark and cold and creepy.

N: And the Dyson sphere is just going through space, minding its own business, when it sees this thing floating out there.

B: So the sphere kind of drifts up slowly, and as it's sliding inside, it goes, "Hello? Hello? Anybody here?"

N: Oh, sure, like it can talk in *vacuum*!

B: It sends radio signals.

N: How 'bout it creates holographic words across its surface?

B: Or maybe Dyson spheres talk with *pheromones*.

N: That's cool.

B: Its atmosphere is filled with this kind of perfume called, "Hello? Hello? Anybody here?"

N: Which is basically what they should call *all* perfumes. "Hello? Hello? Is anyone paying attention to me?"

B: Like Janice Wozniak.

N: Yeah, right, Janice Wozniak. *Swimming* in Chanel or something.

B: Does Ashley wear perfume?

N: She wants to but her mom won't let her. Perfume, makeup, all that stuff.

B: You talk to Ashley about makeup?

N: Oh, fuck off! Fuck right off! I thought we were talking about Dyson spheres.

B: A Dyson sphere sliding into a ghost ringworld.

N: And, like, it gets partway inside when the ring closes up like a bear trap! Boom. And the Dyson sphere is snared!

B: Very psychological.

N: It's not psychological! It's . . . okay, the ring *doesn't* close like a bear trap.

B: It just sits there, dark and cold.

N: And the sphere passes through and keeps on going.

B: Pheromones and all.

N: Off into the blackness.

[Pause.]

B: It's still psychological.

N: I know it's psychological! But what do you want? You want the sphere to turn around and come limping back? No way! The ringworld is the one who's being all cold and dark. It's not the sphere's fault if it's just, like, a friend, and the ringworld is really interested in some jerk of a *nebula*!

B: Ashley likes Justin?

N: As if she talks about anyone else.

B: Maybe she's trying to make you jealous.

N: She could wish. Just wait till you and I are rich, famous writers. We'll be making millions on the bestseller list . . .

B: And she'll be with Justin. Kind of its own punishment.

N: So the Dyson sphere couldn't care less about the ringworld. It doesn't want to get anywhere *near* the ringworld.

B: The sphere just sits back and laughs while the ringworld gets sucked into a huge black hole.

N: Nah. Black holes are *way* too psychological.

B: You're right. How 'bout the sphere goes in and out through the ringworld but it doesn't mean anything?

N: Oh sure, like that isn't creepy. The ringworld isn't *seriously* bad. It's just . . . looking for sun in all the wrong places.

B: So it might smarten up someday?

N: How should I know? I can't even tell what would be a happy ending, okay? Because on the one hand, it's so stupid to care, when it means getting all involved in . . . ringworld stuff. Who wants that? But on the other hand . . .

B: Ringworlds are really really pretty.

N: Yeah.

[Pause.]

B: How 'bout this: what's really going on is there are these two gods, right? And all this stuff with the ringworld and the Dyson sphere, it turns out what's really happening is the gods are just playing basketball.

N: Ooo. Nice twist.

B: Cosmic hoops.

N: Perfect solution.

B: My driveway or yours?

[Pause.]

N: Mine. Ashley might walk by.

Copyright Notices

JAMES ALAN GARDNER is a 1989 graduate of the Clarion West Science Fiction Writers Workshop, and has had several science fiction stories and novellas appear in publications such as *Isaac Asimov's Science Fiction Magazine, Amazing Stories,* and *The Magazine of Fantasy and Science Fiction.* He is the author of seven previous novels: *Expendable, Commitment Hour, Vigilant, Hunted, Ascending, Trapped,* and *Radiant.* He was the grand prize winner of 1989 Writers of the Future contest, has won the Aurora Award, and has been nominated for the Hugo and Nebula Awards. He lives in Canada.